The Bear Pit

S. G. MACLEAN

Quercus

First published in Great Britain in 2019 by Quercus
This paperback edition published in 2020 by

Quercus Editions Ltd
Carmelite House
50 Victoria Embankment
London EC4Y 0DZ

An Hachette UK company

A CIP catalogue record for this book is available
from the British Library

PB ISBN 978 1 78747 361 4

10 9 8 7 6 5

Typeset by CC Book Production
Printed and bound in Great Britain by Clays Ltd, Elcograf S.p.A.

MIX
Paper from
responsible sources
FSC
www.fsc.org   FSC® C104740

Papers used by Quercus are from well-managed forests and other responsible sources.

Shona (S.G.) MacLean has a PhD in history from Aberdeen University, specializing in sixteenth- and seventeenth-century Scottish history. She has written four highly acclaimed historical thrillers set in Scotland, *The Redemption of Alexander Seaton* (shortlisted for the CWA Historical Dagger), *A Game of Sorrows*, *Crucible of Secrets* and *The Devil's Recruit*, and a series of historical thrillers set in Oliver Cromwell's London. The first and third books in the series, *The Seeker* and *Destroying Angel*, have won the CWA Historical Dagger and the second, *The Black Friar*, was longlisted for the same award. S.G. MacLean is married with four children and lives in Conon Bridge, Scotland. Follow her on Instagram @iwritemybike2

Also by S. G. MacLean

THE ALEXANDER SEATON SERIES

The Redemption of Alexander Seaton
A Game of Sorrows
Crucible of Secrets
The Devil's Recruit

THE CAPTAIN DAMIAN SEEKER SERIES

The Seeker
The Black Friar
Destroying Angel
The Bear Pit

To Mairi

PROLOGUE

17 September, 1656

Westminster Abbey, State Opening of Parliament

Boyes stared at the viola case, lying open upon the ground of the courtyard. It was scarcely credible. 'A blunderbuss?'

Cecil was defensive. 'I'll not miss him. Not with this. Not at close range. Besides, what else would you have had me bring? I could hardly have walked openly through the streets with a full-length musket hanging from my shoulder, not today.'

Boyes lifted the weapon out of the case and examined it more closely. It was well made, certainly. The short, large-bore barrel was nicely turned, and the flared muzzle well proportioned for scattering the shot. One musket shot might miss a moving target, regardless of the skill of the marksman, but this would not, at close range. *At close range*. And therein lay the difficulty. A property closer than this house was to the east door of the abbey, from which Cromwell was shortly to emerge, could hardly have been found – its Royalist tenant had been happy enough to take off for his country estate well before today. But still there was the question of whether they would be close enough, and if they were not, how many innocents would suffer in the blast?

Boyes glanced again at the scaffolding they'd hastily erected against the wall of the yard, on pretence of building work being done. It would be substantial enough for their purposes, and they would not be up there long. In all the security checks carried out for this state opening of Parliament, no one had thought it necessary to check a second time the house of the quiet-living old Royalist colonel. So much for the location. The means was another thing, but while the choice of weapon might leave something to be desired, Fish had assured him that Cecil was one of the best shots in England – at least one of the best that could safely be invited to join an enterprise such as this.

The hubbub from the crowd outside had been building all morning, but within the walls of this small courtyard little was said between the three men. Boyes could feel a stillness in the air, a tightening in his stomach, such as they had all three known in the last hours before the commencement of a battle. On different sides, some of them then, but not now. This business had been a year and a half in the planning, first mooted in Cologne then agreed upon in Bruges. His mind went back to the small, smoky parlour of that house in Bruges, where an assortment of men who would never have thought to find themselves sitting at the same table, still less planning an undertaking such as this, had come warily together. Their plan would have its fruition within the next half-hour and they would go their separate ways again – Parliamentarians, Royalists, Levellers; men of so many different views and grievances, but they had all come to the one conclusion: Oliver Cromwell must die. What happened after that, only God knew.

The King had not been told, of course; so unbounded a horror of assassination – even of this usurper – had the murder of his father given him that such schemes were no longer put before Charles Stuart. But the popular rising the young King so waited upon would not happen, not without the crisis that the removal of the tyrant would provoke. Mr Boyes knew this better than most. They would proceed without the King's knowledge, and then Charles would be presented with the fait accompli, and act as a king must.

Boyes studied 'Mr Fish' – or Miles Sindercombe, former Parliamentary soldier and now paid assassin, did his new London neighbours but know it. Fish had made all the preparations from his lodgings recently taken on King Street: selected the time, found the location, brought in a suitable accomplice in the form of Cecil. The presence of Boyes himself was not so much required for the execution itself, but for the aftermath. He would see to events in England, whilst others readied the King for his return to his kingdom.

Boyes brought out his pocket watch and opened the casing. The hand of Chronos went slowly closer to the hour. It was almost time. They had been careful today to arrive at the house by the back entrance, and only after the Protector with his council and family had already entered the abbey. Attention would be turned elsewhere, and Cromwell and his party would discover, when they emerged, that the short walk from the east door of the abbey past Westminster Hall to Parliament House was not quite as they had expected it to be.

Fish had begun to pace. 'If we should fail . . .'

'We will not fail,' said Boyes. But he had already considered their escape routes. They could choose to plunge themselves in to the mêlée and confusion that would surely follow on their success, or leave by the back way, down the narrow alley to the landing stairs and then the river, where a wherry waited, then quickly to Southwark.

The hand of the figure on Boyes's watch now pointed directly to the hour and he snapped the casing shut. 'Now!'

Cecil began to climb the scaffolding, turning to take the blunderbuss once he reached the top. Blunderbuss. *Donderbus*, as the Dutch had it: thunder gun. And what a thunder would sound through Europe, if Cecil should find his mark.

Boyes could feel the excitement mounting in him, the old excitement, as he climbed the scaffolding behind Fish to take his place on the platform. From here, he could see Cromwell's entire short route from the abbey to the hall. Beyond the hall to Parliament House he could not see, but that didn't matter because Cromwell wouldn't get beyond the hall. In the other direction, the crowd that had followed the Protector's progression from palace to abbey was growing, starved of spectacle and eager to buy up the offerings of the numberless traders along their route. The taverns and alehouses of Westminster would be filled fit to burst today, in celebration of their Puritan lord and much-demanded Parliament. Boyes wondered how many of them had come seven years ago to gorge on the murder of their king, only to join in that dreadful groan when they saw the horror of what had been done. He did not wonder long, though, because suddenly the time for speculation was over: the great east doors of the abbey were opening. Their moment had come.

Cecil needed no prompting. His weapon was loaded with shot, and his hand steady as he lifted it. Fish and Boyes scarcely breathed as the doors were fully pushed back and he emerged, first, Cromwell himself. Of course. Everyone should know that the honour and the glory of this moment were his, this black-clad kinglet. A band of gold encircled Oliver's hat, lest any should doubt what they had really done in raising a fenland farmer to be their chief of men.

Cecil glanced one last time at Fish for affirmation, but just as he lifted the gun to take aim, the crowd, which had been converging on the bottom of the abbey steps, surged forward, and Cromwell's Life Guard was instantly around him, itself quickly engulfed by the tide of bodies. Fish cursed and turned to begin descending the scaffold, but Cecil stayed him. 'A moment yet. There are gaps, and that gold band is a beacon through them.'

'He will be wearing a *secret* beneath the hat.'

'I know. I will make my mark lower.'

Boyes began to believe that it might yet be possible and then, as Cecil raised his arm a second time, a figure, a mass on its own almost, pushed through the Life Guard from their side and placed himself between Cromwell and everyone to the left of him. The Protector, hat and band of gold and all, was completely obliterated from their sight.

Again Fish cursed, but Cecil was angry now, and determined not to be deprived of his prey. 'I'll go through him,' he said. 'I'll fell him and get to Cromwell anyway.'

'It's Seeker, Cecil,' said Fish wearily. 'Damian Seeker. You won't go through him and you won't fell him.' He turned away. 'Oliver Cromwell will not die today.'

Cecil made as if he would argue further, but Fish was no longer listening. Cecil lowered his gun and waited for Fish to reach the ground before passing it down to him and following. Only Mr Boyes did not go down immediately. He watched all the way, as the Life Guard and the procession pushed themselves through the crowd until the doors to Westminster Hall had been closed behind them and those of the crowd who had no good business being there were shut out. Boyes watched a moment longer, imprinting on his mind the dark mass, the huge form of the man who had come between Cromwell and retribution.

Fish was calling to him from below, urging haste that they might get to the wherry before any chanced upon them here. But Boyes continued to look towards where Cromwell and his impassable guard had been. 'There will be another day, Captain Seeker,' he murmured before he, too, descended the scaffolding. 'You and I will have another day.'

ONE

The Gaming House

Six Weeks Later:
End of October, 1656

Thurloe shook his head and handed the paper back to Seeker. 'We are drowning in such information. Agents in Paris, Brussels, Amsterdam, Cologne: every one of them hears something suspect of someone; every one of them writes of heated talk against the Protector. The continent is awash with disgruntled officers, Levellers, Royalists, Papists. We cannot chase down every piece of intelligence that comes our way. We have not the manpower. Corroboration is required. This,' he looked again at the paper Seeker had handed him a few moments before, 'this "Fish" is not a priority. Should Stoupe in Paris confirm the report, we will act further upon it, but until that time we do not have the capability.'

Seeker was not ready to be put off. 'Stoupe is seldom mistaken, Mr Secretary, and he states that his information came from Bruges. It speaks of a Mr Fish in the area of

King Street, suspected of plotting against the life of the Protector. It is not the first time I have come across the name.'

'Oh?' Thurloe's interest was piqued.

'Mr Downing's clerk, Pepys, mentioned that name, more than once, in the days just before the opening of the Parliament.'

'Which was six weeks ago, and nothing attempted.' Thurloe's interest was gone. 'I know of this clerk of Downing's – he is too often in taverns and over-fond of groundless gossip. Intelligence, Seeker: what we deal in is hard intelligence.'

Which is what this is, thought Seeker, looking again at the paper Thurloe had just put down.

The Chief Secretary was weary. 'We are inundated with intelligence. What cannot be corroborated must take its place behind what has been. This is but a rumour of a rumour. We cannot run around half-cocked at everything we hear – as well put Andrew Marvell in charge.'

Seeker might have laughed at that, under other circumstances, but there was something in this he did not like the smell of. The source was a good one – he knew it, and the Secretary knew it too, were he not all but overwhelmed. But to countermand Thurloe's orders was not an option: to blunder in where he had been told not to might upset operations of which Seeker was not even aware.

Thurloe had almost reached the door when he turned and cast a wary eye at the great hound stretched out in

9

front of the hearth and blocking almost all the heat coming from Seeker's fire. 'That has the look of the beast I have seen lurking about the gardens of Lincoln's Inn, with the gardener's boy.'

'It is, sir. Nathaniel is fearful it will wander into the city and fall foul of the ward authorities. The constables have been seized by one of their fits of vigilance and stray dogs are about as welcome as stray pigs to the good citizens within the walls at the minute.'

'Though less flavoursome, I'd warrant,' said the Secretary, throwing the animal another grim glance before leaving the room.

The door was hardly shut when the dog's ears pricked up at the sound of a party of riders assembling in the courtyard below, and Seeker's old sergeant, Daniel Proctor, calling instructions to his men.

Seeker opened the casement and called down to Proctor. 'What's on tonight?'

'Gaming house. Bankside.'

'Right then.' Seeker felt a surge of energy. He'd been sifting reports and papers for days, weeks even, and the air in the room had become as oppressive to him as a half-ton weight. He hadn't been on a raid in two months. 'Have them fetch my horse. I'll be down in two minutes.'

By the time he'd donned his cloak and hat, the dog was alert and already at the door. Seeker hesitated only a moment. 'All right, come on then.'

Late October and autumn was finally ceding its place to

winter. Along the Thames, the city had begun to huddle in upon itself. *More manageable, in the winter*, thought Seeker. There was a different quality to the cold and dampness of the air, tempers flared less readily and the fear of pestilence receded for a while. The dog bounded ahead of the riders with their torches. The way down to the horse ferry was boggy like half the rest of Whitehall, its water courses knocked askew by rogue builders as London crept ever outwards. A fug of fog and sea coal hung over the river, and the lights of the hundreds of boats plying their trade, carrying passengers and goods from one place to another, gave it the appearance of a constantly shifting, many-eyed sea-serpent.

The crossing to Lambeth was short and free of incident. The other watermen, whose mouths were often as foul as the silt over which they propelled their vessels, knew to give the ferry carrying Cromwell's soldiers a wide berth. Landed at Lambeth Stairs, the horsemen turned northwards, and soon found themselves passing the eerie wastes of Lambeth Marsh. Across the river, the lights of Whitehall and the grand houses of the Strand glowed and flickered. Proctor shivered and even the dog was more alert as they made their way, shadowing the bend in the river, towards Bankside.

'Cold, Sergeant?' asked Seeker, keeping his eyes trained straight ahead of him.

'The chill of the marshes,' said Proctor. 'Like having the souls of the wicked breathe on your neck.'

Seeker did not mock the sergeant for his superstition. It

was a godforsaken enough place by night. The occasional light twinkled from a lonely dwelling or some rag-tag line of cottages that had grown up, somehow, amongst the bogs and pools of the marsh. He didn't stop to wonder what might drive a person to live there. Disappointment, a course of life gone wrong somewhere, misfortune passed down the generations. They always went to the depths or the edges. The lights and vice and heat of Southwark and Bankside, where the citizens of London had long chosen to indulge the excess of their natures in taverns, brothels and baiting pits, would give way to the misery of the Clink and the Marshalsea, waymarkers on the road to the desolation of the marsh itself. Seeker, too, shivered, and picked up his pace.

Before too long, they were passing Cupid's Stairs and the pleasure garden at the curve of the river, and the lights and buildings of Bankside came into view.

Seeker turned to Proctor. 'So where is it, then, this gambling den?'

'Old gaming house past Paris Garden, between the Bull Pit and the Bear Garden. Shut up long since, but we've had word that it's come into play again – cards, dice, whatever they think is easily hidden. High stakes.'

'Any names?'

'One or two we've heard before – low-level Royalists, stay-at-homes, mostly. Nothing to exercise Mr Thurloe.'

'He's got enough to exercise him as it is. But if they don't come quietly,' said Seeker, flexing the fingers of a gauntleted hand, 'I'm just in the mood for a spot of house-keeping.'

They began to pass houses and gardens, the sounds coming from doors and windows increasing the further along Bankside and towards London Bridge they got. Theatres boarded up, baiting arenas pulled down, the 'Winchester Geese', those long-protected women of the night, thrown a year since from their closed-down stews to mend their ways elsewhere, and yet the miasma of vice lingered. Regardless of the best efforts of the Protectorate, Bankside remained Bankside and Southwark Southwark.

They crossed Paris Garden bridge to a track past the market gardens that backed onto St George's Fields. Proctor brought them to a halt in front of a closed gate in a wall that ran the length of several tenements. Seeker dismounted with three of the men and they tied up their horses, whilst Proctor motioned the other three to turn up the long narrow alley leading to the front of the property. 'Count of sixty,' Seeker said.

Proctor nodded and followed his men up the alley.

At twenty, one of the men levered open the gate, splitting lock from wood. By forty, as the alarm was raised inside the house, the soldiers were past a range of outbuildings and halfway up the yard. At sixty, Seeker was smashing through the back door as the fleeing occupants ran into Proctor coming through the front.

It was difficult to see much to start with. Apart from the embers in the hearth, the only light came from an oil lamp suspended over a square table covered in green baize cloth. The contents of an upended wine jug crept over the cloth and soaked the cards that remained there. Red hexagonal chips and small ivory markers spilled across the floor nearby. A wooden card-dealing box, its contents indiscriminately disgorged, lay on its side, and the distinctive frame of a Faro tally board, its edges shattered and its wooden buttons come to rest far across the room, had kept its last points. The few coins that the gamblers had not managed to scoop from the table as they fled glinted and dulled on the baize as the lamp swung above them.

At the edges of the room, Seeker was aware of sofas, draped in shawls that he suspected would be a deal less luxurious than first glance suggested. The place smelled like a cross between a bordello and a chop house. It was likely both, but Seeker had not the time to consider it for now. Almost over to the front door, he shot out an arm and hauled the hindmost gambler back by the collar of his very fine green velvet coat. As he did so, he caught a flash of movement on the corner landing of the stairs to his left. He twisted his captive's arm up hard behind his back and threw him down against the table, which overturned sending the remaining cards and coins scattering across the floor to land at the feet of two over-painted, under-dressed women cowering by the chimney piece. 'Watch them!' he shouted to the soldier who'd come in behind him.

Seeker began to mount the stairs, moving quickly but carefully. A solitary torch burned in a wall sconce in the upper room. At the far end, a figure was desperately working at the latch of the window. At the very moment he caught sight of Seeker emerging from the stairhead, he hoisted himself up as if preparing to jump. Seeker was three strides into the room when the catch at last gave and the casement opened. His quarry had a foot on the ledge when Seeker drew his quillon dagger from his belt and let fly with it, pinning the flared sleeve of the gambler's coat to the wall. Such was the man's shock that before he had time to think or attempt to divest himself of the coat, Seeker's hands were planted on his shoulders and turning him around to the accompanying sound of tearing silk and velvet.

Seeker looked at the complacent eyes in the handsome face and shook his head. 'I knew it,' he said through gritted teeth. 'I just knew it.'

Ten minutes later, downstairs, the six gamblers, some of them bleeding from the nose or mouth and others nursing swelling eyes or fractured hands, had been manacled and the cart called to carry them the short distance to the Clink. The two drabs were still loudly denying that they were any such thing, even as they were being handed over to the ward constables for escort to the cellars of the White Lion, where they might spend the night with others of their sort. From the back yard came the noise of Seeker's dog, barking.

'He'll have chased down a fox or some such,' said Seeker.

'He's not the only one,' said Proctor, cocking an eyebrow

towards the righted table, to which Seeker's quarry from the upper floor had been secured. 'That one's hardly out of the Tower five minutes.'

'I know it,' said Seeker. 'Barkstead must be going soft over there.' They both started to laugh and then stopped. The Keeper of the Tower and Major-General for Middlesex was anything but soft. 'I'll have a word with this brave lad though, then I'll haul him over to the Clink myself.'

Proctor knew enough not to ask questions he didn't need the answers to, and simply nodded before turning his attention to the loading of the other five prisoners on to the cart.

Once they had gone, soldiers and prisoners all, and the broken door closed as well as it could be behind them, Seeker pulled out a chair at the card table and sat down. He picked up a card, the jack of spades, and turned it over in his fingers, casually examining it. 'So,' he said at last, without looking at the man opposite him, 'want to start talking?'

'It was . . .' the other man began. 'You see, I mean I thought . . .'

'Thought?' said Seeker, smashing the card face down on the table. 'I doubt you thought at all! Mr Thurloe took you on at my word, *my word*. You were to keep a low profile, pass quietly amongst your Royalist friends, make connections with people of quality and influence. You were, under no circumstances, to draw attention upon yourself.'

Sir Thomas Faithly, who had flinched slightly when

Seeker's hand had slammed onto the table, had recovered himself somewhat and attempted his accustomed easy smile. 'I'm sorry, Seeker. I was . . . bored.'

There was a terrible silence for a moment, broken only by the continued barking of the dog in the yard. Seeker considered letting it in, but didn't trust himself not to set the beast on Thomas Faithly. He took a deep breath. 'Bored? You were bored?' The last word was enunciated with such disgust that Faithly's smile evaporated on his face. 'Are you missing the Tower then? Fun and games there, was it? Or are you hoping to slip back off to your old playmate, Charles Stuart?' Seeker paused a moment, in an effort to calm himself. 'I can't believe I wasted my time or Mr Thurloe's taking you down here from the North Riding last year. I should have left you with the major-general in York, and let him show you what happens to captured Royalist spies.'

Faithly's features tightened. 'You know I'm not a spy, Seeker. Not for the Stuarts, anyway.'

'Well you're proving yourself a worse than useless one for us.'

Faithly made to move his hands, but was cut short by the set of manacles binding his wrists. He pulled his hands back. 'I've only been out of the Tower two months, Seeker. These things take time. I've begun to make the connections Mr Thurloe asked me to, I've wormed my way into John Evelyn's circle, for instance, tedious prig that he is . . .'

Seeker snorted. 'You mean he's more on his mind than drinking and whoring.'

Faithly flushed. 'As do most of the King's supporters. But no, Mr Evelyn never did seem quite at ease at Charles's court at St Germains, and it has taken me long enough to counter the ill opinion he formed of me there. I'm beginning to make my way, make inroads into the trust of several persons of note, but for pity's sake, Seeker, a man needs some diversion.'

'Indeed. And how do you think news of this "diversion" of yours will play out down Deptford way?'

'Down . . .?' Faithly gave an uncomprehending shrug. 'You mean at Sayes Court? Why should anyone at John Evelyn's house hear about this? Is that not why you've kept me aside from the others?'

Seeker regarded the man a moment, puzzled, and then realised what Faithly was saying to him. He let out a short laugh of disbelief. 'What? You think I'm going to tidy this up for you, to make it go away?'

'But surely, Mr Thurloe . . .'

'Mr Thurloe? If word gets out, and it will – your companions there looked none too sober, or discreet – that you were taken in a raid here, but that I saw to it that you were let off whilst the others were sent to the Clink until such time as the Southwark magistrates took an interest in them, how long do you think it would take your fine friend Mr Evelyn to work out that you were in Mr Thurloe's pay?'

Seeker saw comprehension dawn on Thomas Faithly's face.

'You'll go to the Clink tonight. You'll damn and blast

me and all my works, you'll tell them I gave you another hiding for trying to run from me.'

At Faithly's mildly alarmed look Seeker pulled a face. 'You can pretend, can't you?'

Faithly relaxed a little and nodded.

'Most of all,' continued Seeker, 'you'll keep your ears open. I'll whistle up a magistrate and you'll be out with a fine before tomorrow dinnertime. And you'll keep your nose cleaner than old Lady Cromwell's bonnet from now on, understand?'

Faithly drew a heavy breath. 'I understand.'

'Right,' said Seeker, bending to undo the link securing Faithly's ankle to the table leg, 'we'll see what's bothering my dog and then you're for the Clink.'

Outside, the fog from the river had made its way down the yard, but it took little effort to find where the dog's barking was coming from. He was standing outside the door of a stone structure built against the far wall. Seeker briefly noted the strangeness of it: a stone outbuilding when the main property, like most of its neighbours, had been constructed almost entirely of wood. The dog's hackles were up, but he wasn't snarling as Seeker had sometimes seen him do with a cornered rat or other vermin.

'Stinks like a French butcher's down here,' said Faithly. 'Must be a dead animal or something.'

'Probably,' replied Seeker, passing the torch to Faithly before reaching down to calm the dog. Then he lifted his horseman's axe from his belt and brought it down heavily to sever the padlock from the building's wooden door. He pushed open the door and the dog bounded in ahead of him. That was when the snarling began. Seeker took the torch again from Faithly and stepped carefully inside, then he stopped.

'What is it?' said Faithly, making to come in after him.

Seeker shook his head. 'Dear Jesus,' he said at last.

He took another step forward, past the dog, and held up the torch that Faithly might also see. A moment later, Thomas Faithly who had fought in the wars and seen men shot through by cannon, was staggering back out of the door to void the contents of his stomach in the yard.

Seeker remained motionless, his eyes fixed on the floor at the far end of the outhouse. 'Out, boy,' he said at last.

The dog gave off its low snarling and cast questioning eyes at its master.

'Out,' Seeker repeated, and the animal slunk out.

Still holding up the torch, Seeker took another two paces forward. There had been no doubt, from the moment he'd stepped in here, what he was looking at: a human being who had been half eaten. At closer quarters, it was clear that what lay mangled on the beaten earth floor, chained at the neck by an iron dog-collar to the wall, one arm torn wholly away, was the remains of a man. Seeker crouched down and brought the torch closer to the gory mess of bloody flesh, bone and rags.

The legs were ravaged, the stomach all but gouged out, and half the face gone, but it was as if whatever had so savaged this man had reached its limits, been restrained somehow. The side of the face that was pressed against the dirt floor appeared to have been untouched, if spattered with blood, as was the remaining arm, also on that side. Seeker reached out and gently turned the head. The hair was sparse, and grey, as was the close-cropped beard. The skin was rough, and deeply lined, the horror-struck eye yellowed, as were the few teeth in the torn mouth. A man of between sixty and seventy years of age, he would have said. Seeker forced himself to look into that face a while, as if somehow to keep company with this nameless stranger in his last, terrible moments.

A sound from the doorway took his attention and he turned around. It was Thomas Faithly, wiping his mouth. Faithly's voice was hoarse. 'What in God's name is this, Seeker?'

Seeker stood up, and cast around for a moment for a rag or some other scrap of fabric on which to wipe the muck and gore from the fingers of his gauntlet. He found none.

'It's . . . a slaughterhouse, Sir Thomas. A man was killed here, chained up and slaughtered like a beast.'

Faithly took a hesitant step in and then another. 'Or by a beast,' he said. 'No human hand did this.'

'No,' said Seeker, surveying again the mauled mess on the ground. 'That you are right about, but when was the last time you saw an animal work a set of manacles?' He held the torch up so that Faithly might see the collar by which the man was chained to the wall.

Disbelief spread over Faithly's face. 'Someone left him here? To die like *this*?'

'Well, he didn't do it himself,' said Seeker, finally coming upon a piece of sacking, on which he wiped his gauntlet as best he could. 'Push that door over and come and take a closer look.'

Faithly shook his head. 'I've seen enough.'

'I need you to tell me what you know of this man.'

'But I . . .'

'Just take a look.'

Faithly swallowed and appeared to steel himself, before taking a couple of steps towards the body. Seeker held the torch up to illuminate the remainder of the man's face. After first instinctively looking away, Faithly forced himself to look back. He bent a little closer, surveyed what was left of the body, then stood up. 'I don't know him.'

'Think. You've never seen him here before, never encountered him anywhere?'

Again Faithly shook his head. 'I'm good at faces, Captain. It's in my interest not to forget who I might have come across before – I need to remember what side they think I'm on. I've never seen that poor devil in my life before.'

Seeker let out a deep breath and straightened himself. 'All right. Nothing more for you here tonight then. I need to get you to the Clink and get a guard on that door.'

Faithly made no protest as Seeker reattached his manacles. There was no need, either, for him to feign weakness or injury from some pretended beating. So pale and shaken was he by what he had just looked on that none would doubt he had been the object of the captain's special attentions. Seeker pulled the door to after them and commanded the dog to stay. No one would be able to enter the outbuilding until such time as he returned with extra men.

As they were going back through the house to access Bankside from the front door, Seeker said, 'I want the names of every man you sat down here with tonight – their real names, mind – and that of whoever owns this house. And you don't breathe a word, to any of them, of what we found here. Understood?'

'Understood,' said Faithly, his voice still hoarse.

'Good.'

Nothing more was said between them as they made their way towards the gaol, the wash of the river on the shore a few yards away from them mingling with the usual sounds of human life drifting from the homes and taverns they passed, just as it must have done when a man was being mauled to death little more than a tenement's length away. They had almost reached the base of the forbidding walls of the Clink itself when Faithly stopped.

'You're going in, Sir Thomas,' Seeker said.

It was as if he hadn't spoken. 'What did that, Seeker?'

'What?'

'What manner of beast killed that man?'

'I think you know as well as I do.' Five lines scored into the remaining skin. Claws. Rows of teeth marks punctured at either side by deep incisors – bites from a massive jaw.

Thomas Faithly wasn't really listening to him. 'I've seen things. Sheep with their guts ripped out, animals savaged by wolves. A man once, but that—'

'It was a bear.'

Faithly nodded. 'But they're all gone, surely?' He contorted his brow. 'They were shot months since, and the arena pulled down.'

Seeker glanced back down the street to the site of the Hope Theatre, once the arena for the bear baiting that had entertained the godly citizens of London for so long, and now rubble, a building plot waiting to be cleared.

'It would seem that there's one of them left,' he said.

TWO

A Holiday

The bells were ringing eight and the fog was already clearing as Seeker once again crossed the river from Whitehall to Lambeth. Rather than go northwards this time, he rode over the bridge and past the sprawl of Lambeth Palace to take the road that skirted St George's Fields. To the north, he could see smoke rising here and there from scattered dwellings on the marsh. It was not so sinister a place now as it had seemed last night, but there was something desolate about those cottages, all the same.

He was hungry, but he didn't slow his horse when the Dog and Duck inn, a mile or so out on the marsh, came into view. He'd come here once, with Maria, in those brief days when it had seemed possible that he might lead two lives – one as an officer of the Protectorate, the other as an ordinary man, in love with a lawyer's sister. But Maria's brother had been a lawyer of the radical element, as much acquainted with the inside of a prison cell as were most of his clients, and she shared her brother's views. It had been a foolish delusion to think that he and she might love as any other man and woman, and they had both suffered for it.

It had been a while since he'd let himself remember: they'd walked out to St George's Fields and to the fort, left over from the first civil war. Maria and her brother had been amongst those citizens of London, men, women and children, who had marched out to the fields, dug trenches, and carried earth to throw up a string of defences to encircle the city and Westminster, protecting the capital from their own King. She'd told him how tired the work had made her, and how frightened she'd been, lying in her bed at night, listening for the alarum that would tell them the dreaded forces of Prince Rupert had breached the bulwarks. But the alarum had never come. Rupert had been ordered to stop before he got to London.

The war was long over, but much remained of those defences, those 'Lines of Communication', the spirit of London's people made manifest. Here, still overshadowing the inn, was the quadrant fort of St George's. They'd explored it that day, he and Maria, while the dog had busied himself chasing wildfowl across the nearby ducking pond. Seeker had tried, for a while, to explain the fort's features to her, as she'd teased and run around him and kissed him until at last he'd given the thing up as hopeless. But that had been over two years ago, in springtime, and now autumn was abandoning the land to winter, and one day what remained of the fort would be crumbled and gone.

Closer to Southwark, the traffic increased once he turned

on to the Newington Road. Carts and riders negotiated past each other with varying degrees of skill and patience as they made their way to London Bridge. Pedlars, merchants, soldiers, honest farmers and hopeful thieves, all streamed towards the city. Others were heading southwards to Surrey, Sussex, the coast, their city sojourn over or with new business to contract. Seeker wondered if amongst those passers-by was the one who had left a human being chained by the neck, helpless in the face of a savage animal. He wondered also where that beast was now, and how it was managed. The darkness of the night and lateness of the hour had not allowed for any but the most cursory search of the outbuildings at the gaming house for tracks or signs, but today he was determined he would go over every inch of the place.

He was about to turn off up the back road to the market gardens when the driver of a cart, passing the windmill on Blackman Street, called out.

'Captain! Didn't think to see you this far south!'

Seeker knew the voice immediately but took a moment to understand that its owner could be here, and driving that cart. 'Samuel! Didn't think to see you beyond Cornhill!'

The old man was already slowing to a stop, earning grumbles from a wagoner coming behind him. Seeker turned his horse across the road and brought it alongside Samuel's cart. Already, the moment after he had recognised Samuel, he had spotted several other familiar figures, ranged alongside and behind the old Parliamentary soldier who kept the coffee house on Birchin Lane. There beside him was Gabriel, of course, the coffee-house boy, taken in off the street by Samuel and his niece years since. Behind them, on sacks of cloth got up as cushions, were a man and two women: the lawyer Elias Ellingworth who had finally, or so Seeker had heard, persuaded Samuel's niece Grace to marry him, Grace herself, and the lawyer's sister, Maria. Seeker could not help himself. The sight of her, in so unexpected a place and at so unexpected a time, deprived him of the ability to say anything further.

The movement and the grumbles of impeded travellers continued all around them, but it was as if Seeker and the occupants of the cart had been suddenly silenced and frozen in that place. Every face in the back of the cart registered shock and then awkwardness. They all knew what was said to have passed between Seeker and Maria and they knew how badly it had ended. It was Samuel who at last broke the spell.

'Well, Captain, we haven't seen you to take your draught down Birchin Lane in a good long day. Truth, we've hardly seen hide nor hair of you since you got back from the north, and I'm sure that must be ten months at least. Don't tell me you've taken to drinking that muck I hear tell they're serving up at the Rainbow?'

Before Seeker could answer, Maria fixed him with a searing look. 'Oh, no, Samuel. The captain doesn't bother himself with coffee houses any more. I hear he prefers what's on offer up at the Black Fox these days.'

At this the boy Gabriel's eyes widened, Grace blushed, and even Elias looked as if he might wish to silence his sister. Samuel cleared his throat. 'Well, Dorcas always did keep a fine table, but I hope you know you'll always be welcome at Kent's, Captain, whatever else.'

'I do, Samuel,' said Seeker, forcing himself to look away from Maria. 'But tell me, what are you doing on the road at this early hour, and so far from home?'

Samuel beamed. 'It's my girl's birthday, and as you know, she don't make a fuss of things like that, nor near enough fuss of herself in general.'

At this his niece tried to chide him, but he wouldn't have it. 'No, I'll say my piece. Best thing in my life you are, child, and by your next birthday you'll be another man's to care for, and not mine. And who knows where I shall be then? You shall have your treat and day out, and fuss made of you, and that's that.'

'Your uncle's right, Grace,' said Seeker. 'So where do you go?'

'Lambeth. Tradeskin's Ark. To see the gardens.'

'And the curiosities,' put in Gabriel. 'Elias is going to take me and Grace and Maria round and explain them to us. They've got a mermaid and a unicorn and all sorts, Mr Tavener says.' Then the boy gave a dramatic sigh and glanced furtively to his right. 'Of course, Samuel won't go in. Nothing in there Samuel hasn't seen on his travels. Or so he says,' he added in an undertone.

'I doubt there'll not be much Samuel couldn't tell you

a tale about,' said Seeker. Before returning to join in the struggle for Parliament, Samuel had fought all over Europe in the Protestant cause, and sacked a good few towns and private strongholds in his time. Samuel loved to tell a story, but Seeker knew that Tradescant's collection of curiosities – 'Tradeskin's Ark' – was displayed on the uppermost floor of a large house in Lambeth. It was the shattered left leg, almost lost to a Royalist's musket, and not arrogance or indifference that would keep the old man outside in Tradescant's garden whilst his family climbed those stairs. 'No point in paying good money to see stuff behind glass cases when you've already seen the real thing, is there?'

'Quite right, Captain. Quite right. Besides, I doubt they'd allow the likes of me around so fine a place, money paid or not.'

Seeker bent lower over his horse's neck. 'If John Tradescant or anyone else takes that line with you or yours, Samuel, you direct them to me.'

The old man smiled. 'Oh, I will that, Captain.'

Seeker's eyes drifted to Maria again. 'You could do worse for your dinner,' he said, 'than the Dog and Duck by St George's Fields. I have passed a happy hour or two there myself, though in better times.'

The studied hostility left Maria's eyes, though only for a moment, before she looked away.

He didn't know what else he could say now, in front of them all, or how he could say it. And then the opportunity was gone. 'Oh, we're to dine at the George, Captain, on Borough High Street,' said Gabriel. 'An old friend of Samuel's, from the German wars, is come up from Sussex.' Again he made a knowing face. 'And *then* there'll be some stories told.'

Seeker laughed. 'I don't doubt there will be. And you mind and listen, Gabriel, for the next time I'm in Kent's, I shall want to hear them.' There was nothing more to be said that could be said there. He swallowed. 'Well, I'd best get on.'

Samuel nodded and set the placid carthorse in motion, and if any of them thought it strange that Seeker watched after them until they had trundled out of sight, none of them said so.

In the gaming-house yard, the men of the local watch were huddled around a brazier. They scrambled to attention when Seeker arrived. He nodded at them.

'Anything?'

The older of the two shook his head. 'Nothing. No one's come near the place all night.'

'And round the back?'

'All's still secure. I've made my rounds every quarter hour.'

'Right,' said Seeker. Ignoring the disappointed looks of the men, who had thought they might be dismissed, he wrapped his sash around his mouth and nose before pushing open the door to the sound of scuttling vermin. What confronted him now was worse, somehow, than what had been illuminated the night before by the shifting yellow and red flames of his torch. In this harsh morning light, nothing could be softened, nothing hidden or even cast into shadow, nothing made to disappear by the simple expedient of moving his hand a few inches to the left or right, consigning the object beneath to darkness. It was all there, still, the unrelenting gore.

He had given orders that the carcass should not be moved from its place chained to the wall, and that no one should be allowed access to the storage house until his return. Now, by the light of the opened door and from a window giving out over the market gardens behind, he looked again at the rust-stained assemblage of rags and human remains on the earthen floor. He crouched down, still keeping his sash muffled to his face, and examined the man's clothing. Shreds of a russet woollen coat, moss-coloured breeches, brown woollen hose. A ripped doublet of hide that had once been tan. A linen shift whose original colour could hardly be determined. Boots flung asunder that looked to have walked many miles. All good, serviceable stuff, but nothing that spoke of luxury or wealth. The clothing of a solid yeoman, perhaps, or honest craftsman. He could see no hat.

Seeker stood, the better to survey the whole space. In the far right-hand corner, beyond what was left of the man's head, was a dark object which he had not noticed in the night. He circled the body and stooped to pick up the item – a long, soft cap trimmed in thick fur. It had a foreign look to it. Seeker considered again the knit of the woollen hose, the stuff of the jacket: these were an Englishman's clothes. It was the hat that did not belong.

'Where did you come from, my friend?' he asked. 'And how did you end up here?'

The earthen floor of the outhouse was soft in parts, and dry where the blood had not soaked into it. It bore the imprints of massive paws and claws, but they did not reach beyond the man's head, and none were visible at the darker end of the outhouse, furthest from the door. The beast had reached its limit there. Seeker went back to the doorway to inspect the area around it, as he had not been able to do properly the night before. There, four feet from the ground, was the heavy iron link to which the animal must have been chained. He paced from there to where the prints stopped, a distance of about fourteen feet. He tried to determine how long the chain might have been, how large the beast it tethered, but gave it up. 'Long enough,' he said to himself. A man had been chained to one wall, an animal to the other, and they had been left to fight it out. The bear's chain had been just long enough.

He left, closing the door behind him. Again, the two men looked hopeful. Seeker started towards the house. 'I'll be back in half an hour,' he said. The younger of the pair appeared to nudge the other.

'It is well past the time for the end of our watch, Captain,' ventured the older.

Seeker was already halfway up the yard. He stopped and turned round.

'I am acquainted with the hours of the borough watch,' he said. 'But this is business of the state you are employed upon, and you will wait here until two of my men arrive to relieve you. Or would you prefer to take your complaint to the major-general? He's generally to be found across the river.' Seeker tilted his head in the direction of the Tower and Major-General Barkstead. 'I'm sure he's nothing else to do with his time of a morning.'

The two men shook their heads vigorously. By the time they had stopped apologising, Seeker was gone.

Bankside was a different place by day. The seductive promises of easy virtue and cheap luxury from lit windows and doorways had given way to another sort of activity – the brisk work of clearing up and stocking up, making ready for another day's profit. London might loom large across the river, its shoulders hunched as if squaring for a fight, but Bankside paid it little heed: there was the business of the day to be getting on with. Seeker could almost have approved.

But then he turned his horse away from the river, down the side of the old Bear Garden. This was the other Bankside – half-hidden, a little beneath where decent men would walk. He made for Dead Man's Place and then the Clink. Trickles of water crawled down walls to become rivulets amongst the cobbles, running not to the river or the city, but away, elsewhere, to elude and disappear and not be found. Southwark leaked, and the spirits of ages past clung with the moss to its stone walls and dank corners. It was a place where men could dissolve into nothingness, disappear.

But Thomas Faithly had not disappeared: Seeker knew exactly where he was to be found. The gaoler who opened the narrow wooden door of the Clink to Seeker didn't ask who he was there for, as he led him down the dimly lit stairs and into the narrow passageway beneath the stone arches that separated the cells. The stench here was almost as bad as at the open sewer running into the river at the end of Dead Man's Place. Faithly and his five companions of the gaming house had been lodged in a small space at the far end of the passage. There was an almost animal shifting and grumbling from amongst the men when the warder turned the key to their cell. Thomas Faithly groaned in relief when he saw Seeker, earning astonished looks from his fellow prisoners. None of them could conceive of a situation in which they would be pleased to see Damian Seeker. Seeker shot Faithly a warning look. 'Less of the wit,' he said, 'or there'll be more of what you had last night.' Thurloe's turncoat Royalist agent made a show of shrinking back and turning his face towards the seeping wall of the cell.

'Right,' said Seeker. 'Up, the lot of you. I have something to show you.'

The men looked at each other, a mix of panic and confusion on their faces, but none of them dared to speak.

The spectacle of several well-dressed gentlemen, their fine clothes stained and stinking, emerging bleary-eyed from the Clink was hardly a novelty, and yet it gave pleasure to many honest folk by the riverside that morning, to say nothing of targets for the street urchins and apprentice boys spying the chance of a moment's amusement. Jeers, catcalls and not a few malodorous missiles accompanied the party as it made its way from the prison to their gaming house back along Bankside. Seeker saw no need to come to the defence of individuals so profitless to the state.

The confusion of the prisoners increased as they were marched into the gaming house and out again at the back door. The grumbling men of the watch had now been replaced by two of Seeker's own men. The man at the front, his fine green velvet suit already streaked with vomit and other things that Seeker did not wish to determine, blanched even further and started to babble, digging his heels into the ground like a stubborn cur.

'No! We did nothing more than have a hand at cards, throw some dice a time or two. You cannot shoot us for that!'

'Keep moving, idiot, you're not worth the powder,' growled Seeker, as one of his men pushed the terrified Cavalier onwards.

At the bottom of the yard Seeker stood in front of the door to the outbuilding. He had sworn Faithly to secrecy over what they had discovered there. 'Were any of you down here last night?'

There was much head-shaking. Seeker looked closely at each of Faithly's five companions; none looked as if he was lying.

'Or at any time before?'

Again outright denial.

'And did you witness anyone, perhaps leading a beast, enter this outhouse at any time yesterday?'

Denial this time was accompanied by a degree of curiosity.

'Right,' said Seeker. 'I want you all to go in there, take a look at what you see, and then tell me what you know of it, whether anything about it is familiar to you.' He turned to one of his men, whom he had known many years and knew to be of a strong stomach. He'd already told him what waited inside. 'You come in with me, Gerald.' To another he said, 'Give us one minute and send them all in in a line, after us.'

Inside, he asked Gerald to pick up some sacking from the corner. 'We're going to shield the body from their sight, and then, once they're all in, reveal it.'

Gerald didn't ask, 'Why conceal it at all?' but Seeker could see the question pass briefly over his face.

'I want them all to see it at once. I want to get their reactions. See if any of them looks less surprised than the others.'

But the actions of five of the men were all of a kind: shouts and groans of horror followed by retching and a dash for the door. The sixth man, Thomas Faithly, had come in last and averted his eyes as Seeker and his man lifted the sacking. He was the first to be back out of the door. Outside, his face was as grey as any of the others.

Seeker waited a while until they'd finished vomiting, until the shaking had lessened, and then told them he wanted them back in, one at a time. Disbelief briefly displaced disgust on their faces.

'I want you to look at his face,' said Seeker.

'Has he even got a face?' said the one in green velvet.

'Enough of one. Come on, you first.'

The man looked as if he might protest but then took a deep breath and offered no further resistance as Seeker led him back into the small building. And so it went on, five men brought in one by one, forced to look, taken out again. Five men denying they had ever seen the victim of the previous night's atrocity. Thomas Faithly was the sixth. Once inside the small stone building and with the door closed, he turned his back on the body on the floor.

'What was said last night?' asked Seeker.

'Nothing of any use – a lot of cursing about damnable luck and even more damnable spies, who'd sell a man out for a grubby coin.'

Seeker couldn't help but smile at that and Faithly's eyes flashed anger. 'I am talking about seedy wretches in taverns or street corners, reporting on innocent—'

Seeker stopped him. 'I'm not interested in your hurt pride. Had they anything to say about this?' He thrust a hand towards the body on the floor.

Faithly still refused to look again. 'Nothing. Nor anything near it.'

'Right. There'll be a justice of the peace to see to you by dinnertime. I've already paid the warder for your keep.

You'll meet me the day after tomorrow, early, the usual place and I'll give you further instructions.'

The luckless gamblers having been returned to the Clink until such time as the local justice had the leisure to attend to them, Seeker called at last for the cart to carry the bloodied remains of the dead man to the Westminster coroner, under whose jurisdiction they lay. Left alone in the now empty outbuilding, he thought again of the horrific scene that must have unfolded here only the day before. It made little enough sense, that a man could have been lured to such a place, unseen. It made even less that a wild beast of the size of one of the Bankside bears could have been brought here without being seen or heard. And yet it had happened, all of it. He determined on finding out who that man had been, and what it was in his life that had brought him to such a terrible end. The earth beneath where the body had lain was dark and sticky, and the bloody iron smell of it reminded Seeker too much of things he had encountered after battle and would rather forget. He would be glad to leave this place. He opened the door, and as he turned to take one last look around him, something light and insubstantial shifted slightly in the draught of air from outside. Seeker walked over to the edge of the stain on the ground beneath where the man had lain, and crouched down. The light and insubstantial thing was a small piece of paper, like a ticket or receipt. Off-white, it was stained a dull brown at the edge, where blood had soaked in before drying. He reached out a hand and gently lifted it from the earth, giving a slight tug where the bloodied part had stuck. Going over to the door, he held the paper up to the light. On it there was a rough stamp in the form of a clock face, and beneath it the letters '*D.K.*' and the previous day's date.

'I think you have left me a message, my friend,' said Seeker, putting the scrap in his pocket and walking back out into the yard.

THREE

The Yorkshireman

Boyes checked that the door behind him was firmly bolted. 'You are sure the information is good?' he asked.

Fish nodded. 'Certain. I paid good money for it on the promise of more to come. All that is required of us is vigilance, and a little patience.'

Boyes, who had had many occasions in his life to learn both, said nothing, but crossed to the window to look out over the Hammersmith street. Fish and Cecil had been lodged in the upper room of this coach house for over a week now, that they might further their enterprise. The street below was narrow, and entered on a bend just as it passed beneath their window. Fish appeared to know London's every nook and cranny, and again, as had been the case on their previous attempt on the usurper's life, he had chosen their vantage point well. Oliver was known to travel this way on occasion, on his journeys between Whitehall and Hampton Court. It would be a fine thing, thought Boyes, a fitting thing that Cromwell, who had mastered armies of thousands, only to descend to a life of luxury and idleness he had not been born to, should at last be brought low here, on this drab thoroughfare, as he trundled his way from one palace that was not rightfully his to another. Boyes pictured him in the carriage, imagined him looking out onto the street, where mortal men and women walked. Would he wave, Boyes wondered, Cromwell, as the carriage slowed to negotiate the narrow bend beneath them? Boyes would like to be there, on the street, watching the man in the carriage as Cecil released the catch on his contraption and opened fire. He would like to see the look on Oliver Cromwell's face when he saw that it was *him* standing there.

One, two, three . . . seven blasts of shot from the seven guns mounted and rigged together on that frame to fire simultaneously. Cecil had been dubious at first and Fish intrigued, as Boyes had explained his idea to them. It was his own refinement of machines he had seen put to use elsewhere, adapted to this place and to their special purpose. There would be collateral damage, innocent victims, but that could not be helped: theirs was a higher, a sacred purpose.

The coach house was next to an inn of no account, and the innkeeper more than happy to accept a generous fee for the sole use of this spacious upper room. Not too much, not so much as would cause suspicion, but enough to secure it without interference or question. Fish had made plain to the innkeeper that the services of the chambermaid would not be required.

Eight days they had been here, waiting for intelligence from Fish's source, John Toope, member of Cromwell's Life Guard. Today, at last, it had come. Whilst Boyes, in the various disguises to which his life had accustomed him, saw to his business around London, making other things ready, one or other of Fish and Cecil had remained in this room at all times, the door well bolted. Early this morning, Boyes had received the coded message that told him he should come today.

Now he turned away from his surveillance of the street. 'Two days from now?'

Fish nodded. 'In the afternoon.'

'Who'll be travelling with him?'

Fish shrugged. 'His wife. A daughter, probably. Does it matter?'

Boyes shook his head. 'Not greatly. The son would have been good.'

'The son's not our concern,' said Fish, the Leveller. 'They'll never make a dynasty of Dick Cromwell.'

'Perhaps not,' said Boyes. It did not seem worth his while saying to this man that dynasties had been built on worse. He didn't expect to have any more dealings with Mr Fish once they had achieved this present enterprise, and he was confident he could deal with the matter of Richard Cromwell himself, should that become necessary.

There was nothing to do here now but wait. For Boyes, there was business still to attend to elsewhere, but he was not inclined to set out on an empty stomach. He and Fish went down to the parlour of the inn, and whilst he ordered a morning draught and a dish of kippers, Fish made a show of returning to the upper room of the coach house with a pot of beer and some watery porridge for Cecil, whom they had given out to be unwell, and not to be disturbed. As Fish was going back out on to the street, the innkeeper's wife called after him, 'Mr Fish?'

He turned around. 'Yes, Mistress Swann?'

'Should I call at the apothecary, for a cordial for Mr Cecil? Some concoction that might ease his belly? It would be no trouble.'

Fish shook his head. 'No, thank you, mistress. A little of your good porridge and peace and quiet will soon put him to rights. If you would see to it that he is not disturbed.'

'Some chance of that in this place,' muttered a man Boyes had noticed when first they'd come into the parlour. He made it his business to notice anyone who might notice him. The grumbler was a young man, aged around twenty-five, perhaps, with a pale face and straggly brown hair that gave the appearance of having been chopped, rather than properly cut, and certainly no effort had been made to dress it. The man's clothes were well made though, if drab, and despite the studied disgruntlement, there was something in his expression that suggested humour.

'You are not pleased with your lodging, friend?' said Boyes, offering the young man a broad smile.

The man amended his disgruntled look slightly. 'Nothing wrong with the lodging, cleaner than some and the ale's all right. But the noise! It never stops – carts, carriages, sheep, cows, chickens, pedlars, washerwomen and I don't know what else. Have they nothing to do but travel back and forth? Can they not just stay in one place and *be*?'

'You've never visited London before, have you, friend?'

'No, I haven't,' replied the younger man with emphasis, as if defending himself from an accusation.

'I fear you will find the city, where all these travellers are bound, a good deal worse than Hammersmith. You are also bound for the city, I'd wager?'

The young man nodded somewhat glumly. 'Inns of Chancery. My master has sent me down to learn all the things he's no time for. I should have been there last night, but I took a wrong turn and ended up here.'

Boyes looked at him carefully. It was such a foolish story for the fellow's presence here that it was probably true. 'And where has your good master sent you down to the Inns of Chancery from?' he asked.

The young man straightened himself, looked Boyes levelly in the eye and said, almost as if offering him a challenge, 'Yorkshire.'

FOUR

The Clerkenwell Clockmaker

Seeker found Thomas Pride in his offices at St James's Palace. Pride, High Sheriff of Surrey and Commissioner of the Peace for London, was a haberdasher by trade. There were rumours that he slept in the bed in St James's Palace that had once been the King's. Seeker's response to any who whispered it within his hearing was to tell them that Colonel Pride merited a good night's sleep in that bed, for his service to the state, as its previous occupant had not. And yet it was an unspoken disappointment to Seeker that Pride, alongside whom he had once fought, should so have lowered himself as to take up the trappings of those whose regime they had fought to end. It was a cause of unease between them, where in years gone by there had been none.

'Seeker!' said Pride as soon as he spied him through the door to the anteroom of his chamber. 'Come in, Captain, come in. You'll be here on Mr Thurloe's business, I suppose?'

'No, Colonel. It's something outside of Mr Thurloe's purview.'

Pride raised an eyebrow. 'Go on.'

'I came across it by chance in a raid last night, on a gaming house on Bankside.'

'With Sergeant Proctor?'

'That's right, sir.'

Pride nodded. 'I ordered the raid. I'll have the pestilence of gambling in this Commonwealth stamped out, come what may. I'll cleanse Bankside of its loose living or I'll have the whole place thrown into the Thames.' The prospect appeared to give him a great deal of satisfaction. 'So you went out on it too?'

'Old times' sake, sir.' Seeker nodded towards the door through which Pride's secretary could be seen. 'I've spent that long with a pen in my hand and a pile of papers in front of me this last while, I thought I was maybe getting rusty.'

Pride laughed out loud. 'We'll all go to the bottom of the Thames before you get rusty, Seeker. And you remembered what to do?'

'Oh, aye, sir. But – it was afterwards. Once we'd sent the culprits off to the Clink.' And he told Pride about the outbuilding, and what he had found there.

Pride's face hardened as he listened.

'It's not possible. I had them all shot.'

'I know. But I'm certain, sir, it was a bear did that, no other beast.'

Pride didn't waste any more time suggesting to Seeker that he might be mistaken. Instead, he went to the door of his chamber and roared at the top of his voice, 'Mowbray! I want Sergeant Mowbray in here right now!'

It was not until several minutes later that a man whose uniform had evidently been thrown on in haste appeared at the colonel's door and stood to attention. 'You sent for me, Colonel?'

'Oh, yes, Mowbray. I sent for you. Now you will explain to the captain here, and to me, how it is that he could have come across the half-eaten body of a man in a hovel on Bankside.'

Every last suggestion of colour drained from the man's pockmarked face. He opened his mouth, but ventured no words.

'Well?' demanded Pride.

'I don't know, sir.'

'Do you not? Then tell the captain what you do know. Tell him what happened that day in February that we took six men and muskets to the Bear Garden at the Hope.'

Mowbray's eyes moved furiously from side to side, and then he appeared to be trying to study his own forehead. He ran a tongue across his bottom lip. 'Well, Colonel, as you know, we got the bears by the nose, joined them through the rings like you ordered and chained them together.'

'And then?'

'And then we lined them up and shot them, sir, at your command. Six or seven of them.'

'Apart from the cub.'

'Yes, sir.' The man nodded eagerly. 'Apart from the cub.

You said yourself, sir, as it was as yet innocent of bestial depravity.' He attempted sympathy. 'To think it has eaten a man. The savagery of beasts, sir. Thanks to God are we raised above them.'

'Oh, you'll be raised very high indeed, Sergeant, if I don't have the truth from you.' Now Pride turned to Seeker. 'What you found, Captain, might that have been done by a cub?'

'Only if that cub was a good two foot bigger than me,' said Seeker.

Pride thumped his hand down on his desk, disturbing the papers there and almost knocking over the inkpot. 'That cub was sold to a travelling showman, and was dancing its way round Ireland last anyone heard of it. It would hardly be big enough yet to take off a man's hand, never mind half his head, even if it has got any teeth left. The truth, Mowbray. I'll have it this very minute.'

Mowbray was terrified. It took several attempts before he succeeded in mastering his tongue. 'It was a fellow supposed to be a philosopher, or a follower of the new science or some such thing. He wanted to keep one of them back, the bears, as a curiosity, and for study.'

Pride's face was almost purple. 'As a curiosity? Do you remember what happened at the Hope last year, Mowbray? Do you remember why we had to shoot those bears?'

Mowbray lowered his eyes.

A second thump. 'You will answer me.'

Mowbray's voice was scarcely audible. 'Because of the child, sir.'

'That's right. Because a young child fell into the bear pit from the viewing scaffold and was killed. And how much more than the price of the life of a child, did this *philosopher* pay you?'

Mowbray looked as if he might attempt to deny having profited from the exchange, but then saw the folly of such a course. He looked at his feet and mumbled something.

'Speak up, man,' ordered Pride.

'Twenty shillings.'

'Twenty shillings. You value the life of a child at twenty shillings.'

'Child, no, Colonel. Surely, you said it was a man's body the captain there found—'

Pride stopped him. 'You're a disgrace to the army.' Then he addressed Seeker. 'Take this man away, Captain. I'm going to have him court-martialled.'

'Colonel . . .'

'Enough, Mowbray. You'll tell the captain everything you know about this *philosopher* you sold that beast to, and if you're lucky, you might end your few remaining days guarding an Irish peat bog instead of up against a wall, in front of a squad of my musketeers. Do I make myself clear?'

A torrent of obsequy signalled Mowbray's understanding.

Half an hour later, Seeker was walking out of St James's Palace, having consigned Mowbray to solitary confinement until such time as he would face his court martial. The shiftless sergeant had told him little of any use. He had never met the alleged man of science, 'the philosopher' to whom the bear had been sold, all contact having been carried out through intermediaries, faceless, nameless characters of the sort that were ten a penny in the liberties and suburbs. A covered wagon had come for the beast, which had already been sufficiently sedated by a preparation provided in advance by the philosopher. They'd hauled the animal onto the wagon, under cover of sacking, and had moved off along Bankside, heading towards London Bridge. Not down behind the arena, no; towards the city. The men driving the cart had paid him what had been agreed and he'd watched them till they were out of sight, fearing they'd cross the colonel's path on the way. He knew nothing more about them and he'd never seen nor heard of men nor animal since.

'"Man of science."' Pride had scoffed at the idea. 'The fellow's running an illicit bear-baiting ring somewhere.' But Seeker hadn't been so sure. If the authorities could sniff out a game of cards in an unremarkable house in Bankside such as Thomas Faithly had been caught in, they would surely have heard of illicit bear-baiting. And the animal had been taken away from Southwark. Where to? Where was this philosopher, and why had he brought the animal back to Bankside? There was no more to be got from Mowbray. The answers would have to be found elsewhere, Seeker thought, in the story of the dead man, and in what he had left behind.

★

Seeker seldom went to Clerkenwell by choice. The very air of the place seemed to retain an echo of the cowled figures who'd given the place its name. St James's, St John's, St Bartholomew's, the Charterhouse. The place had swarmed with monks until such time as Thomas Cromwell had told them to walk elsewhere, and to take their mumbled prayers and chantings with them. The monks might be long gone, but the poor and the sick still came, and the alleyways and courtyards between the houses of the wealthy were filled with the shabby, makeshift dwellings of those the city had no room for.

St Sepulchre's, creeping northwards up Saffron Hill, was the worst. But Seeker wasn't going to St Sepulchre's today. Instead, he tied up his horse, Acheron, in Turk's Head Yard and continued on foot towards St John's. Ahead of him, the streets thinned out, there were more gardens to be seen, and beyond them glimpses of the countryside as it was pushed back towards the sanctuary of Islington. Near the top of St John's Lane he could see the signs of three clockmakers, but a close scrutiny soon revealed that only the second matched the rough stamp on the ticket he had retrieved from the bloodied clothes of the Bankside victim.

He went to the door under the sign of a clock with the letters 'D' and 'K' marked into the bottom corners. Inside, the front shop was small, maybe seven feet deep in all and just as narrow, with a workbench at which the clockmaker sat. Upon the wall ticked a variety of clocks, most weighted, a few in the old style with only the one hand telling the hour across its face, but others with two. The jarring of their mechanisms was out of time, a background cacophony that Seeker wondered did not drive the clockmaker mad. In his boyhood, in the woods and on the moors of the north, Seeker had learned to tell the hour by the quality of light, the length of shadows or position of the stars, the behaviour of animal and birds. Now, in the city, with its endless church bells, it hardly seemed to him worth the trouble of keeping a timepiece, but many clearly did.

The man at the workbench was elderly – almost seventy years of age, Seeker would have said – but his hunched shoulders must once have been broad, and he had a keen eye. At the sound of the bell above the door, he had put down his eyeglass. His hands were long and bony; they shook very slightly as he laid the instrument down beside the mechanism he had been examining. Spread out upon the bench beside it was an array of cogs, weights and lengths of rope which Seeker found bewildering.

'Captain,' the man said, inclining his head very slightly. 'How may I help you?' Seeker couldn't quite place the voice – not English, that was for certain. Dutch, perhaps. Or German.

Seeker held out the torn ticket and placed it on the workbench. 'You can tell me about the man you gave this to.'

The clockmaker lifted his eyeglass again and picked up the ticket. He grimaced at the blood, and looked up to Seeker with a question in his eyes. Seeker simply nodded and the clockmaker held the bloodied remnant closer. He gave it the attention he might give a component he was thinking of inserting in to some complex machine.

'Two days ago,' he said, 'in the afternoon. He left a clock here to be repaired. A very fine pendulum clock of German manufacture. Aside from some minor repairs to its chime mechanism, it was in excellent condition – well looked after.' He handed the ticket back to Seeker. 'A moment, Captain.'

He got up from his stool and drew back the curtain behind him a few inches, revealing a glimpse into the main workshop, which gave out onto a yard at the back. A young man was working a bellows over the fire, where various lengths of metal waited to be heated and beaten into shape. At a workbench next to a large anvil was seated another man, not quite so elderly in appearance as the clockmaker, but whose evident height caused him to hunch even further over his work, who was intent upon what looked to Seeker to be a complex mechanism surrounded by loose cogs, springs and wires. The shopkeeper addressed this man in German, his tone suggesting a question. Without looking up, the other indicated something out of Seeker's line of sight. Seeker suppressed his frustration: he had no interest in the clock, only the man who had brought it, but sure enough the shopkeeper emerged back through the curtain a minute later carrying what did indeed look to be a very fine piece of work, which he set down on his counter for Seeker's inspection.

Glancing back towards the workshop he said, 'My brother is a quick worker, Captain, and he was very taken with the craftsmanship of this piece.'

'I don't doubt it,' said Seeker, not being able to keep from reaching a hand out to the clock, tracing its lines. The case was in the form of a house of gilded metal, the face intricately engraved with lines of classical proportions, as if the whole should bring to mind a temple. The cupola that made its roof was in fact a large bell, and the chains bearing its weights were almost a foot in length. The clockmaker, who informed Seeker his name was Dietmar Kästner, set the whole very carefully on the counter. 'Brandenburg, 1603. A fine piece of German craftsmanship.'

'I won't argue with you,' said Seeker. 'But it's the man who brought it that interests me. Did he give you his name?'

The old man pushed out his lower lip. 'I'm afraid not, Captain. I remember my customers by their clocks – I don't ask their names. The ticket, alongside his face, of course, would have been enough.'

'What do you mean his face? Was there something strange about it?'

'Oh, no, Captain. You misunderstand. I see the face, I remember the clock. The ticket is for their own benefit. Many of my customers entrust me with very valuable belongings, and some prefer to have proof that they have done so. I take no offence.'

'I see. And the man who brought this clock? Had you ever seen him before?'

'Never, Captain.'

'What about your brother?'

The clockmaker pulled back the curtain and addressed the man at the workbench again. 'Josef?'

'*Bitte?*'

And then followed another brief exchange in a tongue Seeker did not properly understand.

'My brother didn't see the man at all, Captain. Only the clock.'

'All right. But you saw him. Tell me about him – his face, hair, build and the like.'

And so the clockmaker described the man, just as Seeker had imagined he must have presented himself to the world before a half-starved bear had torn his body to pieces. They had kept them half-starved, the bears of Bankside, that they might better entertain the citizens who paid good money to see them fight to the death dogs or bulls or some other helpless creature, and Seeker could not believe that an animal that had not been starving had done what he'd seen to the man who had brought that clock to Clerkenwell.

'Where had he come from? Did he say?'

The clockmaker cast his mind back. 'Out of town, the coast somewhere. Sussex? Kent? He was putting up in Southwark for a couple of days.'

'Whereabouts in Southwark?'

'I don't know.'

'And what had he come to town for?'

The clockmaker held out his hands as if it were obvious. 'To have his clock mended.'

Seeker frowned. 'What – all the way from the coast? That can't have been all.'

The clockmaker looked mildly offended. 'It is a very fine piece, Captain. I had not seen one like it in thirty years. A very fine piece, and not to be subjected to the unskilled hands of some village blacksmith. There is a particular delicacy, an intricacy of design to German clocks that English clockmakers are not comfortable with. This man knew what he had and has looked after it well. He knew only a good German clockmaker could be trusted to handle such a piece.'

'Aye well, Clerkenwell's the place to come, I suppose. But the man I'm talking about wasn't a rich man, not by his dress. Respectable, I'd say, but not rich. How would he have come by a piece like this?'

The clockmaker's voice lowered. 'The clock came from Brandenburg, Captain, and the man did not, but he spoke my language well enough. I don't ask English soldiers how they came by German clocks.'

'So,' said Seeker after a pause, 'he was a soldier of fortune.'

'That would be my surmise,' said the clockmaker. 'For whom, I do not know and I did not ask. The Emperor or the Winter Queen. It makes no difference to the clock.'

No, nor to those whose lives were destroyed over the course of those brutal German wars. Years of devastation, set off by a row over the crown of Bohemia. Thousands had gone from these islands to fight in the cause of Elizabeth of Bohemia, the Winter Queen, daughter of James I, sister of Charles I, and wilful champion of the Protestant faith.

She was a silly woman, like all the Stuart women, and she had married a foolish man. Her husband, the Elector Frederick, had lost the Palatinate over his acceptance of the crown of Bohemia in the teeth of imperial opposition. In doing so he has consigned his family to a lifetime's wandering, and hundreds of thousands of men, women and children to their deaths in a war that had lasted thirty years. The Stuarts. Everything they touched corrupted in their hands.

Seeker looked at the clockmaker. Seventy now, short-sighted, stooped, and a hand that trembled. But he hadn't always been an old man.

'How long have you been here?'

'In Clerkenwell?'

'In England.'

'Over thirty years. I fled Heidelberg when Tilly's forces marched in to destroy the place in '22 and I haven't seen my home since.'

'You didn't fight?'

'What? When they killed my daughter? Raped my wife? Burned my father's house?' He rolled up his sleeve to show Seeker the twisted, waxen burns that disappeared up his arm, then lifted his hair to show the scar from what must have been a savage blow, across the back of his neck. 'Yes,

I fought, and when they had finished doing all that they did, and I found to my despair that I was not dead, I came here, where there was no war.'

'And in the late troubles?'

The old man smiled. 'I sat on this bench and I fixed my clocks and I paid my dues.'

Seeker nodded. 'Fair enough.'

The clockmaker indicated the clock sitting between them on the worktop. 'Will he be coming back, the man who brought this?'

'No,' said Seeker, picking the thing up. 'He won't.'

FIVE

Sayes Court

Thomas Faithly felt his heart sink as the masts of Deptford Docks loomed closer into view. The constant building works and expansion of the docks were an unrelenting reminder of the world he had never seen. For all the tales Prince Rupert had brought back to the King's court of the horrors of the Caribbean, Thomas was not sure he wouldn't rather strike out there anyway. But the thought left as quickly as it had come: he wouldn't get away. Seeker would find him, bring him back. And then it would be the Tower again, at best. By the time the boatman drew in to the landing place a little west of where the new dock works began in earnest, Thomas's ill-humour was only surpassed by his discomfort. His bones still ached from a night on the floor of the Clink, his companions having commandeered what passed for bedding. The stink of the sodden, filthy rushes he had lain on was still in his nostrils and his eyes stung through lack of sleep. Although he had returned to Charing Cross to his lodgings at the Three Tobacco Pipes and changed out of his soiled clothing, he had utterly refused his landlady's inducement to take a good dinner 'to set him right and mend his pallor'. He had seen carnage in battle, but he was not sure, after what he and Seeker had come upon in that outbuilding last night, that he would ever eat meat again.

The other passengers having disembarked, the boatman turned a jagged yellow-toothed scowl on Thomas. 'Sayes Court, wasn't it? Shift yourself, then, m'lord, for I've a living to earn.'

Reluctantly, Thomas heaved himself up from the bench and clambered onto the landing stairs. He took one more look at the dockyard and the alternatives it offered, before setting his gaze straight ahead of him again, to the object of his dread: Sayes Court, home of John Evelyn, for whom Sir Thomas had long nursed a mild contempt. Since his return to England, and, more particularly, his release from the Tower, an increased acquaintance had nursed that contempt into something akin to disgust. But Sir Thomas would put up with his lot for now, if that was what it took. He had returned to England last year, having tired of life on the run with the royal court, and sworn to himself he would do whatever was asked of him to be allowed to stay, and perhaps, one day, to return home to Yorkshire and live like an honest Englishman. What was asked of him had soon been made plain to him by Cromwell's Chief Secretary and spymaster, John Thurloe, and then Damian Seeker had made it even plainer: he was to insert himself into the upper echelons of Royalist society – befriend those

Royalists who had stayed at home, those who had returned, and those who claimed they were not Royalists at all. In such circles, Thurloe was convinced, lay the greatest threat of clandestine activity and of danger to the security of the Protector. Thomas was to insinuate himself amongst these people, and he was to learn their secrets.

Such things were not beyond Thomas: long years living on his wits and little else in the train of the Stuarts had taught him to keep his own thoughts to himself whilst gaining the confidences of others. He had not, then, been a man to use the secrets of others against them and had never wished to play the politics of the exiled court. This was something different: he had thrown in his lot with Cromwell's regime as his last hope of coming home, and now his task was to discover secrets as well as to keep them. A little thought, a little patience, and he might have made his entry into more profitable, or at least congenial, circles than those surrounding Evelyn at Sayes Court. And he would probably have done so, had it not been for Clémence.

Thomas had hardly been a week out of the Tower when he had glimpsed Clémence as she flitted from a glover's to a hatter's in the New Exchange. The sight of her had stopped him in his tracks. Clémence Barguil – here, in London. He hadn't seen her in over a year – when the court had been at Aachen – but he needed hardly as much as a glimpse to know for certain that it was her. Once encountered, she was a woman not easily forgotten. A beautiful woman who appeared to have encased her heart in marble, or granite.

She walked with a forbidding, untouchable grace, like a statue come to life. Thomas had seen men all but freeze under her stony gaze, but he had also seen those grey eyes sparkle, like granite, in the sun. One man alone brought that sparkle to her eyes, just one man had ever breached the wall she had built around herself: Prince Rupert had been her sun. Not Thomas – she would shake her head and laugh at the thought of Thomas – but she would tolerate him because he had been Rupert's friend. Thomas had known that day at the Exchange that he shouldn't go after her, no good could come of it, but he had not been able to help himself. He had followed her, and this was where Clémence had led him to: Sayes Court.

As ever, building work, Evelyn's alterations to what had been his father-in-law's home, was in progress. Thomas did not mind that – a fine building he could appreciate, and even he would admit that Evelyn had good taste and a true draughtsman's eye, but the gardens were another matter. Thomas liked a well-stocked orchard and a good vegetable plot as much as any man, but Evelyn's endless disquisitions on plants and the proper design of a garden bored him half to death. Faithly Manor, in the North Riding, had had no pleasure garden – the moor had been Thomas's pleasure garden and the kitchen garden the cook's domain. Why walk through avenues of sculpted hedges to discourse upon the world when you might ride out into it? The time for talk was at the end of the day, by a hearty fire with a good dinner in the belly, a jug of claret to hand and a hound at your feet. But it could not be helped. Thomas had followed Clémence, and this was where she had brought him.

A footman at the door informed him that Evelyn and his guests were in the elaboratory, housed near the western end of the garden. Pausing once at the portico, Thomas closed his eyes and tried to summon his resilience before slipping quietly through the door.

A long bench to Thomas's right was laden with distilling equipment, glass vessels, long-handled metallic instruments, still-pans and mortars and pestles of various sizes. On the shelves above were stored a myriad of jars and bottles, containing an endless variety of dried substances and liquids whose use was beyond Thomas's knowledge or interest. The furnaces, which at times rendered the heat of the place unbearable, were unlit, and all the light in the room was at the far end, where John Evelyn and four other men were gathered around a small stove.

Evelyn and three of the men had their backs to Thomas, and the fourth, who Thomas could see from here was that German pedagogue Samuel Hartlib, was too intent on his demonstration to notice the arrival of the newcomer. From the moment he'd stepped in, Thomas had been aware of a pungent aroma in the air, scents of chypre and thyme, that instantly took him back to another, more congenial place. He could have closed his eyes and imagined himself again slipping in to the parlour of an old acquaintance in Dusseldorf, where many a merry evening had been spent in the King's retinue. But rather than several voices laughing and talking at once, as had invariably been the case on those nights, here there was only Hartlib's voice, as he explained the features of the stove, and its uses in the dissemination of pleasant smells. One of the onlookers – a man whose voice Thomas didn't recognise – asked whether it might not also be used for the dissemination of noxious vapours. Hartlib had looked a little alarmed, and said that yes, he supposed it might, but why should anyone with an interest in advancing the condition of mankind have any notion of such a thing?

'For no good reason, I am sure,' said the man, stepping back a little from his examination of the German stove. Thomas sensed a breaking off in the mood of the gathering and chose this moment to make himself known, coughing slightly. Evelyn turned around and peered up the room towards him.

'Sir Thomas. We had not expected you to join us this evening.'

Thomas doffed his hat and began to walk towards them. 'I found myself at a loss for good conversation, and so turned my feet where I might find it. I hope you will pardon my intrusion.'

Evelyn gave a thin, well-bred smile. 'Of course, Sir Thomas.'

Amongst Evelyn's guests, Thomas had already recognised the scientist and aristocrat Robert Boyle, brother to Cromwell's favourite hostess, Lady Ranelagh, and peering at the machine with the help of a magnifying glass was the

Bohemian, Wenceslaus Hollar. The sight of Hollar lifted Thomas's heart. He had not seen the King's old drawing master in over ten years.

Hollar was equally delighted. 'Sir Thomas! When Evelyn told me you were returned, I thought it hardly possible. But tell me, how does His Ma—'

But then Hollar stopped, at a warning look from Evelyn. For all Samuel Hartlib was their friend and great companion in science, he had been Parliament's man, and some said he, with his contacts throughout Europe, was Thurloe's man. Enquiries after the health of the King in exile would not be entirely wise. Hollar looked down, reconsidered, and then said more softly, 'It is good to see you safe returned, Sir Thomas.'

Evelyn interjected. 'Indeed, but we were about to join my wife and Mademoiselle Barguil for some refreshment, Sir Thomas. Perhaps you will renew your acquaintance with Hollar more comfortably when we are back in the house.'

As Thomas turned to follow Evelyn, he noticed that the man who had asked Hartlib about noxious gases was slipping out of a side door leading from the elaboratory to the western gate of Sayes Court.

'That gentleman is not joining us?' asked Thomas, as Evelyn ushered him towards the other door.

'What? Oh, no. Mr Mulberry has other business to see to this evening.'

Mulberry. Thomas was certain he didn't know anyone by the name, but he was not so certain that he had never seen that man, with his ruddy face and hawk nose, before.

Mary Evelyn and Clémence were waiting for them in the withdrawing room. Evelyn's wife was very young, and pretty at best, her fair curls framing the compliant, slightly plump face from which anxious eyes looked out. The contrast with Clémence could hardly have been greater. The Frenchwoman was almost a head taller, and might have been taken for a Puritan, or a well-dressed housekeeper. Her light brown hair was pulled back and pinned under a simple grey coif, which matched the grey silk of her dress. She's trying to make herself look plain, Thomas thought. And perhaps she did look plain, to those who did not know her. To Thomas, though, the severity of her dress only served to highlight the strength of her features, the intelligent forehead, the firm nose, the wide mouth with its knowing smile. And the eyes, a piercing, sparkling grey. But most of all Thomas's eyes were drawn to the only ornaments Clémence wore – small drop-pearl earrings mounted in silver, with gold fittings. Thomas wondered if he was the only man in the room who knew that those earrings had once belonged to the Queen of Bohemia, and that they had been gifted to Clémence by Rupert of the Rhine.

Whilst servants passed round glasses of good burgundy and dishes of the finest sweetmeats Thomas had had in months, he felt himself begin to relax.

'Do I detect your Breton touch in these very fine galettes, Mademoiselle Barguil?' said Hollar, helping himself to a third. 'I think I have heard you hail from Fougères?'

'Fougères was my childhood home, but I spent much

of my youth at the French court. It was there that I had the good fortune to meet Mistress Evelyn, though she was not Mistress Evelyn then, of course.' No, Mary Evelyn had then been the not-so-simple Mary Browne, daughter to Sir Richard Browne, Charles Stuart's ambassador to the French court. Evelyn's father-in-law was still the exiled King's resident in Paris, and John Thurloe had been very pleased indeed that Thomas Faithly had managed to worm his way into the society of Sayes Court. 'And then,' Clémence continued, 'it was also my misfortune to encounter many rogues, such as Sir Thomas here. But I am delighted to see he is turning his mind to more sober pursuits than he did then.'

Thomas could have sworn he saw a glint in her eye, but he decided it would hardly be worth him taking a chance on Evelyn's sense of humour by rising to the bait.

'A young man's folly, Clémence.' He forced a smile towards Evelyn. 'I hope I may be allowed to make reparation.'

Evelyn said something in Greek.

'I am sorry,' said Sir Thomas, 'but my brother was the scholar. You'll have to enlighten me.'

Evelyn translated. 'Repentance is the beginning of wisdom.'

Thomas said nothing and conversation returned to discussion of Hartlib's stove, and its properties in dispelling noxious odours. This, as Thomas had feared it might, set Evelyn off on his hobby-horse of the poor quality of

London air, the evils of sea coal, and what might be done to improve the quality of life in the city. Move it to Yorkshire, Thomas thought, but did not say. Evelyn's solution, expounded at great length, seemed to involve the creation of gardens and the planting of many trees. Thomas found himself surprised, for once, to be in agreement with his host.

As the wine and the sweetmeats and the warmth of the room took their effect, Hollar began to speak of music, and of the pity that organs had been removed from nearly all the churches, and placed in taverns instead.

'But a private man may still have fine music in his home, Wenceslaus, of that we can be grateful. And there is many a profitable study to be made, of course, of the mathematical properties of music.'

Thomas could not help himself. 'Ah, but is it not better just to enjoy a good old English song for the sheer pleasure of it?'

When Evelyn turned his long gaze on him, Thomas thought it might have been better to have held his tongue. It would serve him ill to fall out with this man without first learning something to Thurloe's advantage. Turning his attention to the others, Evelyn said, 'I have here a manuscript which I think might be of some interest to you gentlemen.' He lifted out a folio and carried it to a nearby side table, where he opened it with some care. Hartlib and the others gathered round, and Thomas bestirred himself to do likewise. 'One of Carissimi's motets, transcribed in his own hand, of course. I picked it up whilst in Rome, in '45.' He glanced over Hartlib's shoulder to where Thomas Faithly stood. 'Is Carissimi known at all, in Yorkshire, Sir Thomas?'

Thomas held his gaze. 'I daresay he is. But,' he added, not quite draining his glass and setting it down perilously near to the manuscript on the side table, 'you have me at an advantage: I was otherwise occupied when you were busy in Rome buying manuscripts. In '45. I'll bid you goodnight, gentlemen.'

Thomas turned away and made quickly for the door, pausing briefly only to make a short bow to Mary Evelyn and Clémence as the footman sprang forward to show him from the withdrawing room. He was down the drive and part way towards the gates of Sayes Court by the time Clémence, her skirts billowing in the chill November wind, was close enough to call out to him.

'Thomas. Wait!'

Thomas stopped on hearing her voice, and waited. When she reached him he turned to face her. 'I am sorry, Clémence. I could tolerate no more.'

'It is possible that he did not realise what he was saying.'

'Didn't realise?' Thomas was incredulous. 'What, that when he was in Rome admiring ruined temples and buying pretty manuscripts I was knee-deep in blood and gore alongside the Prince at Naseby? I watched with Rupert as his Bluecoats martyred themselves in the King's cause, Clémence, and Evelyn can speak to me of manuscripts?'

He was almost overwhelmed with disgust. But perhaps it was beyond her, a Frenchwoman, to understand what it had been to see Englishmen slaughter each other. He held out a hand, as if helpless. 'I don't know how you stand it.'

'For Mary's sake,' she said. 'She is my friend.'

'Then I don't know how she stands it.'

Clémence shook her head as if at an uncomprehending child. 'Because he is her husband, and so she must. And because she loves him, even you must see that.'

Thomas was dismissive. 'Because she has never known any different.' He took a moment to calm himself. 'But you, Clémence, you do not take a husband.'

'Nor shall I.'

'What, even if Rupert should ask?'

Clémence laughed, and it was the saddest laugh Thomas had ever heard. 'You know I would follow the Prince to the ends of this earth, but you also know he does not love me. And so do I.'

Thomas's voice softened. 'Then the Prince is a fool.' He took her hand. 'You could always marry me.'

A glistening he thought he had seen in her eyes intensified and Thomas feared he had made matters worse, but when she looked up at him he could see she was laughing in delight.

'Oh, my dear, kind, Thomas. If I were to marry any other man, it would be you. And what a rogue and a loving, and an unfaithful ne'er-do-well of a husband you would make me! And who knows? Perhaps we would be happy misfits, you and I.' She squeezed his hand. 'I will never forget that you asked me.'

He squeezed her hand back, and she grew serious. 'But we must never compromise, we two, not really. We will say what we must say, and do what we must do, but we will never compromise.'

He was glad of the darkness, because he thought she must surely otherwise have seen his shame, that he had abandoned the cause she never would. 'I will not ask you to come back to Sayes Court,' she went on, 'but please don't abandon me. I'm here not just as Mary's friend, but to advise John on the planting of his gardens. I have some commissions to carry out for him. Will you be my escort?'

Thomas lifted her hand and brushed it softly with his lips. 'While there is breath in my body, Clémence.'

Again she laughed. 'Or until you come upon a prettier face.'

SIX

A Message from Kent's Coffee House

Seeker was making his way through New Palace Yard to his appointed meeting with Thomas Faithly. It was very early, scarcely light, and only perfunctory greetings were murmured as people began to set up their stalls or go to their offices. Seeker liked this time of the morning, despite the cold and murk – people just got on with things and rarely bothered him. But today, it was different; today the sounds of an argument were rising from a doorway beneath an admiralty lodging, and it was no common argument. A young woman was shouting loudly, in French, at a young man who appeared to be trying to take hold of her.

Sighing in irritation, Seeker checked his steps and strode instead towards the arguing couple. The young woman was facing him, and must have seen him, but did not appear to care who might hear her diatribe. The man had his back to Seeker, and was not aware of his approach, until a pair of large hands took him by the shoulder and forced him round.

'You!' said Seeker.

'Captain!' The look on Samuel Pepys's face was something between embarrassment and relief.

'Are you bothering this young . . .' Seeker had been about to say woman, but in truth, the young woman was hardly more than a girl. He turned to the girl, whose face was a study of indignation, whether at being importuned by Pepys or interrupted by Seeker was unclear. 'Is this man bothering you?'

The girl stared at him and began to reply in French before switching to faultless English, with strong overtones of the city. 'Indeed, you might well say he is bothering me and has been this last year altogether. That I should have to tolerate such a man! Such treatment! If I had but listened to my mother!'

'Oh, please, my dear,' interjected Pepys, 'do not go back again to your mother. I shall find us better lodgings, I will be a better husband, I—'

But Pepys got to say no more. 'Husband?' said Seeker in disbelief. 'This girl is your wife?'

Pepys looked slightly abashed. 'Ah, yes, Captain. I have that happiness, since last December, in fact. I have not made it altogether known – young clerks are not encouraged to encumber themselves with a wife until such time as they are—'

But this time it was the young woman who interrupted him. 'Encumber? Encumber?' And so ensued another tirade of French, little of which Seeker could comprehend, other than that the young woman was indeed returning to her sagacious mother.

Once she had left, there was an astonished silence, an almost tangible empty space where she had been, the desolation that succeeds a storm. Seeker looked down at the somewhat dejected Treasury clerk. 'Is it always like that?'

Pepys nodded. 'Most of the time.'

'Well,' said Seeker, finding himself suddenly awkward, 'she is very young.'

Pepys's face lightened. 'Not so very young, Captain. She has turned sixteen now, you know, and oh, she is so very pretty. I am half-mad for her.'

Seeker gave a short laugh. 'I don't think she's half-mad for you, lad. Not just now, at any rate. You won't have had any breakfast yet, I suppose?'

'Ahem, no. I had hoped marriage might bring me some home comforts, and set me on an honest path, if you know what I mean, but alas . . . the comforts of marriage are not quite as I had anticipated.'

'No,' said Seeker, 'I daresay they're not.' He inclined his head across the yard. 'Come on then, I'll stand you your draught and a dish of eggs at the Turk's Head, and you can make yourself useful. I've been wanting to talk to you anyway.'

Pepys's face, which had brightened considerably at the thought of breakfast, fell again. He sighed. 'Lead the way, Captain. Lead the way.'

There were few people in the coffee house. Samuel

seemed to know them all, and they all knew Seeker. It was with no great difficulty that they got a seat near the fire, for which Samuel was volubly grateful, bending over the hearth and rubbing his hands. 'She has much to learn of housekeeping too, I'm afraid,' he said, as if there had been no break in their conversation, 'and I am oftentimes obliged to get my own fire.'

'Astonishing,' said Seeker.

'I *know*. But will she be told?'

Seeker waited until their order had been taken and the food and drink brought. As Pepys fell upon his eggs like a man half-starved, he leaned closer. 'A couple of months back, I heard you mention a man by the name of Fish, with lodgings on King Street.' The intelligence letter from Stoupe in Paris that Thurloe had chosen not to act upon, with regard to a conspirator of that name, was still playing on his mind.

Pepys thought for a moment and then nodded. 'Disagreeable fellow. Nothing much to say for himself.'

'How did you come to know him?'

Pepys paused in his chewing. 'I didn't. Not really. I just found myself a few times at the same pie stall around the corner from Bell Yard. I attempted pleasantries once or twice, just to pass the time as we waited, but he was gruff and hardly gave a word back to me. I soon desisted.'

'How did you know his name?'

'Pie woman called it out,' said Pepys through a mouthful of bread.

'And have you seen him of late?'

Pepys shook his head. 'Not in a good few weeks. I think he must be gone from his lodgings there.'

'Where exactly were those lodgings?'

Pepys made a face. 'Somewhere off King Street, I think. I'm sorry, Captain, perhaps the pie woman will know.'

Seeker heaved a sigh. 'Aye, perhaps. And did you ever see him talking with anyone?'

'I took little notice of him, Captain. He was an ill-mannered fellow and I paid him no more heed.'

'Hmm.' Seeker stood up. 'Well, that'll do for now. You'd best not be here too long, no doubt Mr Downing will be looking for you.'

Pepys became forlorn, but even as Seeker was walking out the door of the Turk's Head, he saw that the young Treasury clerk was already in animated conversation with two newly arrived customers who had greeted him by name.

Seeker soon found the pie stall by the end of Bell Yard. The woman there did indeed remember Mr Fish, and she was also able to direct him to where he had lodged, in a room above a tailor's shop on King Street. As he thanked her, a fresh mutton pasty in his hand, Seeker thought he would check whether the woman was already in their pay, and if not, to suggest that she was put on it.

At Fish's lodgings above the tailor's, the neighbours conferred until they were satisfied with their answers to Seeker's questions. Yes, the man had lived there. He had been there a good few months, three or four, but had not been seen in weeks. Yes, it would have been around the time of the opening of the last Parliament. No, they did not know where he had come here from. One of them, an old soldier himself, was certain the man had been a soldier too. Fish had had few visitors, only one other fellow from time to time, also with the look of a soldier, and an old man, but the old man had only appeared latterly, and none could recall having spoken to him. Fish had not been friendly. No one was sorry he had gone.

Seeker took a description from them, and it tallied pretty fairly with what he already knew from Pepys – of middling height, close-shorn brown hair running much to grey, and of stocky build. His nose was bulbous in parts. His visage was neither pleasant nor ugly, but his demeanour did not invite familiarity. All in all, Fish was unremarkable in appearance, and his description would fit almost every third man Seeker passed in the street. There was nothing more to be done on the matter of Mr Fish, and as Thurloe had pointed out, the rumoured attack on the Protector at the opening of Parliament had never taken place. Seeker left King Street and went towards Hyde Park, where he had instructed Thomas Faithly to wait for him.

It was well after their agreed meeting time, but Faithly was still there, under the appointed oak tree. He was standing with his back to Seeker, a hand casually on one hip, evidently watching something. More alert than Pepys had ever been, he spun round at the first sound of Seeker's approach. 'I had been about to leave,' he said once Seeker was within earshot.

'You'd better not have been,' said Seeker. 'If I can't get to our meeting place at the appointed time, and have sent no messenger to tell you otherwise, you wait.'

Faithly rubbed heavily gauntleted hands together. 'It is perishing cold out here at this hour of the day.'

Seeker looked around him. 'It's not that bad. You must have known colder days than this in the field.'

'Of course,' said Faithly. 'But we are not in the field now, and I can hardly drill on my own.'

Seeker shrugged. 'Why not? I do, often enough.'

Thomas gave him a weary look. 'That I can believe. But if I had a horse—'

Seeker cut him short. 'Perhaps if you'd bring us something useful, we'd give you a horse. But if you're to carry on playing the hard-up, sequestrated Royalist—'

'Which is what I am.'

'Which is indeed what you are,' agreed Seeker, 'you must look and live like one.'

'Whilst the Lord Protector lives like a king, although even his dearest friend, if such he has, would hardly claim he looks like one.'

Seeker drew closer to Thomas Faithly, and spoke to him very quietly. 'If you repent of your change of loyalties, you have only to say.'

Thomas took a deep breath. 'No, no, I don't.' He turned

his attention back to what he'd been looking at before. 'That's a fine horse Oliver rides, though.'

Seeker followed Faithly's gaze and saw what he had been watching. Cromwell was out with his Life Guard of Horse, cantering through the park on a very fine bay. Seeker could see that both man and horse longed for the gallops.

'You're right. It is a very fine horse, and it's the finest horseman in England that rides it. Oliver Cromwell is Lord Protector of England. He doesn't need to look like anything else. But I haven't come here at this hour of the day to discuss horses or politics. Sayes Court – you were there last night?'

'I was.'

'Did you hear anything tending to the bears of Bankside, the old arena, the killing?'

Thomas shook his head. 'Nothing. Evelyn and his circle don't partake in gambling, or speak of the entertainments of the masses.'

'What do they speak of?'

And so Thomas told him of fumigating stoves and planting schemes, and principles of garden design and mining and drains until Seeker held up a hand. 'All right, all right. Nothing worth reporting then.'

'No. Well, apart from Mulberry.' And Thomas told him of the man who had left Evelyn's laboratory in a clandestine manner not long after his arrival.

'Mulberry?' repeated Seeker. 'Are you sure?'

'That's what Evelyn said, but I never knew any man by the name of Mulberry.'

'No,' said Seeker. 'Neither did I.' He took a moment to recall where else he had heard recently of a shadowy 'man of science'. It had been from Colonel Pride's sergeant, who had admitted to leaving one of the Bankside bears alive. 'What did he look like, this fellow?'

Thomas cast his mind back. The elaboratory had been well lit, but the man Mulberry had stood away from the light, and had been heavily swaddled in hat and cloak when he left. 'Ruddy, a little fleshy of face, which did not sit well with his hook nose, and the look of a man in good health. Sixty perhaps. I had the distinct impression that he didn't want to be seen.'

'All right,' said Seeker. Another name for him to track down. 'You can find out more about him the next time.'

Thomas shook his head. 'There won't be a next time.' He told Seeker about his exchange with Evelyn over their respective experiences of 1645, and of the manner of his departure. 'I can't go back there, I've all but broken with him, and it must have been evident to everyone present that I cannot stand the man.' He ground a stick into the earth at his feet. 'It galls me.'

Seeker didn't need to ask why, he already knew. Thomas Faithly had risked all and lost all in the Stuart cause, and now he must wait attendance on a man who had not once lifted an arm in the defence of Charles Stuart or his son. Whilst Thomas had stayed in England to fight one bloody battle of attrition after another, John Evelyn, a man of the same age, had taken himself on a tour of Europe, admiring its gardens, its art and its architecture. While Thomas had endured penury and exile with the man he still believed to be his King, Evelyn had returned home with the paintings and books and artefacts on which he had lavished so much wealth, and busied himself with building projects and the visiting of antiquities and curiosities. Evelyn had lost nothing in the war; Thomas, who by anyone's lights had acted the more honourably, almost everything. The injustice of it angered Seeker too.

'What's done is done, Thomas. You shouldn't have burned your boats there. Evelyn's friend Boyle could have got you in with his sister, Lady Ranelagh, and that would have given you access to everyone.'

'Oh,' said Thomas, 'I haven't burned my boats, not entirely. There's still Clémence.'

'The Frenchwoman?'

'From Brittany. You might say it is to Paris what York-shire is to London.'

'Apart from that you told me she was brought up at the French court.'

'That was how Clémence came to Charles Stuart's notice.'

'Pretty, is she?' asked Seeker.

'Pretty is too base or flimsy a term. Clémence is not pretty, and there are many who would say she is not beau-tiful.'

'But not you?' said Seeker, regarding Faithly with interest.

Sir Thomas smiled. 'No, not me. Clémence is beau-tiful like the moor in winter, like a stormy sea. There's something powerful, seething in her, that most men find terrifying. And she has a seam of virtue going through her like silver through rock.'

'In the minority at Charles's court then,' said Seeker.

Thomas laughed. 'She'd have none of the King, for all his inducements. But the Prince, he could have had her for the taking.'

'Who? Rupert?'

Thomas nodded. 'I was there when she first saw him. I was talking to her when I suddenly realised she wasn't listening, or even looking at me any more. Rupert had just walked into the room and the look that crossed her face – it was like she'd seen her own soul walk in the door.'

'And him? Did he notice her?'

'Oh, he noticed her all right. Came straight over to her as if she was pulling him across the room. He was mesmerised, fascinated, but not as a lover. It was as if he had at last found someone who knew and understood him. He told her all his cares and his troubles, but it was plain to see he did not *desire* Clémence. I think it nearly broke her heart.'

'Nothing came of it?'

Thomas shook his head. 'Only that the most impressive woman at Charles's court followed Rupert around like a puppy. She would have done better to be a puppy – he would have lavished more affection on her.'

'So Mademoiselle Barguil wasn't unsuitable enough for Rupert of the Rhine?'

Thomas was surprised. 'You know his troubled history in that regard?'

Seeker did: his gaoler's daughter, his best friend's wife, his brother's mistress. The romantic misadventures of Rupert of the Rhine were the talk of Europe.

'And so what's this French Royalist doing in England?'

'She's good friends with Evelyn's wife, who spent her childhood in France. But Clémence also has a great knowledge of plants. She learned from Marin, in the royal gardens in Paris, and she's assisting Evelyn with his garden schemes for Sayes Court. I concede I have burned my boats with Evelyn, but not with Clémence. I am to be her escort on her plant-buying trips around the city and the liberties. My days in fine London society aren't quite over.'

'You see that they're not,' said Seeker. 'You're no use to us if they are. And next time you see this woman, you ask her about Mulberry too. I'd like to know what he's about.'

'If he's one of Evelyn's friends, I very much doubt he'll be of any interest to you or Mr Thurloe.'

'I wouldn't be too sure of that, Sir Thomas,' said Seeker, making ready to go his own way. 'You may not know it, but when John Evelyn was passing back and forth between England and France courting that young wife of his, he was carrying cyphers between Henrietta-Maria's court and Stuart supporters here. There might well be a bit more going on amongst his friends than you think.'

★

When Seeker returned to his offices by the Cockpit, a pile of reports requiring his attention had been set on his desk. He took a minute to read through each paper and noted what action would be required. Near the bottom of the pile was a paper which he saw straight away didn't come from within the corridors of Whitehall, and neither did it bear the stamp of the official posts. He opened it and read it then got to his feet to call through to his clerk.

'When did this arrive?' he asked, holding up the paper.

'About an hour ago. Young lad brought it. Full of his own importance. Claimed he knew you.'

Gabriel, the boy from Kent's coffee house. Seeker read through the lines one more time. They were from Grace, Samuel Kent's niece, asking that he would come as soon as he was able to see her uncle, who was in a great state of agitation and in need of help. Grace, who was still so wary of him, and Samuel, who had sat long into the dark hours of the night with Seeker sometimes, just letting him talk, and who asked help of no one.

'An hour?' Seeker turned on the unfortunate clerk. 'You should have sent to find me. Send for my horse.'

Acheron was well used to negotiating the busy streets and narrow lanes of the city, and it was not long before Seeker pulled up at the end of Birchin Lane and threw a penny to a ragged boy with instructions to watch the horse.

Even had he not had Grace's note, he would have known, as he approached Kent's, that something was not right. The familiar smells of the coffee house that habitually snaked from the chimney and doorway of Kent's to mingle with the other odours of the city were missing, the outer door to the coffee house closed. Seeker banged hard on it, and was let in almost instantly by an anxious-looking Gabriel.

'I knew you would come, Captain. I told Grace to write to you and you would come.'

'Where's Samuel?' asked Seeker.

'In the booth. Grace is trying to get him to take a little nourishment, to calm him.'

Seeker went to the one private booth of the serving room. Grace looked up at his approach, relief sweeping over her troubled face.

'Captain, thank goodness.'

Seeker looked from her to her uncle. 'What's up, Samuel?'

The old man clenched his fist and banged it on the table. 'Wickedness, black wickedness. Thieves and murderers, and they think I don't know!'

Seeker took off his hat and slid onto the bench opposite the coffee man and his niece.

'What's happened?'

Samuel started again about wickedness, and Grace put her hand over his and pressed softly, then she looked at Seeker. 'It is Uncle's friend, that we were to have our dinner with that day we saw you.'

'Your birthday?' said Seeker.

'Yes. We were to meet him that afternoon, at the George in Southwark, after we had been to Tradeskin's Ark.'

'And?'

She held up her hands in a gesture of helplessness. 'He wasn't there.'

Seeker looked across the table at Samuel. The old man never complained about his lot, listened to the woes and the glories of the world as they came in off the street to his coffee house. Sometimes, he told stories about his days fighting on the continent, his glory days, although as he had told Seeker privately, they had not all been glorious. The younger ones, customers and friends listened, sometimes agog, and sometimes they laughed, but they only saw the lame old soldier in front of them, not the young man he had been. He told fewer tales of England's own civil wars – no one was ready to thrill to stories of that yet. But there had been a light in Samuel's eye the other day when he had spoken to Seeker of going to meet his old comrade, his brother in arms. Seeker knew that a man held such brothers close in his heart, though others might never hear him say their name.

'I'm sorry, Samuel.'

'Sorry?' There was a fierce look in the coffee-man's eye that Seeker had never seen there before.

'Perhaps he forgot, or was called back home sooner than he'd planned, or ran out of money. It's an expensive business, coming up to London.' Seeker could not see that this was a matter to have called him from his duties at Whitehall.

'Nonsense,' said Samuel. 'Joseph Grindle never forgot anything in his life. Sharper than you or me he was. Sharper even than young Gabriel there. And he never ran out of money, not in all the years I knew him. Run out of money? I should hope he'd know he'd only to come to Samuel Kent if ever he should find himself in need.' Samuel's breathing was coming thick and fast and his hands were shaking. Again, Grace tried to calm him.

'You see, Captain,' she said looking once more at Seeker, 'Joseph was staying in Southwark, at the George, while he came up to do his business in town. But they said he hadn't come back the night before. When we turned up there that day to take our dinner with him, they wanted to charge us for his keep – said he'd left without paying what he owed. But then the chambermaid told me he'd left his bundle in the room he'd been in, as if he'd been planning on coming back. She said the landlord was going to sell it if Joseph didn't appear and pay his dues.'

This was something different, although Seeker had come across it often enough before. He would not tell Samuel there was no cause for concern. When a visitor to London failed to return to his lodgings, leaving his belongings behind, none of the handful of likely explanations were good. And in Southwark, with its proximity to the river and the marsh, its doxies and footpads, con-men and cut-purses, the unwary traveller might fall victim to many misfortunes.

'Was he in good health, your friend?'

'The best,' said Samuel. 'Joseph was as robust as I am, without this pestilential leg.'

Seeker saw the look of pain flit across Grace's face. The passing years had taken their toll on Samuel, and few would have thought of calling him robust. And however able a fighter his old soldier comrade had been, an old man of near seventy would not be a match for the worst that London had to offer. 'You think he has fallen victim to foul play?' he said at last.

'I know it,' Samuel said, again bringing a fist down on the table. 'He was in here, Grace tells me, the day before, very agitated, wanting to see me. But I wasn't here, and so he left in a hurry, and I never saw him again.'

Seeker turned to Grace. 'Tell me about it, Grace.'

'Well, Uncle had told me often about his friend Joseph, what times they had had, but he hadn't seen him since he'd come home from the German wars. And then, the morning before my birthday, in walks this fellow, well dressed and respectable, though wearing the most peculiar hat I ever saw, a grin from ear to ear as he called Uncle's name. Well, poor Uncle there near fell into the fire. Took me and Gabriel a good three minutes to get him steady on his legs again. Oh, and what a hugging and a roaring and a story-telling there was then. Uncle even got up his quarter cask of Canary out of the cellar, that never sees the light of day from one year's end to the next. I think the two of them would have sat there till Doomsday, laughing and newsing and sighing at one another, if Joseph hadn't had business in the city to be getting on with. He left here about two of the afternoon, but not before he'd insisted he would stand us all a good dinner in the George the next day, when we were finished our excursion.'

'And that was the last I saw of him,' Samuel said, his eyes desolate.

'But you saw him again, Grace,' prompted Seeker.

She nodded. 'An hour or so after Joseph left, Uncle went out too, with Gabriel, to buy me a present.' Her hand went unconsciously to the small amber pendant about her neck and Seeker could guess what that present had been. 'They were out a good long time, what with Uncle's leg and making up their minds. But then, just as I was starting to worry for them, Joseph Grindle came rushing back in, looking for Uncle. Very agitated to see him, he was. Made me promise I'd make sure Uncle went to the George the next day, as they'd agreed, and then he left, in more of a hurry even than he'd come. And that was the last any of us saw him.'

Seeker liked this less and less. 'All right, Samuel,' he said. 'You'll need to tell me everything you can about Joseph Grindle.'

And so Samuel told him, about how they'd first met in the Danish service of Christian IV, two young men seeking their fortunes and some adventure in the world, half in love with the idea of fighting in the cause of their princess, Elizabeth Stuart, the Winter Queen. And then they'd joined the ranks of the Swedes, under Gustav Adolph. For years, they'd marched and fought together over half of Europe, seen sights that two young boys from Devon and

Sussex might never have dreamt of seeing. They'd been at sieges, battles, great and small. They'd seen the aftermath of Magdeburg, such horrors as neither hoped ever to witness again; they'd been at Lützen when the Swedish king had fallen, and with him the hopes of the Protestant world; they'd been at Breisach, a siege they thought would never end, and at Vlotho, under Lord Craven, fighting the Catholic Habsburgs. 'That's where young Rupert of the Rhine was taken, Captain. Oh, you should have seen him then: nineteen years old, fighting on in his lovely mother's cause when almost everyone else was killed or fled. I'll never forget it. Me and Joseph were that close to him it's a wonder we never got taken prisoner with him. But they wouldn't have had much use for the likes of us anyway. Never saw such valour as young Rupert showed on that day. Broke my heart when he came over here and took up arms for his uncle against Parliament. Joseph said it near broke his too when he heard of it.' And so it had gone on, story after story, until Seeker almost wished he'd been with these two comrades himself. But time was getting on and the concerns of the present day were pressing.

'When did Joseph return from the continent?'

'Sixteen forty-eight. He'd thought to settle in Germany, but when it came down to it, with all the fighting done, he found he missed home.' Samuel laughed. 'After thirty years away. But it takes you like that sometimes, doesn't it? And he liked the sound of the England we were making too. Said he regretted not coming back sooner, to join in the fight. But I showed him my leg and told him at our age, we were better off out of it.'

'And you hadn't seen him since he'd been back, not until Monday?'

Samuel shrugged. 'Thousands went out. A few of us came back. Then there was the confusion of our own wars here. People just lost touch, didn't know who was alive and who dead. And then, once I settled, well – I never did have much time for the coast, and Joseph never had much time for the city, so I was never likely to chance upon him nor he on me.'

'But he came here on Monday?'

Samuel nodded. 'Out of the blue.'

'What was his business here?'

Samuel puffed out his cheeks. 'Darned if I know, Captain. Joseph had been apprenticed to a saddler as a lad, kept it up whatever army we were with. He took his money home and invested in a saddler's down there in Sussex. Don't think it were anything to do with that that brought him up to town, but I didn't think to ask.'

'There was the clock, Uncle.'

Seeker felt a chill whisper across him. 'What clock?'

'Oh, that, yes. I'd forgotten about that. How I could have forgotten about that old clock, I don't know. Lugged it halfway across Europe with him, I did.'

'Tell me about the clock,' said Seeker.

'Well, it's a lovely thing, still, even after all these years. It was when we took Weisskirchen.' Samuel's face clouded.

'We weren't always as disciplined as we should have been, and the burgomeister and the rest had held out so long, refused us shelter.' He lowered his voice. 'Some of our men were desperate. We sacked the place. Joseph found that clock in the rich merchant's house. Took a fancy to it. I couldn't believe he'd taken it all the way home, still had it.' Then he went on to describe a clock Seeker could picture very well.

'Did Joseph bring this clock to London with him?'

'Well, yes,' said Samuel, holding both hands out towards the table. 'It was sitting just there, only three days since, just where you've put down your hat. He was on his way up to Clerkenwell with it, to a German clockmaker he'd heard tell of, to have it fixed.'

It was almost an hour later, after a desolate Samuel was finally persuaded by Grace to go and lie in his bed, that Seeker made ready to leave Kent's. Down to the very hat that Grace had thought so peculiar, the long, fur-trimmed, often-mended cap that Samuel said Joseph had had off a Croat at Nordlingen in '34, and that Seeker had found lying in the dirt of that bloodied outhouse on Bankside, there could be no doubt: the man whose savaged remains Seeker had so recently come upon with Thomas Faithly was Joseph Grindle.

'I must go now, Grace,' he said, when she returned from settling her uncle. 'But I'll be back. And do not hesitate to send for me whenever you might need me. Tell Gabriel just to come and find me wherever I am. You are sure you remember nothing more of what troubled Joseph Grindle the second time he came in here looking for your uncle?'

She shook her head. 'Nothing. He would not say what it was, and he would not stay till Uncle returned, such was his hurry.'

'And you are certain he didn't have the clock with him when he came back?'

'Certain.'

'All right, Grace. You tell Samuel – I mean this now – you tell him: I will get to the bottom of this, come what may.'

Grace was just assuring him that she would not forget when a new hammering came at the door. Gabriel hastened to open it, to be met by a messenger sent down by Dorcas Wells at the Black Fox.

'Is the Seeker here? I heard tell on the streets he was headed this way.'

'What is it?' said Seeker, getting up from the booth and showing himself.

'Dorcas says you're to come quick, Captain. She says the girl Manon's brother has arrived. From Yorkshire.'

Seeker stared at the man a moment and then grabbed his gauntlets and headed for the door without stopping to tie on his cloak.

'Captain, what's wrong?' asked Grace.

'She doesn't have a brother,' he muttered, before heading out into the street and leaving the door to swing shut behind him.

SEVEN

The Man at the Black Fox

Dorcas was on edge. She'd sent a message to Seeker about two minutes after the man had come into her tavern, but there was no sign of him yet and she had no idea how long the message would take to reach him. It had been a year, almost exactly, since Damian Seeker had entrusted his daughter, his only child, to Dorcas's care. As far as the world was concerned, Manon was Dorcas's niece, orphaned and arrived down from the north. Seeker had too many enemies for him to risk them discovering the identity of his child. Over time, Dorcas had managed to piece together some of the truth of Seeker's past – his other life, before the Civil War, with Manon's mother, who had left him for an itinerant preacher, taking their young daughter with her. She'd learned of his failed searches for them, the trails that had gone cold, the false names Manon's mother and her new husband had adopted to elude him, and their final reckoning, in Yorkshire, only a year ago. The preacher was now dead, the woman supposed to have sailed to the Americas, and the child, by her own choice, had travelled to London, to be close to the father with whom she had been reunited after eleven years. Nowhere, in all of that story, had there ever been any mention of a brother.

He'd come in, the fellow, as if he hadn't a care in the world. Hadn't a clue, more like, thought Dorcas. She'd seen his type before a few times, and beneath all the bravado, they were usually terrified. She'd lay money that he'd never been to London before – he was trying too hard to affect disinterest, but she could see his mind was dancing. So why had he come now? And what had brought him here to the Black Fox, asking for Damian Seeker's daughter and claiming to be the girl's brother? He hadn't asked for 'Seeker's daughter' though, he'd said 'Manon'. Four people in London knew the true identity of Manon's father: the child herself, Seeker, Dorcas and Lady Anne Winter, who had escorted her down here last year from York. And now here was this brash fellow, down to train for the law, he said, swaggering in here and asking for the girl by name, claiming to be her brother. Whether he was a student of the law or not, Dorcas didn't know, but she was certain he was not Damian Seeker's son.

Dorcas ran her hand over the butt of the pistol she had brought through with her from her business room. She'd got Will Tucker out of the kitchen to stand guard at the door and watch the newcomer until Seeker arrived. The worst of it was, Dorcas had been in her work room, setting her accounts, when the fellow had come in asking for Manon, and Isabella had fetched the girl without a thought, and only afterwards come in to tell Dorcas that the strangest thing had happened, because Manon's brother had arrived, and Manon had never said she had a brother, nor Dorcas a nephew.

Dorcas had hurried into the tavern parlour, telling Isabella to send for Seeker without delay, but had stopped short when she'd got there. Manon was seated on the bench beside the man, intent on his conversation. Intent, but not quite at her ease. The fellow looked nothing like the girl, nor like Seeker either. He was tall, but as a willow is tall, as opposed to Seeker's oak, and in place of Seeker's craggy features, which on Manon were refined simply to a good clean bone structure, this chap's face had the smooth lines of a deer or a fox. There was certainly something of the woodland about him. He had not Seeker's black hair, nor the pale yellow that Manon had got from her mother, but a dull brown, like a dried, fallen leaf. He must have been about twenty-five or twenty-six years of age, too old, from what she knew of Seeker's former wife, to be her son, so he was not even a half-brother. Why, then, was Manon going along with this pretence?

Dorcas approached the table, remembering to fix on her smile for the benefit of the other customers who sat around the Black Fox. 'Well, well,' she said, beaming down at the newcomer. 'This is indeed a surprise.'

The young man beamed up at her, but Manon took a moment to respond. Finally she swallowed, and Dorcas could see the lie gave her great difficulty. 'Yes, Aunt, I did not know my *brother* was coming to London.' She looked back to the young man. 'It is a wonder he did not warn us of his coming.'

'Yes,' said Dorcas, fixing the man with an unwavering gaze, 'who would have thought it?' She didn't understand why Manon would play along with this evident lie.

The fellow at last had the grace to look slightly abashed. 'Well,' he tilted his head and gave an awkward smile, 'I thought I'd surprise you.'

Seeker hardly noticed what he rode past and through on the way from Cornhill to Broad Street. It was more to the horse's credit than his that more stalls were not upset, goods trampled and carters and costermongers forced out of their way. Images of almost every enemy he'd ever made sped through his mind as he tried to think who could have sought out Manon in this way, and what harm they might mean her. By the time he reached the door of the Black Fox and threw the reins of his horse to Dorcas's stable lad, half of the city was convinced an attempt must have been made on Cromwell's life.

Seeker pushed through the door, his pistol already in his hand as he shouldered his way past Dorcas's cook, a veteran of many an army mess tent and bigger of build even than himself.

'Where is he?' he demanded.

'There.' Will Tucker pointed.

Seeker surged towards the table around the snug corner,

by the hearth, where he could see Dorcas sitting facing him and only the tops of the heads of Manon and a man, who were seated with their backs to him. He rounded the corner and then stopped. All three at the table looked up. Dorcas stood up, relief flooding her face. Manon looked at him, confused, as if relying on him to explain it to her. 'Captain Seeker. My brother has arrived. From Yorkshire.'

Five minutes later, with Manon and Dorcas in the kitchen, on the excuse of preparing a special dinner for the far-travelled arrival, and Will Tucker guarding the top of the steps to the small parlour with instructions to let no one else pass, Seeker was leaning in very close to Lawrence Ingolby's face. He hadn't seen the steward of Faithly Manor in the North Riding for a year, and had not expected to be seeing him now. He enunciated every word as if he was spitting out a nail.

'And what, exactly, are you doing here?'

Ingolby, as ever, was infuriatingly unperturbed. 'Matthew sent me. Wants me to learn a bit of the law, now that he's taken over the estate – help him to protect his rights against undesirables, any Faithly cousins slithering out of the woodwork, that sort of thing.'

Matthew Pullan, once a Levelling soldier, was Commissioner for the Peace for the villages around Faithly Moor in the North Riding. Following the sequestration, and death in a York prison, of Edward Faithly, brother to Thurloe's newly turned agent Thomas Faithly, Matthew Pullan had taken over their ancestral home and estate, which had been in debt to him for years. Lawrence Ingolby, a young, bright lad brought up in Pullan's household, had been put into Faithly Manor as estate manager by Matthew several years ago as a condition of the mortgage. Whatever Pullan might have told Lawrence about why he was sending him to London, Seeker suspected it was nothing to do with Matthew needing help to run his estate, and everything to do with giving the young man opportunities in life he would never have up on the moor. Seeker kept this thought to himself though.

'Hmm. The law. Just what England needs – another clever lawyer.'

Ingolby grinned the grin Seeker remembered well from his late visit to Yorkshire, and in spite of himself he felt the old liking for the young man start to creep in. He sought to quash it.

'You're not staying here.' It was a statement of fact, not a question.

'What?' said Lawrence, somewhat taken aback. 'Oh, *here*? No, Matthew's set it up for me to lodge at an Inn of Chancery.'

Seeker was conscious of a sinking feeling. 'Which one?'

'Clifford's. Off Chancery Lane.'

'Clifford's. Of course it would be,' said Seeker, his tone grim.

'Why? What's wrong with Clifford's?'

'Oh, nothing,' said Seeker. 'Might as well be there as in amongst some other pack of scoundrels.' It was hardly to the point, and none of Ingolby's business, that Clifford's was also the Inn of Chancery out of which Maria's brother Elias practised, and from where until recently he'd sent out his incendiary pamphlets against Cromwell's regime. But Elias was claiming compliance with the authorities now, or at any rate making a show of behaving himself, and it might do no harm for Seeker to have a set of eyes and ears in Clifford's to report on whether he continued doing so.

'So much for London, then, but what are you doing here?'

Lawrence looked around him, confused. 'But I've just told you. Matthew sent me down—'

Seeker went back to the nail-spitting. 'What are you doing *here*, at the Black Fox?'

'Oh,' said Lawrence. Sitting back, ready to be expansive, and then remembering that in conversations with Seeker discretion was usually better. 'Well, you see, I thought it would look strange if I didn't call upon Manon.'

Seeker felt his hand digging in to the butt of his pistol again. 'You thought what?'

Ingolby leaned in, his eyes checking the empty room in conspiratorial manner. 'With her being supposed to be my sister and all.'

'Your sister? Aye, so I hear. What in the world made you think she was supposed to be your sister?'

Ingolby frowned. 'Well, it was you—'

'Me?' Seeker wondered if the boy had gone mad.

'Aye. You. Manon writes to Orpah, you see.'

'Orpah? The Pullans' servant girl?'

'Yes. That few days you left her at Matthew's house last year, they got to be friends. Manon writes to Orpah now and again to tell her all her news from London and Orpah writes back to tell her all the doings of her little world.'

Seeker was surprised. 'I didn't know Orpah could write.'

Ingolby raised an eyebrow knowingly. 'Ah, well, that's it, you see: she can't. Can't read either. She brings Manon's letters to me to read out to her, and then her and me work away a while at telling Manon all the news of the world of Faithly Moor.'

Seeker gave an amused grunt. 'That'd make for interesting reading. But none of that explains why you thought fit to show up here claiming to be her brother.'

Ingolby narrowed his eyes and spoke through gritted teeth. 'Because it was *you* told everyone down here her name was Manon Ingolby. She told Orpah, her first letter: she was to direct any replies to Manon Ingolby, at the sign of the Black Fox, Broad Street, Bishopsgate, because that was the name you'd given her so's no one would know she was Caleb Turner's daughter.'

Seeker stifled a curse. He'd been determined that Manon should be associated neither with the deeds of her stepfather, the Trier Caleb Turner, nor with his own. It was a moot point whether he or Turner had garnered more enemies over the last ten years and he was determined his daughter should not suffer on account of either of them. And so, when asked, he'd said the first name that had come in to his head. Ingolby. He let out a long breath. 'It was the first thing that came in to my head.'

Ingolby nodded, self-righteous. 'Aye, well. Maybe you should have thought twice. But what's done is done. If she's down from the North Riding calling herself Ingolby, and I'm down from the same, calling myself the same – which *is* my name, after all – then folk down here aren't going to believe we're not related. So,' he took another good draught of his ale, 'here I am, her brother.'

Seeker consoled himself with the thought that if Manon had had to have a brother, he might have been a lot worse.

Ingolby turned his tankard in his fingers, appearing to inspect it very carefully. 'She's come on a bit, mind.'

Seeker felt himself bristle. 'What do you mean, "Come on a bit"?'

Ingolby raised his eyebrows. 'Well, you know – got pretty, bloomed, whatever it is women do.'

'She's a child,' said Seeker, through gritted teeth.

'She's sixteen past.'

'Still too young for you,' said Seeker, dangerously close to leaning over and hauling Lawrence Ingolby out of the Black Fox by the scruff of the neck.

Lawrence stretched out his palms. 'Oh, oh yes, of course. But I'm just saying – I mean it won't be long, you know – her mother's a good-looking woman after all, for all her poor taste in husbands.'

'Manon is *not* her mother."

'No, no.' Ingolby puffed out his lips. 'No. That one

needed watching, no mistake. Manon's much nicer. But I'm just saying – obviously you don't consider such things yourself – she's very pretty, and she's – *nice*, you know. There are plenty of girls married at that age: it won't be long till the lads come calling.'

Seeker was in the process of explaining to an open-mouthed Lawrence Ingolby precisely what such 'lads' could expect should they start bothering the inhabitants of the Black Fox when Dorcas and Manon reappeared with a tray piled high with the finest the kitchen had to offer.

Manon sat down opposite Lawrence and looked at him.

Dorcas placed a hand lightly on Seeker's shoulder. 'Come, Captain, shall we leave Manon and her brother to catch up on all their news? I've got a plate ready for you through the back.'

Seeker was reluctant, but the tavern was becoming busier, and he didn't want to call more attention to Lawrence and his daughter than was necessary. 'All right,' he said, getting up, before turning to Lawrence and saying, 'I'll be calling on you. Clifford's Inn. And don't you forget what I said.'

'About?'

'Lads,' mouthed Seeker.

Lawrence's eyes were still wide. 'Oh, no, Captain. I won't forget.'

Back in Dorcas's business room, Seeker sank back against the door and rubbed a hand over his eyes. 'Thank God,' he said. 'Thank God it was him. When I heard there was someone up here claiming to be her brother, all manner of things ran through my head.'

'And mine,' said Dorcas. 'It's a good thing that message found you at Kent's or I'd have had that young fellow tied up in the cellar by now.'

Seeker laughed. 'He'd be no match for you, Dorcas, that's for sure.' It didn't take long for Seeker to fill in the gaps between what Manon had told Dorcas in the kitchen. 'He's a decent lad,' he said at last. 'Far too pleased with himself, but that's not a bad thing if he's to make his way amongst these reptiles.'

'Reptiles?'

'At Chancery. He's down here to learn how to tie the world in knots for rich men.'

'And he means no harm to your girl,' she said.

She was turning to take the cloth off the tray she'd set down for him when he reached out and turned her back towards him. 'I couldn't do without you, Dorcas.'

She smiled, flustered. 'Oh, you could, Damian. You managed long before me, and you know I'd look after the girl for her own sake anyway.'

He pulled her closer and looked down into her face. 'Not just for Manon. This is the only safe place I know. You are the only home I have.'

'And will be here as long as you want me,' she replied.

As Seeker was finishing off his food, he started to question her about 'lads'. Dorcas laughed.

'Do you think they chance their hands here more than

once, Damian? If that? If the look on my face isn't enough to put them off pestering my girls, I've only to call Will Tucker through from the kitchen to make things plain. The Black Fox is a respectable place, and I hope everyone knows it.'

'They do,' he said. 'It is just . . . the girls.'

'You are like any father, and it is right you should worry. But I tell you, Manon is as precious to me as my own daughter, as is Isabella, for all I took her in to work for me off the street. No one will call upon Manon against your will. But the lad was right – she's not a child any more.'

'She's my child,' he said quietly, before getting up and putting on his hat. 'Besides, it's time he was off to his lodgings – he's been loitering here long enough.'

They were still seated opposite each other, Manon and Lawrence Ingolby, when Seeker went to the top of the steps to the small parlour. But there was something different about them now. Ingolby looked younger somehow, more boyish. He was clearly telling Manon some tale, but he had none of his usual bravado, instead looking up now and again with a tentative smile, as if fearful he might be boring her. But he was not boring her – Seeker could see that. His daughter was watching the young man as if every thing he said was of the deepest profundity, and attempting her own smile in return when she appeared to think it expected of her. Seeker observed them for a moment and then took a breath and went down the three steps into the small parlour. It was a moment before either of them noticed him.

'Oh,' said Manon, standing up. 'Does my aunt need me, Captain?'

'Not just at the minute, but she will soon, no doubt. It must be near time for your brother to get himself back along to Clifford's Inn at any rate. I'll show him down there.'

'Oh, that's all right, Captain. I've been there two days now. I can find my own—'

'Nevertheless . . .' said Seeker, lifting Lawrence's hat from the table.

'Oh. Yes.' Lawrence took the hint and made a show of finishing up his ale.

Manon spoke to Seeker with a little hesitation. 'Lawrence has been telling me of all the strange things he has seen since he came to London.'

'I've no doubt he has. There are a quite a few to see.'

'Women with chalk and paint on their faces, men with powder in their hair, such as was never seen in Yorkshire, a man whose name is "Fish" . . .'

Manon might have rattled on, but Seeker stopped her, addressing himself to Ingolby. 'What?'

'Fish? Yes, there was a fellow in the inn I put up at two nights ago in Hammersmith. Leastways, he was taking his breakfast there in the morning. Went by the name of Fish. I mean, what kind of name—'

'Which inn?'

'Ehm . . .' Lawrence took a moment to remember and then named it. 'You see, I should have got to Clifford's the night before, but I'd taken a wrong turn at—'

'What did he look like?'

Lawrence frowned. 'Ordinary. Stocky sort of build. Close-cropped hair. Grey. Brown maybe. They were in an upstairs room, him and his companion, but the other man was sick, keeping to his room. Cecil, I think he was called.'

'No one else was with them?'

'Older chap by the name of Boyes, but I don't know if he was with them or just knew them.'

'They were still there when you left?'

'Aye,' said Lawrence. 'Like I said, the Fish fellow's companion was sick, didn't sound like they were planning on moving on anywhere just yet.'

'Right,' said Seeker, pulling on his gauntlets. 'You'll have to find your own way down to Clifford's. See you don't get lost again on the way. And remember . . .' Seeker cast a glance at Manon.

'What?' Lawrence looked puzzled then a little awkward. 'Oh. Ah, yes, Captain. I'll remember.'

It was past midday now, but Whitehall was closer than Hammersmith, and Seeker took the gamble that if he made first of all for Whitehall, he might yet be on time.

The coach was ready, the Lady Protectress and one of her younger daughters already inside, and only Oliver himself waited upon when Acheron's hooves clattered in to the

Great Court Yard of Whitehall Palace. The Life Guard of Horse, under the command of Colonel Howard, in which Seeker himself had served before being drawn fully into Thurloe's service, was mounted and waiting to escort the Protector and his family on their journey to Hampton Court. Seeker went directly to the colonel.

'Does he go to Hampton Court, sir?'

The man nodded. 'We should have left by now, but Secretary Thurloe had papers for him to sign that could not wait.' There was a trace of irritation in the colonel's voice.

'You may be thankful for that yet. Do you intend going by Hammersmith?'

Howard nodded. 'It's his preferred route.'

'I'd counsel you to change it today, sir.'

The colonel gave Seeker a long look, then nodded his understanding. He knew enough of the nature of Seeker's business to know that if he asked him to alter the Protector's route, there would be no necessity to ask why, still less to argue about it. He cocked his head towards the carriage. 'And what would you counsel me to say if they should ask?'

'Tell them the road's blocked. A hay cart turned over and the bullocks are causing trouble.'

'It wouldn't be the first time,' said the colonel.

'No. But your men should have a special care to have their wits about them on the road.'

Howard bridled slightly. 'They always do, Seeker. This isn't the Foot Guard.' It was only a matter of months since the Life Guard of Foot, Cromwell's body guard when he was in one of his residences rather than on the move, had had to be purged for suspected disloyalty.

'I know that, sir,' said Seeker. 'But the intelligence I have has come very fresh and I don't know how many conspirators are involved yet. They may well be watching more than one route.'

'They may well be,' said Howard, 'but my men will get him safe to Hampton Court, if it takes every last man in the troop to do so.'

Seeker scribbled a coded note and handed it to a page with instructions that it should be taken to Secretary Thurloe immediately. The sounds of the Foot Guard marching down the corridor were at last heard. Seeker saluted the colonel then wheeled around to go past the protectoral cortège and ride out again at the King Street Gate. He was on the road for Hammersmith before Cromwell ever appeared through the palace doors.

The broth the landlady from the inn next door had sent up had been left to grow cold. None of them had any appetite now that the time was so close at hand. Boyes looked around the room, a pleasant enough little banqueting room that must have seen many good dinners and a few raucous nights. He wondered if Cromwell had ever been here, enjoying a good roast and a bottle and the company of friends and comrades, in the days before he had had no friends, and few comrades, only subjects, and a growing number of enemies amongst them.

Boyes recalled the other times he'd seen Cromwell, across a battlefield, a man transformed into something higher than the ordinary run of men. He would have liked to have encountered him here, sat a while with him, picking over a leg of pork or a rib of beef, downing a tankard or two, seeing the man close up, in all his base humanity. He would have liked to have talked to him, asked what he had truly believed he would achieve by all that he had done, asked him whether he realised he would die, one day, at the hands of a marksman stationed at the window of this very room. Boyes stood up. There would be no time for talk, or beef, or wine. The questions would go unasked. Cromwell would breathe his last on the road outside, without knowing who had done it to him.

None of them had spoken for near a half-hour. A clock on the mantelshelf, an old thing, poorly kept, took Boyes's attention. The ticking was relentless, but the hand moved round too slow, surely. He wondered, suddenly, whether he should go down on the street. What if Cecil missed? What if Oliver, wounded, were to run, to try to get away? But Cecil would not miss, Cecil had fought for the King, Boyes's sources had assured him that Fish had chosen well – Cecil had been one of the best marksmen in Charles's army. And anyway, the contraption they had rigged had seven blunderbusses ready to spray their munition down onto the street: Oliver would not get away. As for Fish, the Leveller, Boyes hoped never to encounter him again once this day was over.

The clock ticked on. 'They should have been here by now,' said Fish.

'Perhaps your source was wrong,' said Boyes, his voice low and deliberate.

Fish turned on him. 'My source was not wrong. John Toope is in the Foot Guard. He could hardly be better placed to know Cromwell's movements, and he's been well paid. I've been putting these arrangements in place for months. Long before you got here.'

'Yes. Months. Too many months. Too many failures.'

Boyes could see a flush of anger creep up Fish's cheeks. He thought it was a good thing he and Fish had not been cooped up here together for days as Fish and Cecil had been, for surely one of them would have killed the other.

By the window, the frame of guns primed, Cecil suddenly lifted a hand to silence them.

'What is it?' said Boyes. 'Is it the coach?'

'Something's wrong,' Cecil said. 'There's a horseman, coming from Knightsbridge direction, much too fast.'

Boyes pushed past to look down the street in the direction that Cecil had been looking. 'They know,' he said, turning on Fish. 'Damn you and your so-called source.' He thrust a finger towards the window.

Fish looked in the direction Boyes had pointed. Any protest he might have thought of making died on his lips. His shoulders slumped, and all he said was, 'Seeker.'

★

Seeker tied up Acheron outside the inn and stormed through the door. A woman carrying a tray of bowls through from the kitchen screamed and dropped them. Seeker ignored her and made for the stairs, taking them three at a time. He barged through one room with six truckle beds set in it, but with no inhabitants, to another, this with only two double beds and overlooking the bend in the street below. There was no one in this room either. Seeker flung open the doors of a wall closet, but found nothing there but linen. Returned to the landing, he climbed a ladder up to the one attic room, which had simple pallets on the floor, and where the only other movement was by mice. He jumped down again and descended the stairs back to the parlour of the inn. 'Where are they?' he demanded of the terrified landlady and her husband.

'Where are who, Captain?' asked the man, his lips quivering.

'The men who slept two nights ago in your front bedchamber.'

'But it was only one man, Captain. A young law student, come down from Yorkshire. He went on his way the next morning.'

Seeker didn't understand. He thought he knew Ingolby well enough, and could not see why the young Yorkshireman would have lied to him.

'You had no one here by the name of Fish? Or Boyes? Or Cecil?'

'Oh, them, yes. Well, Mr Boyes, he has just been visiting

on the other two, and poor Mr Cecil has not been well and kept his chamber these last few days. But Mr Fish has been up and down with food for him.'

'You have other rooms?'

The landlady shook her head, a little less frightened now that she was on surer ground. 'Oh, no. Mr Fish and Mr Cecil did not stay here – they only got their food here. They have had the upper room of the Earl of Salisbury's coach house next door. The coachman has us rent it out from time to time, when it is not otherwise needed.'

Seeker cursed Ingolby for his lack of curiosity as he ran out of the inn and up the wooden steps at the side of the earl's coach house. He pushed through a room that appeared to be filled with stores and tack, to come to a double set of doors, locked. He pulled his horseman's hammer from his belt and brought it down twice on the lock until it splintered away from the wood and the doors fell open. Two pallets with rumpled-up blankets lay on the floor. The room reeked of chamber pot and some old broth that had been knocked over on the table and pooled onto the floorboards beneath. It was the window though, running the entire frontage of the room, that took his attention – or rather, what was in front of it.

Seeker had never seen anything like it – a wooden frame, a good six feet in length, on which seven blunderbusses had been set and primed, their triggers all connected by a series of links to one master trigger. It was a work of genius that, he thought, must have been designed by one with a knowledge of sieges. This contraption was not in a besieged town or stronghold though, but in a small banqueting room, overlooking a village street, on which it could only release carnage. They hadn't been taking any chances, Fish and his crew: neither Cromwell nor anyone else within range of this monstrous weapon could have survived its discharge. Seeker examined the structure closely, but knew it would take more skilled hands than his to disable it. The one thing he knew was that he couldn't leave this for the unwary to come upon, or for Fish and his fellow conspirators to return to. He craned his head out of the window and with relief saw the party of soldiers he'd asked Thurloe to send, heading up from Knightsbridge. Within five minutes, he had a guard set on the contraption, and a master armourer sent for from Westminster to come and make it safe.

Back in the inn, the descriptions he got from the elderly tavern-keeper and his short-sighted wife were a good deal less detailed than he had already had from Ingolby, and of little value. It was with a heavy tread that he went out again into the street to begin for himself the search for the men who so very recently had come close to killing Cromwell.

EIGHT

Tradeskin's Ark

Thomas Faithly could smell snow on the air. Not Yorkshire snow that descended as by right over the moors each winter to catch out those who really had no business being there in the first place, but that delinquent London snow, blown somehow off its course, and spying a place where havoc might be wreaked. Would it fall black, Thomas wondered, through the dirt on the air, or would it offer some respite to the beleaguered citizens, some cleansing of their murky streets? Thomas remembered snow in the city before, when it had silenced the noise of London a while and almost rendered all men equal. He was glad of the fresh cold tang in his nostrils.

The cold in his bones was another thing. It seeped through his clothes, through his boots and his stockings to wrap him in its misery as the boatman's oars powered them up the river towards Lambeth. The cold did not seem to touch Clémence. Her grey silk dress and fur wrappings would have been more expensive than the entire wardrobe he had managed to prise from Thurloe's coffers, and yet it was as if she was trying to disguise herself, merge herself into nothingness against the river and the city beyond. She wore a Puritan's white cap beneath a hood of dark grey velvet, and he knew that there would be no lace or fine cut-work on her cuffs or tucker. Everything about her was calculated to ward off the interest or attentions of the unwary. 'Your eyes would be enough,' Thomas wanted to say to her. Those granite eyes, so focused as they were upon something beyond the grasp of common man or woman, would be enough.

'I'm still at a loss as to why it is necessary for you to do this today,' he said at last. 'I am surprised at John Evelyn giving you this commission in such poor weather. He cannot be in such a great hurry for his plants at this time of year.'

Clémence made a small noise of dismissal as she re-arranged a rug which had begun to slip. 'That is because you know nothing of plants or planting schemes, Thomas. Besides, you may see your friend Hollar there. Wenceslaus has engraved the plates for Mr Tradescant's new catalogue. He is often at Tradescant's.'

How was it, wondered Thomas, that in a city the size of London, surely the biggest on earth, a man could bump into the same acquaintances wherever he went? Was it co-incidence that Hollar had been in attendance on Evelyn only last night, and now might be at John Tradescant's garden nursery this morning? But then, Hollar had fought in the late King's cause and taught the present King to draw, and Tradescant had looked after the Queen's gardens. It was not really such a coincidence that they should associate with one another. There were two worlds in London, co-existing and shadowing one another, from which old Royalists and their former Puritan foes warily watched each other. Thomas felt himself being drawn closer in to both. He should have foreseen it, but only now did it occur to him that while his deepening penetration of Royalist circles might reassure John Thurloe, he himself was not sure how, if ever, he might safely extricate himself from the one, or the other.

The thought of Thurloe recalled to his mind another of last night's visitors to Sayes Court. As the oarsman cut swiftly through the water, Thomas crossed over to settle himself on some cushions alongside Clémence. 'I didn't recognise the other fellow last night.'

'What other fellow?' asked Clémence, putting her hands back into their coney muffler.

'The old chap, hook nose. Marbury? Mulberry? I don't properly recall his name, but I never saw him before.'

'You were out of England a long time, Thomas. It's hardly likely you should know everyone in London.'

Clearly, she was going to say nothing more on the matter. Thomas drew back from pressing her any further. He wasn't entirely sure that Clémence was not a little suspicious of him – not everyone at Charles Stuart's exiled court had been convinced that his mysterious departure from it over a year ago, and his equally mysterious reappearance several weeks later in Yorkshire, had indeed been part of a plot to restore the King. The story he had allowed to circulate in

Royalist circles – that he had left Cologne on a desperate, last-throw-of-the dice escapade, and been captured by the Puritans in the form of Damian Seeker before he had been able to rally anyone else to his cause, was more heroic than it was truthful. Thomas was sorry for that, for he had never been a coward: he had simply had enough of wandering the courts of Europe like a beggar, and he had missed home. And so he had come home. But he still lived the life of a beggar, a genteel one at any rate, and London was scarcely more home to him than Paris or Cologne had been.

Thomas was near enough frozen by the time they reached Lambeth. He wasn't sure why Clémence had chosen him to be her escort. Perhaps his proximity reminded her of Rupert, of the times she had watched them play tennis or joined them out hawking or sketching. When they reminisced about their times at court, something of the near-constant watchfulness lifted from her, and she was almost carefree. But then the reality of their world – that they were here in England, the King counting out his days in Brussels, Rupert wandering from relative to relative around the empire – would weigh down on her again. Clémence's life, like Thomas's and everyone else who had thrown in their lot with the Stuart cause, was one of endless, rootless waiting in a world that no longer had any place for them. Perhaps, not knowing he had turned his coat and was now in Cromwell's pay, she simply thought they might as well wait together.

There was still a way to walk after they had landed by

Lambeth Palace. Whatever it might have meant to others over the centuries, that seat and symbol of power struggles between kings and over-ambitious churchmen, it stood there now as a rebuke to Thomas's own conscience. It hadn't been enough for the Puritans that the last archbishop to occupy it had been dragged from it and taken to the Tower, and thence to eternity, but they must needs defile the place, mock their enemies. It had been turned into a prison for Royalists, and many had died there. Thomas thought of comrades taken prisoner at Naseby and Bristol and Philiphaugh, who had ended their days in the stinking squalor of that palace. 'Died he not revengeless,' he murmured to himself.

'What?' Clémence asked him.

'A line of a poem I once heard.' He looked towards the palace and reeled off the names. He didn't need to explain anything else to her.

Eventually, they crossed a wooden bridge and passed beneath a whalebone arch to arrive at last at Tradescant's garden. Clémence turned off the path to the house and took instead one leading to an orchard. It was a thing of a different order entirely from the sturdy old apple orchard Thomas had known at Faithly. Nearly all the trees were bare now, but Clémence pointed out to him pears, plums and cherries set amongst what, if she were to be believed, was a bewildering variety of apple trees. She showed him where peaches, apricots and nectarines grew in the protection of a south-facing wall, with hardier plums and quinces against the others.

'It must be a veritable garden of Eden in spring and autumn,' Thomas observed.

'Then we should take care that we do not step upon a serpent.'

Thomas would have laughed, but there was no humour in Clémence's voice as she said it.

'And do you think we might?' he asked.

She looked away from him. 'Serpents are everywhere, Thomas. I would have thought all those years in the King's court would have taught you that.'

Thomas was saved from having to make a response by their coming upon a well-made, respectably attired man in his late forties, with unruly brown hair and beard, who was directing two under-gardeners as to the cutting back of some quinces against an east-facing wall. He smiled broadly on catching sight of Clémence, and throwing one last instruction to his workers, he came to meet them.

'Mademoiselle Barguil,' he said, 'I had been afraid you would not come. It would be devilish cold coming up from Sayes Court.'

'Not at all, John. We were well supplied with rugs and extremely comfortable.' She turned her head slightly towards Thomas. 'I have brought with me an old, *old*, friend: Sir Thomas Faithly, who is not long released from the Tower.'

Tradescant inclined his head in a wary bow. 'An old friend from . . .'

'My days at the King's court. Sir Thomas was until only last year abroad, in attendance upon His Majesty.'

At the mention of the King, Tradescant's demeanour towards Thomas changed markedly.

'Sir Thomas. It is a very great honour. I pray daily for His Majesty's restoration to his rights.'

'As do we all,' replied Thomas, somewhat surprised to be addressed so openly on the topic. Something of his surprise must have shown in his face.

Tradescant glanced over to where his men were in debate over the length of a cut. 'We'll not be overheard out here. I've to be more circumspect in the house, to which the generality of the people has access. I must deal with all-comers, in these dark days, if I am to survive.'

'There is no shame in that, John,' said Clémence. 'The King would be sorry to return, and find his gardener gone.'

Tradescant's face was grim. 'He'd weep, mademoiselle, to see what the philistines have done. His father's palace and gardens at Oatlands – pulled down and destroyed. The orange trees all sold. Her Majesty his mother's palace at Wimbledon in the hands of Cromwell's crony, Lambert.'

'May they enjoy their spoils while they can,' said Clémence. 'Pray God, retribution will not be long in coming.'

'Indeed. But come,' said Tradescant, beating his heavily gloved hands together for warmth, 'there is a good stove in my work hut, and we may begin upon Mr Evelyn's requirements in more comfort there.'

Tradescant's work hut was larger and better ordered than Thomas had thought to find it. Over a long workbench were letters sorted into piles, some with rough sketches, presumably of the plants requested by customers who lived away from London. Clémence had clearly been here before and went directly to a lectern by the table, where a loosely bound book was lying. 'Come and see this, Thomas,' she said, beginning to leaf through, a look of delight on her face. Thomas joined her, leaning over her shoulder a little to see. 'The Turke Plum,' he read out, as her finger paused over a watercolour showing five luscious black plums hanging from a branch, a butterfly flitting amongst its leaves and two snails feasting on a sixth. Each turn of the page revealed a new marvel.

'Is this Hollar's work?' he asked.

'Ah, no, more's the pity,' said Tradescant. 'These were made some time ago, by a friend of my father's, as an early guide to his orchard fruits. The ripening times are not quite right, as you will see – my father noted the times they ripened in the places he found them. In our English climes it is generally later. I have just had a new plant list made up, to go along with the catalogue of curiosities. But let us see what Mr Evelyn is thinking of.'

Thomas had no interest in the planting schemes or the bewildering variety of plants under discussion, and continued to entertain himself by leafing through the charming book of watercolours, smiling at the little grubs and insects that had found their way amongst the fruits. The discussion of Evelyn's requirements took a good long time, with several debates over which particular plant might be meant by a particular name, and then where Tradescant might source it, if he did not have sufficient stock to hand. Some of the sourcing required to be far-flung indeed, and Thomas was surprised to learn that the homely gardener had in fact journeyed as far as Virginia in search of his specimens. Thomas was brought out of his reveries about the New World by Tradescant's saying, 'And the other orders, mademoiselle?'

There had been something in the tone of the word 'other' that particularly caught Thomas's attention. He looked up, just in time to see Clémence glance his way. 'That may take a little time, John,' she said, 'and I fear Sir Thomas has but a short tolerance of discussions horticultural. Perhaps he would enjoy to see the curiosities instead?' Before Thomas fully understood what was happening, Tradescant had called down one of his under-gardeners and instructed him to take Sir Thomas to the house, where he might view the curiosities. One short protest that he was perfectly content in the gardener's hut was over-ruled, and he soon found himself being walked back through the orchard towards the house.

'Your master appears to have a very far-flung trade,' he opened, for the sake of conversation.

'We have orders come in from gentlemen all over England for stocking their gardens, and what we do not have, Mr Tradescant will have brought in from the Low Countries. Ships leaving Flushing most months will have something loaded and packed for Tradescant's, and then we have them taken up from Gravesend.' The under-gardener lowered his voice. 'Not just the Low Countries, either. Master John does business in Spain, the Canary Islands. Has done these ten years, although at times the trade's more difficult than others.'

'I daresay the war at sea with Spain doesn't help.'

'No,' the man shook his head in hearty agreement, 'it most certainly does not.'

They'd reached a portico at the front of the house by this time and he tipped the brim of his hat. 'Well, I'd best not go any further. Mistress is a devil for muddy boots, but you just go on in there, sir, and someone'll come to you.'

Thomas thanked him and went in. A wide stairway rose up from the middle of the hall to perhaps three floors above. From a portrait on the first landing, an elderly man, white-bearded and in out-moded dress, gazed somewhat suspiciously at him through what appeared to be a garland of fruit, flowers, seashells and vegetables. Thomas tried to evade the gaze as he paid his sixpence and was shown upstairs by a housemaid. He was relieved to hear that the lady of the household was otherwise engaged, and that she would not be able to show him around the 'cabinet'. 'But I am sure Mr Hartlib will tell you anything you require to know,' the maid added, as she preceded him up the stairs.

'Hartlib?'

'Yes, Mr Hartlib. He has come to look at the new cata-logue. Mr Hartlib knows everything, sir. About everything,'

Thomas sighed. It boded fair to be a lengthy visit, and he was more curious to know what Clémence and Trades-cant were discussing in the gardener's hut. It was not that cabinets of curiosity didn't interest him – he had often found such things fascinating. It had been much in fashion, in some of the towns of Europe where the King's court had for a time settled, for gentlemen to keep their private collections of rarities – coins, shells, the feathers of exotic birds and all manner of other unusual things – in ingeniously constructed and sometimes beautifully engraved wooden cabinets. But gazing upon such things would hardly further the progress of his work for Thurloe, and nothing else would gain him the credit required to be permitted, eventually, to return home. But on entering the room, Thomas could not help but utter an exclamation of surprise. Tradescant's 'cabinet' – the Tradeskin's Ark of which he had heard men speak – was of a different order entirely to those private gentlemen's collections he had seen elsewhere. Tradescant's 'cabinet', it transpired, was a large room taking up almost the whole of the top floor of this fine South Lambeth house. Rows and rows of mounted cabinets and shelves full of objects appeared to run around every wall of the room. Any space between them was taken up with the shells of large sea-creatures or amphibians, if not the skulls, tusks and horns of land-bound mammals. At the far end of the room were displayed incredible brightly decorated robes, some made from the skins of animals Thomas had only read of in books, oddly turned boots and slippers, outlandish headgear and weaponry such as he had never seen on an English battlefield. A long, glass-covered cabinet, full of peculiar artefacts, ran up the centre of the room, and suspended above him hung myriads of stuffed birds and other creatures – a huge fish, even – most of which he had never seen in his life before. Thomas didn't wonder that the cataloguing of such a collection had taken years. He wondered that it had ever been catalogued at all.

Thomas didn't know where to turn or to begin. His eye was taken by a display of items labelled as being African. He had heard stories of quite terrible creatures from sailors who had gone ashore on the Guinea coast, and here indeed were some fantastical and terrifying sights, not least of which was the blackened head of a crocodile, whose vicious jaws looked as if they might open and clamp down upon an unwary passer-by at any moment. Beyond the crocodile head was a collection of small, light arrows with exotically feathered flights. Thomas was reaching out to pick up one of the arrows when a voice called out in alarm, 'Stop, sir!'

Thomas looked around. He hadn't noticed, at the far end of the room, a thin young woman with long dark hair and eyes that were almost black. Had it not been for her pallor, and the fact that he had heard her speak first, he would have thought her a Spaniard. His hand was still suspended two inches above the arrow. 'I was not going to steal it, only to look.' Clearly, Tradescant's wife had stationed another housemaid here to watch for fear of theft.

The girl raised her eyebrows as if he had said something almost impertinent. 'I was not suggesting you were trying to steal it, sir, only that you might do well to read the label beneath before considering touching the item.' Without giving him a chance to respond, she rounded the end of a set of shelves and disappeared from his view.

Thomas felt that a jolt had gone through him, as if someone had prodded him with the end of a hot iron bar. Not since he had first left Faithly had a woman, not Clémence, not the Queen Mother, even, spoken to him in such a way. And he knew for certain that he had never seen such eyes. He was about to go after her when he thought he would do better first to look at the label beneath the arrow, as instructed. When he did, he involuntarily jerked his hand back again. *Arrows used by executioners of the West Indies. Deadly Poisonous.*

Shaken, he turned around to where she had been but there was no sign of her there now. Thomas looked again at the arrow and decided she had been taking him for a fool: an item capable of killing a man on touch would hardly be laid out on public display for any passing Londoner to maim themselves upon. But as he left the arrows and moved on, he made sure he didn't go so close as to touch them.

At the end of the shelf around which the girl had disappeared, he spied her again, now examining some items laid out on a bench. Beside her was indeed Samuel Hartlib, another of Evelyn's guests of the night before. Hartlib smiled broadly on seeing Thomas. 'Sir Thomas! So you are the gentleman so near to putting himself in peril. I am afraid you gave poor Mistress Ellingworth here quite a fright.'

Thomas employed his most winning smile. 'I am very sorry for it.'

Again, the young woman – it would appear, from Hart-lib's demeanour, she was not in fact one of the Tradescants' housemaids – treated him to a look approaching indignation. 'Do not trouble yourself, sir. My concern was for Mr Tradescant's reputation. It would not bode well should so . . .' she assessed him quite openly, 'finely dressed a gentleman come to grief whilst viewing the curiosities. Through his own carelessness.'

'Yes,' said Thomas, accepting his chastisement with a good grace. 'But I am truly grateful for your kindness all the same.'

Some of the antagonism went from the girl's countenance, and Thomas thought he also caught the trace of a blush. Perhaps all was not lost.

Hartlib was oblivious to any awkwardness in the exchange. 'But, Sir Thomas, I had not realised you were to visit the rarities today. We might have come together.'

'I had not realised it myself,' he replied, explaining where he had left Clémence.

'Ah, of course. In fact I must have a word with Tradescant myself. I have just been explaining to Mistress Ellingworth here that the item he has designated a unicorn's horn is in fact no such thing.'

'Oh?' said Thomas, only mildly interested.

'No.' Hartlib became conspiratorial. 'It is the tusk of a sea creature, found off the coast of Greenland. But Mistress Ellingworth does not think her brother's readers will wish to know that.'

Thomas turned towards the young woman. 'Your brother?'

'My brother is the editor of a weekly news-sheet, *The London Lark*. I assist him in its preparation. We thought it would be of interest to our readers to hear of Mr Tradescant's rarities. We have agreed with Mr Tradescant that I should come, once a week, to sketch and study an item to be featured in the next news-sheet.'

Thomas glanced down at the paper she had laid on the table, and, noticing, she placed a hand over it, but not before he had glimpsed the sketch.

'My drawing is not very good, I'm afraid,' she said.

He reached out a hand to the paper and briefly touched hers as he did so. 'May I?' he said.

With a brief hesitation, she moved her hand away and he picked up the paper to examine the sketch more closely. 'It's not so bad, you know – a reasonable likeness, and good enough I'm sure for your brother's newsletter. It is just,' he hesitated, 'untutored. Would I be correct?'

She nodded, all indignation gone now, and he was somehow sorry for it. 'I have never had lessons. We could not . . .'

She didn't need to finish. The austerity of her clothing was clearly born of necessity, not choice. Her dress was of a serviceable brown wool, over a smock of linen that might once have been white but was now dulled to a pale yellow. Both were worn, and both had clearly been mended more than once. Her tucker was clean, but unadorned by lace or pendant of any sort. Only at her cuffs was a small run of lace, a luxury that served not to show up the shabbiness of the rest, but to promise an elegance that might one day be hers. But for all her grace, and whatever learning her brother must have acquired in order to be capable of producing a newsletter, they were clearly as poor as church mice.

Without thinking, Thomas said, 'I could teach you.'

'What?'

'I could teach you,' he repeated. It had startled him almost as much as it had her when first he'd said it, but now it seemed a thing profoundly possible. 'How to draw, more accurately. I did have lessons, and I even remember some of them.'

Hartlib brought his hands together. 'Excellent! Most excellent! Learning is a commodity that will only grow when shared.' He clapped Thomas on the back. 'Well done, Sir Thomas. Well done. I only wish more thought like you. Now if you will excuse me, I must get down to Tradescant and tell him about that unicorn's horn.'

And then the German pedagogue was gone, and Thomas was left looking at the striking young woman and, for the first time in his life, not having an idea what to say.

'Did you mean it?' she said at last.

'Mean what?'

'That you would show me how to draw?'

Thomas took a step towards her. 'Oh, yes,' and he reached out gently to take the pencil she still held in her hand.

Just then, a low, authoritative voice came from behind Thomas's shoulder. 'Maria?'

'Oh!' She looked relieved. 'John. This gentleman was just helping me with my drawing.'

The man, tall, with long dark curls and a sallow complexion, gave Thomas a look that did not imply approval. 'Sir.'

Thomas made a bow. The man merely nodded. 'Maria, I think it is time for us to go.'

And a moment later, with a murmured assurance that she would be back the following week, she was gone.

Thomas was still standing there, looking after her, when Clémence appeared in the doorway. She looked back towards the stairs. 'I saw Samuel Hartlib as I was coming up through the orchard. He was in here?'

Thomas nodded. 'Is something wrong?'

'No. But you must be careful who you mix with. Hartlib is a Republican. The government sometimes uses him to convey messages to his contacts in Europe.'

Thomas shrugged. 'But he had contacts all over Europe even before the war. It's hardly the same thing as being . . .'

'Being what?' asked Clémence.

'One of Thurloe's spies,' Thomas said, keeping his voice steady.

'That's just the trouble,' she said. 'I do not know what one of Thurloe's spies would look like.'

NINE

A New Partnership

Seeker stretched out on the truckle bed in his chamber at Whitehall. He hadn't seen his own lodging on Knight Ryder Street in three days, and he didn't expect to any time soon. The small room he kept there was no longer the sanctuary to him that for several years it had been. Not since Maria Ellingworth. The memory of her so inhabited the place that sometimes he almost thought he felt her breathe beside him, but whenever he opened his eyes she was not there. Even the dog felt the emptiness of the place now, which had not been there before she had first come in to it. In recent months it had become his habit to go instead on up past St Paul's to Broad Street and the Black Fox. He would sit and talk with his daughter there, or don his old carpenter's coat and hat and take her out of London, to show her all the special places in the liberties and villages beyond. And then there were the times with Dorcas, sometimes moments just, when he could glimpse a different kind of life, a life that might one day be possible, if the demands of the state upon his time and loyalties ever lessened.

Tonight though, such a day seemed very far off, and to think of it was to dabble in fantasy. The concerns of the here and now were what pressed upon his mind as he tried to rest. Two days of widespread searches, of thorough questioning of everyone who might have encountered Fish and his fellow-conspirators in Hammersmith, or at his former lodging in the tailor's house in King Street, had failed to result in the capture of the men who had plotted to murder Cromwell. If the last few years in the Protector's service had taught Seeker anything, it was that those who were not caught in such acts would keep trying again until they were.

All the while, though, the matter of Joseph Grindle, and of the whereabouts of the bear that had mauled him to death, wove itself in and out of his thoughts. His promise to Samuel that he would find out what had happened to his friend weighed too heavily on him to allow him to sleep. But how was he to penetrate the clandestine world of animal baiting, whilst at the same time pursuing those who sought to kill Cromwell? The dog, curled up by the embers of the dying fire, was untroubled by such concerns. And it was the dog that gave him the idea.

Seeker had not undressed, not removed his boots even. He planted his feet on the floor and rubbed his eyes. The dog looked up. Seeker stretched his arms wide and rolled his shoulders. 'Come on, boy,' he said. 'Time to get to work.'

Less than half an hour later, they were walking up Middle Temple Lane towards Chancery, the dog loping happily behind Seeker, occasionally disappearing through a gateway to re-emerge from another a good bit further up the street. 'Revisiting old haunts, eh?' said Seeker. The animal knew its way around the city in darkness better than he did himself. As they crossed over Fleet Street, Seeker could see the corner of the wall of Clifford's Inn, jutting into the lane ahead, hanging on to the edges of the law in the shadows of Lincoln's Inn and Gray's, and almost crowded out by all the other Inns of Chancery. There was tenacity in that wall, a stubbornness that Seeker found himself admiring. He called the dog to heel and approached the porter's box by the front gate. The porter, who was finishing off a late supper, stood up and wiped his mouth when he saw Seeker and the hound approach.

'Captain! We've not seen you here a good long while. Is it Mr Ellingworth you're after?'

'Not unless there's something you know that I don't, Bennet,' replied Seeker.

'What? Oh, no, Mr Ellingworth has been conducting himself very properly, with his new news-sheet as they tell me, and Mr Wildman hasn't been here at all of late.'

John Wildman had been a Levelling lawyer more radical than Elias Ellingworth himself, often on the wrong side of the authorities, and one over whom Ellingworth had found himself in trouble several times, for having colluded in the dissemination of his writings and having helped conceal his whereabouts. What the porter Bennet couldn't know, and what Elias Ellingworth almost certainly didn't know, was that during his last incarceration in the Tower, John

Wildman had been turned by Thurloe, and now reported directly to his new master on whatever radical plots and manoeuvres he might come upon. The reason he had not been seen around his old London haunts of late was that he was too busy writing letters to Thurloe from the Netherlands, where his old Leveller comrades happily plotted against Cromwell. Seeker had been astonished when he'd heard the news that he was now in the pay of the intelligence service – if Wildman could be turned, anybody could.

'Well, you be sure to let me know if he does come sloping in here,' said Seeker. 'But no, it's one of your new inmates I'm looking for. Lawrence Ingolby.'

The porter looked surprised. 'Him that arrived a few days ago?' But then he nodded to himself. 'I thought he looked trouble.'

'Oh, never worry, Bennet, he's easily enough handled, if you keep him in his place.'

The man was unconvinced. 'I've seen the likes of him before. That one's no intention of staying in his place.'

Seeker laughed out loud at that. 'You'd best take me to him, then.'

Clifford's Inn was a place of twists and turns and nooks and crannies. Seeker had been here often enough before – usually looking for Ellingworth – but he could never quite be certain of his way around. It wouldn't have surprised him to turn a corner and come upon the cobwebbed form of some ancient lawyer, his quill still in his hand and his existence long forgotten, but Bennet had been there so long he had an unerring sense for where one of his charges would be found, at any hour of the day or night, and within five minutes Seeker was looking down at Lawrence Ingolby.

'Aw, what?' said the young man. 'I'm at my supper.'

Ingolby was sitting at the end of a long refectory table in the hammer-beamed dining hall of the inn, where a dozen or so men of varying ages, in robes of varying degrees of repair, were finishing off an evening meal of bread, wine and cheese. Above them, from flaking gilt frames on the walls, a few of the more notable amongst their predecessors regarded them with a degree of pessimism. A disgruntled servant moved up and down a parallel table, clearing from it the debris of already departed diners. Ingolby's dining companions either made a point of concentrating on the food in front of them, or shifting uneasily further down the benches, away from him and his unwelcome visitor. Lawrence heaved a great sigh and put down the hunk of bread he'd been at work upon. 'I hope it's not going to be like this every time I sit down to a bite to eat.'

'So do I,' said Seeker. 'Now shift yourself.'

As they were rounding a corner on the way to the small library the porter had cleared for Seeker's use, they all but collided with Elias Ellingworth, Maria's brother. The lawyer was about to start on an apology when he looked up and saw who it was he had almost bumped in to. His demeanour changed completely. 'What now, Seeker?'

'Nothing to do with you. Not this time, at least, so you can just carry on to wherever you were going . . .'

But Ellingworth had spied Lawrence behind Seeker's shoulder. His head moved from Lawrence back to Seeker like a dog about to argue over a bone. 'You don't tell me you're here for him? He's only been in London five minutes.'

'Aye, and for some folk five minutes is quite long enough to land right in the middle of it.'

Seeker's tone could leave neither Lawrence nor Elias in any doubt that 'it' meant trouble.

Lawrence's shoulders sagged. 'Come on, Seeker. I've hardly shaken the Yorkshire mud out of my boots. And I've not been near the Black Fox in two days, I swear it.'

'I should think not. But this has nothing to do with the Black Fox, nor with Elias Ellingworth here, so get yourself in there and wait for me.'

Elias looked beyond Seeker to Lawrence again. 'Do you wish me to come in with you?' he asked.

'No, he doesn't,' said Seeker as Lawrence looked as if he were considering it.

Lawrence gave up considering it. 'It's all right. Me and the captain here are old friends.' Another sigh and he passed them both and went in through the library door.

Ellingworth stepped further away from the door and leaned towards Seeker. 'He is seriously a threat to the state?'

Seeker grimaced. 'Heaven help us if Lawrence Ingolby ever decides to take on the Protectorate. Too clever by half. But no, and he's not in trouble either, before you start.' It had been clear to Seeker that Ellingworth had been about to. He looked at the lawyer who had caused him so much work over the past few years. When Elias had been an all-out opponent of the Protectorate, Seeker had known what to make of him. Now that Elias was at least making a show of toeing the line, he was considerably less sure, for all that he was Maria's brother. He decided to take a chance on him. 'Keep an eye out for him all the same. And if ever you hear of a "Fish" or a "Boyes" come looking for him, send word to Whitehall.'

'To you?' asked Ellingworth.

'To any in the Secretariat. There might not be time to find me.'

Elias studied Seeker carefully. 'What would these men want with him, that time should be so pressing?'

Seeker lowered his voice. 'If they come looking for him, it'll be because they're planning to kill him. That's all you need to know.' He allowed Ellingworth to absorb the information. 'Understand?'

'All too well,' said Ellingworth.

'Good. And there's something you can do for me.'

Elias's face set. 'I'm not spying for you, Seeker.'

'Heaven forbid we're ever that desperate. No, I need you to take him,' he jerked a thumb towards the door of the room Lawrence had just gone into, 'down to the Turk's Head coffee house in New Palace Yard tomorrow night. Understood?'

Elias nodded.

'Good,' said Seeker. 'Be on your way, then.' But as

Ellingworth turned to do just that, Seeker put out a hand to stop him again. 'Are you back living here now then?'

'No. I'm still at Dove Court.'

'With . . .'

'With my sister.'

'And . . .' Seeker coughed and looked away. 'All is well with her?'

'It is,' said Ellingworth, his manner a deal less defensive than it was wont to be with Seeker, but there was no encouragement in his tone either.

'Good,' Seeker said. 'That's good. Right.' There was nothing more to be said and he turned away and went into the library.

Lawrence was standing by the fire, examining the bust of a Roman law-giver of whom Seeker had never heard. He put the bust back down on the mantelshelf. 'If this is about Manon, I haven't—'

'It's not,' said Seeker. 'Sit down.'

Warily, Lawrence lowered himself into one of the chairs by the fire. 'So what is it about?'

'Hammersmith. The men you saw at the inn. I need their exact descriptions – height, eye colour, the way they walked, everything.'

'What's so special about them? You were off like a hare out of a trap when I mentioned their names the other day.'

'What is special,' said Seeker, 'is that they're contracted assassins, and whilst you were no doubt slumbering the night away in the finest feather bed that inn has to offer . . .'

Ingolby was about to protest, but Seeker stopped him.

'They were a few yards through the wall, rigging up a frame to train seven guns on the Lord Protector.'

Lawrence's eyebrows shot up. 'What? Cromwell was sleeping next door to me?'

'Don't be daft,' said Seeker. 'They were planning to attack the next time he was being driven along the street below. Which didn't happen, on account of you telling me where they were.'

The expression on Lawrence's face changed completely now, and his colour was ashen. 'Just because I was telling Manon, to make her laugh . . .'

'That's right,' said Seeker. 'A city crawling with paid informants and intelligencers, and we have to rely on you. Something's gone far wrong somewhere.'

'It must have done.' Lawrence was shaken by the revelation of his unwitting responsibility. 'Right then. Well, I only saw the two of them.'

'Two'll do for now,' said Seeker.

'The one I spoke to – Mr Boyes. Now, he was an educated man – you could tell by the way he spoke. Tinge of a foreign accent, too.'

'What kind of foreign?'

Ingolby pursed his lips. 'German? Dutch maybe? Put me in mind of some of the traders that we did business with in York, and most of them were from around the Baltic.'

'All right,' said Seeker. 'What else?'

'Well, he was an older man – sixties maybe?' But then

he screwed up his face, dissatisfied. 'No, though. His hair was grey and grizzled enough, his beard too. He was pale and – he'd lived, if you know what I mean, but his eyes were clear. Refined kind of face. Might have been sixty, might have been younger than you.'

'Did you see his hands?' said Seeker.

Lawrence thought again. 'No,' he said. 'Long grey gloves. Kidskin, good quality. Long fingers though, he had.'

'Rings?'

Lawrence shook his head.

And so the questioning and the description went on, the good grey suit, the long, horseman's boots. Boyes had been seated the entire time of their conversation, but Lawrence had formed the impression that he was a tall man. The other, Fish, had made less of an impression. Average height, forties, short light brown hair, balding and greying, cropped beard, stocky, tan boots, clothing unremarkable. Might have been a soldier once. Who hadn't?

'But you would know them if you saw them again?'

'I'd reckon so, yes.'

Seeker started to put on his own hat and gloves. 'If you should see them about anywhere, have the porter here get a message to me.'

'All right. Is that it then? Can I go back to my supper?'

'No. Come on, out to the gardens. There's something I want to show you.'

Lawrence looked like he might complain, but settled for a petulant 'hmph', and got up to follow Seeker out into the passageway and then through a side door that gave directly into the gardens. It was murky outside, the shapes of trees and shrubs indistinct, and only one or two of the lamps set to light the paths between the lawns had been lit. 'What the . . .?' Lawrence jumped back, hands thrust out in front of him, as a large shape came bounding at them out of the darkness.

Seeker laughed. 'London's turned you soft already, Ingolby. Thought you knew dogs?' and he put a hand out to tousle the head of the hound who'd found them.

Lawrence let out a breath of relief and moved forward, to kneel down in front of the dog. 'Well, you're a beauty, aren't you? Where did you spring from?'

'He bunks down with me, most of the time,' said Seeker. 'Huh, he obviously trusts you.' The animal had pushed its head forward to nuzzle under Lawrence's hand.

'Course he does,' said Lawrence, who was now being offered the dog's belly to rub. 'How's he at hawking?'

'Doesn't get much chance, but he'll bring down anything on four legs, or two for that matter, if you need him to.'

'I bet he would,' said Lawrence, examining one large paw and then another, before moving on to look at the dog's teeth and gums, and nodding. 'I'll have to borrow him off you some time. Take him out on the fields.'

'Aye,' said Seeker. 'You will.'

Ingolby lifted his eyes away from the dog and fixed a suspicious look on Seeker. 'I've heard that tone before. What is it?'

'You might prove to be useful.'

'Ah, no.' Now Lawrence abandoned the dog and stood up, brushing debris from his hose. 'No. I had enough of being useful in York – folk shooting at you, trying to throw you off walls. I've come here to learn to use this better,' he tapped a finger to his forehead, 'and I'd like to keep it attached to my neck, thank you very much.'

Seeker brought his face closer to Lawrence's. 'What you'd like, Ingolby, is not top of my list of concerns. Nevertheless, it's not me you'll be keeping company.'

'Oh?' said Lawrence, betraying his interest. 'Who then?'

'Sir Thomas Faithly.'

Lawrence took a further step back and raised a hand. 'No. Absolutely not. You are not throwing me in the Tower just so I can keep an eye on Thomas Faithly for you.'

'Faithly's not in the Tower. He's been out a few weeks. Not entirely been behaving himself, but nothing that'll get him thrown back in there, yet. I want you at the Turk's Head coffee house in New Palace Yard, seven o'clock tomorrow night. Elias Ellingworth'll fetch you down. Thomas Faithly'll be there an' all, and I'll tell you both then what I want you to do.'

TEN

A Meeting at the Turk's Head

The smoke, seeping out into the street every time the door was opened, was in Seeker's eyes almost before it had reached his throat. He wondered that they didn't have enough of the fog and belching chimneys outside, without they must create their own inside, too, but it was that time of day when the merchants and printers and booksellers, and many of those who worked the corridors of Whitehall, had finished their labours and after a hasty supper at some tavern or cook shop, made for the coffee houses.

He pushed open the door to the Turk's Head to find the noise was worse than the smoke. It did not dip as much here when he entered as it did in other places – the City, Holborn, Southwark – because they were more used to have the soldiery for clientele in Westminster, and for all he was hardly welcome in their midst, they did not always assume the worst when he appeared.

A group of soldiers, members of the Protector's Foot Guard, had commandeered the benches by the fire. It was almost time for the night duty. Seeker came to a halt a yard in from the door and stared at them until they began to make hurried signs of finishing up and returning to their barrack.

'What can I do for you, Captain?' asked Miles, the coffee man, with the look of one who has decided that there is nothing to be done but make the best of it.

'Nothing. It's this lot I'm interested in.' He indicated the main table, a long oval, running almost the length of the serving room. About a dozen animated men were gathered around it, smoking and drinking coffee, and making such a hubbub with their arguments and declamations that they might have numbered twenty at least. Seeker scanned the faces until he found the one he was looking for. Elias Ellingworth seldom ventured this far west, but he'd come at Seeker's bidding this evening. The lawyer stood up when he caught sight of Seeker.

'Did you bring him?'

Ellingworth nodded. 'Over there.' He indicated a small bench near the passage that led out to the back yard of the Turk's Head. Seated at the bench, reading, was Lawrence Ingolby.

'Right. You can wait here till I've finished with him, and then you can fetch him back up to Clifford's with you. Like of him venturing alone into Whitefriars, he'd never be seen again.'

'Lawrence would fend for himself well enough, even in Whitefriars. I think you underestimate your county-man, Seeker,' said Elias.

'Not an inch do I underestimate him. Just if he got in there, he might see things he thought were a better use of his abilities than the study of the law. I like Whitefriars just the way it is – manageable. The last thing I need is Lawrence Ingolby going in there and organising them.'

Lawrence looked up at Seeker's approach, then set his book aside. 'Right,' said Seeker, sliding on to the bench opposite him. 'Thomas Faithly—'

Lawrence interrupted him. 'I hardly know him. I was just a lad when he left Faithly to fight for the King, and he was long gone before I ever went to work up at the manor.'

'Aye, but you know where he comes from, you know the Faithlys, you know his *sort*, is what I'm saying. And you know dogs.'

'What's that got to do with—' Lawrence began to protest, but he was interrupted by the arrival in the Turk's Head of Thomas Faithly himself.

'Right,' said Seeker. 'Get up, go over to him, and greet him like an old friend you haven't seen for years, then take him over here and make a show of introducing him to me.'

Lawrence stared at him. 'But you've already . . .'

'Just do it,' said Seeker.

Lawrence shrugged, pulled a face as he gulped down the dregs of the spiced caudle he'd ordered, and went to do as Seeker had bid him.

He swaggered over to Thomas Faithly with all the ease

of a man with London at his fingertips. 'Sir Thomas! I never thought to see a friendly Yorkshire face so far from home!'

Thomas Faithly looked somewhat startled. 'Ah, Mr . . .? I do not think . . .'

'Lawrence Ingolby, Sir Thomas,' said Lawrence, making a profound bow that Seeker knew would have cost him some pride. 'Your father was very good to me as a boy in the North Riding, and I served latterly as your brother's steward at Faithly Manor.'

Thomas now looked carefully at Lawrence. 'Indeed. I think the name is somewhat familiar to me . . .' Then he broke into a broad smile. 'The foundling of the cave that was taken in by Old Digby Pullan! You've grown a bit in thirteen years, since I first left Faithly. You're attached to Matthew Pullan's household now, are you not?'

'I am, Sir Thomas,' said Lawrence, warming to his performance, which had now attracted some notice, 'and it is Matthew who has sent me down here to learn the law. But come, let's get some warmth and a good drink in you, for your father's kindness, and old times' sake.' Lawrence put an arm around Sir Thomas's shoulder and began to lead him to the table he'd been seated at. 'And let me introduce you to our fellow Yorkshireman, Captain Seeker.'

Before Thomas could say anything, Seeker had stood up. 'Sir Thomas and I are well enough acquainted. And if you'll take my advice, Ingolby, you'll choose your friends better when you're in town. I'll bid you both good day.'

Sir Thomas stood aside with a brisk nod of his head as Seeker went past him, leaving Lawrence looking after him, astonished.

Once Seeker was gone and the noise in the serving room returned to its former level, Lawrence leaned closer to Thomas Faithly and said, 'What was that all about? It was him that called me here to meet you.'

'I know,' said Sir Thomas, also keeping his voice low. 'But it's important, particularly for me, that people think there is no more connection between the Captain and me than former gaoler and prisoner. It is necessary that our public relations be hostile.'

'Oh, I see,' said Lawrence, although he was not altogether certain that he did. 'Well, that should be easy enough, given the way he goes about things. So why are we here then?'

Thomas glanced around once to see that they were not overheard. 'It's clear that Seeker trusts you, so I must also. As you have surely learned, while he knows his way through every murky alleyway his master Secretary Thurloe directs him to, it is not always a simple matter for him to involve himself in the business he finds there.'

Ingolby looked at him a moment, screwing up one eye. 'What you're saying is that whilst he knows where Thurloe's spies need to be, he's a bit on the recognisable side to go there himself.'

'That is, more or less, the situation.'

'And you're employed in his service in some way?'

Faithly lowered his voice even further. 'Nothing that you need to know about, aside from this one thing he would have you assist me with.'

'All right,' said Lawrence, deciding that on balance it was better for him to know as little of Seeker's business as possible.

Just then the server arrived and filled two finians with steaming black liquid from his pot. Lawrence looked in his cup and scowled. Once the man had left he leaned a little closer to Sir Thomas. 'Go on.'

Thomas tested the temperature of his cup and put it back down. 'You looked after my brother's hounds at Faithly, didn't you?'

Lawrence nodded. 'A good pack of dogs. I miss them.'

'You know a good hunting dog then?'

'Course. Don't you?'

'Yes, I do. But the kind of dog Seeker thinks you and I should go looking for isn't the kind you'd send haring off over the moors, if you know what I mean.'

Lawrence felt his lips tighten. 'I don't,' he said, very deliberately, although he suspected he did, but he was going to make Thomas Faithly say it.

Faithly appeared to be paying very close attention to the packing of his pipe. 'I'm talking about fighting dogs.'

Lawrence stood up, picking up his hat. 'Not interested. And if Damian Seeker thinks—'

'Sit down,' hissed Thomas, 'and listen. I have no interest in fighting dogs either – no more does Seeker, or he wouldn't need us to do this work for him. He needs to know about animal fights, who the keepers and the breeders are, which animals are involved.'

Lawrence frowned. 'Surely he knows. Ban's not been in force that long. He must know who kept the cocks and dogs and bulls for the fights and baiting.'

'When they were still legal, yes. But now they're not, and he needs to know who's still putting them on – the worst ones, the most vicious.'

'They're all vicious,' said Lawrence.

'Yes, but they don't all involve bears.'

'Bears?' Lawrence almost splurted out the coffee he'd just tried a sip of.

Thomas Faithly gave him a moment to compose himself. 'A few nights ago, Damian Seeker and I came upon the body of an old man – an old soldier, whose name we later learned was Joseph Grindle. He had been mauled to death. What remained of him was chained to the wall of an outbuilding in Bankside. Seeker is convinced he was killed by a bear that was deliberately set on him.'

Lawrence had put down his cup, very slowly, while Sir Thomas had been speaking. His mouth formed the words 'a bear' once more. Then he shook his head. 'I know nothing about bears, other than that the Bear Garden was closed down long before I got here.'

Thomas drew on his pipe and nodded. 'It was. But at least one of the bears is still, if not on the loose, being kept somewhere. What the Captain wants is for you and me to find our way into the darkest byways of dog-fighting until we're standing in front of someone who can tell us where that bear is. We are to feign an interest in the baiting, in finding ourselves a good fighting dog. Then we have to make it known that we have a very high purse to back this hound against a very particular type of animal.'

'I don't much like the sound of the sort he'd have us consorting with.'

'Neither do I,' said Faithly, 'that's why he needs you to be involved.'

Lawrence put down his coffee and shook his head. 'Ah, no. No. Whatever he's told you, I am *not* a fighting man of that sort. I'll skewer anyone you like with my pen, I can even look after myself in a rumble in an alleyway, but as for dealing with those types . . .'

Thomas smiled. 'Fortunate then, that while you have been learning to keep accounts and order wedders for my brother's flocks and defend yourself in alleyways, I have gained long experience in the use of pistol and knife, and other useful items besides, against properly trained fighting men. However, I am, or so my enemies would tell you, a gentleman, and the search for a fighting dog of *this* nature is not something a gentleman does on his own account.'

A look of mild displeasure crossed Lawrence's face. 'I'm to play your servant.'

'Not in the way of some lackey. But you will be my man, someone I have engaged to assess the quality of what I'm offered, to negotiate terms on my behalf. People around the cockpits and the dog-rings will talk more openly to you than they will to me. The captain says you can pass yourself off in any company, and that no one will get the better of you.'

Lawrence was mollified. 'He said that?'

'Yes, he did, and it's a lot better than anything he's ever said about me.'

'Oh, aye,' agreed Lawrence quite heartily, 'a whole lot better.'

Within a half-hour they had made their plans to meet the next evening at the Bear on Bankside, and there begin their enquiries whilst discreetly making known their business. That done, there was no more to be said. Thomas rose to leave, but as he did so, Elias Ellingworth, who was at that point reading a section of James Harrington's new book aloud to the company, took his eye. He turned back to Lawrence. 'Do you know that man?'

'Which?' asked Lawrence, who had been looking elsewhere.

'There, at the end of the table, the one declaiming.'

'Oh, Elias? Yes, Elias Ellingworth, a lawyer of Clifford's Inn. He's another one that's got some sort of history with Seeker.'

'Of what nature?' asked Thomas.

Lawrence shrugged. 'Not likely to be good, is it?'

'No,' Thomas agreed, 'I suppose not.' He hesitated, then said, 'Do you happen to know if he has a sister?'

'A sister?' Lawrence thought a moment. 'Yes, he does.

I heard him telling Seeker he lived with her. Don't know where.'

'And,' continued Thomas, 'I don't suppose you would know her name?'

Lawrence shook his head. 'Sorry. I'll ask him if you like.'

'Ah, no. Not here at any rate, it might provoke too much interest.'

'It might that. Why *are* you so interested in whether or not he has a sister?'

'Ah well, you see,' said Thomas, becoming quite animated, 'I met a woman two days ago, at Tradescant's Ark – you know it?'

Lawrence shook his head.

'No matter. The thing is, something in the lawyer's face put me in mind of her, something in the look of him, his expression – I cannot pinpoint it. Perhaps I'm imagining it, for since I first set eyes on her I have not been able to get her out of my mind.'

Ingolby smiled; he felt a lessening of the tension that had been radiating through him since Seeker had left. 'Well, I'll find out from him on the way home whether he has a sister, what her name is, if she was at this Ark place, and if she's spoken for. And I'll tell you all about it next time we meet. Take our mind off this business of blood-fights and murders.'

'Truly, I will be much obliged,' said Sir Thomas. 'And Damian Seeker can hardly complain about me paying court to the sister of a respectable lawyer, can he?'

ELEVEN

Maria

'Be careful, Maria.'

Samuel Kent and Gabriel were already at work, roasting and grinding the beans for the first pots of the day at Kent's Coffee house. They would open their doors within the half-hour and already an assortment of lawyers, merchants and visitors would be making their way along Cornhill or up from Blackfriars, eager to fall upon their pipes and news-sheets and to begin the daily process of ordering the affairs of the world. Grace was busy measuring sugar and setting aside the herbs and spices that would be needed for the other beverages – the caudles, possets and infusions – she would be asked for in the course of the day. Maria, as was her habit, had called in to help her for half an hour.

They had spent some time talking of Joseph Grindle, and of what Seeker had told Grace of the circumstances of his death. Grace was not happy about Maria's intention to travel south of the river again, on her own. Maria brushed aside her concerns.

'You need have no fears for me, Grace. I know you love

my brother dearly, but you must know I am left to my own devices from morning to night most days. If Elias is not dealing with his legal clients, he is at work on the news-sheet: he hasn't time to shadow me around London.'

Grace cut another wedge from the sugar loaf and carefully weighed it on her scales. 'But it isn't London, Maria, it's Lambeth. One thing to go to Tradescant's on my birthday visit, or with John Drake when he was selecting his apothecary samples, but I do not think you should go on your own.'

Maria hopped down from the stool she had been perched upon and dipped the tip of her finger into a small spray of spilled sugar. 'John Drake is busy today, up at Cree Church Lane.' A house someway up the lane behind St Katharine Cree had been granted by the city to the Jews of London, who were now at last allowed to live openly, nearly four hundred years after their expulsion from England. Elias had said if Cromwell never did another good thing, he had at least done this. 'Besides, Elias knows I'm going on my own today, and he does not mind.'

Grace continued to set her scales carefully. 'And does Elias know about this Thomas Faithly?' she asked, never taking her eyes from her measure.

Maria felt herself flush. Why had she said nothing of Faithly to Elias? Did she fear what her brother would say about her having anything to do with a known Royalist? No, because Elias might condemn a man's politics, but he would not condemn a man for believing in them.

She swallowed. 'He would not care one way or the other.'

Grace put down her knife. 'Oh, but he would, Maria. I have heard of this Thomas Faithly. He has spent years in the company of Charles Stuart. You know what they say of that man's court, of the mistresses, the drunkenness, the bastards left suckling all over Europe. And Thomas Faithly is hardly out of the Tower, he will not have seen an honest woman . . .'

'He has only offered to teach me to draw, Grace. Besides, he is at Tradescant's as escort to the Frenchwoman we saw about the gardens on our visit.'

'The Frenchwoman?' said Grace. 'Well, *that* is all right, isn't it?'

'Grace! When did you become so staunch a Puritan?'

Grace laughed. 'When first I read your hot-headed brother's newsletters. It was the only way I could get him to notice me, so you must allow me my views on the French. Besides, Maria,' she added, her tone softer, 'for all your wit and your knowledge of London's streets, I have been further afield in the world than you. You must understand, not all men are like . . .'

'Like who?' said Maria, her voice barely audible.

'Like Seeker,' said Grace.

Maria felt herself tremble, felt the tears begin their prickling in her eyes. They had never spoken of Seeker like this, she and Grace, nor she and Elias even. She had never spoken about Damian to anyone. She struggled to find the right words. 'You – you don't know what happened.'

Grace put down her weights and went to take Maria's hands. 'I know what Elias has told me, and that it is what Seeker told him. And Elias believes him. Seeker told him that whatever passed between you was a private thing, of his own will, and yours, and no business of the state's. He swore to Elias there was no truth in the rumour put about by Secretary Thurloe that he had only involved himself with you in order to gain information on your brother's associates.'

Maria could not look into her friend's face. 'He told Elias all of that?'

'You must know how often he was at your door, Maria, before Thurloe sent him north.'

'And cured him of his malady,' Maria said with bitterness.

'Cured him?' Grace stepped back and almost laughed. 'You think he is cured of you? How can you think it? Did you *look* at him when he met us on the road to Lambeth? Did you not see his longing for you, written all across that dreadful face?'

It is not dreadful, Maria wanted to say. Her fingers had traced its lines, its scars. She had lost herself for long hours in the molten dark of his eyes and thought she would never wish to be anywhere else. *It is not dreadful, it is the most beautiful thing I have ever seen.*

Instead, she said, 'If that were true, he would not spend every other waking hour at the Black Fox. Half of London is talking of it, it is a wonder his Puritan masters allow it, him and that woman . . .'

'Dorcas is a good woman,' said Grace.

Maria wrenched her hands from Grace's. 'It does not *help*,' she said, 'to be constantly hearing she is a "good woman". I would rather people damned her for a slattern and a whore.'

'You would not,' said Grace.

'Would I not? Would I not rather think he would grow tired of her, disgusted, and return to me?'

'You would only have to say the word, Maria. The man is in love with you.'

The anger fell away from Maria again and her voice dropped. 'If he loves me, why does he go there?'

'Because you told him you would not have him, and you have given him no cause to think otherwise since his return from Yorkshire. But more than that, despite what people say of him, I think there is a chance Damian Seeker is, at heart, like any other man. No one in this world of ours truly wants to spend their life alone. Not even him. That is why he goes to find his comfort with Dorcas Wells.'

There was silence between them now, nothing to be heard but the sounds of Samuel and Gabriel working in the serving room next door. Maria reached for her shawl and pulled up her hood. 'Then I wish him well of it,' she said at last. 'For myself, I have a drawing lesson in Lambeth to go to.'

Maria didn't know whether Samuel said something to her as she left, almost knocking over a stool that had not quite been tucked under a table, and she could hardly see

Gabriel as the perplexed boy held the door open for her. By the time she reached the bottom of Birchin Lane on her way down to the river, the tears had so flooded her eyes that she couldn't see at all.

Clémence stopped on the first-floor landing to admire the French striking clock, perhaps a gift to Tradescant's father from Robert Cecil. Cecil had been to old Queen Elizabeth what Thurloe was to Cromwell; he had been more, in fact, almost what Richelieu had been to Louis XIII. All that power gone, so many lives destroyed over intrigues long-forgotten, and yet this clock ticked on. She reached out a hand towards its face, wishing she could turn time back. But how far back would she turn it? A year and a half, to when Rupert had still been at the King's court in Cologne, content to let her be in his company, to watch him at his work and at his leisure, to catch an unexpected glimpse of him sometimes? Or would she turn it back further, fifteen years, to before the English War began? No, thought Clémence, because then she would be sitting in Brittany or Paris, with nothing to do but attend to the flattery of foolish women. She had another destiny. Clémence withdrew her fingertips from the brass face of the clock, and continued up the stairs, to the Cabinet of Curiosities.

A visiting merchant and his family were there before her, just through the door, exclaiming upon the sights that greeted them. The father was explaining to his wife how the barnacle goose grew like a tree from the ground in the wild wastes of Scotland. The older son, his eyes gleaming and his hands waving in the air, terrorised his younger brothers and sisters with tales of the items on display coming to life at night, when the ghost of the King of Virginia would don his cloak and headdress and take up his tomahawk once more, in search of English children.

Smiling, Clémence went past the noisy family towards the alcove at the far end of the room, where she spied the blue-velvet-clad back of Thomas Faithly. Thomas appeared to be bent over a table, examining something very closely. As Clémence drew nearer, she saw that a young woman, originally obscured by a wall of shelves, was standing to the right of him, watching intently as he sketched the lines of a feather.

'Thomas?' she said.

He straightened himself and turned around. 'Ah, Clémence. Are you finished so soon? Let me introduce you to Mistress Ellingworth, whose brother is the editor of *The London Lark* news-sheet. Perhaps you know it?'

Clémence smiled at the striking-looking young woman, who was dressed in a somewhat faded yellow linen gown whose hem had frayed and been mended a good few times. The girl looked slightly wary of her.

'It has not been my good fortune to have come across that publication.'

As the women watched each other, Thomas pointed with his pencil to the feather. 'Mistress Ellingworth is composing articles for the interest of her brother's readers, on the many curious items to be found in Tradescant's collection.'

'And your brother's readers will be interested in the Duke of Buckingham's feather?' asked Clémence, picking up the item and holding it towards the window, so that its jewels sparkled in the late morning sunlight.

'Only that it has been plucked, madame,' said Maria.

Clémence could not help but burst into laughter at this. 'Oh, Mistress Ellingworth, I think you will be a tonic. I have not heard such forthright views since I left the King's court.'

The young woman coloured at this, and Clémence held out her hand. 'If you are Sir Thomas's friend, I hope you will be mine,' she said.

The blush went deeper. 'Sir Thomas has offered to teach me to draw.'

'And he has a fine hand for it.' Clémence turned to Thomas, whose handsome face was lit by a broad smile. 'I see now why you attired yourself in your fine blue suit today, Sir Thomas. If Mistress Ellingworth does not mind keeping you an hour or so longer, I have some commissions for friends in the country that I have promised to fulfil from Mr Tradescant's glasshouses and seed stores.' She returned her gaze to Maria. 'Mistress Ellingworth, I hope you will keep an eye on Sir Thomas for me. He has a talent for getting into scrapes when left to his own devices, and there are far too many items in this Cabinet of Curiosities that he could cause havoc with.'

And finally she was rewarded with a smile. 'That is in fact how we met. I will see to it that he tampers with nothing more perilous than a feather, madame.'

As Clémence was descending the stair, she reflected that it might be no bad thing for Thomas Faithly to have a distraction. The girl was evidently capable of looking after herself, and Clémence knew Thomas to be profligate in love, rather than wicked. And in love, a man was less cautious. For all she was fond of him, there was something in the tale of Thomas's return to England that had never struck Clémence as quite right, and perhaps if he were less on his guard, she might find out what it was.

After Clémence had gone, Maria found herself looking into the crinkled dark blue eyes and travel-worn face of Thomas Faithly. She had known him for a Royalist the minute she'd set eyes on him: he walked like a Royalist, smiled like a Royalist, dressed like a Royalist and he had a charm to him that most of her brother's associates thought it beneath their dignity, and hers, to employ. She hadn't known, until Grace had told her, that Thomas Faithly had been a close associate of the King. Even then, it had not really seemed to matter. But here, now, where the rose-scents of the Frenchwoman who could speak with such familiarity of the King's court still lingered, Maria felt that she was somehow losing her footing. The ground beneath the floorboards of this house in South Lambeth seemed to shift a little, and the certainties of her life – the garret in Dove Court, Elias and his news-sheet and his rooms at Clifford's, the coffee house, the city streets – receded. Thomas Faithly was standing in front of her as if stepping momentarily off the stage, or from a painting. He had fought on the side of the supreme enemy, the Stuarts, for years; he had visited all those royal courts that to Maria were just gilded names in a story that was not hers to read, and he had laughed with and danced with and kissed the hand of the King.

He reached out to touch her lightly on the arm. 'Mistress Ellingworth? Maria? Is everything all right?'

Maria recalled herself to the present. 'Yes, yes. Everything is fine, but I think perhaps we should not continue these lessons.'

His face fell. 'Not . . .? But why ever would we not continue them?' He pointed to the sketch alongside his own on the table. 'Look at the progress you have made already this morning. But a few more lessons and you will have perfected it.'

Maria didn't want to look at him. 'We are from different worlds, you and I, Sir Thomas. I think perhaps it is not . . . fitting, that we should continue.'

There was a silence, and then she felt him take her hand. 'Will you look at me, Maria?'

She looked up. The sparkling blue eyes that were usually dancing with humour were not sparkling now; they were intense and serious. She hadn't looked at him properly before. His smile made him seem younger than she now saw he was. He must have been about thirty-five years old, not as old as Damian, but a year or two, perhaps, older than her brother. And she saw in his face that he had lived a life that was more than dancing and gaming and intriguing in foreign courts. A thin silver scar ran from beneath his left eye to just above his jaw, and the pallor of the Tower overlay the ingrained colouring she had noted before in men who had fought and travelled much of their lives.

'I promise you, Maria, I intend you no dishonour, and I would not have you or any other believe that I do.'

She would have said something, but he carried on. 'You tell me your brother is a lawyer?'

'Yes,' she said, not knowing why that should be of any relevance.

Thomas straightened. 'Then I will present myself to him, just like any other gentleman should. And I will engage him on some business I have had in mind for some time now. And your brother will allow that I should give you drawing lessons, and then no one else will have any ground for argument.'

Maria laughed. Sir Thomas's eyes were sparkling again and his smile returned, and it seemed strange indeed that anyone should apprehend anything bad of him. It would be to little purpose to tell him that her brother would not think of disallowing her anything she judged for herself to be right. 'But you know,' she said, carefully extracting her hand from his, 'my brother is a very particular sort of lawyer. His only dealings with professed Royalists have been as their adversary.'

'Then we shall cure him, and he shall make no quibble about our drawing lessons. But oh,' he said, holding the feather once more up to the light, 'you see how the coral on this feather is almost the exact match for the shade of your own lips? How is such a thing to be captured on paper? How is such a thing to be rendered in words? How does a man express his apprehension of a beauty that can only have been created by God?'

Maria could still hear the noisy family as they flitted excitedly from cabinet to cabinet, but the sound of them was muffled now. She was conscious that Thomas Faithly was inclining his head a little closer towards hers. She was caught in time, on the cusp of something. A wave of uncertainty went through her, but then the moment was broken by the sudden, loud arrival of three small children who, shrieking, were running from their brother. Thomas drew back, himself a picture now of uncertainty, a grown man as bashful as a schoolboy. Maria bent her attention once more to the feather and after watching her for a long moment afterwards, he did the same.

TWELVE

Dead Man's Place

Stained red lips on a chalk-white face split open to reveal the remains of two rows of yellowed teeth. A hand shot out and pawed his arm, whilst a knife delved towards the thong that held his pouch. Lawrence spun about and caught his assailant so hard by the wrist that the knife fell from the cut-purse's hand and clattered to the ground. Lawrence kicked it away and watched the small boy go scurrying after it. The stained red smile of the watching foul-breathed doxy collapsed into a scowl.

'Forget it, Grandmother,' Lawrence said. Most of the useful lessons in his life had been learned from Digby Pullan, the North Riding merchant into whose home he had been taken at the age of nine. But some had been learned before then, from a dissolute vagrant mother and a childhood spent wandering across the moors from manor to manor, village to village, begging his bread and stealing his clothes, as his mother plied her trade at the inns and hovels in between. Lawrence doubted there was much that the denizens of Southwark could teach him.

London Bridge though, had been a revelation. Lawrence knew for certain he wouldn't be able to shut an eye at night in a house perched teetering four storeys high over the relentless waters of the Thames, and yet hundreds did, living and working suspended in the air with half the world rumbling past them in wagons, clattering by on their horses, or slinking by on foot, and the other half speeding along beneath in barges and wherries, and never looking up.

'Watch you don't get nipped by a Winchester Goose,' one of the fellows had said to the accompaniment of much bawdy laughter, when Lawrence had expressed his intention of going to visit an old acquaintance in Southwark. 'You'll be diving for the mercury then!' The ribaldry around the table had saved him the trouble of asking what a Winchester Goose was, and now he could see them, craning their necks from hooded doorways, preening their feathers in the upper windows of taverns or as they promenaded along Bankside. He could hear them too, cackling and hissing at one another as they spied a tasty morsel or rich pickings with which to feather a nest. Lawrence batted away their blandishments as easily as he would have done an importunate hen in the courtyard of Faithly Manor.

Passing by what had once been the Bishop of Winchester's Palace, growing moss-green and damp as if born of the Thames itself, Lawrence soon found himself outside the main gate of the Clink. It didn't take much to end up in a place like that, he thought – bad luck, poor choices. Most human misfortune came down to the one or the other in the end. Lawrence wasn't sure the one wasn't consequent on the other. At any rate, he didn't intend to become in any way familiar with this Clink. He moved on. Across the water, London loomed larger and closer than he could have believed from the other side. Judgemental, imperious. And yet the sounds and movement of the place where he was now, the night scents of roasting meat, the snatches of song and raucous laughter, all said that Southwark cocked a snook at London. Lawrence smiled. Perhaps there was something to be said for it after all.

The lights and sounds of the taverns stretched on a good way, tracing the curve of the river where it ran round from past Lambeth, but Lawrence turned left. 'Dead Man's Place,' Thomas Faithly had said. Lawrence came upon it, a lurking, leaking kind of place, winding away from the river, just past the Clink. He made a point of walking down the middle of the road, not just for the sake of keeping his feet from the gutters that ran to the river, but to keep a distance between himself and whatever might be waiting to manifest itself from the unlit walls and doorways as he disappeared deeper into Southwark.

Lawrence wasn't one to seek out trouble, but he wasn't easily frightened, either. Nevertheless here, the knowledge of the death of Joseph Grindle, which across the river had been nothing more than the albeit gruesome cause of the investigation Seeker had involved him in, wrapped itself around him like a cloak. He was glad after about fifty yards to come to the sign of the Bear. The tavern, if such it was,

was as unpromising a hole as he had seen in all his twenty-six years, and not the kind of place he would usually think of setting foot in, but he suspected Southwark might well harbour worse. He ducked his head and went in.

Thomas Faithly was already there, engaged in a game of English hazard with an ancient fellow who looked as grizzled and knotted as an old log just washed up on the Bankside shore. Lawrence could see from the doorway that the fellow was cheating, a third die slipping from his cuff when required. He wondered that Thomas Faithly didn't also see it, but then he thought that maybe he did.

Thomas looked up as the door creaked closed behind Lawrence. 'Ah, my good friend! And in the nick of time to save me from this gentleman who would have every penny from my purse!' The 'gentleman' gave Lawrence a black-toothed smile, which Lawrence did not return. No point in him and Thomas Faithly both looking like they were asking to be taken for idiots. He went over and stood by the table. 'Come on, Sir Thomas, we've business to see to.'

'Another jug of sack, for the love of God, Lawrence, and then I am at your command.' He turned to his gaming partner. 'My man here is the very Devil when it comes to the dice or a hand of cards, he has no understanding of the skill, you see. He thinks nothing worth chancing a shilling on unless it has four legs and a set of teeth that would shred your innards – although he'll look at a cockfight at a push.'

Lawrence stepped forward and planted a hand on Thomas's shoulder. 'Now, Sir Thomas, you know the major-generals have put an end to all that sort of thing. Is that not right, friend?' he added, giving the old dicing cheat a meaningful look.

The old man echoed his look. 'Aye. None of that on Bankside now, may God bless the Lord Protector.'

'It's a pity, all the same,' slurred Sir Thomas. Lawrence knew he was not as drunk as he pretended to be, but he doubted the old fellow would spot it. 'I used to love to watch a good dog. Do you remember my Brutus, Lawrence?'

Lawrence put on a smile. 'Aye, fat old thing. Take down a boar though, if he'd a mind.'

'Best dog I ever had,' said Thomas. He leaned across the table towards his recent adversary. 'Lost him. Marston Moor.'

Lawrence picked up Sir Thomas's hat and handed it to him. 'Lost a lot more than that. Now come on, we've places to be.'

Thomas was making a show of getting up reluctantly from the table, when the old fellow placed a firm hand on his wrist, all the while looking at the heavy purse Lawrence had relieved his master of. 'I can get you a dog. A good dog.'

Thomas made to sit down again, but Lawrence said, 'Sir Thomas isn't interested in your half-bred curs.'

The man shook his head, leaned closer still. Lawrence didn't envy Thomas the reek of rotting breath and Bankside filth he must now be being subjected to. 'No, proper dogs. Bred from the old mastiffs from the baiting.'

Lawrence leaned in. 'The ones that fought the bulls, you mean?'

The man lowered his voice, looked around him as if Colonel Pride himself might be listening in a corner. 'Not just the bulls.'

'Do you mean the ones that baited the bears?' Thomas had now let drop his drunken act. Lawrence saw that the old fellow understood it had all been a game in the first place. Just a game with different rules from the ones with dice, or cards, or peas under a shell. The man nodded.

Lawrence shook his head. 'No. They were all shipped off to Jamaica when the Bear Garden was closed down.'

'Aye, but not before some of them had whelped.' The man looked again at the purse. 'Cost you, mind.'

Thomas slowly turned his hand to grip the old man's wrist. 'I'll not be done. I know my money and my man here knows dogs.'

'You won't be done, your Lordship,' said the man, essaying one brief attempt to release his wrist from Thomas's grip before giving it up. 'You'll want one of these dogs when you see them, I promise you.'

Thomas held the man's wrist a moment longer then nodded and let it fall. 'All right then.'

Less than two minutes later they were out in Dead Man's Place once more, all three of them. Lawrence kept a tight grip on the handle of his dagger and hoped Thomas Faithly was as able a swordsman as North Riding rumour had told. There might be time for the pair of pistols Sir Thomas wore concealed beneath his cloak, but Lawrence doubted it. They went further down the alley, away from the river, then turned sharply to the right. More turns, ever narrower passageways, wooden boards crossing open pools of water, and Lawrence had soon lost his bearings, but Thomas, at least, had the air of one who had been here before.

'Not there then?' Thomas had asked as they'd passed behind the site of the Bear Garden.

Their guide had spat and shaken his head. 'Rubble now. Builder has it. Galleries long burned for firewood. What's the use of building places for people to live, if you take away all of life's pleasures, eh?'

'What did they do with the kennels?' Lawrence asked. 'Burn them for wood too?'

The man laughed, a dry sound from the side of his throat. 'Don't know nothing about kennels. Not there. Cages, though. Sold on somewhere.'

'And the bears?'

'All shot.'

'Aye, so I've heard. But where were they kept?'

The man stopped, as if to consider, then shrugged. 'Dunno. Where would you keep a bear?'

They carried no lantern, yet their guide negotiated with ease the walkways around the pools of Thames water amongst the gardens of Bankside. He did not as much pause nor glance to the side as they passed by the wall of the property in which Thomas and Seeker had only a week since made their gruesome discovery of Joseph Grindle's body. Just past it they forked to the left and Thomas became aware of the water leaching from the ground at either side of their path. They were on Lambeth Marsh.

'I don't like this,' Lawrence murmured just behind him.

'Nor I.' Thomas stopped. 'You!' he called to the man. 'Far enough. Where are these dogs?'

'Yet a little further, master,' said the man, pointing up ahead of him. 'There.' Thomas could just make out the outline of some sort of enclosure or assortment of buildings, from which a solitary twist of smoke wound upwards into the night sky. He nodded, and passed a hand beneath his cloak to take hold of one of his pistols.

As they drew nearer to the enclosure, Thomas began to see the occasional glow of light further back on the marsh, towards the river and Lambeth, the odd rag-tag of cottages or lone houses, as if their occupants had turned their backs on the world.

The path by which they approached the high-walled enclosure was narrow and irregular, and ended in a small wooden door set into the wall. Long before they reached it such a barking had set up that Thomas would have given up any thought of examining the creatures making it, had not his purpose been getting to the owner of those dogs. Loud curses and the sound of a leather leash whipping swiftly through the night air were followed by a yelp, then a whimper, then silence.

At a series of knocks the small wooden door was opened

to them. Their guide went in untroubled, but both Thomas and Lawrence had to stoop. When they straightened up again it was to be confronted by a man twice the size of their guide and a head taller than either of them. His chest alone was broad enough for two men. A pelt, Thomas thought, and the fellow might have passed for a bear himself.

A short exchange between guide and guard ensued. 'Have they money?' Thomas heard the giant say. The answer in the affirmative was followed by a swift body search that soon relieved Thomas of his sword and his pistols, but not, to his surprise, his purse. Almost as surprising was the failure of the search of Lawrence to turn up any weapon at all, when Thomas knew for a certainty that his companion was carrying a knife.

'You'll get these back when you leave,' the man growled, throwing down Thomas's weapons and powder flasks on the lid of a water butt near the door. Thomas tried not to imagine the damage that would be done to his powder, or indeed to his fine new flintlock pistols should the lid of the water butt choose to give way beneath them.

'Glad to hear there's a chance of us leaving,' Lawrence muttered as their guide disappeared back out of the door and onto the marsh again.

The place stank. It was a stink beyond the usual stink of London, which had receded the further from the city they got. Beyond the different, dangerous miasma of Southwark too, overlaid as it was with all the pulsating potential of human sin. This place stank of dog piss, and shit and fear.

Like a field hospital, or one of the prisons Cromwell had had packed with taken Royalists. Thomas felt an old nausea rising within him. 'What kind of beast can be kept in a place like this?' he asked.

'One that will kill,' said the kennel master. 'That's what you're here for, after all, isn't it? Let us not pretend you didn't understand what you were coming to.'

'And for that you keep them in filth?' Lawrence's voice registered as much disgust as Thomas felt.

The kennel master stopped, and turned around to loom over them. 'This is not the place to find a lady's lapdog, nor the season to waste my time.'

'We're not here to waste your time,' said Lawrence, in a tone that cut by a couple of inches at least the difference in height between them, 'but I have my doubts what manner of sorry specimen can be kept in a condition like this. Sir Thomas has no mind for a sickly runt, nor I the humour to nurse it.'

The man simply laughed and continued on ahead of them. A growling then a barking set up again, and this time he did nothing to quiet it. At the far end of the yard was a palisade of brick, broken at intervals, floor to ceiling, by sets of iron bars. The barking grew and became frantic the closer they got to the cage. Such was the leaping and tussling from inside, desperate animals pressing their muzzles through the gaps in the bars, that they could not at first tell how many hounds were in there.

'The last three,' the man said proudly. 'Last three mastiffs whelped off the Bankside bitches before they were shipped off to the Caribbean. Magnificent beasts, they are.'

And Thomas had to admit that they were. The largest of them, at full stretch against the bars, was almost face to face with him and might have placed its massive paws on the shoulders of a man as tall as Seeker even. The muscles across neck and chest looked powerful enough to pull a cart, and the teeth revealed by the huge, gaping jaws would have ripped a man's throat out in seconds, had the beast been so ordered or inclined. Even Lawrence, drawing closer to the cage and making calming sounds as he did so, looked impressed. The dogs continued to bark and scramble as Lawrence got closer, but gradually the barking became less aggressive and the scrambling less threatening. The smell, though, as they drew almost up to the cage, was worse. The worst of it was coming from an empty cage to the right of that in which the dogs were kept. Thomas wondered when its last occupant had left the manure-ridden hole.

'What say you, then?' asked the kennel master of Lawrence, recognising the servant as the man of the two newcomers who really knew dogs.

Lawrence shook his head. 'Never seen anything like them. Are they trained?'

'Enough, but they need an expert handling.'

'Aye. And have they fought?'

'Not yet. Not ready. Nearly, mind, but not yet.'

'How long?'

'Another month maybe.'

Lawrence looked at Thomas and Thomas shook his head. 'Too long. I'd get in to the business sooner. I have – patrons – who would take an interest in this venture.'

The man was back on his guard. 'Private patrons?'

'Are there any other kinds, in these benighted days?'

'Fair enough. They got money to spend?'

'Plenty,' said Thomas. 'I assure you.'

'Take all three dogs?'

'One,' Lawrence said, 'we'd start with one. See how it did.'

Thomas wondered if Lawrence, mesmerised as he evidently was by the beasts, had forgotten that they were not in fact there to purchase a hound.

'We might extend to the three,' Thomas put in, 'if the first proved promising.'

'The others on deposit, like?' the kennel master said.

'Aye, something like that.'

'Full price for the first, and the other two on deposit. For a fortnight. I've other customers interested.'

'Oh?' said Sir Thomas.

'Aye, but I won't give them to just anyone, not beasts of that quality. Has to be someone who knows what they're about.'

'Oh, I know what I'm about,' said Lawrence, who had now got one of the beasts to sit in front of him, on the other side of the bars.

'That's the best one,' the man put in quickly. 'Cost a bit more.'

'You don't say,' murmured Lawrence.

'Full price for that one,' said Sir Thomas, 'and the others kept here on deposit for two weeks. If this one shows promise, we'll take the other two, but the price has to be agreed today.'

The man mentioned a number. Sir Thomas laughed and mentioned another. They haggled this way and that a full two minutes until they arrived at the figure they had both known from the start they would agree upon. Higher than most fighting dogs were worth. But Sir Thomas, who had lost and won several purses on dog fights in his time, could see that these were no common fighting dogs.

Leaving Lawrence with the dogs, Thomas went with the kennel master to what passed for the man's office. He missed his pistols, but he reckoned the promise of further money to come two weeks hence would keep him safe enough. He counted out the coin Seeker had given him, with the admonition that every penny should be accounted for. In his head, Thomas added his necessary losses to the old gambler on Dead Man's Place, and the price of a decent late supper in some agreeable tavern for himself and Lawrence when their business here was done.

'I'll keep these other two in prime condition for you, have no fears of that,' said the man, locking the coins away in a small iron chest. 'Two weeks' time, they'll be just about perfect.'

Thomas knew that now they had come to the most delicate part of the whole evening's venture. 'Only remember,' he said with exaggerated caution, 'the first must show promise.'

'Certainly, it will show promise. Your man out there sees that for sure.'

'I would have it proven,' said Thomas.

The expression on the man's face showed that he was at last beginning to understand. 'Ah, you mean to put him to the test.'

'Exactly so,' said Thomas. 'As you may know by our speech, my man and I are down from Yorkshire. We've come to London for this specific purpose, but we are not familiar with the *particular gentlemen* here in the south who might be willing to assist us. In putting our dog to the test.'

The kennel master nodded, a man of the world. 'I can put you in the way of some other gentlemen, businessmen like myself, who would be happy to assist you in matching your dog.'

Thomas shook his head. 'It is no common dog fight that my patrons are interested in.'

'I'll get you the best of dogs to try him against.'

Again Thomas shook his head. 'Not dogs,' he said. He held the man's gaze a full minute.

'Bulls?' the kennel master offered at last, but Thomas could see from his face that the man knew he wasn't talking about bulls. A third time he shook his head.

The man's jaw slackened. 'There aren't any left.'

'Not what I've heard,' said Thomas.

'What have you heard?'

'There's at least one wasn't shot.'

The man turned away. 'Rumour. Rumours'll get you killed.'

'Or make you very rich, if they're true.'

There was a pause. 'How rich?'

Thomas nodded towards the iron box into which the kennel master had put Seeker's money. 'So rich you can afford to throw away money like that on a dog that'll have only one fight, and throw in two others just to secure it. Like I said – or maybe I didn't – my patrons are *very* wealthy men, and they have *very* particular interests.'

The man's eyes travelled to the locked iron box. 'It might take a while – need to be careful. Protector's spies are everywhere.'

'So I'm told. Too long and I go elsewhere. A message within the week to me at the Three Tobacco Pipes, Charing Cross, with the time and place to conclude our bargain, or you never see me or my money again. Now, I'll have a leash off you, if you please. My man can handle a hound, once he has it trained, but I wouldn't like to take a chance on letting that thing run loose on Lambeth Marsh.'

Their guide long since having vanished into the night, Thomas also demanded a lantern from the kennel master, who, the promise of more money to come his best guarantee, was happy enough to return their arms and see them off his premises.

The small door back out on to the marsh had not long been closed behind them when the sound of a cart trundling along behind them took their attention. It was making directly for a large set of gates at the far end of the enclosure they had just left. The cart was covered, and its sole visible occupant the driver, who was hunched over the reins, with his large hood pulled up. He brought out a long staff and rapped, in a distinct pattern, on the double gates in front of him. A moment later, the gates had been opened, and the kennel master was holding up a lamp to speak to the newcomer. Not far into their exchange, which appeared ill-natured, the kennel master pointed towards Thomas and Lawrence. The carter looked around towards them once, and that quickly, but it was enough: the movement had caused his hood to slip, and the light from the kennel master's lamp had illuminated the man's ruddy face, with its hawk-like nose.

'Who's that, do you think?' asked Lawrence.

'I don't know,' answered Thomas. 'But the last time I saw him he was slipping out of the back door of John Evelyn's elaboratory at Sayes Court, and people were calling him "Mr Mulberry".' Thomas shook his head. The vapours of the marsh, or the effects of the foul wine he had drunk in that fetid inn on Bankside must be affecting his eyesight or his wits. How could it be that one of John Evelyn's associates would have any connection with the murder of Joseph Grindle?

'And just where am I supposed to keep this?' asked Lawrence, as he brought the hound to heel on a leash wound short around his hand. 'They won't let me have him at Clifford's – half of them are such milksops they'd pass out at the sight of him.'

'You're not keeping him at all,' said Sir Thomas, who was holding the lantern.

'What? I'm not turning him loose.'

'No. But remember, we didn't come out here to get a dog. We came here to find out where that bear's being kept that mauled that old soldier to death. That fellow knows, I'm certain. The purchase of the dog was just a necessary means to that end.'

'Use all the sophistry you like, Sir Thomas, but what's on the end of this leash is a means to an end weighing a hundred and seventy pounds if it's an ounce and strong enough to kill a man. It needs food, exercise, training, and secure lodgement. It can't be neatly filed away in a book, "My accounts to Damian Seeker".'

'No.' Thomas thought a moment. 'But you're right – it was Seeker's money, his work we were on.'

'So?'

'So, this beast is Damian Seeker's problem. We'll take it up to the Mews on St Martin's Lane. Tell them Seeker ordered it in for Cromwell's Master of Hounds.'

Lawrence snorted. 'Huh. This one would eat the Lord Protector whole.'

THIRTEEN

A Question of Strategy

They had gone their separate ways and lain low since the debacle of Hammersmith. Boyes was in no doubt – had Damian Seeker not made the mistake of going first to the inn next door, they would have been taken for sure. And then what would Cromwell have done to *him*? He'd wondered sometimes what would happen, if he were caught. And then he would laugh to himself – he would have escaped, of course. But there were no 'of courses' now, the trampling of the law under the major-generals did not bother itself too nicely over questions of justice. Cromwell's justice could be swift, and often had been, long before the major-generals had ever been thought of.

As well, then, that they had escaped from the upper room of the coachman's house, though it had been with only moments to spare. Boyes could still hear the sound of Seeker's boots thumping up those stairs as he'd fled with Fish and Cecil out of the back door of the coach house. The loss of the shooting frame, abandoned as it had been in that upper room, had been bad enough, but the loss of the seven guns attached to it could hardly be made up without drawing unwelcome attention on themselves.

And they were already subject to unwelcome attention. Half the city, it seemed, was on the lookout for men of their description. So, Boyes had taken the precaution of varying his appearance, removing his grey wig from time to time and putting on finer clothes when he went out and about. Today he would be a north country gentleman, should anybody ask. There was little the other two could do, or in fact would need to: so unremarkable, the pair of them, as to be anonymous, and that would be the saving of them. Two English soldiers, not worth the asking even which side they had fought on, getting on with their lives under the Protectorate. They would be his servants, come down south with him as he attended to his business in London. But if any did ask? If any should guess at the truth?

Fish. Or Miles Sindercombe, as his mother might have known him. Leveller. Had served the Protectorate under General Monck in Scotland, until, that was, Monck had dismissed him as 'a busy and suspicious person', bent on ill designs. What person of any worth, nowadays, was not? Monck had advised his arrest in England, but Sindercombe had taken ship instead for the Netherlands, where he had met with other disgruntled Puritans intriguing with the Stuart court towards their mutual aim of removing Cromwell. And so here was Sindercombe, returned to England a hired assassin with a heavy purse, and going by the name of Mr Fish. Fish had then found Cecil, a former Royalist soldier with time on his hands and no taste for foreign travel. Cecil sometimes had a bored look to him, as if there was little in these peaceful times that could interest him. The money, of course, would always help. And here was he, Boyes, entrusted with seeing to it that their bungled attempts to rid England of Oliver Cromwell did not become a catastrophe.

It had been Cecil's idea to meet in South Lambeth. He had done right to suggest a rendezvous away from the city, where Seeker's interest in them was still ringing around the taverns and coffee houses. So the ill-assorted companions had made their separate ways to South Lambeth, and Tradescant's.

People didn't go to Tradescant's to look at each other, but at plants, seeds, fruit, trees, or the curiosities. Furthermore, gardeners had no great interest in the doings of other people, unless a spade or a poor choice of soil be involved. As for the more crowded confines of the Cabinet of Curiosities, they would stay well away from that.

And so here they were, affecting to examine specimens of fruit trees, whilst discussing their failure, as yet, to rid England of Oliver Cromwell.

'Your source is compromised, and has taken us for fools,' said Boyes, all the while turning in his hand a hard yellow fruit, just plucked from a Portingale quince. He bit into it. Bitter, suffering from the season. He recalled for a moment the luscious fruits of warmer climes, and the swamps, disease, unforgiving seas that were their price. 'A good English apple,' he said aloud, discarding the quince. 'That's what we need: a good English apple.'

They waited whilst a gardener's boy trundled past trailing a cart full of gnarled old roots, just dug up. 'There's nothing wrong with the English apple we've got,' muttered Fish.

'No?' asked Boyes, reaching up to turn another fruit, twisting it on its stem, waiting for the snap. 'I think the worms have got at it.'

'They have not!' said Fish with some vehemence.

'Then how did Seeker find out where we were?'

Fish kicked at a twig that had caught on the buckle of his boot. 'I don't know. But it wasn't John Toope. I served with him in Ireland and in Scotland. He wouldn't betray us.'

Cecil, who'd said nothing since they'd passed beneath the whalebone arch into the garden, gave a soft, tuneless whistle, which Boyes was coming to recognise as the prelude to the statement of his considered opinion. 'If this Toope, in the Life Guard, of all things, was prepared to betray Cromwell for ten pounds . . .'

'He's been promised fifteen hundred,' retorted Fish.

'Indeed. But the fact remains that he's done it for ten. My point is, if he'll betray Cromwell for ten, what makes you think he wouldn't betray you?'

'It's not about the money,' retorted Fish, his old Leveller pride bubbling up.

Cecil pursed his lips. 'But is it not? If it wasn't about the money,' he said, 'your friend Toope wouldn't have asked for it before he agreed to alert us to Cromwell's planned movements. I think we must allow that he did it for the money, and that Seeker has made him a better offer.'

Fish scoffed. 'Damian Seeker is not in the habit of making offers.'

Cecil gave a bored sigh. 'I don't mean of money, Fish, I mean of his life. If Toope would betray Cromwell, whom once he fought for, he'd surely betray you. For his life.'

'We shall know soon enough.'

There was a dangerous, slightly nervous look in Fish's eye that Boyes had noticed there before, and it seldom heralded good news.

'What do you *mean*, Mr Fish?' he asked, as he abandoned his examination of the fruits and began to pull back on his gloves. 'How shall we know?'

'He's coming here to meet us. He'll be over soon, off the horse ferry.'

'What?' Cecil spun round, his usual nonchalance having deserted him. He looked over Fish's shoulder down through the orchard towards the entrance to the garden. 'Have you lost your mind? You have set us up to be taken!'

Fish spat as he snapped back. 'No. It was not John Toope gave us up; he swears it. He will be here at any time, alone. He'll tell you himself.'

Just as Cecil was declaring his intention that neither John Toope nor any other in Cromwell's livery should set eyes on him, Boyes caught sight of a soldier of the Foot Guard hurrying up a path towards them, looking anxiously to the left and the right as he did so.

His heart sank. 'Tell me this is not your friend,' he said. Rarely had he seen a man so openly proclaim his business to be clandestine. 'He's your informant – you see to him. I've not come this far to make the acquaintance of one of Cromwell's Foot Guard, nor Cecil either. Come, Cecil,' he said, turning to the other, 'I am a north country gentleman, and you my steward. Let us consider what cherries we might buy for my orchard.'

They left Fish to deal with John Toope and anyone else Toope might have seen fit to bring with him. An orchard was not a bad place to avoid notice, as Boyes knew full well, but the time of year was against them, leaves and fruit almost all gone, and bare brown trunks and branches their only camouflage. Nevertheless, he felt that as he and Cecil made their way out of the orchards and towards the glasshouses at the top of Tradescant's land, they were unobserved. Certainly, if Toope – who was now in earnest conversation with Fish – had brought any of Seeker's men with him, there were none yet to be seen.

'You're not, though, are you?' asked Cecil as they climbed the slope towards the glasshouses.

'Not what?'

'A north country gentleman?'

Boyes had been expecting this. There had been intermediaries, in Brussels, between himself and those who had hired Fish. And yet a man liked to know who it was that was at his side as he risked his life in a cause, this good old cause, and in Cecil he saw a love for the cause, not simply a hatred for Cromwell such as Fish displayed. Even so, if Cecil did not know who he truly was, Cecil could not betray him.

'I am a gentleman,' he said at last, 'and I have fought for the King as I fought for his martyred father before him. I will keep on fighting for him until he is restored to his throne, or until my body draws its last breath.'

Cecil looked at him strangely, as if he thought he might know him from some other time and place. 'Then you shall never have cause to fear betrayal by me.'

There followed a period examining tender plants in the glasshouse with a visit to the plantsman's workshop. They'd waited until they'd seen John Tradescant leave with a dibber in his hand and a sack of bulbs over his shoulder. Tradescant had had charge of Henrietta-Maria's gardens, if Boyes remembered right. He couldn't have picked out the Queen's former gardener, but that wasn't to say the fellow wouldn't remember him. Still, there was a thrill in the danger of being recognised, even by one who might wish their enterprise well.

In the workshop, they found the plant lists and the catalogues, and it wasn't long before Boyes could truly believe that he was a gentleman down from Northumbria, with a garden to stock. 'Oh, I would plant some of these, Cecil,' he said, turning the pages of the fruits catalogue with a smile. 'Look, here, "the Bell Coronation peach", or here, "the Grand Coronation peach", still better. We might plant them, might we not? I think it is almost the season. I would even go so far as to allow some space for this "Queen Mother plum", although it should certainly be kept strictly in its place.'

Cecil gave a low laugh, but then became serious. 'But what if another should seek to pluck those fruits before our time is ripe?'

'You mean Cromwell.'

'There are rumours that he aims at the crown, and that others seek to encourage it.'

Boyes shook his head. 'Cromwell will never be king.' He turned a few pages until he found what he was looking for. He extended an expensively gloved finger. 'I prefer this one for him.'

Cecil peered down at what was written below the image of the coarse-looking, ugly round fruit. 'The Russet Blood'. A fitting choice for Cromwell. 'Aye, sir, I think you have chosen well.'

'Well, let us make our order then.' Boyes, watched by a somewhat mystified Cecil, closed the catalogue and called over Tradescant's apprentice, who had been busy sorting corms at a long workbench at the far side of the room. He found he greatly enjoyed the next quarter-hour spent explaining to the young lad exactly what he would require, and was particularly pleased with his ingenuity in selecting the appropriate name and delivery address to be written in the order book. He was on the point of asking to be shown some examples of the latest innovations in gardening tools when a cough from Cecil took his attention.

Boyes followed the direction of Cecil's glance to see Fish

hurrying up the slope towards the workshop. Assuring Tradescant's apprentice that he would return soon to complete his order, he swept outside, followed by Cecil, to head Fish off.

'Well?' Boyes demanded when they met at the top of the path.

Fish shook his head. 'It wasn't him who gave us away.'

'He was hardly likely to say otherwise,' said Cecil.

'No, but it was not him. He said the Lady Protectress and her daughter were already in the coach, and Cromwell expected any minute, to commence their journey to Hampton Court by way of Hammersmith as planned, when Damian Seeker came storming into the palace courtyard and told the Horse Guard to go by another route. Toope made enquiries – for he knew we would suspect him. He has some friends in the Secretariat who have no fondness for Seeker, and who make it their business to know his whereabouts. Seeker was known to have come in haste from the Black Fox, on Broad Street. He had been in conversation there with a young Yorkshireman, and left of a sudden at something the Yorkshireman said. Toope believes it is this Yorkshireman that gave our plan away.'

Boyes felt something cold strike him.

'Who was this Yorkshireman?'

Fish shrugged. 'How should I know, or Toope for that matter?'

'There was no Yorkshireman,' said Cecil with scorn.

'Oh, but there was,' said Boyes. 'At the inn in Hammersmith, one morning, two days before our planned attempt.'

Fish and Cecil took a moment to consider this information. 'And how should he have known what was planned?' asked Fish, before a thought appeared to come to him. 'Unless you told him.'

'Don't be ridiculous.' But then the scene from that morning in the parlour of the inn in Hammersmith played out once more in Boyes's mind. 'Seeker was already looking for a man called Fish by then – I had a report he had been asking questions around your old lodging on King Street. And that morning, in the breakfast parlour, the landlady called after you by your name.' He could see the blood drain from Fish's face. 'You should have taken another, as I told you to,'

'Ach,' Fish spat in frustration. 'False names, secret lodgings, changing of wigs, waiting for instructions from overseas – let the thing only be done!'

Boyes looked at him coldly. 'You'll be dead before it's done if you don't use greater caution than you have employed thus far.'

'We'll all be dead,' said Cecil. 'But I daresay our chances would be improved, were we to remove this "witness" – this friend of Seeker's who told him of our whereabouts. He has seen both of you, and Seeker will have him primed to recognise you, should he set eyes on either of you again.'

'We haven't time,' said Fish. 'Our priority is Cromwell.'

'True,' said Boyes, thinking carefully now on what Cecil had said. 'Our next attempt may be a few days in the preparation. It would not be wise to call attention upon ourselves, particularly if this Yorkshireman is known to Seeker. It would do no harm to find out where he is, but anything more definitive might risk exposing us further and endanger our enterprise.'

'We need to see to his silence.'

Boyes knew Cecil was right, but he did not like it.

The elderly couple who ran the inn at Hammersmith were discounted as a threat, for that she was of such poor eyesight that she could hardly see her hand in front of her face, and he had never ventured close enough to take a look at their guests.

The matter of the Yorkshireman was left to Cecil's discretion and they proceeded to discussion of their next attempt on Cromwell.

'Toope said something that has given me an idea,' said Fish.

The others waited.

'It is known that the Lord Protector is a great judge and admirer of horseflesh.'

'Go on,' said Boyes.

'He rides out in Hyde Park every morning that he has the chance.'

Cecil was dismissive. 'This is hardly news, Fish. We'd never get near him, for the Horse Guard all around him.'

Fish shook his head, a sly smile crossing his face. 'Cromwell doesn't let them hem him in, out in the park – likes to ride free, likes to show them what he's got. The colonel doesn't like it, Toope says, but who's going to tell Oliver Cromwell what to do on a horse?'

Boyes was getting interested, and he could see that Cecil was too. Fish nodded, encouraged.

'Toope says if a fine horse catches his eye, the Lord Protector's off like the wind after it, for a closer look. Of course, he has the finest mounts himself, and he can still out-ride any of his guards.' He looked now to Cecil, who had been no mean cavalryman in his day. 'One good fast horse. One thrust of a knife, and that'd be it.'

'I'll do it,' said Cecil.

'The risk would be great,' cautioned Boyes.

'I'll do it.'

There was little more to be said. Fish knew of a dealer on the Downs from whom a horse fit to take Cromwell's interest might be had. Boyes undertook to provide him with the necessary funds. They would meet again when the horse was procured. Meanwhile, Cecil, the only one amongst them whom the Yorkshireman had not seen, was to deal with that problem.

The other two left to go about their separate business, but Boyes found himself reluctant to return so soon to the city. He was hardly a stranger to small rooms and cramped accommodation — confined quarters had long ceased to bother him, although pain from an old head wound at times made him crave fresh air and open spaces; it was his roving, questing mind that lacked sufficient stimulation in his present circumstances. This cabinet of curiosities kept by the Tradescants could do nothing to rival those he had seen or knew of on the continent — the Ambulacrum at

Leiden, Morin's collection in Paris, or the Wunderkammer of Rudolf II in Prague that his mother had told him of when he'd been a child. All the same, it might relieve the tedium of his London existence for an hour or so, give cause for reflection, or further enquiry.

Boyes surveyed the grounds of Tradescant's property. The gardener himself, John Tradescant, was a good way away, on hands and knees, planting, with a young apprentice a few yards further up from him apparently engaged on preparing planting holes. They looked like men at the beginning of a task, not nearing its end. It should be safe enough. Boyes adjusted his posture, composed his face, and headed towards the house.

The clock on the landing was slow. He could never understand why people would not keep up their clocks properly. He was almost tempted to unlock the side panel and adjust the mechanism himself, or to wind it at least. But caution, even as he was reaching for the catch of the panel, got the better of him, and he continued up the stairs towards the top floor, and the Cabinet of Curiosities.

To begin with, he thought he was alone in the room. He stood a few moments just in the doorway, letting his eyes take in the displays laid out before him the length and breadth of the walls, and on tables down the middle of the room. He passed by the trays of shells − West African, Caribbean − they were no curiosity to him, he had seen them lying on the beaches of Guinea and St Lucia, Cape

Verde and Guadeloupe. There was, however, a beautifully carved nautilus shell with birds and flowers engraved on its surface, its edge worked as if trimmed with lace. Then he caught sight of a shell labelled as from St Kitts. The very sight of it recalled to his mouth the bitter taste of the bread they'd had to eat there, the flour pounded from cassava fruit. The men had grumbled at it, until rations of even that, too, had begun to run low, and they'd kept their grumbles to themselves.

He paused to examine a plum stone on which was carved in intricate detail the passion of Christ. A tiny thing it was, and on it so much suffering, the price of the Saviour's shared humanity. He set it down again. A stoppered glass jug at his eyeline took his attention, something forever suspended in the liquid inside. A female hand. Boyes felt revulsion at the grotesquery of it, but then, against his will, he read the label, and it became to him a thing of beauty. 'Hand of a Mermaid', it said. 'Where did you swim?' he wondered. 'Where did you come ashore?' Had that hand held the hand of his brother? Had the gentle touch of those fingers comforted him as he'd plunged, helpless, to the depths? Had Maurice not died alone? But then Boyes shook himself. Maurice was not dead; he would find him, one day. And their cause was not lost.

The sound of female laughter broke into his thoughts. It was coming from around the corner of a shelf that he had not realised led to another small section of the room. Boyes stood still a moment, not certain what to do. Then he moved a few steps closer, and listened. A man's voice. 'It's true, I tell you.'

The woman's voice again. 'It cannot be. Those are the boots of a child.'

'I assure you, they are not. Tradescant has marked it right – they were the boots of Henrietta-Maria's dwarf. His name was Jeffrey and she was sooner parted from her children than she was from him. The King presented him to her in a cake.'

The woman's voice changed now from incredulous humour to scorn. 'A cake? Dear God, these people were debauched.'

Boyes remembered it, remembered the Queen's initial fright when the huge confection had started, of its own volition, to crumble before her, and then her delight when the little man had sprung out from inside. He remembered, too, the look of fear on the man's face that he was so desperately trying to hide. The anxiety that he would not please, and would instead be condemned to a life of fairs and travelling circuses. But he had pleased, and he'd performed, and been made a pet of, when it had suited her. And yes, the Queen had given old John Tradescant a pair of Jeffrey Hudson's boots to display amongst his other curiosities.

Boyes moved quietly to the edge of the shelf. The man's voice was familiar to him, but he could not be certain that he was right. Carefully, he peered around the corner. The couple were at the far end of the passageway, bent over a table beneath the window. Hudson's old boots were on the table, and the man was showing the young woman how to draw them. Boyes saw what the young woman did not – that the teacher's glance lingered longer on the curls at the nape of her neck, where the petrol-black hair had been pulled back, and at the delicate curve of her arm, than it did on what she drew. He smiled, wanted to step forward, reveal himself. 'Oh, Thomas, will you never change?' The words were on his lips, and he had to make himself silence them. He retreated quietly back around the corner and then turned and went quickly from the room. Thomas Faithly. Clémence had not told him about this. He would need to consider it, and give thought to what it meant.

FOURTEEN

Rendezvous Are Made

'You'll be one of her lot, I take it?'

Andrew Marvell was used to lack of preamble with Seeker, but on this occasion he was at a loss as to what he was being asked about. 'You'll have to enlighten me, Captain.'

'Artists and the like. Lady Ranelagh. Over by St James's. Milton's forever over there, and all the alchemists and philosophers and new scientists and such that hang around her brother. Don't tell me you haven't got your foot in that door as well.'

Marvell bridled a little. 'Mr Milton was good enough to introduce me to her ladyship, and she has been kind enough to invite me to some of her gatherings, to converse with other – like-minded – people of her society.'

Seeker nodded. 'Like I said. One of her lot. Good.'

'*Good?*' said Marvell, surprised. 'I thought you'd summoned me here to warn me to stay away from such gatherings.'

'Stay away?' said Seeker. 'Now why on earth would I do that?'

And that was when Andrew Marvell felt the first suggestion of a smile start to creep across his lips. 'Ah. Might I sit, Captain?' he enquired.

Seeker looked surprised. 'What? Aye, of course you can sit. There's no standing on ceremony here.'

Marvell reflected that ninety-nine in a hundred of those who'd had the misfortune to find themselves standing here would be surprised to hear that, but he chose not to share the thought. He manoeuvred himself around the huge Irish hound that seemed to have taken up residence in the captain's quarters, and sat down in the room's only available chair.

Seeker was examining a piece of paper on his desk and began to make marks against notes on it. 'There's a gathering over at Lady Ranelagh's house tomorrow evening. Are you going?'

Marvell puffed up slightly. 'Yes, Captain, as a matter of fact I am.'

Seeker nodded. 'Excellent.' He continued writing on the paper in front of him.

Marvell sat forward. 'You see, the Lord Protector himself suggested Mr Milton and I should accompany him.' He lowered his voice. 'He is not always confident in matters of poetry, and he doesn't like it when those around him break into foreign tongues.'

'I should think not,' said Seeker. 'Those speaking in foreign tongues are seldom up to any good.'

Marvell sat back again, wondering whether Seeker

included in that number the ambassadors who now came flocking to Whitehall from all corners of Europe. He suspected that he did.

Seeker finally put down his quill pen and pushed the paper aside. 'Well, the Lord Protector's not going to Lady Ranelagh's tomorrow night any more, not after the planned attempt on his life at Hammersmith.'

Marvell felt his enthusiasm deflate. 'Oh, I see.'

'But you can still go. There's a few things I'd like you to keep an eye on for me.'

'Things?'

Seeker shrugged. 'Things. People. Anything that strikes you as odd, anything amiss.'

'Like?' said Marvell carefully.

'Like things out of place, things that don't look quite right. Like folk speaking to folk they shouldn't be speaking to.'

'But that is the nature of Lady Ranelagh's gatherings. She brings together people who interest her, without regard to their politics or past connections. It is their genius, their gifts, what they can contribute to the conversation that she admires.'

'Doubtless,' said Seeker, a look of mild distaste on his face. 'And that's exactly why it's just the sort of thing that needs keeping an eye on.' He picked up the sheet in front of him and handed it to Marvell. 'Guest list.'

'Even Lady Ranelagh refers her arrangements to you?'

'Only when the Protector's involved. Well?'

Marvell cast his eye down the list. His own name was there. Of course. Seeker had already known he was going. There was also a handful of names on it that he had never come across, but only one or two surprised him. 'Sir Thomas Faithly?'

He felt Seeker's gaze assess him very carefully.

'What about him?'

'Well,' Marvell tried to think how to put it, 'it seems somewhat odd, that's all. He's not long out of the Tower, as I hear.'

'Hmm,' said Seeker.

'And he's not entirely the sort I would expect at her gatherings. His reputation, even as a young man when I was still in Yorkshire, was of a man of action rather than of thought. He has the name of being a Cavalier, and her ladyship is of a more Puritan cast. Perhaps she has asked him there to add some colour all the same? I've heard he's a very handsome man.'

'I wouldn't know,' said Seeker. 'But yes, that's one for you to keep an eye on. Make yourself known to him, fellow-Yorkshireman, that sort of thing.'

'You could as well do that yourself, Captain.'

Seeker gave one of his low laughs. 'Oh, yes. I'd be just what Lady Ranelagh was looking for, for the poetry, wouldn't I? Besides,' he continued, 'nobody would do anything if I showed up. The gathering would be over in ten minutes, and nothing learned.'

It was true. Marvell had seen it himself. People didn't

just carry on regardless when Seeker turned up. There was a tendency to silence, a hiatus in movement, before everyone suddenly found reason to be elsewhere. It was not just amongst the guilty that such was the case. Those of blameless life were equally dumbstruck and guilt-ridden at the captain's arrival anywhere. Even in the guardrooms of Horse Guards Yard it was the same. Marvell wondered how it made Seeker feel, this power he had to arrest the motion of others, kill dead their conversations. He wondered if the man was ever lonely. At his feet, the dog snored rhythmically in its sleep, and Andrew Marvell thought he began to understand Damian Seeker a little better.

'So,' the voice recalled him to the matter in hand, 'you'll go and keep an eye on Thomas Faithly? And anything about anyone else that strikes you as not quite right?'

'Yes, yes, of course, Captain.' Marvell took a breath as if to say more, but found the words eluded him.

Seeker had already turned to something else, and nodded towards the door. 'You can go now. But close the door behind you when you go out, will you? The dog doesn't like a draught.'

After Marvell had left, Seeker surveyed again the list of names of those expected to attend Lady Ranelagh's gathering. Among several groups of the prominent citizens of Westminster and London and those known as great intellects there was indeed Andrew Marvell, alongside Secretary Milton. And from Deptford would travel John Evelyn and his wife, with Mary Evelyn's French companion, the woman Clémence Barguil. And there, too, was the name of Thomas Faithly himself. His eye was especially drawn to Faithly's name, and he didn't know why. Neither could he have said for certain why it was in Faithly he had told Marvell to take an especial interest. John Evelyn, who was known to have smuggled cyphers for the dead King and suspected still of involvement in clandestine correspondence, or the artist Wenceslaus Hollar, who had fought for the Stuart cause at Basing House, would surely have been more profitable subjects of surveillance. So why, Seeker wondered, was it his own man, Thomas Faithly, doubly compromised, that he had set the poet to watch? Why did he trust him enough to use him in his search for the killer of Joseph Grindle, but not to mix with his own kind? He didn't have a satisfactory answer to that question, save to acknowledge that he had seen a look of late in Thomas Faithly's eye that suggested the former companion of the exiled King was no longer certain which side he wanted to be on.

Just at that moment, a falling log disturbed the hound, and it bestirred itself, alert for trouble. Seeker sighed and stood up. 'Aye, lad. I think you might be right. Come on then.'

The Black Fox was busy and had the air of often being so. Cecil could see why: the ale was good, the food better, and the place cleaner than most. The landlady, moreover, was an exceptionally comely woman, more than capable of running a well-ordered house. Cecil was feeling well satisfied at this moment. It had been a pleasant surprise, a change from the one misstep and disappointment after another that had dogged his enterprise with Fish and Boyes that here, in this tavern, his prey had more or less fallen into his lap. Cecil himself had been barely seated, just wondering how exactly to begin his discreet enquiries about the young Yorkshireman who had been seen here talking to Damian Seeker only a few days ago, when the young Yorkshireman himself had walked through the door.

The voice was the first thing, a grudging apology mumbled by the fellow to a man whose foot he had stepped on. Very Yorkshire, defiantly Yorkshire, as if it were the man's fault for having a foot. The age was about right too – twenty-four or twenty-five years old, perhaps. Skinny but not scrawny, a few pockmarks on the pale skin, hair neither long nor short, and chopped like ruffled sparrows' feathers. Nose just on the safe side of being a beak. The suit of good woollen cloth was the same colour as the hair, as if there were no other colour but brown, and no shade but dun. The collar and cuffs were the plain white linen of a Puritan, but there was a carelessness to them. This fellow doesn't care about anyone's opinion, thought Cecil.

The next thing was the recognition. Dorcas, the land-lady, was the first. She glanced up from a table she was scrubbing to see the young man come down into the parlour. Her nod of greeting was attended by a distinct hint of unease.

'Lawrence,' she said, 'we hadn't thought to have a visit from you today.' She gave an involuntary glance towards the counter, where two of the young girls who served in the tavern were loading tankards and jugs onto trays.

'I thought I'd just call in, Aunt,' he said, a little cocky, 'and see how you and my sister did, and let you know how I've been getting on.'

'Of course,' said Dorcas, still not altogether pleased, it seemed, at her nephew's arrival.

As Cecil pretended not to notice much of the exchange, he saw the younger of the two girls at the counter, a healthy, strong-boned and clear-skinned child of about sixteen, with flaxen hair, look up and after a moment cast an uncertain smile in the way of the brown woollen knight.

She was rewarded with a very broad smile in return. 'Manon.' He didn't appear to notice the extremely pretty, slightly older girl beside her.

'Lawrence,' the younger one said at last. 'It's been so long since we've seen you.'

'Five days, he hasn't been here,' corrected Dorcas. Then her manner seemed to soften. 'Sit you down, Lawrence. Will you have some rabbit fricassee?'

The young man affirmed with enthusiasm that he would.

'I'll have Manon fetch you a dish, then, and you can tell us of all your adventures at Clifford's Inn.'

The fellow rewarded her with a grin that Cecil had

to admit to himself was not unengaging. 'Thanks, Aunt Dorcas. I'm half-famished with what passes for food down there. No wonder lawyers are all so miserable.'

Cecil thought there was no harm in him raising his glass to the young man at this remark. A likeable fellow, with a ready wit, it seemed. It was a pity he'd have to kill him.

'Who's he?' asked Lawrence, his head bent forward across the table.

'Who?' said Manon, looking about her.

Lawrence lowered his voice. 'Don't look just now, but the man over there by the organ.'

It was with a great deal of effort that Manon kept herself from turning her head and looking in the direction of the organ. She in turn leaned a little towards Lawrence. 'The man wearing the green felt hat with a goose feather in it?'

'That's the one,' he said, scarcely moving his lips.

'I don't know. He's not been in long. I've not seen him in before. He's very polite.'

'Hmm.' Lawrence's face was writ large with distrust as he raised his tankard to his mouth.

'What's wrong?'

'Smiled over here a couple of times, trying to draw me in to his conversation. A bit too friendly.'

Manon's eyes sparkled and she tried to stifle a grin.

Some of the tension went out of Lawrence and he returned his tankard to the table with a cautious smile. 'What?'

'You're just like my father,' she breathed.

He almost dropped his ale. 'Me? Like . . .' He remembered in time to lower his voice to a near whisper. 'Me? Like Seeker? How?'

'I think you don't trust anyone you don't know. Especially if they make the mistake of trying to be friendly.'

Lawrence wiped the back of his hand across his lips and gave this some consideration, then nodded, not displeased. 'Well, perhaps he does right not to. Mind you, he doesn't trust anyone he does know either, apart from you, and Dorcas.'

'And you.'

'Me?' he said, forgetting this time to lower his voice, such was his surprise. He shook his head. 'The captain doesn't trust me.'

'Oh, I think he does.'

'Why do you think that?'

'He is at his ease with you, for all he pretends otherwise. I saw it that first day, up on the moors. You're the only person I've ever seen him at ease with, aside from Dorcas. You must know he just has his gruff way. I don't know why you would think he doesn't trust you.'

He gave a small, awkward laugh, looking away from her and back again. 'Oh, just because I think he knows me.'

'Then he will like you,' she said quietly.

Lawrence found himself suddenly incapable of making any response, and was relieved to see Dorcas come towards them. 'Now, Manon, you must let your brother finish his dinner. No doubt he's in a hurry to return to his studies, and we don't want to be getting a bad name from the masters of Clifford's Inn for keeping their young gentlemen from their books.' She looked across the parlour and Lawrence saw her eye alight on the man in the green felt hat. 'Besides, you've tables to clear and customers ready to die of thirst. Lawrence'll be back up here amongst us soon enough, I don't doubt.'

Manon stood up quickly. 'Oh, of course. I'm sorry, Aunt.'

Dorcas clearly regretted her chiding. She touched a hand to Manon's shoulder. 'We shall have Lawrence up to supper another night soon, just family, but I expect Captain Seeker's arrival at any minute, and you know, the captain doesn't like to see young men idle.' She gave Lawrence a meaningful look. 'Especially those that would be lawyers. Lawyers he keeps an especial eye on.'

Lawrence needed no further encouragement. 'He does that, Aunt.' He lost no time in rising from his bench and putting on his cap.

Cecil gave it a minute, but no more, before he too got up, having left a generous pile of coin to cover his food and drink. Back out on Broad Street, it didn't take him long to catch sight of the brown woollen knight threading his way through the passers-by who were going in the other direction. Cecil knew the side alleys and shortcuts of London well, and had done from childhood. He could be standing in his quarry's path in less than five minutes, and any who'd seen him leave the Black Fox just now ready to swear he had made off in the other direction. Up the road, into Austen Friars and down through the churchyard of Peter the Poor and he'd be out in front of him at the top of Throgmorton Street. Then, passing amongst the throng, a knife through the back, right into the kidneys – that brown woollen cloth was so giving – and drifting away again in the flow of people, away down through the lanes of the city, long before any noticed the flailing, dying man.

Cecil's feet were moving as fast as his mind was working, and he already had a hand slipped beneath his cloak to check for the dagger, the Yorkshireman still in view, when further down Broad Street, into his line of vision, loomed Damian Seeker.

The young fellow had evidently spied Seeker too, and tried to slip into a doorway, but not quickly enough to evade Seeker, or the huge hound who bounded away from the captain's side and through the crowd to sniff out and greet him as he lurked in the doorway. So they did know each other, Thurloe's henchman and this young lawyer. Any doubts Cecil might have had – and they had been fleeting – about how he should proceed now, vanished. He turned casually and strolled off in the other direction, and through the gates of Gresham College. The deed could not be done this afternoon, but it would be done before morning. He had this Yorkshireman's name, this 'Lawrence', as the mistress of the Black Fox and her niece had so unwittingly made clear. And they had been kind enough to inform him too, although they didn't know it, that he should make his way to Clifford's Inn tonight, to get his business done. Cecil began to whistle, a jaunty tune that was a favourite of his: it had, after all, been a remarkably good dinner.

FIFTEEN

An Evening at Lady Ranelagh's

'Fetching, I must say. Have to keep your wits about you though, wearing those red ones, especially down around Bankside.'

Lawrence stepped back from his intense examination of the side panel of the haberdasher's window, himself crimson with embarrassment at being caught lurking in the doorway, apparently fixated by the pair of red women's drawers on display. He wasn't able to step back very far, for the excited proximity of Seeker's dog made it almost impossible for him to move. Lawrence flicked his hair to the side and pushed back his shoulders in an attempt to recover his dignity. 'I, eh, was just . . .'

But Seeker was enjoying himself far too much to let him wriggle out of his mortification just yet. 'Of course, you'd need to be careful about the stays, that you got a set to match. Very fetching, all the same.'

'All right,' said Lawrence, conceding defeat. 'You were looking for me, I take it?'

'No,' said Seeker, casting the lurid drawers a last glance

of distaste, and making a note to have a word with the constable of the ward. 'But you'll do for now. Come on.'

The dog loped on ahead of them, turning at Seeker's whistle down an alley that led to a small abandoned garden at Austen Friars.

'It's a wonder they haven't built on this,' said Lawrence, casting his eye around the precious patch of open space, half-enclosed by crumbling walls, that had slowly been encroached upon by nature.

'They'll try, I've no doubt. Anyway, tell me about your trip south of the river.'

Lawrence settled more comfortably on the large slab he'd sat down on, and leaned back against what remained of the wall behind it. 'Right. You've seen the dog? The one Sir Thomas and I brought back.'

'Oh, I've seen it, all right. Nearly had the arm of the kennel master's boy up at the Mews. It'll be a good long time before that thing's allowed anywhere near Oliver.'

Lawrence's eyes took on a misty look Seeker had seldom seen there. 'Oh, but it's a beauty,' he said. 'Just needs proper handling and it'll be fit for a king.'

'Only if the brute's having him for supper,' said Seeker. 'That's the only use we have for kings nowadays.'

Lawrence swallowed and carried on. 'Aye, well. It's a good dog, but it was bred and being kept for baiting, and for people prepared to pay high prices to see it. The sort of people that wouldn't like it noised about, how they really spend their leisure hours. All the same, the dealer did look surprised, when he finally understood what we were really asking about. But the more Sir Thomas got me to wave his purse at him, the less surprised he got.'

'And you're convinced this dealer's telling the truth?'

Lawrence nodded. 'I've dealt with a trickster or two in my time on the Pullans' business, but that man was definitely telling the truth. He knows where there's a bear to be found; I'm just not entirely sure yet that he knows exactly how he's going to lay hands on it, that's all.'

'Did you get the sense he knew anything about the death of the old man?'

'Joseph Grindle?' Lawrence shook his head. 'Not specially. He knew our business was murky, but nothing he asked suggested he had any idea we were there about that. He believed our story, I'm sure of it. Sir Thomas is no mean actor, you know. Must be all those plays and masques the Stuarts spend their time on to keep themselves from being bored. That dealer believed him. What's more, he believed your money.' Lawrence tapped the place where he kept the remains of the purse Seeker had given them.

Seeker reached out a hand, and with an exaggerated sigh Lawrence handed it over.

'And this place on the marshes, Sir Thomas had never been there before?'

Instead of saying, 'Why do you ask?' as most people would have done, Lawrence took a minute to consider. 'I'm not sure. I don't think he could have found his way there himself, or that he and the dealer knew each other, nor he and the old fellow who guided us there. But . . .'

'But what?' said Seeker.

Lawrence shook his head briefly as if he were trying to dislodge an irritating fly.

Seeker waited until he saw he had it. 'What?' he repeated.

'Just after we left the compound, a few minutes after the kennel master had seen us out, a cart came trundling out of the darkness, from further out on the marsh. It was headed for the breeder's compound, but the breeder met him at the main gate, and turned him away. The light caught the carter's face just as he was looking over in our direction. Sir Thomas recognised him. Said his name was Mulberry or something.'

'All right,' said Seeker. 'Description of this man you saw driving away?'

Lawrence gave him what he could: hunched beneath a woollen cloak, hood up, sixty or so maybe, hook nose.

The light was starting to fade, and Seeker had other places to be. 'When you or Faithly hear again from this dealer, you get word to me immediately. And wherever this fellow tells you he wants you to go to, you don't go there until you have my say-so. Understand?' Lawrence nodded. 'Right. You get yourself back down to Clifford's Inn. No more stopping to look at women's drawers and petticoats and the like, and don't stop to talk to anyone.'

'Why?' said Lawrence.

Seeker leaned down towards him. 'Because this isn't

Yorkshire, and that mouth of yours is more likely to get you into trouble here than out of it. Some folk might be a bit less impressed with a cocksure so-and-so down here than you'd like.'

Lawrence lost the cocksure demeanour and gave Seeker a penetrating look. 'Who, for instance?'

'The men you saw in that Hammersmith tavern, that were all set up to kill the Lord Protector. They'll not be happy if they get wind it was you who told me their plans . . .'

'But I didn't . . .' Lawrence began to protest.

Seeker shrugged. 'Good as. Just keep your eyes open and your wits about you. If you see either of them again—'

'I know, I know,' interrupted Lawrence. 'I let you know.'

'That's right,' said Seeker. 'Once you're back at Clifford's tonight, and you've had your supper, you get into your chamber, you lock the door and you stay there.'

Lawrence nodded and started to make his way through the stone archway that led to the lane and out on to Broad Street again. 'I've already had a good dinner though,' he said, obviously trying to lighten the mood, then instantly regretting it.

Here it was; this was why Ingolby had been trying to avoid him. Seeker had suspected as much anyway. 'At the Black Fox, I take it?'

Lawrence's response, an affirmative, was scarcely audible.

The bell tolled the half-hour and Seeker looked again at the falling shadows. 'You just get down to Clifford's. And remember what I said.'

'About what?' asked Lawrence.

'Everything,' said Seeker, his voice very deliberate. 'You remember what I said about everything.'

Andrew Marvell saw to it that Secretary Milton was comfortably seated in the chair Lady Ranelagh had appointed for him and took up his position at the great man's shoulder, ready to assist with anything that Milton might require. He wondered how it must be for Milton to have the sparkling beauty of such surroundings as Lady Ranelagh's reception room reduced to nothing but flickering impressions of warmth and light. Milton, though, he reminded himself, saw far beyond what other mortals could.

Once the old Latin Secretary was settled amongst congenial company, there was a familiar squeeze of Marvell's fingers, the understood sign between the old poet and the young that the latter might be released from his duties. Marvell made his bow to the company surrounding John Milton and receded into the throng.

Marvell surveyed the gathering from a pillar that separated the reception room from a balcony overlooking the garden. When he and Milton had arrived, there had been a hiatus in the suppressed excitement of perhaps forty voices as all turned to look to the entrance hall. Faces had fallen and an audible sigh of disappointment escaped the crowd when Milton had made the austere announcement that His Royal Highness, the Lord Protector, would not in fact be coming tonight. But that initial disappointment, once expressed, had not been long in floating away to nothing, to be replaced by a relaxed chatter. Marvell allowed himself to drift around the edges of the gathering, listening for any who might become too relaxed at the unexpected absence of the Protector, who might let slip something that would be of interest to Damian Seeker.

He had been occupying himself in this way for several minutes when his ear picked up a conversation going on in French. So accustomed had he become to the tongue during his recent sojourn with his pupil in Saumur, that it took Marvell a moment to realise he was not following the conversation in English.

'So, we are to be deprived of our sighting of his elegant personage.' The slight sneer, and the slighter trace of an English accent alerted Marvell to the proximity of John Evelyn. Although Evelyn's disdain for the Protector was well known at Whitehall, it was also considered that he liked the comforts of his life too well to risk setting his own head above the parapet these days in support of the Stuarts. Marvell considered it unlikely he would hear anything of interest here and was about to move on past Evelyn's group when his eye was caught by the movement very close to him of the most striking woman. It was as if one of the marbles, some Roman goddess from Arundel House, had come to life and walked from the Strand to Pall Mall and Lady Ranelagh's gathering. Athena, perhaps, or Judith. Before Marvell knew what he was doing he found himself offering the so-gracefully-moving statue his deepest bow. The lady turned her extraordinary stone-grey eyes on him and then, glancing towards her companion, whom Marvell recognised as John Evelyn's wife, very slightly inclined her head in return. Marvell was in the middle of paying his compliments to Mary Evelyn when he became aware of having drawn the attention of the man who had been standing with his back to her, talking to someone else. Marvell had already noticed the particular blue of his velvet suit, and the soft folds of the fine Flemish bobbin lace at his cuffs. From Seeker's description, he knew even before the man had fully turned around that this was Sir Thomas Faithly.

Faithly's eyes found his instantly, and the handsome mouth broke into a broad grin. 'My, but it does my ear good to hear a Yorkshire voice, even in French!' He thrust an elegant though not unscarred hand towards Marvell. 'Thomas Faithly, of the North Riding.'

'Andrew Marvell,' Marvell replied, and then, 'of Hull.'

'Or Kingston upon Hull?' Faithly suggested with a wicked grin, slinging an arm around Marvell's shoulder. 'Now, Clémence, if you will excuse us, I have found a fellow-countryman, and I would quiz him for news of home.'

The striking woman who had first taken Marvell's attention dipped them a curtsy, accompanied by what Marvell considered a most becoming smile. 'You are indeed excused, Sir Thomas. I have heard more from you of this Yorkshire than would do me many lifetimes, but no doubt Mr Marvell is better prepared against such wonders.'

She moved softly away, and Marvell found himself rooted to the spot, like a well-trained puppy whose master has left it for other more pressing business. Beside him, Thomas Faithly sighed, and reverted to English. 'She is of a different order of woman, is she not, my friend? But come, let us find the punchbowl and you can tell me all the news from the north.'

A comfortable bench near the balcony and Lady Ranelagh's orangery, and the engagement of a biddable footman who knew the shortest way to the punchbowl, ensured that within the half-hour, Thomas Faithly and Andrew Marvell were the best of old friends. Marvell found his tongue loosened to an eloquence usually reserved for his pen, and discovered his new acquaintance to be an excellent conversationalist. Their continental travels had taken them to many of the same places, and the Royalist sympathies Marvell had held to in the early years of the war meant they had several acquaintances in common. Inevitably, their talk fell to others they had met from home, bringing Thomas Faithly to a sombre pause.

'Marvell, I fear I must broach an unpleasant subject.'

Marvell felt their political differences were about to drive a stake through their new-found friendship. He prepared himself.

'Damian Seeker,' Faithly said at last.

'Seeker?'

'The same,' said Sir Thomas, as if there was nothing further to be said.

And, in fact, Marvell could not quite think what further there was to say. Eventually, the silence became too much for him. 'Ah, yes. Seeker,' he said.

'Exactly,' said Sir Thomas, with some emphasis. 'You know him, our fellow Yorkshireman. Who doesn't? But how is a man to make his way in this town without his every step is dogged by Damian Seeker?'

Marvell gave thought to the question. 'In all,' he said at last, 'I think it is better not to try. It only annoys him, and to be quite frank with you, Sir Thomas, cooperation saves a tremendous amount of time.'

Thomas's face became even more sombre. 'I feared as much. But does the man never sleep? Is he never distracted by the pleasures of life?'

Marvell felt his eyes widen. 'Pleasures?'

'Oh, you of all people must know – the sorts of things you poets are always going on about. Wine. Gardens. Music. Love.' He leaned in closer, though without lowering his voice sufficiently for Marvell's liking. 'I mean, surely Seeker has a woman?'

Marvell coughed on his punch and set down the exquisite Austrian crystal cup he had been drinking from. 'It is – ahm – not something I have considered.' His own voice fell to a near-whisper. 'It is probably better not to ask about such things.'

Faithly leaned back, disappointed. 'Ah well. But it is not good for a man not to be in love, don't you think?'

'You are in love? With Mademoiselle Barguil?' enquired Marvell, hoping he was steering the conversation onto safer ground.

'I believe I am,' said Sir Thomas. 'But not with Clémence. I have met the most astonishing woman, Marvell. She haunts my dreams. I have travelled Europe and . . .'

Marvell was not entirely listening. Too often, he found himself the object of such confidences, and he had long lost any real interest in them. But suddenly, he became aware that his companion had stopped talking.

'Are you ill, Sir Thomas?' he asked, looking round for the biddable footman or a suitably empty receptacle.

'What?' asked Faithly, distracted. 'No, no. I am perfectly well.' But without any further address to Andrew Marvell he stood up and walked away through the crowd, ignoring any greetings that came his way, out of the reception room and eventually disappeared into the entrance hall of Lady Ranelagh's fine house. Andrew Marvell did not see him again that night.

SIXTEEN

Clifford's Inn

Lawrence lay with his hands behind his head, looking up at the stains and cracks in the plasterwork above him, and at the spiders at work in the cobwebs spanning the cross beams of the ceiling. The branches of the great elm outside his window cast eerie shadows in the light through the casement. It was gone midnight; the bells of Clifford's and all the other chapels of the Inns of Court and Chancery round about had told him that, quite insistently, some time ago.

'You'll get used to them, eventually – the bells,' Elias Ellingworth had assured him as Lawrence had yawned his way through their first learned discussion together. It wasn't the sound of the bells that was keeping Lawrence awake tonight though. It wasn't even Seeker's warning about the men from Hammersmith – though that had been plain enough to make him take the precaution of bolting his door, locking his window and making sure he had his knife beneath his bolster. A simple Scottish dudgeon dagger, serviceable and easily hidden, that Matthew had given him before he'd left for London.

Lawrence shouldn't have come to London. Matthew wouldn't have insisted upon it. He would have let him go to Leiden, or Utrecht or wherever he'd wanted. But when Matthew had suggested London, and the Inns of Chancery, Lawrence, like a fool, had said yes. Maybe before Manon he wouldn't have done.

He wasn't certain how it had happened, or even exactly when it had happened. It hadn't been that first time they'd met, that was for sure: she'd been a terrified child, hiding in an upper room in an inn high on the moors, and he the bemused companion of Damian Seeker, sent into the inn to find her. Perhaps it had been later that day, as the sun was going down over Blakey Ridge, setting earth and sky aglow, when he'd glanced out from an upper window of the Lion Inn and seen that same girl sat on a bench beside Damian Seeker and somehow rendering Seeker a mortal man, like any other. The girl had smiled and said something, and the mortal man had laughed, and a crack had appeared in the carapace where Lawrence had carefully stashed his heart. Just a crack.

The next day, he'd glanced over at her once or twice as they'd ridden away from the Lion Inn and down off Blakey Ridge, and he'd seen in the way she possessed herself as she sat her horse, in her strong, clear face, that she wasn't quite a child. But Seeker had kept her almost out of view as they rode, and shielded her from any conversation but his own. And then it hadn't been long after they'd arrived back at Faithly Manor that Seeker had taken her away, down to the village, and the next day to York, and at last to London. Lawrence had watched her ride away from Faithly Manor and patched over the crack in the carapace. He'd told himself to forget he'd ever known a girl called Manon.

But then the letters had started to come. Letters from Manon, in London, to Orpah, Matthew Pullan's soft-hearted, simple-minded housekeeper. Poor Orpah, who could speak to the animals and claimed to understand every sound or movement they made in response, could not read a word that was written, and had taken her letters to Lawrence, with a plea that he would read them to her and write down her replies. How long had it been, Lawrence wondered, before he'd started adding in little things from himself, things that he thought Manon might like to know of, that Orpah would never consider? How long before the letters coming back from London were as much for himself as they were for Orpah? He had them all, here, in a packet locked away in the drawer of his writing desk. The black shadow of a branch moved gently to and fro across the panels of his ceiling, driven by the light, invisible wind: Lawrence could no more have said 'no' to coming to London than that branch could say no to the wind.

And then there was Damian Seeker. Seeker had been gruff at any enquiry about the girl. He'd been protective of her, but in the same way as he was protective of his horse, or, in London, his dog. Lawrence had wondered who Manon might be to Seeker, but Seeker had made it plain he would give him no answer. And so he had come to London, and he'd sought out the Black Fox as soon afterwards as he was able to, and found her there. Knowing she was going by his own name, Ingolby, he'd blurted out that he was her brother. Could he not have said cousin, second cousin, at least? But too late, and he had called himself her brother. And then Damian Seeker had come in and made plain he was not happy even with that. Seeker's warnings about Manon were the warnings only one type of man would give about a girl. And at last, today, she had confirmed it, saying it without thinking, and not even noticing she had done so.

He saw again her face, the mild amusement in her eyes. 'You're just like my father.' And he'd known it then, said it: 'Seeker.' She hadn't contradicted him, hadn't even realised she shouldn't have said it.

Lawrence scrunched up his eyes and let out a long groan. Of all the bad hands fate had dealt him, and there had been a few, this was surely the worst: how could it be that he had fallen in love with Damian Seeker's daughter?

He must have slept, for it was to a new, deeper darkness that he awoke, and a deeper silence. The evening and late-night sounds of Clifford's – murmurs of voices, snatches of songs, servants bustling back and forth along the corridors, old lawyers grumbling – had given way to the special silence of the night. Beyond that silence, out in the courtyard and gardens of Clifford's, he could hear the flying and creeping things that shunned the day, and he could have imagined himself back in his chamber at Faithly Manor, listening to the creatures of the woods and the moor assert their nocturnal dominion. But here, in this room, if he listened harder, further along through the archways, down the alleyways and out at the gate he could hear the occasional footfall of those whose business was conducted by night. He was no longer at Faithly Manor.

Outside his door, the old wood of the corridors and doorways creaked a little, as if Clifford's itself was having trouble settling to its own sleep. There was a heaviness to the silence beyond the creaks, like a presence. As Lawrence listened, that heaviness grew, and he knew for a certainty that he was not alone.

Slowly, and as silently as he could manage, Lawrence slid his right hand underneath his pillow, and brought out his dagger, which he just as silently unsheathed. He felt the chill air of the chamber touch his skin as he drew back the bed-covers and quietly swung his legs over and out of the bed. For a moment, he sat there, his feet firm on the bare wooden floor, staring at the door, whose contours came more clearly into his view as he did so. Lawrence stared at the handle, waiting for it to turn, convinced there was a presence on the other side of that door. He could feel the presence. Seeker's warning came back to him. His mind darted around a moment, and then he settled on what seemed the only possible plan. He would stand against the wall, so that he was behind the door as it opened, and thus take his assailant by surprise as he entered. The knife would do the rest. Two men he had seen in the breakfast parlour of that Hammersmith inn, and yet he felt the presence of only one, and against that one, he did not mind his chances. Lawrence gripped the fluted oak hilt of his knife all the tighter, and began to raise himself up from the bed. And then his room exploded.

Before he could turn around towards the glass shattering behind him, Lawrence felt a hard loop of rope come down over his head to his neck. He tried to call out, but was silenced by the crashing of a fist to the side of his face. Another explosion, this time of the wood in the door to his chamber and he felt a jolt at his neck, and the rope around it begin to hoist him into the air. Lawrence struggled, dropping his knife and putting his hands to the noose in a desperate attempt to free himself. The breath was being choked out of him as the rope burned his skin. The higher it pulled him towards the beam over which it had been slung, the more Lawrence kicked. And the worse the choking got. Lawrence could feel his eyes bulge; he was scarcely conscious of the huge mass stumbling towards him through the shattered door. There was a moment's confusion and hesitation before two strong arms reached out from the sides of the mass and gripped him under the arms, holding him up as a familiar voice bellowed for help. A scrambling noise and a sudden sharper tug at the rope and Lawrence saw only vibrant colour, felt death rush away with him, and then looseness, before a fall, and finally, subsidence. The two strong arms were beneath him now, the rope slack, and Damian Seeker, looming over him, was laying him carefully down on his bed.

'Don't try to speak,' Seeker said for the second time in as many minutes.

The physician, who had been greatly disgruntled at being roused from his bed at such an hour, finished applying the poultice that had been made up in the inn's kitchens.

'The captain is right,' he said. 'Your throat will feel raw for a good while.' He handed Seeker the script he had quickly scrawled. 'You should have these powders fetched from the apothecary in the morning, and see that he swallows them down, in accordance with my instructions. The poultice should be changed daily for a week, and the salve applied. You will have my bill by dinnertime.'

And then the physician was gone, and the porter with him. The porter had been in something of a quandary as to what to do about the door to Lawrence's chamber after he had stepped through the smashed centre of it and back out into the hall. He stretched a hand towards the handle, which was hanging loose on its barrel, as if he might attempt to close the broken skeleton of the door behind himself.

'Leave it,' Seeker said with impatience, and the man did.

Now there remained three of them in the devastated room: Seeker, Lawrence, and Elias Ellingworth.

'Well, Captain,' began Elias, who had been first to the door at Seeker's calls for help, 'should I ask what any of this means? For I am sure it must mean something, I am just at a loss to know what.'

'You should start by telling me what you're doing here.'

'Doing? Well, when I heard the smashing of the door and the rumpus coming from this room, I thought I should hasten to see if someone was being murdered. Which it appears they were.'

Lawrence opened his mouth as if to say something, but at a glance from Seeker, shut it again.

'I meant,' said Seeker, channelling more patience than he felt, 'what are you doing here, at Clifford's? I thought you stopped the night with your sister, at Dove Court.'

Still surveying the shattered room Elias said, 'Usually, I do. But sometimes there is a late supper, or debate that goes on to an hour that would have me in trouble with the men of the watch should I try to make my way back in at the city gates afterwards, so I stay here.'

'And what of your sister?'

'My sister, as I'm sure you will recall from the many occasions you had me incarcerated in one of London's more secure establishments, is well used to seeing to herself, and not in need of *anybody's* protection.'

Seeker was working himself up to a suitable response when a pained clearing of Lawrence Ingolby's throat recalled them both to the present.

'Right,' he said. 'Well, you'll remember I told you Ingolby here had told me something it wouldn't do well for people to know he'd told me?'

Elias gave a drawn-out, 'Yes.'

'Seems someone did find out that he'd been talking to me and took it into their heads to make sure he couldn't tell me any more, or at least identify them if ever I should lay my hands on them.'

'And you just happened to be here to see them off? Have you been waiting outside his door every night?'

Lawrence swept an astonished look from Elias over to Seeker, and raised his own eyebrows as if to ask the same question.

'No I have not,' replied Seeker. 'Better things to do with my time than act nursemaid to this one on the off-chance he's set off an assassin. I just received some intelligence earlier this evening that suggested the attempt would be made tonight.'

Lawrence's eyes widened to their greatest extent and some sort of indignant squawk issued from his throat. 'I did warn you,' Seeker said. 'But too late. You'd already walked right into a trap, carrying your own flag, just in case they didn't spot you.'

Elias righted the only chair in Lawrence's room and sat down. 'How did you come by this intelligence?'

Seeker stared at him. How had it come to this, that Elias Ellingworth expected he would discuss such a thing with him? 'I may have gone soft, Ellingworth,' he said, 'but I haven't actually lost my mind. What in the name of all that's holy makes you think I'd start telling you where I get my information?'

Ellingworth's face fell a little. 'I just . . .'

'What?' said Seeker, 'thought I might like to give you a few titbits for your news-sheet?' He shook his head. 'Oh, no. We're not there yet, not by a long shot, nor ever will be. Now take a tip from Ingolby there and keep quiet a minute. I need to think.'

Seeker looked around the room. The shattered door, half off its hinges, its wood splintered into a mess of lethal shards, he could ignore. He had only meant to force the lock, but he seemed to have demolished the entire door and damaged its frame too in the process. Well, it could be mended. It was the window, though, that most interested him. Holding up the lamp Ellingworth had brought, he stepped across the room, glass crunching under his boots. The window had been forced open from the outside. Ingolby's chamber was three floors up from the ground. How his assailant had reached to such a height was no mystery: the rope that had first been attached to the lower branches of the great elm in the courtyard, and then slung over a beam for a noose to the law student's neck, before finally being employed in the would-be murderer's escape, still dangled down the outer side of the wall. It was anchored by the bedpost around which Seeker had flung it when he had got it off Ingolby's neck. Seeker had rarely come across such ingenuity. He looked more closely at the shattered casement and felt a shiver of cold night air as he plucked the grey goose feather that had caught there. If it hadn't been for Manon, Lawrence Ingolby would be dead now.

★

He should have gone up to the Black Fox sooner, but every time this week that he'd set out, he'd turned back again, telling himself that he hadn't the time. These last few months he'd let himself almost believe in the possibilities of that world he found when he went beyond the private parlour door of the tavern. They'd spent hours there, just him and Manon, talking and not talking, making up the losses of the years. He'd tell her of his own family – mother, father, sister, brother – dead now or scattered he knew not where. They'd even talk, sometimes, of how, an itinerant carpenter, he'd met her mother, and he would tell her of the house he'd built for the winter times, and of their summer travelling, and the cradle he had carved for her with his own hands. Then he and Manon would stop, not long after the cradle, before the shadow of Caleb Turner fell on their clearing, and they'd go on to talk of the doings of the Black Fox, or what Manon had learned of London. Sometimes she would tell him of things she had taught Dorcas – uses of herbs, ways of dressing game – that Dorcas had not known before, and that Manon had learned of necessity in her long years on the road with her mother and Turner. Of the rags of their separate pasts, they'd woven together something new in which to clothe themselves.

Seeker would often whittle at pieces of wood as they talked, and Manon would watch him, entranced by the dexterity of those enormous hands. It would often be a figure of a person, or an animal, once or twice something from the very rare occasions he risked going out with her in London, he in his carpenter's garb. Once, he'd taken her to the garden of a crumbling Royalist mansion on the Strand. Amongst the overgrown lawns and roses run wild, they had found marbles, statues from so far away and long ago they could neither of them properly comprehend it. One in particular had entranced Manon, a figure of a girl who was out hunting, with a quiver of bows across her back, and a small greyhound dog at her feet. 'What do you think the dog's name is?' she'd asked him. It wasn't the kind of thing he'd normally consider, but eventually, casting around him for inspiration in that neglected, overgrown Royalist garden, he'd settled on 'Nettles'. The name had delighted Manon and she'd chattered about Nettles all the way back to the Black Fox. That night, he'd carved her a dog, a greyhound, the best he'd ever done.

Seeker always set what he had been working on down on the floor by his chair at the end of the night, and never looked at it again. He'd learned from Dorcas that Manon would gather up the pieces next morning, and put them in a small basket she kept under her bed. When Dorcas had asked her about it she'd said, 'My father is making a family, but I don't think he knows it.'

And that was why Seeker had turned back, every time this week that he had set out for the Black Fox. That family he was thoughtlessly making, that would inevitably be made, by his putting his only child into the household of Dorcas Wells, was a thing he could destroy as easily as he had destroyed Lawrence Ingolby's door. Since his return to

London, he had told himself to forget about Maria, but the sight of her that day, on an outing to Lambeth with her friends, had almost been enough to rip him open. And if Dorcas looked too long in his eyes she would see the truth there, and the pain that he felt would pass instead to her. He'd have found an excuse tonight, too, not to go to the Black Fox, had his growing fear that Lawrence Ingolby had made himself a target for Fish and Boyes not forced him there. Dorcas had seen in his face straight away that this was no domestic visit, and had ushered him quickly into her business room, and locked the door behind him.

'What is it?'

In a very few minutes, he had told her of the danger that Lawrence was in, because he had unwittingly alerted him to a plot to kill Cromwell, and because he might recognise again two of those involved. He didn't tell Dorcas of the additional danger he himself had placed Lawrence in, by sending him to Bankside and out onto Lambeth Marsh in the search for the bear that had mauled Samuel Kent's old friend to death; that was something different, and not something she had cause to concern herself with. Seeker gave Dorcas the descriptions of the men Lawrence had seen in the Hammersmith inn, but no such characters, nor anyone else, in fact, had come in to the Black Fox asking questions about the young Yorkshireman. Seeker warned Dorcas to use great vigilance, and to have her girls tell her straight away should anyone come in to the tavern asking such questions.

And then he had allowed himself a half-hour with his daughter. Usually, her easy presence around him was enough to make him feel as if the concerns of his day were slipping from his shoulders, and that there was no great necessity of picking them up again. Tonight, however, she was more quiet than usual, and seemed preoccupied. When she did speak, it was to ask about Lawrence Ingolby, and whether Seeker thought he would always stay in London, or return soon to Yorkshire, or even travel abroad. Seeker, in response, said he thought the first the more likely, the second a possibility, and the third a very bad idea. The accompanying caustic remarks he felt compelled to make upon Ingolby's boots, his hair, and general demeanour, in the hope of lightening her mood, fell utterly flat, to the point that she began to try to explain to him that he was wrong. And then she had said,

'You know, for all you think yourselves so different, he is just like you, Father.'

'What do you mean?' he'd asked her.

And so she had told him about the man with the green felt hat who had been in the Black Fox earlier that evening that had never been there before, and who Lawrence had been convinced was watching him.

Now, here, in Lawrence Ingolby's room in Clifford's Inn, the broken glass crunching under his boot, Seeker looked down at the grey goose feather he had plucked from the crack between broken window-pane and casement in which it had caught.

'It was a green felt hat with a grey goose feather, Father,' she had said. And then with a little more prompting, she had recalled that the man had left the Black Fox very soon after Lawrence himself had done, about a half-hour or so before Seeker had arrived. Yes, she thought she had called him by his name, Lawrence, and Dorcas too, though only by his first. A little more thought, a question or two more, and Manon thought that Dorcas might well have said, aloud, that Lawrence should return to Clifford's Inn.

Seeker had been on his feet in seconds, so that Manon had thought she had done something wrong. 'No, Manon, you've done nothing wrong, but very right, and I must go now and see to it.' He'd told Dorcas that should the man in the green felt hat ever return to the Black Fox, she should have her cook, the massive Will Tucker, restrain him, and then send word to Whitehall to himself. And then he had left, and run the whole way through the streets, pausing for no one, until he was on Fleet Street and through the gates of Clifford's Inn. He'd reached Lawrence's corridor just in time to see him disappear into his room, and by the time Seeker had reached the outside of the door, Lawrence had been happily whistling. Seeker had then taken up his position in a darkened recess a few yards along that corridor, from which he'd watched all the comings and goings until all at Clifford's had settled themselves for the night.

That had been three hours ago. 'I thought he'd come by the front,' he said to Ellingworth. 'I can't believe what a fool I was.'

'But surely that's how he did come,' said Elias, turning to look behind him. 'In through that door and then out through the window.'

Seeker shook his head. 'It was I who came through the door, after I heard the smashing of the window. He must have moved very fast, this man in the green felt hat, and be a person of some ingenuity, to make the means of execution the means also of his escape.'

Elias got up from his chair and came over to examine the rope. 'Why this, and not a knife?'

'Perhaps because he had it to hand. He would have needed it for the ascent of the tree and for getting away again. And a knife will not always incapacitate a man as a noose around the neck will.'

Lawrence croaked some sound of agreement.

Elias glanced over in his direction. 'He can stay in the chamber set aside for me tonight, and then can come and lodge with us at Dove Court until he is well.'

Seeker paused in his task of coiling the rope. 'Have you actually lost your wits? Men who would murder Cromwell are after this fellow's skin, and you would expose your sister to them? Lawrence Ingolby is coming down to Knight Ryder Street, with me, where I can keep an eye on him.'

Lawrence began to make some sound of protest, but stopped, the knowledge of what had just happened and the realisation of what it meant sinking in at last. He nodded, gave his neck another rub, and rose to begin the painful process of dressing for the night journey from Clifford's

Inn to Knight Ryder Street. Seeker watched him struggle for as long as he could, as Elias Ellingworth went through the process of putting Lawrence's belongings into a leather sack that had been hanging from the bedstead, and eventually went across and awkwardly helped him shuffle into his doublet.

When he'd heard the shattering of glass come from Lawrence Ingolby's room, Seeker had experienced a surge of dread that he hadn't quite recognised. It had grown, become more urgent, as he'd run down the corridor and charged at the lock. In his head, he was certain he'd been praying. He shook his head now, as if to dislodge whatever it was, but he could not shift it, this anxiety that this cocksure, infuriating young man should come to no harm. He watched as Ingolby painstakingly pulled on one boot and then the other. An image of the figures he whittled as he and Manon spoke, the family she said he didn't know he was making, came into his head. He let out a heavy sigh and picked up the bag Elias had packed for Lawrence. 'Come on then,' he said.

SEVENTEEN

Elias Has a New Client

The air was fresh as Seeker crossed over Knight Ryder Street next day. He liked these November city mornings – too early, too cold and too miserable for trouble-makers. They'd be sleeping off whatever debauchery or intrigues they'd been up to the night before, and only honest folk, with work to do, would brave the damp grey streets in the wake of the scavengers and the night-soil men.

Lawrence Ingolby was sleeping it off too, although, Seeker conceded, he was only slightly to be blamed for his own misfortune in being the subject of an attempted hanging. There was an irony, Seeker thought, in Lawrence's having survived a trip to an illegal dog-breeder's on Lambeth Marsh unscathed, only to come so close to death in his own bedchamber in the hallowed surrounds of the Inns of Chancery. Seeker had left him in the small, sparsely furnished room, down the back passageway of the unremarkable house on Knight Ryder Street which he himself used as a retreat from the demands of Thurloe's work. The dog had been happy enough to stay lying guard across the door.

On finding that his friend Drake was not in his apothecary, but engaged on the supervision of works at Cree church, Seeker left the prescription for Lawrence with Drake's sister, not long arrived from France. He could have done without walking all the way up to Leadenhall before he set out for Whitehall for the day, but something Lawrence had said to him earlier had resurfaced to trouble him. On Cornhill, he glanced uneasily down Birchin Lane. It was almost a week since he'd promised Samuel he would get to the bottom of the murder of his friend, but there was no time at the moment to go down into the coffee shop to explain he was a little closer to tracking down the whereabouts of the savage animal that had been used to such brutal effect. As well, perhaps, since for now all he had that might lead him to the killer were the disparate frayed ends of something that he had not worked out how to put together. Once he had spoken to Drake, though, he might be a little closer to seeing how that might be done.

Across from Hartshorn Alley, Seeker turned up past St Katharine Cree. This was the London Cromwell wanted, the London Cromwell had made. Along the lane, beyond the church, a group of people were busy at work on a house. There was an industry to them that said they needed no overseer; this was *their* house. Seeker waited as two labourers passed him carrying a ceiling beam, a good twelve feet long, to replace one that had rotted, then he crossed to where Drake was standing, watching a slater begin the leading of the roof.

Seeker followed the line of his gaze, gave a nod of

approval, then let his eye travel further down, to where a jutty was being erected over the street. 'They'll need to watch that,' he said. 'The aldermen don't like anything that narrows the common passageway.'

The apothecary laughed. 'That is what the aldermen are for, is it not? Not liking things?'

Seeker started to explain the need for good government and regulation of the city wards, but soon saw his friend was baiting him. 'Well, anyway,' he finished, 'they'll need to watch it, all the same.'

'Do you wish to see inside?' asked Drake.

Seeker shook his head. 'I'd only see things that would annoy me – work not done right, that sort of thing, end up wanting to sort it myself.'

Drake appraised him a moment. 'I forget sometimes that you were a carpenter, in another life.'

'Not when you wanted shelves put up in your elaboratory, you didn't,' said Seeker. Drake laughed and then his face became serious. 'But I think you have not come here as a carpenter today?'

'No, I'm here about something else.'

'About our synagogue?'

'What? No. You've Cromwell's say-so for this – no one'll touch you. You're not getting any trouble, are you?'

Drake shook his head. 'No.' As he did so, Seeker noticed that the pendant he had always worn beneath his shirt he now wore openly. He'd seen it properly only once before, when he'd been helping Drake with the carpentry for the fitting out of his stillroom. Hanging from the links of the gold chain around the apothecary's neck was a ring, large enough for a man's finger, and wrought with exceptional intricacy. Vines of gold twined around tiny pearls and painted enamel flowers to meet at a small structure at the top, in the form of a tiled roof. When Seeker had asked him about it, Drake had opened the roof, to reveal a Hebrew inscription beneath. 'It is from the *Song of Songs*,' he had said. 'This was my wedding ring.' Drake's sister and his nephew had come safe at last to England, but Seeker knew that his friend's wife never could.

Today, though, Drake was taken up with thoughts of the present and the future. 'And we have secured an old orchard too, out at Mile End, for our burials. The people at St Katharine's here have offered to lend us their pall, and to toll the bell for our burials. You cannot know what it means, Damian, to have somewhere we might call home. But come, tell me, what is it that has brought you here?'

Seeker put his hand on Drake's elbow and guided him down the small passageway leading from the street-front of the house to the overgrown garden behind. He brushed the debris from a weather-worn bench beneath an old pear tree and sat down, gesturing to Drake to do likewise.

'It's to do with the murder of an old soldiering friend of Samuel Kent's.'

Drake nodded. 'I heard of it. Abominable savagery.'

'Aye. Well what I need from you is whatever you know about the scientific lot that hangs about John Evelyn.'

A look of astonishment crossed Drake's face. 'You cannot think John Evelyn is involved in this.'

Seeker's shoulders sank. 'No. But one of his friends has been keeping some very bad company.' He went on to tell Drake of Thomas Faithly's two sightings of the shadowy 'Mr Mulberry'.

Drake considered. 'I've never heard of this Mulberry,' he said at last, 'but I'll wager that this fellow, who is so anxious to avoid being recognised, has a greater interest in the – *old* – science than the new.'

'Alchemy, you mean?'

Drake shrugged. 'There is a fine line between what you would call alchemy and I science, but there are some practitioners of alchemy who are prone to err a little on the – how should I put it . . .'

Seeker helped him out. 'You're talking about magic.'

Drake was hesitant. 'I don't speak of witches and warlocks, and spells, but everything in the science of the natural world is magic, until we fully comprehend its properties and what action upon them causes them to change. I accept as science only what I can demonstrate and explain. Others do not.'

'And you think this Mulberry is one of those others, who dabble in darker things?'

'If he is anxious not to be seen, and fears accusations of witchcraft, that is certainly possible. Let me make some enquiries – discreetly. I'll let you know what I discover.'

Seeker stood up, making to leave, when Drake coughed

and, with some awkwardness, introduced a new subject. 'Ahem, I was at Tradescant's last week, in South Lambeth.'

Seeker made a face. 'You an' all? Seems half the world's got nothing better to do than go south of the river.'

'John Tradescant keeps the best supply of herbs and simples within miles of London. I frequently go over there, when I have the leisure. Last week I had a little time to spare, and I was glad of it, for I was able to accompany Maria.'

'Maria?' Seeker asked before he could stop himself. 'But she was only there the week before. What was she doing going back?'

Drake explained to him the planned articles for Elias's news-sheet, and the sketches she was attempting to make to go with them.

'Well, I suppose it's better than all that seditious rubbish he used to spread in his old paper.'

Drake laughed. 'Let us wait and see. I think Maria is as driven as her brother and can find seditious things to say about the most innocuous of objects. I was treated to a long harangue on our journey back into the city about a pair of hawking gloves in Tradescant's collection that had belonged to Henry VIII. Maria was able to extrapolate a great deal of outrage from their very existence.'

'Was she?' Seeker felt something loosen in himself, fall. He thought of the times he had watched her, as she'd worked herself into a fury of righteous indignation over some injustice she had seen, remembered how it had felt to pull her close and gently soothe her, trying not to let her see how amused and enthralled he was by her passion.

Drake must have seen it in his face. He put a hand on Seeker's shoulder. 'She is unchanged, my friend, you know. Behind the anger, there is . . .'

'More anger, for me,' said Seeker.

'No. There is hurt, and fear, and determination to protect herself from it. And it is all because, behind it all, there is love.'

Seeker regarded the dusty toe of his boot for a while. 'I don't know how to break through, John. I don't know if I can. And besides – there's Dorcas.'

Drake said nothing.

'But,' Seeker said, raising himself to his feet, 'I am glad her halfwit brother at least has the sense to have you keep an eye on her, rather than let her travel the roads and the river alone.'

Drake frowned. 'I think that was a fortunate coincidence. Elias does not attend to her welfare as much as he ought. He puts too much faith in her own good sense and her disposition. But sometimes, her good instincts are misplaced. That day at Tradescant's, when I went to see to the purchasing of my simples, I left her in the Cabinet of Curiosities, taking her notes and making her sketches. I was gone perhaps an hour. When I returned there was a man . . .'

'Bothering her?'

Drake wrinkled his brow. 'She said not. She claimed he was offering to teach her to draw.'

Seeker could feel the blood begin to pound in his chest and down his arms. 'To *draw*?'

Drake made a calming gesture. 'It's all right, I warned her. And I made it quite clear to Elias: good-looking Cavaliers with fine blue velvet suits and battle-scarred hands do not befriend young women in order to teach them to draw. I told Elias he must not allow her to go to such places alone, no matter how respectable those places might seem.'

But Seeker wasn't listening any more to what Drake might have told Elias. He felt that his mind had slowed to a state of the barely functional. Tradescant's. The blue velvet suit, the scarred hands. 'This Cavalier,' he managed at last, 'did you discover his name?'

'Faithly,' said Drake. 'His name was Sir Thomas Faithly.'

Maria dropped the small earthenware pot containing the last of their salt. It smashed to the floor. 'Damian?'

Elias nodded. 'Got in there just in time. Half a minute more and Ingolby would have been dead.'

'But Damian was not hurt?'

Elias gave her a rueful smile. 'I have just told you my pupil was less than a moment from death, and all your concern is for Seeker? Rest assured, sister, that hulk of Yorkshire granite demolished all around him without a scratch to his own person. Two hundred years old at least, that door was, and now it's hardly fit for kindling.'

Maria looked down, bemused by the broken pieces of earthenware at her feet. 'And the assailant?'

'Escaped, out the window. Seeker couldn't go after him until he had Lawrence safely down without snapping his neck or choking the last of the life out of him. He seems to have a better idea of who he's looking for now, though.' He shook his head, smiling. 'I can't believe you think that anything could touch Seeker.'

Could it not? thought Maria. She remembered almost a year ago, when he had finally returned from his exile in Yorkshire. She had heard the rumour first from Kent's: Seeker was back from the north, badly hurt, new scars from knife and musket ball, bones broken, flesh torn, dragging his right leg like a man just home from war. She'd run through the streets when they'd told her, tried to find him. Gone to Knight Ryder Street, to Drake's. Sent the boy Gabriel from Kent's to Whitehall looking for him, gone at last to the gardener's hut at Lincoln's Inn, where the young man who kept Seeker's dog was to be found. And it was Nathaniel who had told her: Seeker was at the Black Fox, on Broad Street, being tended to by Dorcas Wells.

Maria bent to start picking up the broken shards of the pot. She looked at her own fingers, wondering if they might be cut by the sharp edges, as she sought to avoid their jagged points. Nothing could touch Seeker.

Elias appeared not have noticed her distraction, or the broken pot. He pushed aside the trencher she had set out for him, with its remnants of the bread and cold beef, to make room for his papers, then got up to rummage on the shelf above his bed for one of the new quills she had made up for him earlier.

'I have a new client coming this evening,' he announced.

If she had not already dropped the pot, Maria would probably have done so again. Elias's clients were few and far between, and only those actually in hiding from the law came to their small dwelling at the top of the old house in Dove Court.

'I thought you had decided to keep to the right side of the authorities from now on? Did you not say you would spread your views through subtlety, in papers that are permitted, rather than loudly in news-sheets which are not? What manner of client is this?'

'Oh,' said Elias, 'one with no more intention of coming to the attention of Mr Thurloe than I have. He, like your chastened brother, has learned his lesson, and is anxious not to return to his former quarters on Tower Hill.'

'Tower Hill? Who on earth are you bringing here, Elias? You cannot risk being sent there again yourself!'

Elias smiled. 'A gentleman. Maria. My new client is a repentant Royalist who is desirous of changing his ways. He wishes to do nothing more than return to his home to lead a quiet English life. He has engaged me to assist him in trying to recover some of his family's lands, in Yorkshire, that were lost to him through his poor choices during the war.'

Maria pulled out the stool across the table from him and sat down. 'A Royalist? Elias, not three weeks ago, in this very room, with half a dozen of your oldest friends, you said there was no such thing as a repentant Royalist, and the only ones who slunk back to England claiming to be so were out only for themselves.'

He waved his quill at her. 'Ah, but this one is different, Maria. He is genuinely chastened. And he lost much of his patrimony due to the duplicity of his brother – for it seems that it is not only good Republican women who have troublesome brothers.'

Maria felt herself warming. Elias always had a way of getting around her more cautious instincts.

'And you know, he is a friend of Ingolby's too – another Yorkshireman.'

'Another . . .?' Maria didn't finish her sentence. She knew now who this new client of Elias's was. She had thought Thomas Faithly had just been speaking nonsense, saying he would present himself to her brother as a client as a means of gaining Elias's trust for – what? What did Thomas Faithly really want of her? What foolishness had she allowed herself to indulge in, to be charmed by the flattery and fine manners of a Cavalier? Maria stood up abruptly and put on her cloak.

'Where are you going?' asked Elias in surprise. 'Don't you wish to meet my new client?'

'No, I, that is, I do not have the time, at the moment. I promised I would call on Grace.'

'But I am just back from Kent's,' he said, 'and Grace certainly made no mention of expecting you.'

Maria was fumbling at the ribbons of her hood. 'She must have forg—'

But it was too late. The sound of footsteps coming up the stairs was followed by a firm knock on the door. As Elias went to answer it, Maria sank back down on her stool, her ribbons still undone.

'A small estate,' Faithly was saying, 'left to me by my grandmother – my mother's mother. I remember her as an ancient lady when I was still a boy, but I suppose she would have been fifty or so then. You see, I had already returned, and surrendered myself to the Protectorate, before she died. Do you think I have a chance?'

Elias nodded. 'Assuredly. It may take some time, for the wheels of justice move slow at Chancery, but if you had already made your peace with the regime before you were even bequeathed the estate, and your grandmother gave the authorities no cause for concern?'

'None,' said Faithly. 'She was the most dread Puritan I ever saw, and would never have left me the place had I remained with the King.'

'Good, good,' said Elias, 'then you most certainly have a very strong case. But as to your patrimony . . .'

'Oh, there is no hope of Faithly Manor. Had it not been for my brother's duplicity and bad management . . . But, well, that is done now, and cannot be undone. The place is in the hands of another and I make no claim on it.'

Maria had retreated to the window overlooking the small

back yard of Dove Court. After Sir Thomas had come in, and Elias begun to make the introductions, Sir Thomas had stopped him and told him they had already met. He had gone on to tell Elias a version of their acquaintance that, whilst it might not say everything, at least told no lies.

Thomas had not put on his fine velvet suit today, but a more sober, though still well made, affair of russet wool. Even so, in their small, bare apartment, his long, fair, Cavalier hair and his lively eye made a centre of warmth, and colour. The scars on his hands and the slight lines around his mouth and eyes alluded to stories yet to be told, that she could not help but feel intrigued by. He spoke with ease and humour of foreign towns, different peoples, their customs, their clothing, their incomprehension of English ways. He made them laugh. He made her laugh.

Elias had brought home a jug of good burgundy from the Mermaid, but an hour had not long passed before it was empty. So at ease was he with his new client, who was already halfway to becoming a friend, that Elias declared he would go back down to Bread Street for another. He didn't seem to notice the look in his sister's eyes that implored him not to go, and didn't even let her finish her offer that she would go instead.

'And what would Drake say, and others – and you will know of whom I speak – that lecture me night and day that I have no regard for your safety, if I were to send you out, alone, to a tavern at this time of night? No, you stay here with Sir Thomas, and I will brave the unruly streets alone.'

The door shut behind him, and she and Thomas watched each other as the sound of Elias's steps faded down the stairs and disappeared onto the street. When at last it was certain her brother was gone, Sir Thomas took a step towards her. Involuntarily, Maria shrank a little further back, but the window being just behind her, there was really no further she could go. Thomas stopped where he was. 'Maria, do not fear me. Please, do not fear me. And I implore you, do not judge me by the reputation of those with whom I have associated.'

'I don't mean to,' she said, her voice very quiet.

'I told you I was determined to do things properly, so that your brother might not object to my presence around you, and I will not deceive him. I ask only that you believe what I feel now, here, for you, is utterly sincere.' He took another step towards her. In the small attic room, he was now quite close, a foot away at most. She was aware of him looking down at her, but was scared to look up. He reached out his right hand and took hold of her left, holding it very lightly. 'Tell me you believe me, Maria.'

She felt a wave of something – panic, excitement, fear – she didn't know, that rendered her immobile. Thomas took one step more forward and passed his left arm around her waist, pulling her gently towards him. A slight movement of his foot crushed beneath it the one remaining piece of the broken salt pot she had missed, and rendered it dust.

EIGHTEEN

Flowers Out of Season

Dawn was just creeping through the window of his room high above the Cockpit when Seeker put down the last of the reports from the Netherlands that he'd had lifted from the records room. This thing had been brewing for months – easy enough to see that now, when the plans were being put in to action, more difficult when their beginnings were just being mentioned amongst a hundred other things. And Thurloe had known it too. Seeker looked again at the copy of the letter, written six months ago by Thurloe to Henry Cromwell in Ireland:

The Spaniards, Cavaliers, Papists and Levellers are all come into a confederacy. What monstrous birth this womb will bring forth I cannot tell.

That was what had almost overwhelmed Thurloe: the enemy was everyone. Floods of intelligence had come from all corners of Europe, reports on every possible suspicious movement, so that those charged with bringing forth this 'monstrous birth', this murder of Oliver Cromwell, had managed to slip in under cover of the deluge. Thurloe could talk of confederacies, use terms – 'Spaniards, Cavaliers, Papists, Levellers' – investing those who went by them with a dignity and a cause that made them somehow stronger and more noble than they were. But Seeker knew these men for what they were: fallible individuals, ineffective killers who had huddled in the upper room of a coaching house in Hammersmith, for days on end; he sought, at the end of a frayed rope, the failed assassin of an insignificant Yorkshire law student. Seeker hunted not causes but men, flesh and bone, who had shown themselves capable of failure and prone to making mistakes. He sought Boyes, a man whose face, according to Ingolby, was younger than his demeanour would have onlookers believe him to be; he sought Fish, a man who'd rented modest tailor's rooms on King Street and bought pies from a woman in Westminster; he sought Cecil, a man whose grand cause might yet be reduced to ashes by the wearing of a green felt hat that had lost its grey goose feather. These men would not be found in reports of clandestine meetings in Paris, Brussels, Madrid; they would be found amongst the heaving inns and cold corners of London's lanes and alleys, and that was where his men were hunting them.

For himself, he was set for south of the river. His first port of call would be the George, in Southwark. The attempts on Cromwell had left him no time, up until now, to go south of the river to conduct his own enquiries into the death of Joseph Grindle, and the enquiries being made by Ingolby and Thomas Faithly were not progressing fast enough for his liking. Besides, he was becoming increasingly uncertain that he fully trusted Thomas Faithly, and what Drake had told him about seeing Faithly with Maria at Tradescant's had done nothing to assuage his distrust.

The George was seething already, with travellers anxious to get on to their business in the city, taking their breakfast or their morning draught. The landlord himself was attending to the better-off patrons in the small parlour, and not best pleased to see a soldier evidently set on business at so early an hour. His face clouded over all the more when Seeker told him why he was there.

'I told the folk that came looking for him – Joseph Grindle left and never paid his bill, so I'm in my rights to keep his belongings.'

'Sold them already then, have you?'

'Nothing worth selling, was there? Only thing he had worth selling was that old clock he took with him, saying he was going to have it mended. All he left here was a leather bag that had seen better days and a change of shift and hose.'

'He'd been expecting to stay then?'

'Another two days or so, as long as the clock took to be fixed. Didn't speak about any other plans, apart from going into the city to look for a coffee house I'd mentioned – seemed to think he might know the fellow that ran it. Must have been that old game-legged fellow that came here with his family next day, looking for him and making such a fuss, but I told him: Joseph Grindle never came back here after that first morning.'

'Had he spoken of going over to Bankside, asked about gaming houses, shown any interest in anything of that sort?'

The man shook his head. 'Didn't look the type at all. Sober, respectable sort. Canny with his money. Stayed in quiet the night he arrived, took an early supper, only drank moderate and didn't converse with anyone out of the ordinary. Said he hadn't been to London in many a long year. It was only when I was telling him about the coffee houses, and mentioned Kent's on Birchin Lane, that he showed any interest in the sights of the town. Next morning he was up with the larks to go looking for his old friend. Left with that clock under his arm and that was the last I saw of him.'

Having viewed the room Grindle had slept in, established that the other two beds in it had been empty the night of Grindle's stay, and got even less helpful answers from the chambermaid than he had done from the landlord, Seeker left the George and set off back for Whitehall. Taking the road that skirted the marsh, he resisted the temptation to cut across and see for himself the dog-breeder's compound visited by Faithly and Ingolby. The sight of him taking too close an interest in the place might raise suspicions and put the pair in unnecessary danger. He thought back to the day after Grindle's murder near the Bear Garden, when he had met Samuel Kent's party making its way along this very road, to view the curiosities at Tradescant's. He thought of Maria, and Thomas Faithly. Things that should be separate were getting mixed up in his head. Instead of carrying on to the horse ferry, Seeker turned Acheron towards South Lambeth.

By the time he was passing beneath the whalebone arch of Tradescant's, Seeker was regretting having come here, but it was too late to turn back. He would ask Tradescant whether he had ever been offered bear's teeth, claws or suchlike for his collection of curiosities, and then he would leave. Whether Maria was here, or Thomas Faithly either, could be no concern of his. At Tradescant's stable he dismounted and left Acheron in the care of the lad there. A little way into the gardens he came upon two boys busied in digging out a drainage trench that had threatened to become clogged with fallen leaves and other debris. 'Where's your master, lads?'

The older of the two took the chance of respite from his digging to lean on the end of his shovel. He nodded towards a long hedge separating lawn from path, leading to an ornate iron gate. 'Up there, working on the hawthorn, near the rose garden.' His face took on a look of excitement. 'Is there trouble?'

Seeker frowned. 'Should there be?'

'Two soldiers in two days. Sounds like trouble to me.'

'Oh? What soldier was here yesterday then?'

The younger boy, who had now also stopped work, chimed in. 'One of the Foot Guard – the Lord Protector's. Came here yesterday and spoke to a man.'

But the older one shook his head and addressed his

companion with scorn. 'Wasn't the Foot Guard, fool, it was the Horse Guard. I told you.'

But the younger one was determined on his point. 'No, I tell you it was the Foot Guard. Grey coat, that's the Foot Guard. Velvet collar and black lace. And he didn't have a horse, either.'

'You're right,' said Seeker, going a little closer to the younger boy. 'The Foot Guard is grey. So what did he want here yesterday, this soldier?'

The boy shook his head. 'Don't know. He was just talking to a man, then went away.'

'What kind of man?' asked Seeker.

The boy thought a minute. 'Ordinary. About your age, but smaller. Brown, grey hair. Gurn on his face.'

'Wasn't wearing a green felt hat, by any chance?'

The young boy shook his head, and turned back to his digging. 'No. That was one of the fellows that was with him.'

Tradescant put down his cutters and removed his heavy leather gloves at Seeker's approach.

'Captain.'

He looked wary. Seeker knew him for a Royalist who had quietly worked at his trade through the wars and the beginnings of the Commonwealth without giving any concern to the authorities. John Tradescant and his father were men who'd raised themselves in the world through the work of their own hands, and when that world had turned upside-down, they'd just kept on working.

'You'll not be here to talk about roses,' said Tradescant as Seeker drew up to him. He pushed up the sleeves of his coat and rolled back the plain cuffs of his shirt to reveal browned workman's wrists and hands marked by the scars of their labour. Seeker felt this was a man with whom he could do business. 'Warmer in there,' Tradescant said, and Seeker followed him to a gardener's hut nearby.

The hut was a long, thatched wooden structure with row upon row of shelves bearing hessian sacks in which Seeker assumed bulbs and roots were kept. Apart from at the far end of the structure, where a young woman appeared to be working on some ledgers, the place was very poorly lit.

Seeker nodded towards the woman. 'Your daughter?'

Tradescant raised his eyebrows and shook his head. 'Frances is married these ten years, in the city, and has her own household to run. That's Mademoiselle Barguil, a Frenchwoman here to advise Mr Evelyn on the design of his gardens at Deptford.'

Seeker looked over again. There was something not quite right though, in her intense concentration on her work, in the fact that she had almost made a point of not looking up when they'd entered: he felt she was more aware of their presence than she would have them believe. He lowered his voice. 'John Evelyn has her keep long hours, it seems. It's a fair way up river from Sayes Court, for a young woman to be here so early, and on her own.'

'She's usually escorted here – an acquaintance of Mr Evelyn's, Sir Thomas Faithly, but she came especially early today to arrange for some packages to be sent away with the carrier.'

Seeker frowned. 'To Sayes Court?'

'Sayes Court? Oh, no. Orders for Sayes Court can be sent down to Deptford at almost any time. These are orders – bulbs, rose roots, seeds and the like – for gentlemen in the north and the Midlands.'

'Bit late for bulbs, isn't it? Roses should be planted by now too.'

Tradescant nodded his agreement. 'It's out of my hands, though, Captain. I've come to observe that there are some gentlemen who prefer to take their own advice, and not that of a humble labourer.'

'A fool and his money are soon parted,' said Seeker. He'd seen it himself, often enough, in his carpentering days. 'Can they not get what they need closer to hand?'

Tradescant laughed. 'Perhaps what they need, but not what they want. Tulips and roses put in too late are the least of it: your northern gentleman would grow orange trees, have his own lemons and pomegranates. Let his neighbour have the Rose of York; he will have the Rose of Muscovy. My father scoured Europe, to Russia itself, in search of species and varieties. I myself have been to the Caribbean and the new world.' He waved a hand around the utilitarian shed. 'From here, I've done business with nurserymen in the royal gardens of Paris and Brussels, with traders in the Canaries. We have connections that were begun when my father worked for Lord Cecil and King James was still on the throne. Mademoiselle Barguil undertakes to fill commissions for many of her friends and for Mr Evelyn's acquaintances who live far from London but who would have the best all the same. I think they like to pretend nothing has changed.' His expression said what they both knew – everything had changed. 'We've a carrier going to Hull from Gravesend tomorrow afternoon.'

'Is that right?' said Seeker. Faithly had put it somewhere in his report that Clémence Barguil was sourcing plants at Tradescant's for friends and acquaintances of John Evelyn, but Seeker hadn't considered that she might be involved in the sending as well as the finding of these items. He'd need to have enquiries made at Gravesend about what exactly was in those shipments going north. Oranges, pomegranates, or something else?

But he hadn't come here to talk about fruit. 'There was a soldier here yesterday, a member of the Lord Protector's Life Guard of Foot, according to your boys down there. Seems he was talking to a man who appeared to have come here with two others – one with a green felt hat and another, a north country gentleman who gave himself out as their employer. What were they doing here?'

Tradescant went to his order book. 'I was working out in the orchard most of the day, and had no dealings with customers. I'll see if there's anything in the order book.' He opened the book and made a face of displeasure. 'I don't understand,' he said, before pushing the book across to Seeker.

Seeker scanned the entry Tradescant had had his finger on, once and then once again, before slamming shut the covers. '"Alterus MacDuff. Thane of Fife." What idiot wrote this?'

'It would have been Edward, the lad I left in charge in here yesterday. He's working in the hothouse this morning.' He took the ledger back from Seeker. 'You can hardly blame a gardener's boy, Captain, in these your Puritan days, for that he doesn't know the works of William Shakespeare. Enough for me that he can read and write. I daresay he thought "Thane of Fife" was a place.'

Tradescant was right. How should a gardener's boy, with dirt still under his nails and hardly a trace of a beard on his chin, not be taken in by one so cleverly, openly almost, pro-claiming himself the avenger of a murdered king? Whoever was behind this conspiracy was no ordinary adversary and he was laughing at anyone who might come looking for him. Seeker felt a tension creeping across his head, like a metal band that was starting to tighten. He had come here to ask about bear's teeth or claws and found instead the unmistakable traces of Cecil, Fish and Boyes. He needed to get back to Whitehall.

'One more thing,' he said as he gathered up his gloves. 'Over in the house there you keep a cabinet of curiosities.'

Tradescant nodded.

'And I daresay you get folk now and again offering you stuff for it, at a price.'

Another nod. 'Now and again.'

'Anyone offered you a bear's tooth, claw, anything like that, of late?'

As Tradescant shook his head, Seeker noticed that the pen in the hand of Clémence Barguil paused in its motion across the page, just for a short moment, before it recommenced its journey. He'd need to ask Sir Thomas Faithly a few more questions about that young woman.

Despite the winter chill in the air, and the first flakes of a light snow, Tradescant's gardens were far from bare. As he made his way back down to Tradescant's stable, where he'd left Acheron, Seeker stopped a moment to examine a small yellow flower growing on straggly, leafless stems up the side of the stone wall by the path. It looked so delicate a thing, to withstand the north winds from which it had no shelter, yet it seemed to thrive. There was something defiant in it. He stooped to touch the dainty yellow head of one of the flowers, fearful it might break off under the pressure, but it was resilient. He took out his knife and carefully cut a thin green stem, thinking to go back and ask John Tradescant what it was. He'd like to plant it somewhere for his daughter.

As he nicked the stem, a voice behind him said, 'A gift, Captain?' He stood, motionless, almost afraid to turn around.

'Maria?'

Then he did turn, feeling such a rush of warmth to see her there he was hard put not to reach out and take hold of her. 'Maria,' he repeated. 'I didn't think to see you here today.'

'I hardly think you would. You have more to take up your time than considering my movements.' She looked at the stem in his hand. 'I hope Mistress Wells will like the token.'

He too looked down at it. 'It . . . it isn't for Dorcas.'

There. He'd said the name, an acknowledgement, and the very articulation seemed a barb to her. Her face fell, the defiance left her eyes and she looked away. 'Well, I must not keep you, at any rate. Excuse me, Captain . . .'

She turned and began to walk away, and he felt panic rising in him. 'Maria!' he called, loud enough that the two apprentices stopped in their digging again. Then more quietly as she stopped. 'Maria, please.'

He saw her shoulders set, and she turned around. 'What, Damian? What is it you want of me?'

'I . . .' What could he tell her – that he wanted to be another man and this to be another time? That he wanted to wipe out every mistake he had made, every wrong thing he had said, and just hold her, one more time? He hadn't the words for any of it, and stood helplessly with his hands by his side.

'Whatever you wanted of me, Damian,' she said, tears brimming in her eyes through her anger, 'you might have had, but you walked away because you did not want it.'

'But you wouldn't see me, Maria, before I went to York-shire. You must know that I tried.'

'And when you came back? How hard did you try when you came back? I looked for you, ran through the streets like a harlot trying to find you when word came that you were back in London. And I didn't find you because you had gone to Dorcas Wells!'

Seeker felt the stem drop from his fingers, felt nausea in his stomach. 'I didn't know,' he said, his voice hollow.

As she looked back at him some of the anger seemed to leave her face. 'And would it have mattered if you had?' she said at last, almost inaudible.

'Mattered? Oh, yes, Maria, it would have mattered.'

They stood looking at each other for a moment, one as hopeless as the other. Then Seeker knew that regardless of the consequences, he had to take this one chance. She was looking up at him and heedless of the gardener's boys or whoever else might observe them, he took a step towards her, reaching out his hand.

'Maria, you must know I could never—'

'Maria?'

Maria froze and Seeker let his hand drop. Thomas Faithly.

'Ah, Maria, there you are.' He came and stood very close to her, something proprietorial in his proximity.

Seeker looked at Maria and saw in her eyes all that he needed to know. He had left it too late. He took a step back. 'Faithly.'

'Captain.' Thomas Faithly's face took on a stony look. 'I trust you are not subjecting Mistress Ellingworth to harassment over her brother's publication. It can hardly trouble your great Cromwell that a young woman should sketch an item or two for the interest of her fellow city-dwellers.'

'No,' said Seeker, stepped back a pace now, 'I doubt that it would. Mistress Ellingworth is free to make her own choices. I'll bid you both good day.' Nodding briskly to Maria, he stepped past Thomas Faithly and walked away, and did not see her bend down to pick up the fallen stem of winter jasmine.

By the time Seeker was back in his office in Whitehall, he was still scarcely capable of putting together one coherent thought. If anyone had asked him, he would have had no recollection of riding away from Tradescant's, taking the ferry back across the river or leaving his horse at the stables, and it was only when he became conscious that his clerk was standing in front of him, a concerned look on his face and evidently repeating something he had already said, that he recalled himself properly to his surroundings.

'What?' he said.

His clerk, looking relieved, handed him the paper he was holding and explained again. 'It came an hour ago, from John Drake, the apothecary.'

'Oh, right,' said Seeker, forcing himself to focus on the business of the day. Before opening the note he said, 'Have a man on a fast horse sent down to Gravesend, with orders to open and inspect any packages sent this morning from Tradescant's garden in Lambeth for shipping north.' Then he sat behind his desk and opened the note.

Drake's script was so near-illegible that it might as well have been in code, but Seeker's eye was well-accustomed to it, and it didn't take him long to decipher the salient phrase. *Discreet enquiries amongst some alchemical friends suggest that the man calling himself 'Mr Mulberry' is, in fact, the mining engineer, Thomas Bushell.* In a moment Seeker was on his feet again, calling for Thomas Bushell's file to be brought to him.

Bushell was well over sixty years old. As a boy, he'd been page to Francis Bacon, and was reputed to have learned many scientific secrets from the Lord Chancellor. On the wrong side in the late wars, he'd had charge of the royal mines in Wales, and of the mint at Oxford under the King. He'd held Lundy Island against Parliament until 1647 and then been forced into hiding abroad over some treacherous publications for which he should have hanged. But the Protectorate needed Bushell: it needed his knowledge of mines, and his expertise. Four years ago, he'd given security for his good behaviour and made his peace with Parliament. And now he again held the lease of the Crown mines, this time from Oliver himself.

So why should Bushell, thus rehabilitated, hide his visits to John Evelyn's laboratory, and masquerade by another name? And what had he been doing at a disreputable dog-breeder's compound in the middle of Lambeth Marsh, in the middle of the night? Seeker was uneasy. Secretive behaviour by a known Royalist with a good knowledge of explosives could only suggest he was engaged upon something that, if discovered, might lose him his licences, his liberty, or possibly, his life. And then Seeker came to the last page of the intelligence record, which reported a rumour that had been circulating for a good long while: Thomas Bushell had never left England for the continent when he'd gone into hiding. He had lived, secretly and for years, in his own house, on Lambeth Marsh.

NINETEEN

A Supper at the Black Fox

Andrew Marvell was not quite sure how he had found himself in this situation, nor, indeed, what its precise nature was. He considered the matter as Thomas Faithly chattered all through the city on their way up to the Black Fox, throwing in the occasional response of affirmation or sympathy as Faithly's tone dipped or rose.

As Sir Thomas spoke, Marvell arranged the problem in his mind. He was on his way to take supper at the Black Fox, on Broad Street, at the invitation of Sir Thomas Faithly. This much was plain, and might appear to the casual observer to be simple enough. But whilst Marvell was often an observer, his interest was rarely casual, and he knew his situation was not simple in the least. Sir Thomas Faithly was in the pay of Thurloe's intelligence service, and under the control of Damian Seeker. Sir Thomas did not know that Marvell also acted, from time to time, in Thurloe's service and at the direction of Seeker. Neither did Sir Thomas know that Marvell had made his acquaintance at Lady Ranelagh's house on

Seeker's express instructions. And now Sir Thomas had, of his own volition, invited Marvell to accompany him to supper. Did Seeker know? Had he authorised it? If so, why had he not told Marvell of it himself? Those were the questions, and none of them were questions Marvell could ask Thomas Faithly.

Still, it was an opportunity, and not one that he should miss. 'I was very pleased to receive your note today, Sir Thomas. After your sudden departure from Lady Ranelagh's I feared I had said something to offend you.'

Faithly looked a little uneasy, just for a moment, but then put an arm around Marvell's shoulders. 'Oh, you know how it is, Marvell: one moment you are happily carousing with a friend, not a care in the world, and the next your stomach threatens revolution upon you, and you must dash for safety.' He raised his eyebrows and gritted his teeth in a grim smile. 'I'm afraid by the time my revolution was over, my suit was sadly besmirched, and I not fit for decent company.'

Marvell had seen men aplenty taken by the sudden need to vomit, and the look on Thomas Faithly's face had not been as theirs usually were. No, Faithly had seen something, across the crowded reception hall of Lady Ranelagh's house, that had drained the blood from his face and made him forget everything else around him. All Marvell could see in that direction was an old clockmaker, attending to the large bell-tower clock in the hall, which Marvell hadn't even noticed had stopped. When Faithly had got up suddenly and left Marvell, to cut through the swathes of people in that hall, he'd looked neither left nor right, but kept his gaze fixed on whatever it was that he'd seen. He hadn't staggered or stumbled, and he most certainly hadn't looked backwards, for if he had done, he would have seen Andrew Marvell following him. And Andrew Marvell had been gaining on him, and would have caught up with him, had it not been for the importunity of the Frenchwoman, Clémence Barguil, who'd insisted on having his opinion of some plant she intended for John Evelyn's garden, and a flustered Marvell had lost sight of Thomas Faithly.

But tonight, as they made their way to the Black Fox, Thomas Faithly was talking about something else, and Marvell resolved to be on his guard to notice things. To that end, he decided he should pay attention to what Sir Thomas was actually saying.

'. . . to dispel any doubts her brother might yet entertain.'

'Oh, I'm sorry, Sir Thomas. The racket of those butchers' boys has near enough rendered me deaf, and I have hardly caught a word.' They were almost at the end of Pentecost Lane, and the rowdiness of the apprentices of St Nicholas Shambles as they hurled abuse at each other whilst scrubbing down and closing up their masters' booths and shop-fronts was considerable.

'It's her brother,' Thomas Faithly repeated, more loudly this time. 'To accept me as a client is one thing, but to trust me with his sister quite another. I fear he still harbours some doubts about my loyalties and leanings. There are those amongst the Republicans who believe once for the King, always for the King.'

Marvell began to understand now that his own presence tonight had been secured in the hope of bolstering Sir Thomas's new-found Republican credentials.

'It is known that you are an associate of Mr Milton, and you have been tutor to Cromwell's own ward. I'm certain that to be able to present you as my friend will do a great deal to raise my credibility in the eyes of her brother.' Sir Thomas lowered his voice. 'Between you and me, Marvell, my Republican friends are few and far between, and it seems her brother was until lately of the more radical Republican persuasion, almost a Levelling tendency.'

Marvell's mouth pursed in distaste. 'You don't want to get caught up with the Levellers, Faithly. You'd have no hope of getting your family lands back with them.'

'No, no. But as I say, he has distanced himself from them of late, and taken a line more in accordance with the views of the government. You'll know his news-sheet, *The London Lark*, I'm sure.'

Marvell did not know it. New publications, weekly and twice-weekly news-sheets, were like weeds in the cracks of an old well – they appeared, flourished for a day or two, and then died and were seen no more, their seeds blown on the wind to land and spring up elsewhere. 'I've been out of the country a long time. I haven't yet had the chance to become familiar with all the new newsbooks.'

'Oh, you will come to know this one. I believe it will be

quite exceptional, and in quality much above the rest.' Sir Thomas leaned in closer. 'I have been helping Maria with her illustrations and . . .'

Maria. Marvell suddenly felt he had been hit in the stomach with a large stone. He stopped. 'Tell me again,' he said, 'what her brother's name is?'

'Ellingworth,' Thomas replied, as he stepped out of the way of a hawker with a basket of pies on her head. 'His name is Elias Ellingworth.'

Sir Thomas continued to talk of how he would reform his way of life, and how his intentions were nothing but honourable, all the way up to Broad Street. By the time they had passed the Drapers' Hall and the dancing yellow glow from the windows of the Black Fox was in view, Marvell felt sick to his stomach, his own appetite for the coming supper quite gone. When he followed Faithly through the door of the tavern, however, to be greeted by the sight of Damian Seeker's great hound stretched across the front of the hearth, it was all he could do not to turn and run.

Elias's sister was certainly pretty, but Lawrence was forming the opinion that she might be quite hard work. When the Ellingworths had arrived to collect him from Seeker's lodging at the back of the little house on Knight Ryder Street, his first reaction had been one of surprise that anyone should know where Seeker's fox-hole was, but he'd learned in York that it was futile to enquire into Seeker's personal business or motivations, so he didn't ask them. His next, almost simultaneous, thought was that they had come to enquire after his welfare, but he soon realised that he was mistaken, insofar as the sister was concerned, at least. Elias showed a natural concern for how he was feeling, whether he had slept, whether the burn from the rope on his neck gave him much pain, whether he could swallow, and so forth. His sister, however, once her tumultuous greeting from the dog was thoroughly acknowledged, appeared at first not to notice Lawrence at all. She spent a full minute looking around the small, spartan room, as if she had never been in anyone's bedchamber in her life before. She walked over to the mantelshelf, and let her hand hover a moment over the old, dead red rose that lay there, something Lawrence, even in the bewildered state in which he had woken earlier in the day, had found incongruous.

'I'd have tidied up a bit, thrown that out,' he said awkwardly, picking up some of his own outer garments that had fallen to the floor, 'but I thought he might be keeping it for something.'

'You shouldn't touch his things,' she'd said, as if he was a scullery boy unaccountably let loose in an earl's bedroom. 'Enough that he takes a risk by letting you stay here.'

Had his throat not still been giving him some difficulty, Lawrence might have treated her to his views on who had put whom at risk, but he merely put a hand to loosen the linen band around his neck a little and said nothing.

Seeker, it turned out, had sent Elias a message, or 'issued an instruction', as the lawyer put it, that as he was unexpectedly constrained to be elsewhere that night, Elias should assume the watch over Lawrence's safety.

'It would astonish the man, no doubt,' Elias said, 'to learn that other people have friends, private lives, do not sit at home to be at the beck and call of the state. I am already engaged tonight to take supper with a client, and fortuitously he is known to you too – in fact, Seeker had me bring you to the Turk's Head in order that you and he might meet – so I thought he could hardly complain if instead of staying here, watching you, I take you along there with me. If you think you are able for it, that is.'

Lawrence had not been sure whether he was able for it or not, and hadn't much felt inclined to abandon the quiet warmth and relative safety of the small room for the darkness and unnamed dangers of London's as yet unfamiliar streets. He'd been about to tell Ellingworth that he'd be just fine here for the night, alone with the dog, when the lawyer had added, 'It's not too far from here – the Black Fox, just up on Broad Street.'

And so here he was, ensconced in the most comfortable corner of the Black Fox, only the dog between him and the fire. Dorcas had insisted upon it, once she'd recovered herself. There had been an odd moment, just after they'd come in the door – Elias in front and Maria and the dog behind him – when a look of shock had registered on Dorcas's face. She'd greeted Elias, and then looked at him, and he supposed at Maria beyond, and it was as if she'd suddenly forgotten his name.

'Hello, Aunt,' he'd said, as a prompt.

Still she did not seem instantly to register that he was speaking. He was about to say it again when she recovered herself. 'Lawrence. And Mistress Ellingworth, is it not?'

Maria had given a 'yes' so muted Lawrence doubted Dorcas could even have heard it. The two women remained looking at each other, as if struck dumb. Elias was scanning the parlour for some sign of Thomas Faithly and appeared unaware of the strange encounter between the two women, but Lawrence found it peculiar to the point of unsettling. Yet London was not Yorkshire, he reminded himself. Maybe that was just the way things went here.

Dorcas eventually looked at him again, looked at him properly. 'Lawrence! Dear Lord, boy, what has befallen you?'

He started trying to explain, but his voice failed him and so Elias stepped in to fill in the details. By the end of it, Dorcas was almost trembling with fury, which she then vented on the group of travelling wool-merchants occupying the nook nearest the fire. 'You've had your supper and you've been nursing those tankards this last hour. Off with you, before I have you thrown out. My nephew needs to be in the warmth!'

The men had shot off without needing another telling, and Dorcas, still furious – at whom, precisely, Lawrence was uncertain – propelled him to the fire seat and demanded cushions. When she had got more of the detail of the attack from Elias, and assurances about Seeker's safety – Seeker again! – she calmed a little, and fussed gently around him as if she were in reality his aunt, or even his mother. Lawrence shuddered a moment at the idea of the kind of tavern his own mother would have run, and settled into his cushions.

'I should never have made you go down to Clifford's Inn,' she said. 'If you'd been lodged here, that fellow would never have got past Will Tucker.'

Lawrence thought it better not to tell her that it had been in the Black Fox, under the very eyes of her admittedly imposing cook, that his assailant had first spotted him. Dorcas had treated him with a decided air of mistrust since the first time he'd set foot in here, but now all that was gone, and he was determined not to do anything to endanger her new-found concern for him.

'Or if Seeker had been here,' she murmured.

Lawrence was beginning to realise that Seeker was at the Black Fox more often than might be expected, and to suspect that it was not only the presence there of his daughter that brought him to the tavern. 'Where's Manon?' he asked.

'Oh,' said Dorcas, looking around. 'She must be in the kitchen. I should warn her of what's happened. She'll not want to hear it first in front of all these people.'

When Dorcas left, Maria moved up the bench to sit next to him. She glared at him for an unnatural period of time, as if attempting to read a particularly troubling proclamation nailed to a church door. Thomas Faithly had yet to arrive, and Elias, having spotted an acquaintance at the other end of the taproom, had got up and gone over to greet the man, thus leaving Lawrence at this strange woman's mercy.

Lawrence shuffled forward a little. 'Mistress Ellingworth,' he began – there had been no indication from her that he might call her Maria. 'There, ahem – there appears to be something about me that troubles you.'

She looked at him even more closely. 'I can assure you, sir, there is not.'

'Right,' he said. But his head and throat were too sore to put up with such nonsense. 'Well, back on Knight Ryder Street, you looked at me as if I'd just broken into the place, and now you're staring at me as if you expect me at any moment to sprout horns. I'm new to these parts, so you'll excuse me if I'm not familiar with what passes for manners round here.'

Maria's look grew even more indignant. 'Are you all like that?'

'Who? Like what?'

'From the north. Ill-mannered. You, Seeker—'

Lawrence cut in. 'Aw, now, I hope you're not going to class me along with Seeker. I mean, he's not so bad, I suppose, once you get to know him a bit, but . . .'

This seemed to Lawrence to anger her all the more. He was at a loss, and in his exasperation abandoned all attempts at subtlety. 'What is *wrong* with you, woman? What in the name of all that's holy have I done?'

'Done?' she said. 'First, I am told you are my brother's pupil. Next I am informed that you are mixed up with dangerous assassins, who have pursued you almost to his very rooms at Lincoln's Inn and that you are presently hiding out in Damian Seeker's own lodging. And now, at last, you announce yourself to be the nephew of Dorcas Wells.'

Lawrence was saved from further uncomfortable inter-rogation by the arrival of Thomas Faithly, resplendent in a beautifully cut black velvet suit with pristine Flemish lace at collar and cuff. Lurking behind Faithly was another, less well-dressed man. On this other man's slightly pudgy face was a look of alarm, which seemed to be directed mainly at Seeker's dog. Lawrence sighed. It was going to be a long night.

But, half an hour later, despite his painful throat, Law-rence and the man with the pudgy face, who, it transpired, hailed from Hull, were thoroughly enjoying exchanging tales of mutual acquaintance and avoiding any too detailed mention of their connection to Damian Seeker. That this Andrew Marvell knew Seeker had become evident in the course of their conversation. That he didn't wish to elab-orate on the nature of their acquaintance struck Lawrence as being entirely sensible. Thomas Faithly's concern after hearing of Lawrence's experience was, to Lawrence, a reassuring reminder of home. But there was more than fellow-feeling in it – Sir Thomas appeared as eager as Seeker had been for a description of the assailant, and seemed particularly relieved that there had been only one.

After his experience of the night before, Lawrence was

finding Thomas Faithly's supper quite convivial. Whatever Dorcas had put in the warm spiced caudle she'd insisted he take for his throat, it was not very far on in the evening that he felt able to confide in Marvell his doubts about their friend Thomas Faithly's romantic choice.

'I mean, she's a very fine-looking woman, of course. If that's where your taste runs – dark eyes and ebony locks . . .'

'Engines more keen than ever yet adorned a tyrant's cabinet,' murmured Marvell.

'What?' said Lawrence.

'Oh, nothing of consequence, I assure you. So you are not seduced by such charms? You prefer a fairer blush?'

'Ah, well,' said Lawrence, not knowing what to say and looking down at his tankard.

Marvell leaned a little closer. 'Your feelings tend elsewhere?'

Lawrence caught sight of Manon appearing from the kitchen. 'What, me? No, no time for all that. Never mind me, though. What are we going to do about Sir Thomas? Look at him: he's entranced. He'll regret it, I'm certain of it.'

Marvell nodded in deep agreement. 'But who is to tell him? I mean, we are not even supposed to *know*. Yet if Seeker should get wind of it . . .'

Lawrence was about to ask what on earth it could have to do with Damian Seeker, when Marvell said, 'Ah, here she is, the green girl.' Manon was in a blue gown Lawrence hadn't seen her wear before, with plain white tucker and cuffs. Her hair hung perfectly, white blonde from beneath her cap, coming almost to the small of her back.

'Green girl?' queried Lawrence.

Marvell wrinkled his brow. 'One – that is untouched by the cares and corruptions of life. One who is closer still, to another, purer, world.' He nodded towards Manon. 'That girl.'

Manon approached their table and had no interest in Lawrence's attempted introductions, such was her concern about the attack on him. Elias, who knew her from his previous visits to the Black Fox, took a moment to reassure her about her 'brother's' safety. 'Damian Seeker, you see, takes an interest in it, and if Seeker's for you, you have no need to fear.'

Manon didn't appear to be listening to him. Her eyes never left Lawrence's. 'What if you had been killed?'

He tried to smile at her. 'I wasn't though, Manon. It's like Elias says, the captain was there, and no real harm came to me.'

'But he can't always be there, can he?'

'If only,' said Thomas Faithly. 'To get rid of the man would be the trick.'

This was greeted by a snort of amusement as Elias almost choked on his wine, a nervous laugh from Marvell and such a look from Manon that Lawrence wondered they did not all transform into pillars of salt. Lawrence had never seen her look so like her father as she did at that moment. Something in it seemed to suddenly chill the air, and the rest of the party fell silent. Only Maria, who was now staring at Manon, looked as if she might say something. She started to, but it was as though her tongue wasn't working right, or whatever she'd thought she was going to say died somehow on her lips.

'You'd best get back to the kitchen, Manon,' Lawrence said, glancing towards Maria. 'Aunt Dorcas will be needing you there.' Manon nodded, as if she understood how close she might just have come to revealing herself. But as she picked up Lawrence's empty trencher, Maria put her hands on Manon's wrist. The attention of the others round the table was now taken up by a man who had sat down on the organ stool, and commenced a hearty rendition of 'Old England Grown New', in which he was joined by several of Dorcas's other patrons.

'You remind me of someone,' Maria said, searching the girl's face.

Manon's eyes darted towards Lawrence for help.

'Oh, she's always getting that, my little sister. Just one of those faces that looks like lots of other faces. You go off now, Manon.'

But still Maria wouldn't move her hand from Manon's wrist. 'Are you certain Mistress Wells is not your mother?'

'I should think we should know our own mother,' said Lawrence, his voice rising in irritation.

But Maria wasn't looking at Lawrence. 'And your father? Who is your father?'

Discreetly, Lawrence put his hand, covered by his napkin,

over Maria's and with a very firm grip removed it from Manon's wrist. 'Go back to the kitchen, Manon,' he said, never taking his eyes from Maria's.

Manon did so, quickly. She looked frightened. When she had disappeared through the door, Lawrence said, 'I'll thank you not to meddle in my family's affairs again.'

'She's not your sister,' said Maria.

'What?' said Lawrence.

'She's not your sister. Not your full sister, at any rate. You may have shared a mother, I don't know, but I am certain that you are not Damian Seeker's son.'

The others had now joined in with the singing. Lawrence leaned towards Maria and spoke quietly, so that none but she would hear.

'I don't know what your problem with me is, or with Dorcas. And I don't know why you are quite so prickly about anything you imagine to be to do with Damian Seeker, but if you have any feeling for him – and I'm beginning to suspect you have – you'll say not one more word about Manon. About *my sister*.'

Maria looked down at her wrist and Lawrence realised he was squeezing it more tightly than he'd intended to. He quickly released it with a mumbled apology.

The expression on her face was different now. The hostility was gone. 'I'll say nothing,' she said at last. 'But he's not *your* father, is he?'

Lawrence sighed and shook his head. 'No.'

The song came to an end, to tumultuous applause.

The face Thomas Faithly now turned towards Maria was glowing with enthusiasm, his eyes bright and his smile such as would have swept any other woman out of the clutches of any other man. And Maria was trying to smile back, Lawrence could see that. She was trying, but her eyes looked as if they had filled with tears. As Sir Thomas demanded another song, Lawrence leaned towards Andrew Marvell. 'Elias Ellingworth's sister,' he said.

'Yes?' said Marvell rather warily.

'She's not – engaged elsewhere?'

Marvell swallowed and spent some time brushing crumbs from the table in front of him onto the floor. 'Not that I'm aware.'

'It's just, well, she seems to take a bit more interest than is natural in Damian Seeker.'

Marvell opened wide his eyes, his mouth. Closed his mouth and raised his eyebrows. Took in a great breath. 'Oh dear,' he said, once he had exhaled again. 'Oh dear.'

Lawrence felt exhausted now, and wondered whether Elias might agree to just leaving him at the Black Fox, where Dorcas had made it clear he would have a safely guarded bed for the night. He was about to suggest it when a young boy came bursting through the door of the inn, scanning quickly about him, until his eye fell on Thomas Faithly.

'Sir Thomas!' he said, pressing through the gathered patrons to reach him.

'Yes?' said Sir Thomas, clearly with no idea who the child was.

'This come for you, to the Tobacco Pipes. Mother said I was to take it up here to you straight away.'

Sir Thomas took a coin from his pouch and thrust it into the child's hand whilst taking from it the letter clutched there. 'Wait!' he ordered the boy, tearing open the seal. He read the contents once, then again, a look of confusion overtaking his face.

'When did this arrive?' he said, looking up at last. His face had paled and all trace of his former jollity was gone.

'Not more than half an hour ago. Mother said I was to take it to you, and I run nearly all the way.'

'All right then, you get home,' said Sir Thomas, absent-mindedly giving the boy another coin from his pouch.

'What is it?' asked Elias. 'Is there trouble?'

'Ah, no. No, not trouble. Just something I must attend to – I think our friend Ingolby too.'

Lawrence felt himself groan, and Elias protested vigorously. 'It'd be more than my life's worth, if Seeker found out.'

'I will square it with Captain Seeker,' Sir Thomas replied, adding quietly, 'More than mine's worth, if we don't go.'

And then Lawrence knew, without being told, what the note was about. 'From Southwark?' he asked.

Sir Thomas nodded. And so that was it then, their breeder of fighting dogs had found what they'd told him they were looking for. Ingolby checked in a hidden fold of his doublet for the purse of Seeker's – or the state's – money, which he'd had the presence of mind to take from Knight Ryder Street with him, and reached for his hat.

It took a few minutes to negotiate the protests of the others that Lawrence was not fit to go, and Sir Thomas himself, who appeared uncharacteristically distracted by the note, at one point seemed on the verge of joining in their protest, but Lawrence was insistent.

'Where?' he said to Sir Thomas as he followed him out of the Black Fox and into the street, leaving their bewildered supper companions behind them.

'Lambeth Marsh,' said Faithly, 'exactly half a mile due south of the Bear Garden.'

TWENTY

On Lambeth Marsh

They were hardly halfway over London Bridge when Thomas Faithly pulled up. 'No, this is wrong. You are not fit for this. I can do this alone.'

'What? You think I'm going to risk Seeker finding out I just handed his purse over to you? Be lucky if I ever saw you again.' Lawrence could think of a good few places he'd rather be going on a night like this than Lambeth Marsh, but he'd taken a liking to Thomas Faithly, and wasn't inclined to let him face whatever they were about to face on his own. Nevertheless, that Faithly surname was weighted with distrust, and Lawrence was not altogether convinced Sir Thomas's unease and eagerness to get rid of him were entirely born of a concern for his health. 'I'll be fine,' he said, giving his neck an involuntary rub. 'I doubt they'll be asking me to sing, any road. And these horses are pretty docile beasts – they won't give us much bother.'

Lawrence wondered if perhaps Sir Thomas's nerve was going, faced, as they were now, with the prospect of meeting the individuals who had control of the bear, and who had not shrunk from chaining Joseph Grindle to a wall to meet his horrific death. Before, their search for the bear's handlers had had an air of adventure to it, but now it was becoming all too real.

'I've never seen one,' he said to Sir Thomas.

'What – a bear?'

'Aye. Bess didn't hold with travelling circuses and the like.'

'I'll bet she didn't!' said Sir Thomas with a laugh. 'Bess didn't hold with much.' It was a boon to Lawrence, despite the odd circumstances of their association down here in London, to have someone from home to talk to sometimes, someone who'd known the family that had taken him in, and the old Puritan woman who'd brought him up.

'I had the back of her hand across my ear more than once,' said Sir Thomas. 'What a woman! The Puritans wouldn't have needed a major-general in the north, if only they'd put Bess Pullan in charge.'

But Bess was dead now, like her husband long before her. Her ward, who had been like a sister to Lawrence, was dead too, and Matthew, the Pullans' son, could manage his life well enough without Lawrence, whatever Matthew might say different. The 'home' Lawrence thought of was no more real now than was the one Thomas Faithly dreamed of getting back. And so they were natural companions for one another, he and Sir Thomas.

'Have you ever seen one?'

'In Germany, Spain, France – all on the ends of chains

and rings on their noses, dancing to pipes or mauling a hound twice the size of that one.' He pointed to Seeker's dog, who was lolloping along beside Lawrence's horse.

'Well, I doubt the one that savaged Joseph Grindle danced much.'

'Joseph Grindle – I'd forgotten the name.'

Lawrence regarded Sir Thomas with disbelief. Was this the difference that birth and wealth had made between them, that Joseph Grindle's lack of them were enough that Thomas Faithly couldn't even bother to remember his name? He wondered about Joseph Grindle too, and the kind of life that could end up like that. After a moment he said, 'I still think we should have waited till we heard back from him – Seeker. He was quite insistent that we weren't to set out to encounter these people without him.'

Thomas shook his head. 'No time. Too much time was lost already, by my landlady's boy having to come up to the Black Fox to find me.'

'We should have sent back a message to him all the same,' said Lawrence. 'He'll skin us when he finds out.'

Sir Thomas laughed. 'You're too much the lawyer already, Lawrence. The stakes will have altered by then. When you've lived the life I have, you learn to think on your feet, take your chance when it comes.'

Lawrence thought that if he'd lived the life Sir Thomas had – picked the wrong side in the Civil War, been forced into nine years of exile, been thrown into the Tower of London when he'd dared to show his face back home – he'd have been a deal less inclined to hand out advice. But that was the gentry for you, and Lawrence had long been of the view that most of them were idiots.

'Besides,' Sir Thomas continued, 'tonight will just be about the arrangements for the fight, between that monstrous hound we bought the other night, and their own ursine prize-fighter. It's the time and place arranged for *that* event that Seeker will want to know.'

'It'd better be,' said Lawrence. 'And they'd better not get any ideas about this one.' Despite Lawrence's best efforts, Seeker's dog had refused to remain at the Black Fox, to be returned to Seeker's lodgings by Elias and Maria as he'd suggested.

Elias had argued vigorously with Thomas Faithly too, that Lawrence was in no fit state to go anywhere but to his bed. 'If Seeker thinks you are in need of its protection,' he said, 'then you are quite assuredly in need of its protection. He values that hound more than most men do their wives. Should you choose to wander the streets of London tonight without it, I can only imagine it is because you do not wish to see another morning.'

And so, although neither had wanted to, Thomas and Lawrence had taken the dog with them.

The streets of Southwark were not as empty as they should have been at that hour of the night, and the taverns and brothels facing the water and the alleyways leading off from it were not empty at all. The major-generals still had a deal of work to do south of the river.

'I like an adventure as well as the next man,' Sir Thomas

was saying, 'but this business of Seeker's has set back my wooing, and I could see tonight that I still have much work to do upon it. Maria paid me very little attention.'

Lawrence went over in his head again what Marvell had told him just before the message for Sir Thomas had arrived, and how he might best communicate the import of it. There was no easy way to say it.

'I think you'd do best to set back your wooing yourself. Set it right back – in fact, forget about it. I think you must give up Maria Ellingworth.'

'Give her up? Lawrence, what kind of man would I be to give up a woman like that for lack of a little encouragement? Maria will be the making of me, of my future, in this new England. I just need to try harder to convince her that I'm—'

'It's not a question of convincing her, Sir Thomas,' Lawrence broke in, 'but I'd counsel you, for your own sake – give it up for a very bad idea.'

Thomas's astonishment was written over his face. 'On what grounds? Has her brother said something to you?'

'Her brother? He has said nothing, although it might have saved some grief if he had. No, it's Andrew Marvell that told me.'

'Told you what?'

Lawrence heaved a great sigh, that hurt his throat as it passed. 'About Maria Ellingworth,' he said. 'And Damian Seeker.'

★

The damp from the river clung to the back of Thomas Faithly's neck and seemed to seep through his gloves to his fingers. He couldn't remember when last he had felt so cold. He had been cold of course, very cold, many times in his life before now. When he'd joined with Montrose's forces had possibly been the worst time, when they'd marched across Scotland through snowbound mountain passes that surely had never been meant for the foot of man. There had been the time, too, when he'd been tossed from a small rowboat into the twenty-foot waves of the Irish Sea. How he'd been saved then, God only knew. But never had he felt as cold as he did now, and the chill was at his very centre.

Since the day he had met her he had built such castles in the air that an army could not have taken them. It had seemed plainer to him than almost anything in his life before: this business for Seeker would be finished and he would be granted leave to return to Yorkshire. Surely he could spy as easily for the government there as he could in London? Maria would come north with him, with her brother's blessing or without, and he would live once more the life of a proper Englishman. The King's cause was finished, and this was Cromwell's England now, but it could be Thomas Faithly's England too. Thus had Sir Thomas's thoughts run.

But if an army couldn't have taken that castle in the air, six words from Lawrence Ingolby had brought it crashing down around him. Thomas's mind went to the day he had come upon them at Tradescant's, Seeker and Maria, and he saw it all now with different eyes. He didn't press Lawrence for any more details; he knew that it was true. His memory raced over Maria's every gesture. She had, somehow, never been completely with him, even when there was no other living soul in the room. He had thought perhaps there was a lost love, hoped for a dead love. Never in his wildest fears had he considered it might be Damian Seeker.

Lawrence was still talking. 'It's what got Seeker sent north last year, apparently. To get him away from her.'

'And it's not over between them.' Thomas said it as a statement, not a question.

'Who knows? But Marvell senses – unfinished business. Give her up, Thomas. You don't want to come between Damian Seeker and his unfinished business.'

They rode on in silence after that, the sound of their horses' hooves their only accompaniment as they made their careful progress through the darkness and mists of the marsh. It wasn't too long until they caught the first glimpses of the breeding kennel where they had bought the hound. Further away were the occasional glints of light from other dwellings. If anything else was moving on the marsh tonight, Thomas couldn't see it, and all he could hear, save the sounds of their own progress, was a sort of heavy seeping, as if something large and ungodly waited, dormant, in the marsh itself.

Thomas wondered what would happen should he decide to wheel around, speed his horse back towards the river and down to Deptford, and then on to Gravesend.

Lawrence Ingolby would have no chance of catching him, even should he want to. Sir Thomas had made sure that he had the better horse, and he knew that at a gallop he would be a better rider than the law student anyway. And there would be little anyone else could do about it. Thomas could be away in a boat and off to the continent before Damian Seeker even knew he was gone. But then what? Back to the Stuarts to tell them that what they dreamed of would never be, and would hardly be worth the having anyway?

And yet, there was what he thought he had seen at Lady Ranelagh's, and there was the handwriting of the note he'd received tonight. He might be mistaken in it, but he didn't think so. It was not the hand of a dog-breeder, but of one he knew well that had written that note. In the noise and light of the Black Fox, he had not been sure of it, but with every step of his horse further out onto the marsh he became more certain . . . Sir Thomas did not wheel around. Perhaps there was just the chance of one more adventure, of a final redemption, to come. He followed carefully in Lawrence Ingolby's wake and waited.

It came soon enough, when they were about halfway between Bankside and Lambeth, almost at the middle of the marsh and close to the lights of the breeding kennel. It was the dog that heard them first – heard the other dogs, and then the horses. By the time Seeker's hound had dropped on his haunches and started to growl, they could hear it plainly themselves, the determined yelping, the thunder of hooves, coming straight for them. Docile or not, Lawrence had spun his horse round and geed it towards Bankside before Thomas had even had time to think properly.

'Come on, Sir Thomas. Our new friends are nothing of the sort. Come now, if you don't want to be dog-fodder!'

Still Thomas hesitated. The riders were coming closer now. There was something about the way the lead rider sat his horse . . .

'Sir Thomas!' Lawrence yelled. But there was no time now, he'd left it too late. Thomas's horse might be the better of the two but it scared the more easily. Thomas tried to turn it, half-tried, but he could feel the animal tense beneath him, at the barking of the dogs. Thomas saw now that they were loose and running ahead of the four oncoming riders. He knew it was going to happen even as it happened, but he was powerless to stop it. The horse reared up in panic, screaming as terrified horses in battle scream. He tried desperately to master it, to calm it, as its hooves flailed in the air. What felt like a struggle minutes long must, in reality, have lasted only a few seconds, for the next Sir Thomas knew, he was on the ground, rolling away from the flailing hooves, and the next after that there were two massive paws on his chest, and a set of teeth inches from his face, ready at any moment to rip it off.

Thomas dared not take his eyes away from those of the snarling dog, but he knew somehow that Lawrence had turned back, to try to help him. He opened his mouth to shout to Lawrence to go, but the moment he did so the beast above him snarled more menacingly and ripped a claw across his face as if to shut him up. One of the riders shouted to another to call the animal off. The pain seared like four blades of steel ripping through the flesh of his cheek, but in the midst of it he knew that it had missed his eye. Thank God, it had missed his eye. There was a terrible whinnying and snarling and thud and then worse snarling behind him, but he dared not look back. Dear God, Lawrence, why didn't you run? he thought, as he heard his companion's incoherent shouts. But then Thomas heard a voice, the breeder's, call off the mastiff that had him under its claws, and he felt himself dragged up by the shoulders and lifted on to the back of a horse that was not the one he had come on. He gripped the belt of the rider in front of him. To struggle now would be death – his flesh ripped from his bones or those bones crushed beneath the stamping hooves of the horses.

He managed to summon up the voice to shout, 'Lawrence, go!' but he knew, as he turned his shredded face to look behind him, that Lawrence could not go. All he could see by the light of their assailants' torches was a writhing shape, a snarling mass of vicious mastiffs, jaws gaping and claws gouging, and Lawrence's riderless horse galloping away. Somewhere in the middle of it all, as the rider he held fast to sped away across the darkness of the marsh, he could hear Lawrence's cries, and the desperate barking and yowling of Seeker's dog.

TWENTY-ONE

Mr Mulberry

It was an old two-storeyed wooden-framed house set behind a high wall towards the north-west edges of the marsh. The roof was well tiled, with three octagonal chimneys at its centre. The iron gates and railings surrounding the property were a little rusted, as if it were not inhabited. Ivy clambered over wall and gateposts and crept up around the base of a stone statue – some Roman goddess, Seeker supposed – in the middle of the lawn to their left. To the right, there was a pond, with a fountain at its centre, but the fountain did not run. The narrow-mullioned windows were darkened, not a hint of light glinting in their diamond panes. Grass and weeds grew on the path leading to the main door. But Seeker knew the place was not, in fact, neglected, not abandoned, whatever its inhabitant might wish any who wandered this way to think. A wisp of smoke not quite smothered drifted into the night air from one of the three chimneys, and through a narrow gateway to the side of the house he could see a well-kept path leading to orchard walks behind.

'This is definitely the place?' asked Proctor.

Seeker nodded. It was the house of Thomas Bushell, the banished Royalist mining engineer and alchemist who'd never actually left, but instead hidden here, until Cromwell had called him home to put his skills to the use of the Commonwealth.

'So why keep this place secret? Why go out under the guise of "Mulberry"?'

'Because he's up to something that would have him right back out of favour. Something to do with a bear that should have been shot and wasn't, and I'm determined to find out what it is.'

'Right,' said Proctor, who'd served under Seeker long enough to know what came next. 'Better get started then.'

He beckoned to two of the men they'd brought with them to follow them down the path to the front door. The door-hood was supported by corbels carved into the shape of men, poised as if ready to take flight. Something in the look of them put Seeker in mind of Charles I, who'd taken flight too late. The door itself was sturdy, moulded and ribbed, good workmanship. It had probably hung there fifty years. It was a shame to damage it. The long strap hinges were newer, well-kept, no sign of rust. But there wasn't time to unhook them from the door jamb. 'There,' he said, indicating to the two men with the short battering ram where the door would give most easily, and with least damage. The foremost of the two nodded. Seeker and Proctor stepped back and then the men swung the ram with all their force. The sound of the latch inside splintering from door and jamb was accompanied by shrieks from a chicken coop somewhere around the back, and the hissing of a black cat as it shot out of the gaping doorway and past them in to the night.

Inside, all was darkness until he and Proctor went in with their torches. Seeker set his up in a bracket on the wall and surveyed the partially illuminated room. A typical gentleman's hall with good oak dining table and chairs, and settles bedecked with embroidered silk cushions at either side of a recently quenched fire. The hangings on the wall were very old, if Seeker was any judge of arras. A dresser at the far wall held good pewter, and silver too. Near one end of the table was a large salt, and the evidence of an unfinished meal.

'Someone left in a hurry, said Proctor.

'I doubt it,' said Seeker. Somewhere, he could hear someone trying not to move, someone trying to cover their own breathing. He stood stock-still a moment, listening, and then strode quickly to a door in the corner of the room, wrenching it open. Backed into the far corner of the kitchen, and brandishing a long-handled bird-roaster, whose lethal-looking red-hot tines had lately been planted in the embers of the cooking hearth, was an elderly woman. The expression on her face left Seeker in no doubt that should he come any closer, she would lance him like a joint of meat.

'Easy, Grandmother,' he said, holding up a cautious hand.

'I'm not here for you. It's your master I'm looking for. Where is he?'

The old woman said nothing, but merely scowled the more, and jabbed the tines of her roasting fork in his direction.

'All right then,' he said, calling one of Proctor's men in to watch her. 'I'll find him myself.' He was about to go back into the main body of the house when he noticed the old woman was not only brandishing her weapon, but backed up against a small door in the corner of the room. 'Out of the way,' he said, only provoking another thrust of her fork. Seeker sighed and reached for the handle of a broom set against the wall near him. He'd done this a hundred times, a thousand maybe, in drills. The disarming of the old woman took less time than the hefting of a bale of hay, though the process was noisier. She was still squawking when he broke the lock on the door she'd been so carefully guarding.

This room was larger even than Bushell's hall. Like a barn, almost, but brought into other uses than had first been intended, the floor beaten but the walls dressed as if for the inside of the house. One wall was almost entirely lined with books, two others were covered in charts – not maps, but astronomical and scientific charts – and the fourth supported shelves stacked with more liquids, powders, plants and metals than would have filled John Drake's apothecary five times over. A table ran down the centre of the room, and on it were all manner of stilling apparatuses, small stoves, spouted alembics, flasks and other vessels of peculiar shape and size. A larger stove was positioned at one end of the table, and at the far end of the room stood not one, but three brick furnaces, varying in size. A large stack of wood for burning dried near the furnaces. No doubt this was the place in which Bushell and his cronies conducted their experiments. Seeker put a hand out towards the nearest furnace and felt the warmth. 'He's about some-where,' he said.

It was in the attics that they finally found him, but when Proctor's light began to illuminate the long room under the eaves of Bushell's house, Seeker thought he had descended rather to Hades. It was a gallery, such as he had seen before in wealthy men's houses, and at the same time was nothing like he had seen anywhere else. Black drapes were suspended from the rafters and hung in swags over the one small window, set in the far gable end. Beneath the window was a bed, also draped in black. Seeker went cautiously towards it. It was empty, but painted on the wall just above it, as if in fact lying on it, was a dead man, his bones almost poking through taut and luminous flesh. That the man was meant to have died in torment of the soul was very clear. Seeker looked at it longer than he should have done then turned away.

'What's up that end?' he said.

'What we're looking for,' said Proctor.

Seeker didn't know what he was looking at to start with. His first thought was that someone had erected a tomb inside the room. A Gothic arch, intricately carved like something in a Romish chapel, and painted black, took up most of the opposing gable wall. The light from Proctor's torch this time showed not a dead man, but a skeleton, and as Seeker became aware of it, he realised that there were death's heads positioned all around the room. But he didn't pay much attention to them, because beneath the archway was a couch, on which a man was sitting, watching them with an amused detachment. This man was very much alive. Seeker knew him from descriptions given by Thomas Faithly and John Drake: well made, about ten years older than he looks, ruddy of face with a nose like a hawk. 'A hawk that would charm the birds from the trees, before devouring their nests,' Drake had said. The man was looking at them as if considering whether or not to buy them.

'Thomas Bushell,' said Seeker.

'I cannot deny it,' said Bushell. 'And you, I imagine – from the delicacy of your entry, and what I have heard of your, ahem, form – are Captain Seeker.'

'Why are you hiding up here?'

Bushell raised his eyebrows as if extremely surprised by the question. 'Captain, I can assure you, I am not hiding. I am sitting in my own house. Giving thanks for my many blessings, and contemplating my mortality, like any honest Englishman.'

Seeker jerked a thumb towards the image at the other end of the room. 'What kind of honest Englishman has something like that on his wall, or has his housekeeper threaten the Lord Protector's soldiers with heated roasting forks?'

'Perhaps the kind who has encountered Cromwell's soldiers before,' said Bushell, the charm in his voice barely concealing the hostility underneath. 'What are you doing in my house, Seeker?'

This was better. Seeker had no desire to be led through the dusky labyrinth of this man's mind. Straight out with it was the best way. 'First, you can tell me why you've been going about by the name of Mulberry.'

Seeker could see that this question surprised and somewhat displeased Bushell. 'You refer to my visits to Mr Evelyn's house, I think.'

'Amongst other places,' said Seeker.

Bushell didn't much like that, either. 'I hide my identity on certain occasions when I am not entirely certain of the company I'm in. I was on the late King's side in the war, and many of your persuasion choose not to forget it. Despite being in the Lord Protector's favour, I know I'm not trusted. I would not have the opprobrium attaching to me attach itself to friends who are innocent of any malice towards the state.'

Seeker gave a dismissive grunt. 'Same could be said for half of England. We'll leave Mr Evelyn aside for now. What were you doing at the dog-breeder's out on the marsh three nights ago?'

Seeker could see that for all his bravado, Bushell had not expected this.

'Breeder's? I-I don't know what—'

'You were seen,' cut in Seeker, 'so don't waste my time. The man breeds dogs for illegal fighting. You were seen arriving there, with a cart. What, exactly, were you doing there?'

Bushell's mind was obviously working for an explanation that would satisfy, no doubt constructing a thing of brilliance with which to put off the unlettered soldier. Seeker decided a prompt was required. 'Tell me what you know of the bear.'

Now the man's ruddy face blanched. His eyes darted from side to side in one last attempt to extricate himself by obfuscation, but then Seeker saw the sinking of the chest, the lowering of the eyes, those gestures he had come to recognise as preceding someone deciding to tell the truth.

'I never saw it,' he said.

'But you know of it,' said Seeker.

Bushell nodded. 'I had heard of it.'

'Who from?'

Bushell shrugged. 'Rumours had begun to circulate amongst my alchemical associates that one of the Bankside bears had escaped Colonel Pride's firing squad, but no one knew where it was to be found.'

Seeker frowned. 'But why should you care? What interests could alchemists have in an animal like that?'

Some of the confidence returned to Bushell. 'Oh, there is little in this world that is not of interest to the man of science, and there is much that can be learned from the study and observation of an animal carcass. But as to bears, it is believed that their bile has many curative properties, and it is in this in particular that I was interested.'

'Their bile?' said Seeker, with some disgust. 'And how did you propose to get hold of that?'

'Well,' said Bushell, becoming more animated by the minute, 'it is, as you know, stored in the gall bladder. It can be obtained by the removal of the gall bladder from the animal's carcass. *However*, I am very interested in the possibility that it might be milked from a living animal, you see . . .'

But Seeker held up a hand to stop him. 'How did you propose to get hold of the beast?'

'Ah, now that was the difficulty. It took several months of enquiry, in some very dark places, I might add, before I discovered that it was housed not a mile from me, with a breeder on the marsh.'

Seeker and Proctor exchanged looks. 'The one you were seen arriving at the other night.'

Bushell nodded. 'The breeder was very wary at first. He didn't appear at all for our first arranged meeting, and on the second occasion I had to endure the spectacle of watching the poor beast tear some dogs to pieces before he was convinced that my interest was genuine. A good deal of money it cost me, just to attend those fights.'

'He was baiting it?'

'Yes. After the closing of the Bear Garden last year, that

animal has become very valuable – there are plenty of people who will pay good money to watch it fight.'

'So what happened, once he realised you weren't there to report him?'

'We made a bargain. I was to have access to the animal, for one week – at a quite scandalous price, I might add – in which to conduct my experiments. I was also to furnish him with sedative preparations for use when the beast was being transported. Afterwards I was to return the animal to the breeder's property.'

'And you did this?'

Bushell shook his head. 'I was to have collected the animal from the place on the marsh that night – the one when I was evidently seen. But when I got there, the breeder told me not only that the animal had been moved elsewhere – somewhere north of the river, I believe – but that he had changed his mind. Another client had offered him a higher price.'

'For what purpose?

'I didn't ask, but I doubt it was to further the ends of science. I was greatly disappointed and not a little angry, but there is not much you can do when the object of your anger has a pack of snarling mastiffs at his back. It was a great disappointment to my scientific friends. Several of them had lent me money to facilitate the bargain.'

Seeker had no interest in Bushell's financial dealings, but he was interested in Bushell's friends. 'Sergeant Proctor, would you be good enough to go back down those stairs and fetch up some of the paper, pen and ink in that first bedchamber. Mr Bushell here's going to write me down a list of those friends of his, the ones he told about that bear.'

It was nearing midnight when they finally left Bushell's house, having made a thorough examination of grounds and outbuildings as well. They should have been tired, all six of them, but they weren't. Proctor's men were hand-picked, and they wouldn't tire until he told them to. Seeker himself was invigorated: at last he was making some progress in the hunt for the evil individual who had left Joseph Grindle chained in a shed on Bankside, to be mauled to death by a tormented bear. Within an hour that dog-breeder would be his prisoner. Within two, the man would be telling him who he'd sold that bear to.

Bushell's dark sentinel of a house receded into nothingness behind them. The mist on the marsh hadn't cleared at all. Had Seeker not seen the place once or twice ablaze with flowers and alive with dragonflies and wildfowl on a bright summer's day, he would wonder if the mist ever did lift. The horses placed their feet carefully as they worked their way across the paths towards the breeder's compound. Their ears were pricked as carefully as were those of Seeker and Proctor. It was the kind of night and place where wickedness might take its chance and be away before dawn.

The first thing was a sudden alteration in the rhythm of Seeker's horse beneath him, a stutter and then a soft whinny. The next was a huge shape leaping towards him out of the mist, only to come to a halt at his horse's side and begin jumping and barking dementedly. One of Proctor's men already had his horse-axe off his belt and was raising it into the air when another shouted, 'Stop! It's the captain's dog.'

Seeker leapt down from his horse to try to calm the animal. He had a moment of confusion, in the darkness, before he knew the wetness beneath his hand as he smoothed the dog's flank was not moisture from the air, but blood from the animal's side. Its ear, too, was torn and bleeding profusely.

A deep groan went through Seeker. 'What's happened to you, boy?' He looked around him as if expecting a response. 'Who's done this?'

Proctor too was now down off his horse and examining the agitated animal. 'Dog fight,' he said. He scanned a wound by the spread of his hand. 'Mastiff.'

Seeker felt more anger than he thought he could control. He started to undo his riding cloak, but one of the other soldiers was already there, by the dog's side, trying to put his own round it. The dog shook him off and continued to bark relentlessly at Seeker.

'Lead my horse,' said Seeker to the man with the cloak. 'All right, boy, show me.'

The dog, a leg clearly injured, lurched ahead, and Seeker, his torch raised, jogged along to keep up with him. Proctor and the others followed with the horses, their torches sweeping the ground around them. It didn't take long, ten minutes at most, and Seeker wasn't even sure what direction they'd gone in, but suddenly the dog had disappeared off the path and run over squelching mud to stand and bark at the edge of a shallow pool. Seeker followed, the mud sucking at his boots in a way that took him back over ten years, to the bloody battlefields of Naseby and Marston Moor.

What he saw when he got past the dog, who at last ceased his barking, also took him back to what he had witnessed on those fields. Lawrence Ingolby was lying on his side, part-submerged in the shallow pool of water, blood mixed with mud streaked down the side of his face. The hair that Seeker had always thought half-chewed-looking and mud-coloured was dark and flat against the waxy skin of that face where it, too, was not also matted in mud and blood. The one arm of the jacket not submerged was shredded, and bloodied rags of linen from what had once been Ingolby's shirt poked through into the night.

Seeker collapsed on to his knees at the pool's side, the memory of a brother soldier who had died such a death all those years ago coming blindingly in to his mind. He felt inside him the silent howl, an echo of that old grief. Summoning a deep breath to overcome it, he reached out his hands to take the body by the shoulders and pull it from the pool. Lawrence's head lolled to one side, and a small sound, like a groan, the last gasp of the soul leaving the body, escaped him. Seeker shifted the weight of the torso slightly to get a grip with his other arm beneath the legs.

Another loll of the head, a breath, the flicker of an eye, opening only long enough to register his face.

'Took your time, didn't you,' the young man murmured, before passing out again, cold.

TWENTY-TWO

Hyde Park

Cecil could feel himself shivering. The morning was cold enough as it was, but he'd slept less than two hours in the night and his body yearned for rest. He was getting too old for this. His eyes smarted as if they'd had gravel thrown in them, and his stomach was sick from fatigue. This was the worst of days to do it, after the night they had had, but Boyes was almost out of patience – especially after the business of the dog. It was to be done today, or they would have no choice but to put into action their only other plan, and not one of them truly wished to do that.

Fish, though, had no reservations about how the day would unfold. 'It will be done, and none but Cromwell suffer. So simple a thing, it is a wonder it was not done before.'

'It has been tried,' said Cecil. Tried, and failed, like every other attempt upon the charmed life of Oliver Cromwell.

'Not by us,' said Fish. Cecil made no response to this. That old Leveller certainty of Fish's, that Puritan arrogance. How had he come to be mixed in this business?

'Though he might have come,' Fish added.

'Who?'

'Boyes – who else should I mean? An extra man on watch, or to provide a diversion, would more thoroughly ensure our success.'

'He has other things to attend to this morning,' said Cecil. 'Besides, there would have been a greater risk of us being noticed, if he'd been here, upon a horse. His height alone would have attracted attention. I half-feared that he might demand to do the thing himself.'

The gate at which they had met was little used, being on the less fashionable side of the park, and one rarely used by Cromwell. It had been left open for them, as had been arranged.

'Toope was as good as his word,' said Fish, leading the way through it.

On this occasion, thought Cecil, remembering the debacle of Hammersmith, where Toope's information had proved false to the extent they were almost taken by Damian Seeker. Instead of voicing his thoughts, he said, 'The gate is open, granted. But will Cromwell come?'

'He'll come,' said Fish. 'And Damian Seeker will have other business on his hands today, I'd warrant.'

Seeker splashed cold water over his face from the ewer on the side table. The room was too hot already.

'He must not get a chill or take a fever,' Drake had said, as he'd finally left half an hour ago, after stitching and dressing

Lawrence's wounds. Lawrence had been too far gone to feel half of it, and what he had felt had been doused by liberal quantities of the best brandy to be got hold of, or what Seeker had been able to make him swallow, at any rate. 'I must return to Knight Ryder Street to make up more medicines, but I will leave my sister here to nurse them – if you have no objection?' Seeker had none. 'My nephew will come back with the medicines, when they are ready, and I myself will return before suppertime.'

The apothecary's sister sat on the floor, not by Lawrence, who slept in the truckle bed of Seeker's Whitehall apartment, but near the hearth, beside the dog's head. Once she had cleaned Lawrence's wounds for her brother to stitch, she had turned her attentions to Seeker's dog.

'Leave him,' Seeker had said to her, his voice choked. 'He'll not mend.' His pistol and powder were ready. There was a place down by the Garden Stairs that the dog had always liked to swim from. Seeker would carry him down there, once Drake and his sister were gone. But the woman had looked at the pistol, set out already on his desk, and put her hand over it. 'No,' she'd said. 'He mend. I mend him.'

She'd spent as long on the dog as Drake had spent on Lawrence, the boy going between them in response to mur-mured words of Hebrew. At times when Seeker was not needed to hold man or dog, he simply looked on, crushed by his own helplessness. Eventually Drake had said to him, 'See to your business, Seeker. There's nothing more you can do here, and you make me ill at ease, looming like that.

Michal too, I think.' But Michal, so recently arrived in England now that Cromwell had said the Jews might live here openly, hardly seemed aware of Seeker's presence, so intent was she upon the animal. Seeker had gone and sat at his desk and begun to write his report of the night's events. He was pressing down too hard, though, and had split three quills before he had them into Thomas Bushell's house.

That had been an hour ago, and now as Drake was leaving, satisfied that he had done all that could be done for Lawrence, Seeker asked him, 'What are his chances, do you think?'

Drake had merely furrowed his brow. 'Who knows? Only God. I have given him a draught to make him sleep and obscure the pain. We will have a better idea when he wakes.' And then he had left, and Lawrence, sleeping soundly now in clean linen, hadn't stirred. When the laundry woman had seen Lawrence's clothes, soaked through with so much of his blood, she'd said there was nothing for it but to burn them.

Seeker went to stand over the dog for a moment. He wanted to stroke him, but there was hardly a place on the beast that was not shaved and bandaged or would not hurt. There'd been almost as much blood from the dog's ripped ear as there had been from Lawrence Ingolby's arm and leg, but Drake had told him that was because Lawrence had come so much nearer to death than had the dog. 'The blood was hardly moving in him. A few minutes more, and it would have stopped.'

The report from Proctor's men contained little good

news. The breeder's compound on the marsh had been deserted, by man and dogs both. There had been no sign, either, of Thomas Faithly. Proctor offered to take a fresh party out on the marsh, now that daylight had broken, but Seeker told him not to bother. They hadn't the resources, and it would like as not be a waste of time anyway. The fact that Faithly had not been found alongside his badly injured companion suggested two things to Seeker. Firstly, Thomas Faithly was still alive, and secondly, he was no longer on Lambeth Marsh. What exactly the pair had been doing there in the first place, when Lawrence had been supposed to be sleeping soundly in Seeker's lodging on Knight Ryder Street with Elias Ellingworth keeping watch over him, was another thing altogether.

'One thing at a time,' Seeker said to himself, 'one thing at a time.' The first thing would be to work out what had happened to Thomas Faithly.

Calling for someone to bring some breakfast, he sat back down at his desk and pulled from the pile to his right all the reports he had from Sir Thomas. As an afterthought, he reached to another pile and picked up that written by Andrew Marvell, detailing the evening at Lady Ranelagh's house which the poet and Sir Thomas had attended, and which Seeker had not yet had the time to read.

It was a long report. Marvell had clearly been determined to miss out nothing. All the names Seeker would have expected to attend one of Lady Ranelagh's gatherings were there, a mix of Republicans and old Royalists, brought together by more interests now than had separated them before. Science, music, philosophy. 'Hardly one of them that works for a living,' he murmured to himself, before reading on.

'Sorry?'

The woman's voice startled Seeker. He had forgotten Drake's sister was still there. 'Nothing,' he said. 'Just talking to myself.'

She nodded, while appearing unconvinced, and after laying her hand upon Lawrence's forehead and wrist, returned her attention to the dog. To his further discomfort, Seeker noticed the crumbs and apple core on the now otherwise empty plate at his elbow. He cleared his throat awkwardly.

'Ahm, are you hungry?'

She glanced at the empty plate and once again indulged her small, amused smile. 'No, thank you, Captain. I am not hungry,'

He returned to Marvell's report. Marvell had managed to detach himself from his duties to Milton and insinuate himself into Faithly's company at an early point in the evening. Faithly had drunk copiously and been very much at his ease, but given nothing of interest away, other than a dislike for John Evelyn and a great admiration for the Frenchwoman, Clémence Barguil. Marvell was fairly certain that their relationship went no further than admiration on his side and benign indifference on hers. All had been well until suddenly, something away on the other side of the room, in the entrance hall in fact, had taken Faithly's attention. He had stood up abruptly, and left, cutting a determined swathe through the groups of people gathered there. Marvell had not been able to see anyone of possible interest in the direction that Faithly had been looking. Nobody but an elderly clockmaker, engaged in working upon Lady Ranelagh's bell-tower clock, and even he had been gone by the time Marvell reached the hall.

Seeker stood up. 'If you need anything – anything at all, you tell him next door, and he'll sort it for you.' He jerked a thumb towards the door where his clerk worked.

Michal looked towards the clerk's room. 'I understand.'

Less than five minutes later, Seeker was crossing Horse Guards Yard. The Protector's Horse Guard was already assembled.

'His Highness going out riding this morning, is he?'

The captain nodded. 'Hyde Park. And if it's off, you can be the one to inform him this time. He's talked of little else for days.'

'No, you can go on ahead. Just make sure you stick to the park, and whatever else you do, don't think of going anywhere near Lambeth.'

The man laughed. 'It's the other direction, Seeker.'

'I know that. But I'm telling you – no matter what he says in the next few days, steer clear of south of the river, until you have my say-so.'

'Understood. Fancy coming out with us?'

One or two of the captain's men looked so uncomfortable

at this prospect that Seeker was almost tempted to say 'yes'. He couldn't remember the last time he'd had Acheron out for a good run in the park, but his horse was exhausted from the night's adventures, and he'd be taking another from the stables today.

'If I could, but I've got other places to be this morning.'

'Ah, come on, Seeker. Where's better than the park on a morning like this?'

Seeker sighed. 'I doubt it'll be Clerkenwell.'

On this visit to Tradescant's, Maria found herself drawn to the item said to be Anne Boleyn's night veil. She had looked at it before, and been scared even to touch it. It was so light, like gossamer, and yet so dark, like the Boleyn's dark heart, or so people had said. Now, she touched her fingers to the edge of the lace, imagined how the dead queen must have touched her fingers to it too. What had she seen, Anne Boleyn, through that gossamer filter? What had she hidden behind that veil? Not enough to save her. Maria had no veil – she had learned, this last year and a half, to make a mask of her own face. And she had no filter through which to look at the world. It had always been her lot to see the stark and solid truth of it. She'd seen the truth last night, in the Black Fox Tavern, and in the look on Dorcas Wells's face when she'd come in. And she'd seen the truth in the eyes of the girl given out to be Dorcas's niece. Damian's eyes. He'd told her he had no past, whenever she'd asked him. 'All I am is this, what you see, now, in front of you.' Fool, fool that she had been. Fool to believe him. He could have told her anything, and it wouldn't have mattered, but he hadn't told her, because *she* hadn't mattered enough.

Maria let drop the edge of the veil. Elias had said dead queens were not what the people needed to read about just now. She went instead to the little box cabinet in which Mistress Tradescant had shown her the cherry stones, with faces carved upon them. 'Two faces on each, that you might choose which one you prefer.' Maria opened a small drawer in the cabinet, took out a stone, and chose her face.

Sir Thomas was late this morning. He'd left the Black Fox so hurriedly last night, with that Yorkshireman, but the last thing he'd done before he'd left was to seek her assurance she would be here for their drawing lesson at Tradescant's. Maria went to the window that looked out towards the orchards and rose gardens. Sir Thomas had spoken of the orchards at his home at Faithly. When she'd asked if there was also a rose garden, he'd said no, but he would plant one for her, whenever he should come at last into his inheritance. It was fresh and cold and clear outside, and the murk of London across the river couldn't be seen from here. Her eyes caught for a moment the stone bench, with the winter jasmine growing against the wall behind it. Maria quickly looked away. She thought she might like to have a rose garden.

She'd been standing there a while, looking out, when a movement in grey took her eye. Clémence Barguil. The French woman looked up to the window as if she had expected to find Maria there, and waved. Maria waved back. A month ago she had yet to set foot in Tradescant's, and now a woman who had danced with the King was smiling up at her, and waving. She hardly recognised her own life any more.

A few minutes later, the door to the curiosities room opened and Clémence came in, a little flushed from the exertion of climbing the stairs so quickly, and from what must have been an early morning ride, for Maria could see that she was still in her riding habit. Clémence's hair was pulled back as tight as ever in a net beneath her hat, but her eyes were sparkling, even in the paltry glints from the low winter sun. She looked like a woman in love, Maria thought.

Clémence took a step towards her, hesitated, then spoke. 'Mistress Ellingworth. I am so pleased to find you here.'

'You're looking for me?' Maria asked.

'Just so,' said Clémence, sitting down on a stool and taking a little moment to catch her breath. 'Sir Thomas said you would be here.'

'Oh,' said Maria, 'you have seen Sir Thomas?'

'Just this morning, yes. He asked that I find you, and bring his apologies. He met with an accident last night, and cannot come here today.'

'An accident? Is he badly hurt?'

Clémence looked awkward. 'He says not, but he is barely able to walk. He fell from his horse last night, and I think took a knock to the head. But still it was all I could do to prevent him coming here to see you himself.'

'But that would be foolish,' said Maria. 'Has he seen a physician?'

Clémence reached out and took her hand. The kid of her gloves was the softest Maria had ever felt. 'He will not, but is very desirous to see you, Mistress Ellingworth, and I think he might listen to your advice, for he will not take mine. Will you come with me?'

'To Deptford?' Maria said. She knew that that was where Clémence Barguil was staying, at the home of John Evelyn.

'Deptford? Oh no, he is much closer than that.'

Fish screwed up his eyes and looked into the distance. He had the better eyesight, though Cecil was the better shot. 'They're coming,' he said.

'Definitely them?' Cecil asked.

'Definitely.'

Cecil looked harder. Yes, he could see something far in the distance too – the glint of their breastplates as the early sun caught them through the branches of the trees. And he could feel them, feel the increasing tremor through the ground, through his own horse's legs, into his own. At their head, as always, Colonel Howard. Cecil felt his mouth twist at the sight of him. Howard, that had once been for the King, and now abandoned his loyalty for this usurper. And there he was, right in the middle of them, the usurper himself.

'Ready?' asked Fish, picking up the reins of his horse.

Cecil adjusted his hat, his old favoured green hat, that

had come off last night, battered now and besmirched by mud, its feather lost. Blood on it too. He would buy himself a new one, when this was over. 'Ready,' he said, moving his heels just slightly to set the horse forward at a walking pace. It was a magnificent animal – the best he had ever sat – and how much Boyes had paid for it he didn't know. All he knew was that should he succeed today, Boyes had told him he might keep it.

The group of horsemen was getting closer, and Cecil kept his eye on the one in the middle, the one that was Cromwell. But the plan was not that Cecil should approach Cromwell, try to get into that middle – he'd be cut to pieces before he got past the first horse. No, the plan was that Cromwell should come to him. 'The finest judge of horseflesh in England,' Boyes had said, for all he loathed the Protector. Hence Cecil was riding out into the park now on this finest of horses. 'I'd stake my life on it, he'll come after that horse, for a closer look,' Boyes had said. And Boyes would have staked his life on it, as well. But Boyes's life was worth more than Cecil's, Cecil was almost certain of that now, and so he had insisted that it would be he who would be the bait to draw Oliver Cromwell away from his guards.

They had their mounts going at a gentle canter, and the Horse Guard came closer. A hundred yards away now. 'Wait till it's fifty,' Boyes had said. 'Close enough for Cromwell to see the horse, too far for them to be able to catch him.'

They counted silently, he and Fish, counted down to

almost fifty, then Fish said, 'Now!' and that was it, heels into his horse's flank, a bit of the spur and it flew. Cecil had rarely felt such power beneath him. Cromwell's horse would have to be a Pegasus to catch them. Cecil hardly dared turn to glance behind him. Already Fish was falling back, unable to keep up, but yes! There, amongst the thunder of hooves, steel and leather, a finer horse than even that on which Cecil rode emerged from the crowd, a true Pegasus, and upon him God's own Englishman. Cecil could let the horse have its head, for Cromwell would catch them, and the Horse Guard be too far behind, until it was too late. He bent further over the animal's neck and they shot towards the copse as had been planned. Fish would be peeling off now, to ride around and open the further gate, beyond the trees, for Cecil's escape.

The closer they got to the trees, the closer Cecil could hear coming the hooves of the Lord Protector's horse. Another thirty yards, another twenty. And then Cecil started to slow his horse, got it to veer to the right, to turn, and stop. The edge of the wood was behind him now. In front of him, having eased to a slow trot, was Oliver Cromwell.

Something happened in Cecil's stomach. Not the nausea from the fatigue of last night, but something deeper, like when he had been a boy, standing at the edge of a waterfall, and his brother had urged him to jump. He had jumped, and the shock and the cold of the clear, rushing water had been magnificent. Cecil had fought for the King from the start, never a notion in his head for Republic, never an ounce of respect for the title Lord Protector. But here before him was something more; here before him was Oliver Cromwell. Naseby, Marston Moor, Worcester, Dunbar. Here the victor, the Lord General, who had made himself invincible. Here, he had heard him called it, our Chief of Men. The shock was again cold and clear, and overpowering. At Cecil's right hand, the knife that he was to have plunged into Cromwell's neck remained sheathed, the pistol that he might, if required, have had recourse to remained in his belt, and Cecil found himself bowing his head before this man of flesh and blood, this specimen, bewarted as he was, of human greatness.

The Horse Guard was coming closer, and Cecil hardly knew what answers he gave about the horse. Cromwell got down from his own, the better to examine it, and Cecil did likewise, as was right in the presence of Highness. In a moment they were surrounded, and Cromwell calling upon his men to admire the horse's fine flank, his good teeth, the hold of its head. Colonel Howard had come closest to Cecil, and never looked at the horse once, for that he was keeping his eye so exactly upon Cecil and the weapons that hung from his belt.

Ten minutes. Ten minutes of England's time and Cromwell was back on his horse, his Horse Guard around him like a Roman phalanx, and riding away, the colonel's eye still on Cecil, and Cecil's feet still planted on the ground, the knife never taken out of its sheath.

Fish had been waiting in the trees. Cold fury was written on his face. 'What have you done?' he said.

'You don't understand. You didn't see him.'

'Oh, but I do. I saw him and I saw you. And I understand what must be done now, what Boyes, you and I will have to do. There is no option, now. And then we'll see Oliver Cromwell, all three of us, in Hell.'

TWENTY-THREE

The Brother of Charterhouse
and the Searcher of St John's

By the time Cromwell and his Life Guard had entered Hyde Park, Seeker was well along Theobald's Road towards Clerkenwell. To his right the city spilled out from its walls to encroach on the fields and commons – Lincoln's Inn, Red Lion, Gray's – there were more houses being snuck up in their fields, more passageways that once had been paths, every time he looked. To his left he could still see clear over Conduit Fields, as far as the old fort at Black Mary's Hole and almost to St Pancras. Healthier entertainments there for the townspeople than all the illicit pleasures on offer south of the river. Men could run, hunt, wrestle, swim – he did himself sometimes. Only a few months ago, he'd taken Nathaniel – the gardener's boy from Lincoln's Inn who often looked after the dog for him – swimming out at Parlous Pond.

There was something about the memory that eluded him. It was as he passed over Saffron Hill that he remembered: after their swimming, they'd gone up by the New River

Head and on to the fort, because Nathaniel had never seen it, and then they'd taken their supper in a tavern at Hockley-in-the-Hole. It was the name of the tavern that came back to him now: the Bear Garden. Seeker shook his head as if to clear it. The place had been there since before Queen Elizabeth's time, and there had been no bears there since long before Pride had shot the animals on Bankside. It was just a name, and on the wrong side of London entirely, but the name was still playing on his mind by the time he got to St John's Lane. When he got back to Whitehall, he'd send some men up to Hockley-in-the-Hole to search that place.

He was soon at Dietmar Kästner's shop, which Joseph Grindle had visited on the day of his disappearance, but even before he brought his horse to a halt, he knew the place was empty. The door was firmly closed, and the shutters still up on the windows. Nothing strange in that, given it was early enough for folk to be thinking about clocks. But it was a perishing cold day, fair set for snow, and no smoke came from the chimney either. Seeker dismounted and banged on the door. Nothing. He banged louder.

A neighbour from next door stuck her head out of an upper window. 'No one there.'

'Where are they then?'

The woman made a face. 'Don't know. Off to foreign parts somewhere. Anna came round yesterday morning, with some food they weren't taking with them. Said they wouldn't be back.'

'How many went?'

The woman looked at him as if he were stupid. 'All of them, of course – Dietmar and Anna and those two young lads he had for apprentices.'

'What about his brother?'

'Brother? Well, he'd have gone as well, I suppose, wouldn't he?'

Seeker was back on his horse by the time the window slammed shut. His mind was working quickly. Dietmar Kästner had told him he'd been settled in London over thirty years. In all the shifting populace, the comings and goings of those years, there was one man Seeker could think of who would know everything there was to be told of London's clockmakers. He went back up to the top of the lane and turned the horse's head towards the Charterhouse.

Bernard Dunn had been a brother of Charterhouse for three years now, sent there by his failing sight and the benevolence of an old patron. Dunn was not blind, but he could not see well enough any more to work on the mechanisms of the clocks he'd spent a lifetime caring for and seeking to understand.

It always made Seeker feel uneasy, going into the Charterhouse. It wasn't the ghosts of the monks who'd been there, or the tales of the deaths they'd suffered at Henry Tudor's hands, for refusing to give the place up. He'd seen a few bad deaths himself, and he didn't believe in ghosts. It was the date over the entry way: 1611. 1611 was the year Thomas Sutton had bought the old Carthusian Monastery and endowed it as a hospital for the indigent and elderly, men of good repute, who became the Brothers. It was also the year Seeker had been born. Each time he passed into the entry, beneath Sutton's arms and that date, it was a reminder to him of time passing. But Seeker wouldn't finish his days in a place like this. The musket ball on the battlefield, the knife in the night: those or something like them would be his end, he told himself as he passed under the archway of Charterhouse court.

The Brothers had finished their breakfast and those that were able dispersed to their tasks for the day. Seeker found Bernard Dunn in the Great Cloister, sweeping out the leaves that had blown in from the mulberry trees of the court-yard. The old man looked up as Seeker's shadow spread over the flagstones and the fugitive, heart-shaped leaves. His face broke into a smile. 'Captain. Haven't seen you here in a good long while. Have we trouble here in the Charterhouse?'

'None that I know of, Bernard. It's you I've come to talk with, if you can spare me five minutes?'

Dunn laughed. 'Five? I can spare you all the minutes there are, and more besides. The sun will be round that dial on the wall and back again a time or two before anyone else needs Bernard Dunn.'

Seeker leaned against the wall. 'Then they'll not mind you sitting a while,' he said, indicating one of the stone benches that lined the cloister.

Dunn set down his broom, sat down carefully, and waited.

'There's a clockmaker I need to know about.'

Dunn nodded. This was his territory. The captain didn't waste time asking you questions you knew nothing about.

'Dietmar Kästner,' said Seeker.

'Ah, Dietmar. Good man, knows his craft. Best man for a German clock. If you have a German clock, you take it to Dietmar, and I even said that myself sometimes, to them that brought me theirs. German clocks can be tricky devils, if you don't know what you're doing.'

'What can you tell me of him?'

Dunn puffed out his cheeks. 'Just about anything you want to know. I've known that man over thirty years. Not much about old Dietmar I couldn't tell you. What'll you have?'

'Where did he come here from?'

'Heidelberg,' replied Dunn, without hesitation. 'Came after the Habsburgs took it in '22. He told me about it once, the things they did – the Habsburgs – when they took the city. Never spoke of it again, but then, there are some things you only need to hear the once. The castle and gardens though – he was never done speaking about them. His father had been clockmaker to the Palsgrave, and Dietmar learned his craft at his father's shoulder. A place of wonders it was, that palace, to hear him talk of it, and the gardens especially, fountains that played music, statues that sang. I should have liked to have seen it. And of course, he loved our Princess Elizabeth, though there was plenty amongst the Germans didn't.'

'You mean King James's daughter?'

Dunn nodded. 'Queen of Bohemia. Dietmar kept a por-trait of her – not on show, not in these late times of ours, but before, when her brother Charles was on the throne. Always said he'd never go back to Heidelberg unless her children were restored to their inheritance – Charles Louis and Rupert and all of them. We near fell out about it, him and me.'

'About Heidelberg, the Palatinate?'

Bernard scoffed. 'No, about the Stuarts, for I was all for Parliament, as you know, Captain. Still am. But once Prince Rupert and his brother Maurice come over here to fight for the King, well, Dietmar he declared for him too – quietly, mind, amongst his friends.'

'He was a Royalist?'

Dunn nodded. 'On account of the Heidelberg family.'

Seeker didn't like where this was leading. 'And his brother?'

'Brother?'

'He had a brother, lately come from Germany, who worked alongside him.'

Dunn shook his head. 'Dietmar never had a brother. Sisters now, he had those, but gone, all three of them at the hands of the Habsburgs. But a brother? No, Dietmar never had a brother.'

Fifteen minutes later, Seeker was back on St John's Lane. It was no surprise to find Dietmar Kästner's shop still closed, the window shutters and doors still bolted fast. Seeker looked around him for something to break down the door with, but found nothing suitable to hand. He sighed, and took an extra step back, before charging, right shoulder down. As the lock gave way and the door swung inwards, he told himself he was getting too old for this. The place was in darkness with no candle or flint to hand. Seeker was still forcing open the shutters when a terrible noise pierced the air.

'Who are you? What business have you here? Robber, thief, housebreaker!'

Seeker spun round to confront the source of the screech. An ancient woman, bent of back and missing more teeth than she retained, was standing in the doorway, a crook raised in her hand. As he stepped forward further into the light coming through the doorway she raised her crook higher but then let out a laugh, almost more disturbing than her screech. 'You're the Seeker.'

'And who are you?' he demanded.

'Me?' the old woman asked, still cackling. 'I'm the Searcher. The Searcher and the Seeker!' She craned her neck further into the darkened room. 'I wonder what we're looking for?'

A few minutes later, Seeker having secured the door to Dietmar Kästner's shop, he was sitting facing the crone in an alehouse in Turk's Head Yard. She had her own pot with her, a mark of her trade, a gift of beer being the prerequisite for her and those of her calling to do their duty. She was indeed a Searcher, one of the old women employed in every parish to view and search the bodies of the deceased. They were to establish the cause of death, and report it to the vestryman of the parish, that any pestilence or other dangerous infection might be kept under control. They were supposed to be sober and discreet matrons, and perhaps some of them were, but what sober and discreet matron, unless she be desperate, would perform a task such as that? The Searchers. Their discretion could be bought, or discarded, if the price was right, and there weren't many households whose uncomfortable secrets they didn't know.

'A shilling,' she said.

'A shilling? Dream your dreams, old woman, you've had your pint of ale. Tuppence a household, you lot get paid.'

'Aye,' she said, a very cunning look in her eye as she observed him sideways whilst sipping at her ale, 'but there's no *body* there, is there? And I get paid to report on bodies that are there, not ones that aren't.'

Seeker reached into his money pouch with a sigh and slapped a shilling down on the table. 'Let's have it,' he said.

The shilling was whipped away in a flash, to some crevice of her filthy apron.

'What would you know?' she said, all business now.

'Who was in the household?'

She went through the clockmaker, his wife, their two apprentices, all in short fashion, and then watched him.

'The rest,' Seeker said.

'What rest?' She eyed Seeker's pouch again.

'No chance. Tell me the rest or I'll have you in the Bridewell.'

'The brother,' she said.

'That's right. Everything you know about the brother.'

'Well,' she leaned in to him, a trusted associate, 'big tall fellow – tall as you – although he tried to hide it with a stoop. He wasn't any brother, not of Dietmar Kästner's at any rate. Dietmar nor his wife – that he married after he came here from Germany, by the way – never mentioned any brother, not in thirty years, till that fellow turned up. Brother?' She made a noise of disgust. 'Old enough to be his son, perhaps.'

Something Lawrence Ingolby had said came into Seeker's head. It was about the conspirator Boyes – that he wasn't as old as he gave the impression of being. 'The man I'm thinking of was about the same age as Kästner,' Seeker said, recalling the stooped, grey-headed man he had glimpsed at work in Dietmar Kästner's back shop the first time he'd gone there to ask questions about Joseph Grindle.

'From a distance, maybe, but I've the habit of looking at people close up, very close up, and I got myself close up on that fellow a couple of times.' She fixed him with a raven-like eye. 'You remember you had this from me, mind – that *brother* of old Dietmar's was no more than thirty-five years old or so, though at a distance he'd pass for sixty or more.'

'What else?' said Seeker.

'Had a woman.'

'Woman? What kind of woman?'

She gave her horrible smile. 'Kind some men like. Fancy

woman – all plain and proper-looking, but eyes like a cat that let them know she's on the lookout for a mouse.'

'Street-walker?'

'Pah, not her. Though no doubt she knows a trick or two. No, this was a *lay-dee*. Went into Dietmar's shop the first time with another *lay-dee*, who was all twittering and chattering about a watch that she was going to have made for her husband. Well, by the time they came out, that other lady, she was still fluttering and twittering, but your fancy one had a face like chalk, as if she'd just seen into her own grave.'

'You were positioned outside Kästner's door, I take it?'

The woman missed Seeker's note of sarcasm and merely took another swig of her ale before shaking her head. 'Opposite. Bell Cullen's cookshop. Bell's got a nice little bench outside, brings me a scrap of this and that to eat now and again, and I make sure everyone roundabouts knows no one ever got ill from eating at Bell's cookshop.'

'Hmm.' Seeker imagined the grim delights that would be on offer in such a place. 'You saw this woman again, this "fancy woman" you'd seen at the clockmaker's?'

'Oh, yes. Very next day, and the day after that. She'd pretend she was looking in some other shop window, but she never went into any of them, just always kept one eye on the clockmaker's door. She was watching so hard she didn't notice me, watching her. Third day, back she came, in her furs and her grey silks. And then out he came . . .'

'Who?'

'The clockmaker's brother, of course.' The old woman was annoyed to have her narrative interrupted by so stupid a question. 'He come out, doing that old man walk of his, and she waited a moment, then followed him down the street.'

'Did you go after them?'

The Searcher was astonished. 'Go after them? Why should I have done that? None of my business where they were going or what they were doing. My business is St John's, what happens anywhere else is none of my concern.'

Seeker sat back against the wall of the alehouse taproom and screwed up his eyes in frustration.

'Followed him back, too.'

He opened his eyes.

'Followed him back. Went on for days – her following him around like a little puppy. Then one day he came out of the shop, unexpected. Went right over to her, had urgent words.'

'Warning her off?'

The woman shook her head. 'No, just urgent. Like there was a worry. He even forgot to walk old. After that, I never saw her again.'

'I don't suppose you remember when that was?'

'Oh, but I do. It was the day Aubrey Goode's wife died. Used to be the feast of St Jude, before you lot decided such things weren't allowed.'

The feast of St Jude: the 28th of October. The day before Grace Kent's birthday. The day Joseph Grindle had taken his clock to Dietmar Kästner's shop.

But the Searcher remembered nothing of Joseph Grindle. Old soldiers were ten a penny around London nowadays, surely Seeker knew that? Back then to the clockmaker's brother and the strange woman.

'You didn't hear what they were saying?'

'I heard all right, heard every word.'

Seeker felt his hopes rise. 'And?'

The woman shrugged. 'Who knows? Everything they said was in French.'

Seeker stormed up the stairs of the Cockpit and into the clerks' room.

'Where's that report?' he demanded.

'Which one?'

Why was he forced to deal with idiots? 'The one from Gravesend. The plants shipment from Tradescant's.'

The frozen clerks suddenly broke into motion, and a moment later he was back on the stairs, the required report in his hand. It didn't add up to very much: a list of north country gentlemen for whom Clémence Barguil had ordered plants, a list of the plants ordered for each client, along with Mlle Barguil's notes on planting, blooming and fruiting times. All were now in transit, the ship for Hull having weighed anchor the previous day. Seeker studied the names and recognised a good few among them: all Royalists of one colour or another. He looked up from the paper in time to see Andrew Marvell coming out of the anteroom to his own chamber.

'Ah!' said Marvell, the startled look with which he perennially greeted Seeker upon his face. 'Captain. I have been just visiting your rooms – I heard about the terrible events of last night. Poor Ingolby is in a bad way. Has there been any word of Sir Thomas?'

'I've been out the last two hours. Nothing this morning, I take it?'

Marvell shook his head.

'How are they all in there?' asked Seeker, nodding towards his own door.

'Drake has sent more medicines, and Lawrence and your dog are both asleep. The lady tending to them is vigilant, and full of hope.'

'Good,' said Seeker. 'Very good.' Perhaps that hope might see them through. 'Tell me what you know of last night.'

And so Marvell did, in detail – other than his awful discovery of the object of Thomas Faithly's affection – down to the point at which the note for Sir Thomas had arrived at the Black Fox, prompting him and Lawrence Ingolby to leave soon afterwards.

'And they never sent a note to me, nor a messenger?'

Again Marvell shook his head. 'Not unless they did so after leaving the tavern.'

'All right. You can go.'

Marvell was about to continue down the stairs and Seeker about to check on Lawrence and his dog, when another thought struck him. 'No, wait, Andrew. You know all about flowers and gardens and things, don't you?'

'Well, yes,' said Marvell, 'although my interest is more in—'

'Good,' said Seeker, handing him the report of the Tradescant shipment from Gravesend. 'Take a look at this for me then, would you? See if there's anything about it doesn't look right.'

Marvell went on his way, and after receiving guarded assurances from Drake's sister about her patients, Seeker finally went to the Chief Secretary.

Thurloe was putting his signature to a document when Seeker appeared at his door. A mound of other papers awaited his clearance. 'Seeker?'

Seeker closed the door behind him. 'It's Rupert.'

Thurloe put down his quill pen and gave him his full attention.

'Rupert of the Rhine. He's in London.'

Thurloe's head moved slightly, as if he might dislodge the information that had just entered there. 'He can't be. We'd have heard.'

'I don't know that we would, sir. Only last week, one of our Dutch agents reported that a Royalist could get through a Kent port for as little as twenty shillings.'

Thurloe was utterly motionless, apart from his mouth. 'But Rupert? He'd be recognised in minutes. He wouldn't dare.'

'I think he would,' said Seeker. 'Things he's done in the past. The man that would buy a basket of apples off an old woman then walk through an enemy camp selling them to Parliamentary soldiers knows how to disguise himself.'

'That was just a rumour, Seeker.'

'I know good men that say it's true.'

'Even so, why would he be in London now?'

'That report we had in a couple of months ago, from Stoupe in Paris, warning of an assassin named Fish who'd taken lodgings in King Street.'

Thurloe nodded. 'Go on.'

'Fish was behind the planned attempt on the Protector from the coaching house in Hammersmith. He had two associates with him – one who kept to the chamber where the blunderbusses were rigged, feigning illness, and another who went by the name of Boyes. This Boyes was seen by a man I know. He described him as having a slight foreign accent, and of looking much younger than he purported to be. Such a man has been masquerading as the brother of a German clockmaker who I am assured has no brother, and who I have learned was an old retainer of Rupert's family in their Heidelberg days. All are now disappeared.'

'That still doesn't mean it's Rupert, Seeker. You'll need to give me more than that.'

What could Seeker give him? A woman in grey silks, with eyes like a cat's, who Thomas Faithly had told him was in love with Rupert of the Rhine, and had 'followed him around like a puppy'? An old crone who had watched just such a woman follow a man around Clerkenwell 'like a little puppy'. An old clockmaker from Heidelberg who had been a closet Royalist? The name 'Boyes'? It had been in Andrew Marvell's report, of his evening at Lady Ranelagh's:

Thomas Faithly, in his cups, had spoken with some emotion of Prince Rupert, whose life had been loss after loss, and who had told him once, 'I am master of none, Thomas, save this little dog, Boy. I am Boy's master.' Boy's Master. Mr Boyes. Rupert was a man with nothing left to lose.

None of it would be enough for Thurloe, and Seeker was still calculating how to persuade him when an urgent knocking on the Chief Secretary's door heralded the entrance a moment later of a breathless Andrew Marvell.

'Captain, Mr Secretary, please excuse the interruption, but I thought you would want to know straight away.'

'Know what?' said Thurloe, with an unwonted hint of impatience.

'The Flanders Cherry.'

'Marvell, I have enough to occupy me that I—'

But Seeker could see that Marvell was brandishing the report of the Tradescant shipment. 'No, sir, I think he may have something.'

Marvell nodded. 'Yes, indeed. It's the Flanders Cherry. It most certainly does *not* ripen in December.'

It took less than an hour for the Cypher Office to translate the coded messages Clémence Barguil had sent out to almost a dozen dormant Royalists in the north of England, explaining to them that they would not be dormant much longer. The 'Flanders Cherry' – the seeds of which had been planted in a Bruges inn several months before – was about to come to fruition. Each plant listed, in her handwriting, in Tradescant's shipping order, was a code for a place – a rendezvous for those named as having ordered it, each ripening or flowering day code for the date and time of meeting.

Thurloe looked at the paper again, as Samuel Morland, the Protectorate's chief cryptographer, returned it to him. 'Tomorrow,' he said. 'Whatever their plan is, it is to come to fruition by tomorrow.' He held the paper out towards Morland. 'And nothing said here about the place, or time where the thing is to be done? The means even?'

He didn't need to elaborate on what 'the thing' was – they all knew, it was what they'd had intelligence of months before – the plot, involving Mr Fish, with the aim of murdering Oliver Cromwell.

Morland shook his head. 'These detail only what is to be done in the aftermath, not where, how or exactly when the assassination is to be carried out.'

Thurloe turned to Seeker. 'Have the woman Barguil taken in, and have her accomplices found, at any cost. If the stay-at-home Royalists should think Rupert of the Rhine is returned to rally them, the Lord alone knows what will happen. With the alliance Charles Stuart has made with Spain . . .' He didn't need to say any more. The successful assassination of Cromwell at the hands of the Royalists' most feared general, and the promise of Spanish help, would be more than enough to embolden Charles Stuart's supporters at home to a concerted rising, where all previous efforts had failed.

Seeker was already halfway through the door when Thurloe called him back.

'Seeker?'

'Sir?'

'Thomas Faithly. Is he with them?'

'I don't know, sir. I don't know.'

TWENTY-FOUR

The Guard Room

Clerks and messengers moved out of Seeker's way as he went quickly down the stairs from Thurloe's corridor and along the passage to the Tilt Yard and then Horse Guards. He was heading across the yard to the guardhouse, and then to the barrack room where Proctor and his men rested between duties. A small detachment would be sent to Tradescant's, and another to Sayes Court, in search of Clémence Barguil. The rest would be tasked with hunting down Prince Rupert and his accomplices. That done, Seeker had business with the Foot Guard: in all that had happened since, he had almost forgotten what had first alerted him to possible trouble centring on Tradescant's garden – the remark by one of John Tradescant's young apprentices that a soldier of the Foot Guard had been there the day before, talking with the man Seeker was now certain was the conspirator, Fish.

The raised voice of Colonel Howard took Seeker's attention as he passed the Horse Guard's barrack.

'If it's any one of you, I'll have you garrotted by your

own innards. Truth, now, or you're all on double duties for a month.'

The chorus of protest and denial stopped on the instant Seeker walked into the guardroom, and Howard turned around.

'Captain.'

'Colonel Howard. Has something happened, sir?'

'Something or nothing, Seeker. Just a suspicion of something that didn't feel right.'

Seeker waited.

'It was this morning, on the Lord Protector's ride out in Hyde Park. His Highness got away from us – rode off after a fine bay gelding he'd caught sight of. By the time we caught up with him, he was off his own horse and examining the other, talking to its rider.'

'Who was this rider?' asked Seeker.

'I don't know. But something wasn't right. He didn't have the look of a man with the means to be on a horse like that.'

'The horse was bait then. Where have you got him, this rider?'

The colonel looked like he'd rather be having his teeth pulled. 'My only thought to start with was to get the Protector back on his horse and away. By the time I sent someone back to apprehend the fellow, he and his companion were gone.'

Seeker felt his muscles tense. 'Companion?'

The sergeant now spoke up. 'One of our men noticed

him as we rode away. Watching from the woods. Saw him leave with the other fellow, by the east gate.'

'The east gate? Isn't that supposed to be locked, early morning?'

The sergeant nodded. 'But today it wasn't.'

'What did they look like, this pair?' asked Seeker.

As he had known they would, the descriptions accorded with those he had of Cecil and Fish. 'Was either of them wearing a green felt hat?'

The expression on the colonel's face told him everything he needed to know.

Seeker bit back an oath. 'They were waiting for him.'

'Looks like it,' said the colonel. 'And they might have done it on chance, for everyone knows Oliver likes to ride. But the matter of the gate aside, we haven't been out in Hyde Park for weeks. They'd need to have been waiting there every day.'

'And they weren't, I take it?'

'If they were, it was never reported.'

Because if it had been reported, they would have already been taken in and questioned, and Oliver would never have been riding out there this morning. Seeker surveyed the guardroom. 'It's not one of your men that's passing on details of the Protector's movements: it's one of the Foot Guard.'

Colonel Howard took a moment to process this. 'Does Captain Strickland know?'

'No. I'm going over there now.'

Seeker strode across the yard in a maelstrom of anger. The traitor was somewhere here, under his very nose. Before he even reached the Foot Guard barrack, he saw through the door two men seated at a small table in the corner, examining some object that one of them held in the palm of his hand. As he entered, there was the usual standing to attention, but not before one of the men he had noticed snatched back the object he had been showing to his companion.

Seeker went no further than the doorway and picked the man out.

'John Toope.'

Toope was rigid, but his gaze was shifting around the room like a trapped pigeon trying to find its way out of a cellar.

'What's that?'

'Sir?'

'In your hand.'

The man looked down at his hand as if he had forgotten there was anything in it.

'Now, Toope!'

Toope uncurled his fingers to reveal an object the size of a large walnut, glinting like silver.

Seeker put out his hand and jerked up his chin. Toope walked over like a man going to the gallows and put the object into his palm. It looked like a pill box, or some similar trinket, but it was heavy. The silverwork was very fine, the engraving of a repeating vine. Seeker clicked the catch on the side and the casing sprang open, to reveal not a pill box, but a watch, its face edged in gilt marked with roman numerals. Seeker looked from the watch back to Toope's face, which had utterly drained of colour. Seeker gave his attention back to the watch. The nearest in quality he'd seen to this was one carried by Oliver himself. He let out a breath of appreciation and shut the casing with such a snap in the now near-silent room that Toope flinched.

'Oh, I'd jump as well if I were you, Toope. Now, I don't know much about hallmarks, but I'd be willing to stake my back pay that when I take this up to the Goldsmiths' Hall in Aldersgate they'll tell me that this is a finer piece than a soldier of the Lord Protector's Foot Guard could afford in several lifetimes. And I'll wager something else, that when I take it up there they'll tell me that hallmark's German.'

Toope was trying to speak now, but nothing came out save an incoherent babble. Seeker could hardly look at him for disgust. Only a few months ago, Toope had survived a purge of the Protector's Life Guard, and now here he was, one of a small number of men who knew in advance the Protector's movements, showing off a valuable German watch.

Seeker sent one of the other men to fetch Walter Strickland, Captain of the Foot Guard. When he arrived Seeker told him to have John Toope put under restraint. 'He's suspected of passing information of the Protector's movements to malignant parties.'

Strickland turned a look of loathing on Toope and

ordered two of his men to put him in manacles and march him to an interrogation room.

Toope looked as if he might protest, but Seeker stopped him. 'Don't bother. I've two witnesses saw you at Tradescant's garden, talking to the conspirators. I'll be back here in ten minutes and you're going to tell me everything you know.'

It was a little longer than ten minutes before Seeker had returned to the Horse Guard's barrack, having issued orders for search parties that were to go out to Sayes Court, Tradescant's, and the city, with as detailed descriptions of those they sought as could be given, including one of Thomas Faithly. He'd also warned them that Rupert would almost certainly be in disguise. 'He's six foot four though, same height as me, and there's only so much you can do to hide that.'

The captain of the Foot Guard had had John Toope secured in a small room with only one high, barred window. 'Shall I stay, Seeker?' he'd asked.

Seeker looked at Toope, already attached by a manacle to the wall. 'No, I think I'm up to managing this one. You could ask the rest of them what he's been like this last couple of months, if he's been acting different, throwing his money about, that sort of thing.'

Strickland nodded. 'Oh, I know the sort of thing.' Then he brought his face up close to Toope's. 'And if I find that he's sullied the name of my Guard, he'll be screaming to get sent back to your tender mercies.'

The door closed, leaving only Seeker and his ashen-faced prisoner in the room,

Toope tried to take a step forward but was checked by his chain. 'Captain, there's been a mistake . . .'

'There certainly has,' said Seeker, 'but you and me are about to put that straight. First off – the watch.'

The answer came too quick. 'A gift from my father.'

Seeker feigned admiration. 'Oh? A wealthy man your father, then?' Toope was opening his mouth as if to confirm this, but Seeker carried on talking. ''Cause last I knew he was an ostler in Sarum.'

Toope ran a tongue across his lips, his eyes following thoughts across his mind and away. 'He . . . it was . . . a grateful patron.'

'Grateful indeed, that gave him a solid silver cased watch.' Seeker turned the watch over, opened it, smoothed a finger across its face. 'German was he, this patron?'

Again, Toope sought to moisten his lips.

Seeker held the watch up. 'I'll ask you once more: where did you get this watch? And don't give me any more rubbish about your father, or I'll have him fetched here and ask him myself.'

'I bought it.'

Seeker snorted. 'On your wages? You'll never earn what this is worth till your dying day.' He held the watch up again and let the sound of its ticking take over the small room. '*You* are running out of time. Who gave you this?'

Toope kept his eyes fixed on the watch but said nothing.

'You got this from a clockmaker in Clerkenwell, didn't you?'

Toope began to deny it, but his words tripped over themselves and fell into a heap of nothing.

'Didn't you?' repeated Seeker.

Toope shook his head. 'Never went to Clerkenwell. Never went near it.'

'So how did this watch, which your whole troop put together couldn't afford, come into your possession? Who gave it to you?'

'Don't know. Don't know him.'

'Do you not? Oh, but I do,' said Seeker. 'I know him, and when I get him he'll give you up faster than your friend Cecil's horse was galloping this morning.'

At the mention of Cecil, Toope's eyes widened in fear, and then his shoulders sank.

'That's right,' continued Seeker. 'That green hat of his. And your lumpy little friend, Fish, waiting in the woods. Hirelings, that's all they are. Ten a penny, the pair of them. And it probably won't take as much as that to get them to put all of this on to you.'

Toope began to shake his head, to pull on his manacles. 'It wasn't me. I just gave them a tip or two. The planning was nothing to do with me. It was all them.'

'Fish and Cecil.'

Toope was panicking. 'Yes. No. Not them. Boyes.'

'Boyes was running it?'

Toope nodded. 'Boyes was master of all.'

'The man who gave you that watch?'

'Fish gave it to me, but he got it from Boyes.'

'They'd run out of money?'

Toope nodded dumbly.

'To pay you to tell them when the Lord Protector would be riding in Hyde Park.'

Toope looked as if he would say something, but then Seeker could see that a new thought had crossed his mind. 'Yes, yes,' he said, a little too eagerly, 'for the foreknowledge of His Highness's ride in Hyde Park.' A kind of relief flooded Toope's face, and relaxation seemed to spread through his body. It was as if Seeker had gifted him something that had shown him a way out of all his problems. And that was when Seeker knew that Toope was hiding something worse.

Just then, a hard knock came on the door and the sergeant of the Foot Guard walked in. He gave Toope a look that would have shrivelled most men, then turned to Seeker. 'There's a message from your chambers, Captain. A lawyer, Elias Ellingworth. Come to report someone missing.'

Missing. Twelve hours at least since they'd come upon Lawrence Ingolby half-dead in a ditch on Lambeth Marsh and only now did Ellingworth, in whose worthless care he'd left him, report him missing. 'You can tell him I know all about it,' said Seeker. 'I haven't got time to see him just now, but when I do, he'll have more of my attention than he could ever wish for. As for now though, no more disturbances, not unless it's Mr Thurloe or the Lord Protector himself that's asking for me.'

It took almost two hours. Seeker would never have imagined Toope to be so resilient. There was a deal of time at the beginning getting over the pretence that Toope had thought Fish, Cecil and Boyes only to want intelligence of Cromwell's whereabouts in order that they might waylay him and plead their cause. Seeker wondered how such a specimen had ever got into the Life Guard in the first place.

'And what cause would that be?'

'Well,' Toope had stuttered, 'Fish is a Leveller.'

'So our intelligence suggests, but the Lord Protector is done with Levellers, and as for Cecil and Boyes, well, I don't think Oliver ever started with them, not unless it was at opposing sides of a battlefield, with his sword in his hand.'

'I, ehm, I don't know . . .'

'Oh, but I think that you do. I think you know very well. Cecil's a Royalist, and as for your watchmaker friend Boyes, he's one of the biggest Royalists of them all.'

Toope had gone even paler. 'I didn't know about Cecil. It's Fish I've dealt with, and Cecil is of little account. Boyes is just an old clockmaker from Clerkenwell, works with his brother.'

Seeker came around the table he'd been leaning on and looked very close in to Toope's eyes. 'You really don't know?'

'Know what?' Toope was stuttering with some regularity now.

'Your Mr Boyes, your old clockmaker from Clerkenwell.'

'Yes?' said Toope, attempting to shrink back from Seeker but being impeded by the wall behind him.

'He's Rupert. Rupert of the Rhine.'

There was a strange movement of Toope's mouth, and then it widened, in a question and then a laugh. 'You're not . . . Captain, Prince Rupert? What on earth would Rupert of the Rhine want with men like Cecil and Fish? Why would he walk right in to the heart of London, within a stone's throw of the Tower and of Tyburn Hill?' Toope shook his head. 'I think you are mad, Captain.'

Seeker slammed his hand against the wall behind Toope's head. 'It's not your place to think, Toope, it's your place to tell. So start telling. What information did you give them in return for that silver watch?'

Toope held out a while longer, but eventually, as the light outside was greying and dusk falling over Whitehall, he began to tire, and to run out of the ability to maintain his silence.

Seeker was tiring of the whole thing too. It was a waste of time, and that time would be better wasted by Major-General Barkstead and the men of the Interrogation Committee at the Tower than by himself. He opened the door, with the intention of making arrangements for Toope's transportation eastwards when Toope said, 'The chapel.'

Seeker turned round. 'Which chapel?'

Toope glanced to the side and said in a low voice, 'The Palace chapel. Whitehall.'

Seeker closed the door again. Went back to stand in front of Toope. 'What *about* Whitehall Palace Chapel?'

And then Toope told him.

Seeker was running. The Life Guard of Foot, minus Toope, who was now even more securely shackled and under lock, key and close observation, was on its way to secure the person of the Protector and escort him to the river. The Horse Guard was to make its way directly to Hampton Court, where the Protector would be sent.

Passing his own rooms in the Cockpit on the way to Thurloe's, Seeker was waylaid by the young soldier who acted as his clerk.

'Captain!'

'I've no time just now, Robert.'

'But, Captain, the lady says it is a matter of great urgency.'

'I've no *time*, Robert, for ladies or anything else, now . . .'

The boy's face flushed. He half-stepped in front of Seeker to stop him, a thing he'd never done before. 'It's Mistress Wells,' he mouthed, just as Seeker was preparing to propel him by the neck of his jerkin back through the door.

Seeker loosed his grip on the young man. Dorcas had never once breached the gates of Whitehall to come looking for him. He felt a wave of fear in his stomach. 'Where is she?' he said.

The young man, trying to rearrange his jerkin unob-trusively, led the way back into the anteroom to Seeker's chamber. Dorcas rose as soon as they entered. She was dressed not in her town outfit, a good, plain-looking green dress and velvet jacket, but in the serviceable brown gown she wore in the tavern, with her old woollen cloak thrown over.

'Leave us,' he said to his secretary, without turning to look at the boy.

Dorcas took a step towards him, but he held up a hand. 'Dorcas, I have not time. Lawrence is safe, he is in my chamber, but I have not the time to see you just now.'

Her face was ashen. 'It is not Lawrence, Damian.'

'Not Manon?'

Dorcas shook her head. 'No. She's safe, back up at the Black Fox, but I've closed up. It's Maria, Damian. Elias came to me because he couldn't get access to you. Maria Ellingworth went to Tradescant's early this morning and has not been seen since. Grace Kent had been expecting her at the coffee house before three, and she never came. They're all distraught, Damian, after what happened to Samuel's friend, and then the attacks on Lawrence.'

Seeker felt his blood course through his body with such force that he thought he might explode. Thoughts of the two assaults on Lawrence, the disappearance of Thomas Faithly, who had so openly courted Maria, Tradescant's and Clémence Barguil, whirled into his head. He closed his eyes and gripped the back of the chair behind the secretary's desk, feeling he might gouge it through. When he opened them, Dorcas was still there, her face expectant.

'Dorcas, there is an attempt on the life of the Protector

in preparation as we speak. I have no time, and not a man to spare.' He put his hands on her shoulders. 'You must go back to the city. You must rouse the constables and watch of your own ward at Broad Street and of Maria's at Cheap. They must spread the search for her through the city. Tell them they will answer to me if they don't. Tell Ellingworth there are searches already under way for those most likely to have taken her, at South Lambeth and across Southwark . . .'

'Taken her? Dear God, Damian, what do these people want?'

'They want Oliver dead, and they don't care who else they have to sacrifice to do it. Maria has become entangled with it, all unknown to herself, through her visits to Tradescant's and her acquaintance with Thomas Faithly. I have men looking for the culprits, but go, now, Dorcas, and rouse the watches.'

He opened the door for her, but stopped her as she was only part way through it.

'Yes, Damian?'

He let his eyes trace her face and touched a rough hand to her cheek. 'Thank you,' he said.

He ran now, shouting at people to get out of his way. The sense of the commotion travelled through passageways and up stairways so that the Chief Secretary himself was standing in his own doorway by the time Seeker got there. Anxiety was written on his face.

'What is it Seeker?'

Seeker nodded into the room behind and then followed Thurloe through.

Thurloe closed the door behind them. 'Damian?'

'A plot, to set light to the chapel during tonight's service, when the Protector and all the Committee of State are at worship. I have John Toope under close guard, in the Foot Guard's barrack. He has confessed to passing information on the Protector's movements and security provisions to Mr Fish, who he says is the Leveller, Miles Sindercombe.'

'Sindercombe.' The name meant something to Thurloe. General Monck in Scotland, dismissing him from the army, had warned about him over a year ago. More intelligence that had slipped through his fingers.

'Sindercombe and his fellow-conspirator, John Cecil, a Royalist, are in the pay of a man Toope knows only as Mr Boyes.'

Thurloe's gaze was unwavering. 'Rupert.'

Seeker nodded. 'Rupert has been behind the attempts at Hammersmith, and in Hyde Park this morning.'

'This morning?'

'Averted. But their money is almost done, and Rupert angered at their failures. Tonight is their last chance, it seems, before Rupert seeks other collaborators, other funds.'

Thurloe sat down. 'Tell me everything, Seeker.'

Seeker spoke quickly. Bribes had been paid for access to parts of Whitehall where feet such as those of Fish and Cecil could never have hoped to tread. Rupert, of course, knew his way around the palace from his days as favoured nephew to the dead King. The door to the chapel was to be left open, to allow Cecil, Fish and Rupert to lay the long, slow-burning fuse devised by the Prince, whose expertise in munitions was well known, and who had honed his devices in the backroom of a clockmaker's shop in Clerkenwell. Holes would be drilled through panelling and walls to stimulate draughts and encourage the conflagration. The incendiary device itself would be placed under General Lambert's seat – it was known that the Protector's own place was checked, but none usually made of those of his companions, and Lambert always sat close to the Protector. If the blast and fire failed to kill Oliver, amongst the confusion, Cecil would be waiting at the vestry exit, to shoot him as he was being led out. Toope was to arrange for fast horses to help the three make their escape.

Thurloe seemed to sink further into his seat. 'At the very heart of the palace, in the very centre of government. That it has got so far . . . we had warning from a source in Holland that Charles Stuart had placemen nearer the Protector than we imagined – but in his own Life Guard?'

'I think we must act *now*, sir.'

Thurloe shook himself and straightened. 'Yes, Yes, of course, Captain. Now, let me see: the service is to be at ten tonight.'

'That's two hours,' said Seeker. His heart was pounding faster with every moment's delay. 'They might still be there. I'll take some men and . . .'

'Yes of course,' said Thurloe again. 'Go. I will see to the rest.'

As Seeker was storming out of Thurloe's room and back down the stairs, the Chief Secretary was already sending messages to Major-General Barkstead at the Tower, and making arrangements for extra men to be put on every gate and roadway out of London and Westminster, and at every river port. He was just leaving his room to warn Cromwell, when Andrew Marvell appeared again at his door.

'Marvell. I have not the time!'

'I'm sorry, Mr Thurloe. I was told I would find Captain Seeker here.'

'You're too late. What message do you have for Seeker anyway?'

Marvell swallowed. 'That the men he sent out to the Bear Garden tavern at Hockley-in-the-Hole have returned and report there is clear evidence of a large animal having until very recently been kept in an old cellar there. One of them swears the scrapes on the door of the cellar are too large and deep by far to have been made by a dog. There are five grooves. He says they are the claw marks of a bear. He swears he can still smell it.'

Thurloe looked at Marvell as if he had lost his mind.

'Bears? Go home, Andrew. Go home and rest. You are of no use here.'

TWENTY-FIVE

The Chapel

Rupert had never seen the chapel from this perspective before. In countless others he had taken refuge, found a hiding place, somewhere to rest for the night, for England had made itself a land of defaced, abandoned churches. The sacred had fled, beauty was banished: there was only the Word. Rupert had respect for the Word, and he had respect for beauty, but his uncle Charles's passion for the elaboration of the sacred had not quite been to his taste. Still, though, there must surely be something blasphemous in the desecration of places dedicated to the worship of God that the Puritans had inflicted on England.

Their progress concerning the chapel had been less difficult than he had feared it might be. Most of John Thurloe's resources and Seeker's search parties were focused on the city, and around Lambeth Marsh. The money paid to Toope to meddle with the palace guard duties had done the rest. Those who should have been guarding the chapel had been bribed by Toope to take themselves elsewhere. Rupert had told Fish and Cecil to wait in the outward vestry, on the pretence that he needed a moment alone to think clearly, to select the best places for the drill holes and the devices. But Rupert did not need to think; he already knew. He had a sketch of this place in his head, precise as by the best of draughtsmen. Fish and Cecil seemed unaware he had any existence in London than when in their presence, any other acquaintance but them. He had made a plan, of course, from his memories of his own attendance at services in this chapel. Twenty years ago, himself seventeen years old and already baptised into war on the battlefields of Europe, his brother Maurice just a year younger. They had had nothing in their heads but adventure and the promises of life. All had seemed possible then – they would return in triumph one day to their lost inheritance of the Palatinate, and England, under the benevolent rule of their uncle, would be to them a second home. Rupert stood where the altar had been, and looked down the body of the chapel. If he closed his eyes he could see it all now: his uncle the King, rapt in devotion, his cousin Charles struggling to hide his boredom, the other, younger ones, doing better. The Queen, of course, was seldom there, preferring her Romish chapel at St James's, which Inigo Jones had started for another princess and finished for her. Rupert's mother might have let them stay in England then, but for her great fear that Henrietta-Maria's popery was infectious. Rupert could see it so clearly, that twenty-year-old tableau, in all its majesty, and he had made his sketch, his first sketch, accordingly.

They were gone, though, those people he could see here when he closed his eyes. His uncle, murdered by the usurping Cromwell; his cousin Charles, a wandering refugee denied his crown; Maurice – but Rupert wouldn't believe that his brother was truly gone. Had he not twice been told that Maurice had died in battle, only to find later that it was not so? It had only been four years since that storm at sea. Men had been found alive after more than four years. Rupert would not give up searching until Maurice was found. And then he would tell him of this night, when, in this very place, he had blown Oliver Cromwell to eternity.

Of course, when Rupert opened his eyes, the chapel he looked upon told a different tale from that in which he had worshipped twenty years ago. Since Cromwell and the generals had taken up residence in the royal palaces, countless treasures from the King's collections had been sold, churches stripped, their organs torn out and put in taverns, windows smashed. The windows had not been smashed in this one though, and the organ remained – for the Lord Protector, it was crowed, as if the fact somehow made him a gentleman, had a great love of music. Nevertheless, much had been altered here, much was gone, beauty removed, its very memory all but erased. But Rupert had known that the plan he'd made of the chapel would need some amendment before it could serve their present purposes. Consequently, he had taken his sketch to one of his other acquaintances in London, a loyal supporter of the King, and she had taken up her own pencil, and marked for him where alteration would have to be made.

Lady Anne Winter was less than a year returned to the capital from enforced exile in the north. Contacts on the continent had given him her name as one who could be utterly relied upon, and one who knew the design of Cromwell's Whitehall. Since her return from the north, she'd lived very quietly, respectably, so as to give no cause for concern to the agents and watchers employed in Thurloe's service. Rupert had gone to her lodgings near Lincoln's Inn when first he'd realised that they might indeed need to implement this, their most dangerous and audacious scheme. When Lady Anne had got over her shock at realising who he was, this clockmaker who had called at her door on the pretence of returning a mended clock that she knew for a certainty she'd never put in to his shop, she had said at once that she would do whatever was required of her. She'd taken care, she said, to let the authorities see how well she had learned her lesson, and that she had finally learned to behave, so that they might not notice when she did not. So quietly had she lived that even Damian Seeker seemed to have given up watching her. 'A pity,' she'd said, 'for I miss our old game.'

She'd understood straight away what Rupert required. She could easily see where the differences were between Rupert's plan of the chapel and the way it was under Cromwell. In her time living at Whitehall Palace, the wife of a high-ranking Republican officer, she had been obliged at times to attend church services in the presence of the Lord Protector. So bored had she been by the Puritan dronings of Oliver's preacher, that she had taken great interest in the design and furnishings of the chapel.

Rupert had found himself thinking occasionally about Anne Winter since that afternoon in her lodgings. Something in her beguiled him. At another time or in a different place, perhaps their interest in each other might have been different. But they lived here, now, and they both had the one, higher priority: the restoration of the King. Anne Winter had altered his sketch, and he, for such things did really interest him, had taken out his little case of instruments and shown her some of the tricks the old clock he had brought with him could be made to do. It was the most pleasant hour he had spent since returning to London.

But the clockmaker's days were over, for now, and time was pressing – the guards bribed by Toope would soon be replaced by others less amenable and more curious. In the chapel, Rupert looked into his bag, the carpenter's bag that he had carried right through the streets of London, out at its gates and on into Westminster and then Whitehall Palace itself. He took out the auger, and the brace and bit, and called for Fish and Cecil to come in. To Fish, he handed the auger for boring holes into the panelling and beneath seats, in order that the resultant draughts of air would perform the work of bellows once the fire was started. Cecil began to unscrew the back panel of General Lambert's seat, behind Cromwell's own. Rupert reached again into his bag and brought out the device he had spent so many hours in the back room of Dietmar Kästner's shop working upon. It really was a well-made piece, quite ingenious, and it was a pity neither Cecil nor Fish had the knowledge to understand its mechanisms. He had wondered about showing it to John Evelyn, or even Robert Boyle, who delighted in ingenuity, but Clémence had counselled him very strongly against it. He checked that the necessary parts were in contact with one another. He also checked that the powder was properly dry, for it had begun to snow again as they'd made their way down the Strand. Then he affixed the device, as planned, to the underside of Lambert's seat.

He glanced up at Cecil. 'Ready?'

Cecil nodded. 'Ready.'

Rupert took the fuse from the bottom of the bag and began, carefully, to unravel it. Lambert's seat, against the wood-panelled wall a few feet from the pulpit, was closest to the vestry door. The palace chapel had two vestries: one, the outward vestry, was on the north side and connected the chapel with the Great Hall. The other, the smaller of the two, was to the south, and opened on to Whitehall Palace Stairs and so the river. It was this second, smaller vestry that was key to their plans. Rupert had stained the long, thin fuse cord a deep brown, to accord with the dark oak beading of the wall. One end he affixed to the powder casket of the device beneath Lambert's seat, the other he pushed through behind the panel that Cecil had unscrewed. As Cecil worked quickly to replace the panel, Rupert, on hands and knees, began laying the camouflaged fuse along the bottom skirting of the wall. They would run it beneath the vestry door and so to the outside where, just before the Lord Protector and his Council entered at the west door of the chapel, they would light it. The plan had been that Rupert and Fish would then leave – Fish to rally his Leveller friends, Rupert, or Mr Boyes as they still thought him, to rally his fellow Royalists. Cecil would remain behind, outside the vestry door, to shoot Cromwell should the Protector survive the blast and seek to flee the fire. That had been the initial plan, but Cecil's bewilderment when face to face with Cromwell in Hyde Park had forced a change – he could not be trusted not to fail a second time, and their cause be lost. Fish, to his credit, had said he would remain behind and do it, but Rupert had his own debts to pay to Cromwell, and he would not stand amazed in the face of the tyrant when the time came to pay them.

The place was almost entirely in darkness. The sliver of new moon between the snow clouds gave little light. Cecil crouched above him, holding up a candle that he might see what he was doing. Snow was lying on the ground outside. Inside, the chapel was cold as a Puritan's heart. Rupert's fingers trembled a little. He told himself it was because of the cold. He had almost finished securing the fuse line around the other side of the vestry door. It would be easier from here on, few would pay attention to the skirting of the vestry. There were just a few yards left to go. And then they heard the sound of boots on the snow, and Cecil's candle went out.

They went two abreast down the passageway between the pantry and the Great Hall. The outward vestry and the chapel beyond it were in darkness. Once past the Great Hall, Seeker positioned four men at the entrance to the outward vestry and motioned for the rest to follow him around to the west door. There, he took up position with three of the men, sending the remainder to the smaller vestry door that gave on to Whitehall Palace Stairs. At the count of thirty from their leaving the first group, they were to enter the chapel, leaving a man at each door.

At twenty-nine, Seeker raised his arm. At thirty, he dropped it. All three sets of doors to Whitehall Palace Chapel were forced open, and his men, heavily armed, poured in. Light from torches trailed over the walls, then spread up the chapel by degrees as candles in sconces were lit. The soldiers were well ordered, yet everywhere there was movement in shadows, everywhere noise in a place that moments before had been silent and still. He himself stopped at the bottom of the chapel. His eyes swept the rows of pews, the galleries above, the choir ahead of him where Cromwell and the Council were to gather to hear the sermon. He listened through the clattering of boots on flagstone floor and the clanking of arms for some other noise, the noise of breathing, of something that did not wish to proclaim itself, the noise of a thing hidden.

Seeker's flintlock pistol hung in its holster at his waist, but a pistol could be a slow thing to use, and was not always to be relied upon: he preferred his mace with the shaped steel flange and conical finial. His old sergeant, who had carried it around the bloody fields of Germany, had gifted it to him at Dunbar, the sergeant's last battle. Seeker liked the weight of it hanging from his wrist, liked the way the shaft, with its worn, twisting pattern of leaves and flowers, fitted in his palm. Hand to hand, face to face, man to man – that was what the mace was for. Let them keep their muskets: Seeker liked to look his enemy in the eye. He turned his wrist and wrapped his fingers around the mace.

Suddenly, there was movement ahead. An arm shot out from behind the pulpit and a musket was discharged. To his left, one of his men went down, clutching an arm. Seeker and three other soldiers were then running towards the pulpit when the sound of another shot filled the air, this one coming from the left-hand side of the choir. In the ensuing confusion, a man sprang from behind the pulpit, sword drawn, and made for the south vestry door. Just at that moment, the door swung open and another soldier ran in, sword also drawn, and planted himself in the fugitive musketeer's path. The fight that ensued was brutal and without compromise, as it had to be, the rebel giving all or nothing for lack of a choice. He had clearly been a soldier and he handled his sword as one who knew what it was to fight for his life. For all that, he was no match for an opponent who was still a soldier and who drilled every day. Seeker had no fears over who would prove the victor. 'Take him alive!' he shouted, over the din of clashing steel. The shout appeared to distract the plotter just momentarily, but that was enough: the mildest turn of his head had left him exposed, and the point of his opponent's sword moved quickly across his face and removed the end of his nose. The maimed man dropped his sword and fell to the floor clutching his face as blood poured through his fingers and down his arm. Before he could reach across the floor for his dropped weapon, a second soldier had kicked it out of the way and was yanking his arms back behind him, and fitting manacles.

Seeker registered all this as he ran the remaining distance up the chapel to the choir, from which the second shot had come. This part of the chapel was not yet lit and was a confusion of shadows. Three of his men had already vaulted the side rail and their shouts and the sounds of the scuffle told him they had the second marksman cornered. As Seeker stepped over the side gate into the choir, the man dropped his weapon and a glance at the green felt hat and the shape of a head he had last seen disappearing out of Lawrence Ingolby's Clifford's Inn window told him this was John Cecil. He looked back at Cecil's bloodied, manacled co-conspirator. 'Fish', of course. That was two: Cecil, 'Fish', but no 'Boyes'. Seeker quickly scanned the opposite side of the choir. Empty. His men would have found anyone lurking in either vestry as they'd come in. He wheeled back around and took hold of Cecil by the collar, hauling the terrified man off his feet.

'Where is he?'

'Where is who?'

Seeker slammed him full body into the seat he'd been cornered at. 'Rupert! Rupert of the benighted Rh—'

Cecil gasped and cowered. He started to shake his head but then realisation dawned and a smile broke over his face. 'Rupert! Of course! I knew it! Who else could it have been? To think I served the Prince . . .'

Even as he said it, something over Seeker's shoulder caught Cecil's eye and he looked away too quickly. Seeker spun round. At first he saw nothing, but a slight scuffling sound made him look up. A man was standing on the wooden balcony of the organ gallery. He was as tall as Seeker himself, but slimmer, more graceful of build. No grey clockmaker's wig now, but long chestnut locks falling to broad shoulders, a swordsman's shoulders. The man was dressed in a simple linen shirt and buff jerkin and hose, a carpenter's belt was at his waist, but he was no carpenter. From that belt Seeker could see protrude no chisel or rule, but the butt of a flintlock pistol and the shaft of a horseman's hammer such as he himself kept at his saddle. Seeker's mind went back to the last time he had seen this man, who had been no carpenter then either, but commander of the King's cavalry and general of the Royalist forces. It was eleven years ago at Naseby that he'd first seen Rupert of the Rhine, son of the Winter King and Queen of Bohemia, brother of the Elector Palatine, and nephew of the executed King Charles I. Seeker remembered him that day, twenty-five years old, swathed in a scarlet cape and leading the Royalist cavalry in one of the most gallant charges he had ever witnessed. Ordered to fight by his uncle, Charles I, Rupert had taken an army of nine thousand men out against one almost twice its size and had believed he could win. But he had not won; slaughter had been done that day. The lesson Seeker had left the field with, his horse picking its way through the bodies of Rupert's martyred Blue Coats, had been that there were few things more doomed to end in disaster than valour without discipline.

Seeker's hand went to his mace as Rupert's went for his pistol. As Seeker drew back his arm to throw, he saw Rupert pull back the trigger on the snaphaunce pistol. As Seeker released the mace, there was a flash and then a bang from above. He ducked instinctively, but a crash behind him told him Rupert had fired not at him, but at the heavy candelabra suspended from the ceiling. The shot split the link from which the ornate arrangement hung and all – brass, wood and crystal – came smashing and splintering down on to the floor inches from his feet. Almost as Seeker registered this, he saw Rupert jerk to the side to try to avoid the mace before throwing out a rope from the organ balcony to loop around the chain of the matching candelabra further across the chapel. The mace just glanced the prince's shoulder, and there was a moment of stillness before, to Seeker's disbelief, Rupert leapt from the balcony rail. The Prince held momentarily to the rope he had slung around the candelabra as he swung, before releasing it a moment before that too came crashing down, and he fell the last ten feet to the floor, just behind the huddle where Seeker's men were still securing the profusely bleeding Fish. There was no one now between Rupert and the vestry door, and only one man still on guard outside it. That was at least two men too few for such a fighter. The shock of the shattered chandeliers was still resonating around the marble-floored chapel as Seeker drew his dagger from its sheath and yelled at his men to come after him.

A twisted arm of burnished brass sticking out from one of the stricken candelabra almost sent Seeker flying on his face as he ran for the door of the small vestry, but he righted himself and called out a warning to the men coming behind him. At his first attempt to get through the door, it would not budge, and it took a shoulder charge to get it to open. Once through, he almost went over again, this time caught by the prone form of the man he had left to guard it. The man was conscious, but bleeding from a wound to the temple that looked to have come from the butt of a pistol. Seeker stepped over him and shouted that someone should see to him. The door leading from the vestry out on to the passage for Whitehall Palace Stairs had also been rammed shut, and it took the shoulders of two men this time to dislodge whatever Rupert had stuck against it.

Once out into the passageway, Seeker could hear the muffled sounds of boots running through the snow, which was now falling heavily. The sounds were getting more distant, and they were going in the direction of the river. 'Get over to the Cockpit, tell Mr Thurloe what's happened, and tell him Rupert's headed for the river.' Then the man, and his torch, were gone. Seeker ran too, in the direction of the river. By the time he got to the Whitehall Stairs, a boat, with Rupert in it, was already being rowed at speed towards the south bank. Seeker stifled a curse. The only other boat at the stairs was a small rowboat with a floating pallet, stacked with other pallets, attached, and no sign of its oarsman. All other vessels had been pressed into the service of getting the Lord Protector and his household to Hampton Court. The snow was lying, thickening on the steps. Every moment that passed was a moment more in which Rupert could disappear. Seeker flexed his shoulders and swung his axe down to sever the rope between the small boat and its laden pallet. He could wait no longer: there was nothing for it but to cross the river himself.

TWENTY-SIX

The Bear Pit

Seeker's hands were frozen, and his face stung with the cold, but the snow was getting lighter, and what at first had looked set to be a blizzard had gradually let up. By halfway across the river, he could see Rupert's boat ahead of him. The Prince was pulling not upriver towards Lambeth, where lights flickered through the snow from the palace windows, or further south to Tradescant's as Seeker had thought he might, but north, towards the darkness of the marsh. There was something odd in the Prince's rowing action, and Seeker realised that not only was Rupert alone, but he was also clearly injured.

With each pull on his oars, Seeker was gaining on the Prince, and by the time Rupert reached the other side, the distance between them had almost halved. The lamp Rupert must have taken from the vestry guard was a beacon to Seeker, marking out his quarry. Once on land, Rupert picked up speed, his injured arm hampering him less on foot than it had done on the water. Seeker redoubled his efforts to power himself across as Whitehall receded further behind him, and the cries of some of his own men as they commandeered a boat died away to nothing through the snow.

By the time Seeker reached the far side, the light from Rupert's lamp was just an intermittent glimmer, but it was enough. The Prince was heading not on to the marsh but towards Bankside. It took Seeker a moment to adjust his stride to the snow lying underfoot. Large, fat flakes flew into his eyes and seeped through his boots as he ran, but he dared not take his eyes from that lamp for a moment, for fear of losing sight of it altogether.

Rupert was slowing by the time he reached Cupid's Garden, and it wasn't long before Seeker was able to make out the form of the Prince himself. They were almost within sight of the first straggle of houses along Bankside when Rupert looked back on his pursuer for the first time. Without hesitation, he hurled the lamp away from him and Seeker lost sight of him altogether. Seeker took a gamble that Rupert would not go onto the marsh and kept to the road. At last some light began to appear from the windows of the Bankside houses, and Seeker saw that his gamble had paid off, and that the distance between himself and Rupert was down to forty yards. The way the Prince was moving, he'd have him in less than two minutes. But then, just as he was about to pass Paris Garden, Rupert veered right and disappeared.

Seeker cursed and turned down the first alleyway he came to at Paris Garden. He was now amongst the high walls and back yards of the depths of Bankside. Rupert could have ducked in to any lane or doorway. Seeker stopped running and listened. There was sound everywhere – singing from a tavern somewhere, sounds of an argument nearer the river, a woman's voice raised and a man's in response, drunk and conciliatory. 'Where are you, you German dog?' Seeker murmured to himself, and then he heard it, the sound of feet landing from a height, of a man having cleared a wall. It sounded to be about three gardens away. It was difficult to tell in the darkness, but he knew he must now be very near the place where he and Thomas Faithly had found the bloodied remains of Joseph Grindle. And what was clearer to him now, on this snowy night, than it had been before was that he must be less than eighty yards from the site of the old Bear Garden.

Seeker vaulted a gate into the back yard he thought the noise had come from and stopped to listen. He tried to cut out the sounds drifting down to him from the Bankside, from the taverns and stews, tried to cut out the sound of a cat mewing to be let in, of pigs shifting and grumbling as they slept in their pen nearby, of a horse whinnying in its stable. He listened for movement, outside. Dogs huddled in their kennels, birds kept to their nests, rats sought warmth and better pickings indoors. Nothing. Nothing out in these back yards but the particular silence of snow relentlessly falling. His eyes were growing more accustomed to the outlines of the yard and its buildings, and he could just make out traces of bootprints in the snow, sliding and gradually being covered, leading from one side of the yard to the wall on the other.

Seeker was already standing on a barrel, and reaching to the top of the wall, when he heard it: a slamming, muffled by the snow, but a slamming all the same. It didn't sound like a door, but a shutter or something of that sort. He gripped fast to the top of the wall and hauled himself over, dropping ten feet to land on the other side. His feet went from under him in the snow, and he lurched sideways, falling hard on to his side and hearing the crunch as the wooden gunpowder flask he wore at his belt split beneath him. The measure of powder spilled to the snow and was gone.

Seeker heaved himself up and cast about for where the slamming might have come from. The back door and windows of the place were firmly shuttered and no light coming from them, nor from the range of outbuildings. He looked at the ground, and there they were, bootprints. It didn't make sense at first – they seemed to just disappear, about six feet from the far wall, and then he saw, a few inches from the ground, the handle of a hatch door, as for a coal cellar or some other underground store. Some snow had slid off it into a pile – it had very recently been opened. Seeker examined the ground around the door: only one set of prints, and they went nowhere but to the door before disappearing. He bent his head to listen. Nothing. Slowly, he began to raise the handle, and as he did so, a dim glow of light filtered out from the darkness below, illuminating not a coal chute but a set of steps. Again Seeker listened:

this time there was something – a muffled sound. It was the sound of someone who had been bound with a gag and not quite silenced.

'Who's there?' he shouted.

Movement, scuffling, and a more high-pitched muffle.

'Sir Thomas? Thomas Faithly? Are you down there?'

A sudden flare of light illuminated not only the steps but a level gallery six feet below the hatch, looking down over the darkness of a deep pit. A voice reached him from the other side of the gallery and Thomas Faithly stepped into the light. 'I'm sorry, Seeker,' he said, and as he said it Seeker felt something hit his back with tremendous force, sending him tumbling down the steps to land on the beaten earth floor of the pit fifteen feet below. He tasted dirt and almost gagged on air so foul it was worse than in a barn full of dead sheep he'd once come across. The whole side of his face stung, and he could feel the blood begin to seep out of the cuts to mix with the dirt. He tried to right himself, wincing as he realised, too late, that his ankle was twisted and his arm was broken. And then he heard a scuffle, a scream, and Maria Ellingworth cry his name.

She was there, near the edge of the gallery above him, a few feet from Thomas Faithly, and Clémence Barguil was standing behind her.

'Maria?' His voice was so hoarse the first time he had to say it again. 'What are you doing here? Why have you . . .?' And then he saw that Clémence had her arm around Maria's neck, and that in her hand she held a knife.

He forced himself to his feet and lunged at the wall, succeeding only in further injuring his ankle. He roared in frustration. 'Harm her and I'll kill you. I'll kill you all.'

Thomas Faithly came further into the light. 'Steady, Seeker. We mean her no harm.'

Rage almost overwhelmed Seeker. 'I'll start with you, Faithly. I'll tear you limb from limb. You'll wish I'd shot you the minute I first saw you. Tell that French trollop to let her go. Now.'

Clémence Barguil merely brought the knife closer to Maria's throat. There was terror in Maria's eyes as her lips silently mouthed his name.

'Clémence,' a voice warned.

Seeker spun round and felt his ankle scream again. He was behind him, Rupert. Still in the workman's clothes, his hair was sodden, and blood was seeping through the sleeve of his shirt from a wound just below his shoulder. Somehow, though, he managed to retain the bearing Seeker remembered from the battlefield.

'Discard your weapons, Captain, and she will come to no harm.'

Seeker shook his head. 'I mean it,' he said, 'prince or no prince, I'll kill you if you cut a hair on her head.'

'I see my poor carpenter's disguise has not fooled you.'

'Nor your clockmaker's, either. It's done, Rupert, over with. Fish and Cecil are both taken. They'll give you up without another thought.'

'Ah, will they?' Rupert sounded almost sad. 'Have you

any notion how many times I have been given up, Seeker? My own parents forgot about me as they fled their palace in Prague, did you know that? I was only a few months old, and yet here I am. A servant found me rolled off the sofa onto the floor, and threw me through the window of a moving coach, to land amongst the baggage. I have been throwing myself through moving coaches and escaping ever since. God has not protected me thus far so that I might make my obeisance to your Puritan oaf, who sits on my cousin's throne.' He picked up a cloak that had been lying over the rail of the gallery. 'My friends and I will soon be leaving, and you and this young woman will also find your way out of here, in time. It was not my choice to involve her, but Mademoiselle Barguil felt her presence might serve for us as a bargaining counter, should you trace me here. I am truly sorry to have caused her this distress. I am sorry too, that we have not been able to test each other's valour in a more fitting arena, Captain.'

'Valour?' Seeker's voice was contorted with scorn. 'What valour was it to shackle an old man to a wall and leave him to be savaged by a wild beast? What generalship was that?'

Rupert looked at him with genuine incomprehension. 'I don't know what you're talking about.'

'His name was Joseph Grindle. He fought with you many years ago, in Germany, for your brother, and he recognised you, didn't he, the day he took an old clock to Clerkenwell, to be fixed in Dietmar Kästner's shop?'

Rupert's brow furrowed, and Seeker expected another

denial, but it didn't come, not as he'd expected at any rate. 'Joseph Grindle recognised me, yes, I am fairly certain of it. But he was not – what? Chained to a wall? To be savaged by a beast? Clémence paid him for his silence, and he left London the same day he'd come into Dietmar's shop.'

Rupert turned to Clémence Barguil for affirmation, and Seeker saw now that Thomas Faithly was also looking at her. His face, even in the yellow light of this cavern, was like chalk.

'Clémence . . .' Faithly said. 'The old man, that Seeker and I found . . .'

'Would never have kept his silence,' Clémence said. 'He would have betrayed the Prince the minute he found someone to tell it to. This enterprise would have failed, as the others before it have failed, and another gracious prince would have ended his days on earth by the axe of Cromwell's executioner.'

Thomas Faithly's face was suffused with horror. 'But how . . .?' He couldn't articulate his thoughts.

Rupert was more collected, although there was a deadness to his voice as he spoke. 'What did you do, Clémence?'

'I followed him, as you asked me to. That Croat's hat of his was like a marker. I came upon him on Cornhill – he had darted into a coffee house but come out again soon afterwards. I told him I was looking for him. I told him I had followed him from Dietmar Kästner's shop.' Now a look of triumph spread across her face. 'I told him,' she said, her eyes glittering, 'that I was in the service of Secretary Thurloe, and that myself and other agents had been watching the clockmaker's shop for some time. He almost vomited his story over me, such was his eagerness to tell what he had seen.'

'And you brought him here,' said Seeker.

Clémence nodded, as if it were the most reasonable thing in the world. 'I brought him – well, not here, exactly, but to the yard of the gaming house along the street. I knew Thomas had engaged himself there with some acquaintances for the evening, and would be arriving just after dark. I had no idea, really, what I should do with the old man – he had clearly been a soldier, and retained a great deal of vigour. I did not think I would be capable of overwhelming him alone, but I knew Thomas would have no difficulty in dealing with him.'

'Dealing with him?' said Seeker.

She narrowed her eyes. 'Come now, Captain, thousands, hundreds of thousands have died already in this struggle. Who would miss an old soldier whose fighting days are past? He'd had his chances and his time, and his life was nothing compared to that which he threatened.'

Now Seeker turned his disgust on Thomas Faithly. 'You said you'd never seen him before.'

But Faithly was shaking his head. 'I never had. I swear it, Seeker. And I didn't see Clémence that day either.'

Clémence Barguil gave Seeker a fixed look. 'Your manners are truly dreadful, Captain. If you didn't keep interrupting me, you would not be led into these misunderstandings. I told the old man – Grindle? – that those who worked for Mr Thurloe used the house on Bankside as a safe house, and that he would need to wait in the outbuilding until I had permission to take him inside, to meet my superior. I opened the door, and then I hit him on the head with a brick.' She smiled. 'I am not without ingenuity. When he went down, I hit him again. I hoped he might not come to before Thomas arrived, and then I saw the old dog chains. It was perfect. It took some effort to drag him across the floor close enough to clamp him by the neck, but my gardening activities have given me more strength than most men might imagine. Then I covered him with some sacking.'

Faithly was still staring at her in horror. 'Seeker, I swear—'

But Clémence interrupted him. 'Thomas is telling the truth, Captain. The most extraordinary thing occurred as I waited for him to arrive at the gaming house. Just as darkness fell, a cart came trundling into the yard. The man driving it was very concerned that I should leave, just as concerned as I was that he should. He threatened me, and I him, and we raised our threats and our promises awhile until I had gained his trust. He told me the nature of his cargo.'

'Which was?' asked Seeker, although he was certain he already knew the answer.

'Oh, I think you have guessed that, Captain. A bear. A brown bear. A particularly fine specimen too, or so the man claimed. As you will imagine, I was not able to verify this because, it being no easy thing to transport a live bear across London Bridge to Bankside, its keeper had taken the trouble to render it tranquil through some preparation he had got from the man who wished to examine it.'

'Mulberry,' said Seeker.

'Yes,' said Clémence. 'The friend of Mr Evelyn's in whom you took so much interest had contracted with the keeper to examine the animal, to assess its fitness for his scientific purposes. The examination was to take place in the very outbuilding in which I had secured the old man.'

'Why there? Why take the risk of transporting it from where it had been kept? Surely Mulberry,' then Seeker corrected himself, 'Thomas Bushell, could have examined it wherever it was being kept?'

'No doubt he would have done, but the keeper seemed to have become nervous about the interest lately shown in the animal and had moved it to a location he was not willing to make public. Also, as I understand, he and his charge had business on Bankside that night.'

'He can't have been baiting it. The bear pit's been demolished.'

Now Clémence Barguil's smile was truly frightening. 'The one at the Bear Garden, yes, it has. But this one has not.'

'This . . .?' And then Seeker understood. The beaten earth floor, the gallery fifteen feet above, the streaks he had noticed on the walls and at first thought to be fungus but now realised were blood, the smell. 'They've been having private fights here.'

She nodded. 'Well done, Captain. Yes, and to great profit, I understand. I don't think you had anyone examine the coal-hole of the gaming-house yard, did you?'

Had he? The place would have been looked in, as part of a general search afterwards, but if nothing was found in it, no further examination would have been made.

She was far too amused. 'If you had done, they would surely have found the hatch at the back, rather like the one by which you entered here, but necessarily larger. A passageway leads down beneath the houses and gardens to come out behind us. London is full of such tunnels and passageways, as I'm sure you know.'

Seeker knew.

'Anyhow,' she continued, 'once Mr Mulberry – Thomas Bushell – had finished examining the animal in the out-building, the keeper planned to transfer it here, by that passageway. I told the keeper that I was a friend of Mr Mulberry's, and that if he deposited his charge securely in the outbuilding, he might go and get himself some supper and I would wait till Mr Mulberry was finished.' She raised her eyebrows. 'I furnished him and his men with enough money that would have done them for ten suppers. I believe they went away and got very drunk.'

Seeker was just considering what justice might be served on Thomas Bushell for his involvement in the murder of a defenceless old soldier when Clémence Barguil forestalled him. 'Of course, when Bushell arrived, I told him I had been asked to convey to him a message that the animal would not be available for experiment that evening, due to the major-general's planned raids of Bankside. Colonel Pride had, after all, been threatening for some time to clean the place up. And so Bushell left, much disappointed.'

Rupert spoke very quietly. 'And what did you do then, Clémence?'

She shrugged. 'Nothing. I just waited. In time, I heard sounds of the animal waking, and then the man. And then there were other sounds that suggested this Grindle would present us with no more problems, and so I returned to Sayes Court. I think the animal's keeper must have returned some time soon afterwards, because I do not think you mentioned having come upon the bear when you found the old man, did you, Thomas?'

She might have been enquiring as to whether he had remembered to lace up his doublet.

Thomas's voice was a husk. 'Clémence – how could you do that?'

She looked as if she didn't properly understand his question. 'I would do anything, Thomas, for the Prince. You must know that.'

Thomas Faithly looked appalled, and Rupert's face was grey. 'Clémence,' he said, staring at her. 'Oh, Clémence.'

Seeker still couldn't hear any sounds from outside to suggest his men had tracked them down here. He scanned his surroundings, but there was nothing, not so much as a foothold to help him scale the stone walls of this pit, even had he the use of more than one good arm. His powder was gone and so his pistol useless, and his knife had clattered from his hand as he fell and now lay eight feet or more away, across the earthen floor. He had little doubt that if he moved towards it, Clémence Barguil would sink the tip of her knife into Maria's throat. The only way back up to her was the stairs, and a heavily armed Rupert was standing at the top of them. Seeker scanned the figures on the gallery. Clémence radiated triumph, but the two men were like players who had found themselves in the wrong play.

Thomas Faithly swallowed. 'Come, Clémence,' he said, 'it's time for us to go.'

But the woman merely shook her head.

'Clémence . . .' more urgently this time.

'No, Thomas. I will wait here until you and the Prince have got safely away, then I will come.'

'But then you will be taken,' said Rupert. 'Come, Clémence, we go now. We'll lock and weight the hatch, and be long gone before Seeker and this woman find their way out or are found.'

Again Clémence shook her head. 'Not him. He will find a way. I have heard it of him.'

'Clémence,' Faithly urged again.

Rupert changed tack. 'Will she come with us, the girl?'

Faithly turned towards Maria, pleading. 'Will you, Maria? Will you come with us? Will you come with me?'

Seeker felt time stop.

They were all looking at Maria now, waiting for her to speak. Clémence had even lowered the point of the knife and adopted a look of interest. Maria's eyes darted from one to the other of them and then settled on Sir Thomas. 'I think you are mad.'

He took a step towards her, and Seeker noticed Clémence tighten her grip on the knife. 'No, Maria. I have told you: I love you. We can have a life . . .'

'I have a life,' she said. 'And you cannot love me because you do not know me.'

Thomas Faithly looked as if she had struck him. 'And he does?' he said, indicating Seeker. 'Cromwell's thug? A man with no principles but what he can test with the toe of his boot, the swing of his fist? What life can he give you? You cannot *love* him, Maria.'

Tears were pricking Maria's eyes, and she was looking at Seeker. 'I love every part of him.'

Rupert had heard enough. 'Thomas, we must go now. Release her, Clémence.' He was turning away, had his hand below the hatch door, ready to push it up. Still Clémence did not move. She appeared to be considering something.

'Now, Clémence. I order you.'

'All right,' she said at last. 'You go after the Prince, Thomas, and then I will let this woman go.'

And so she did. As Thomas Faithly moved past her, Clémence lowered the hand that held the knife, and cut the rope that bound Maria's wrists together. But instead of following Rupert and Thomas, she turned back, towards a dark recess behind the gallery.

'Clémence! We must go now,' said Rupert.

'A moment,' she said. 'Less, even.'

And then she was gone from sight, with Thomas calling after her. There was no reply, save a sound of sawing, as of a knife through rope, and then a snap. Something fell, something clanked, like chains on a pulley run out of control. Seeker followed the direction of the sounds in time to see a gate at the far end of a passageway behind him fly up. At the same time, he heard a scream, and spun round in time to see Maria falling from the gallery, pushed by Clémence. She hit the floor of the pit with a cry and a thud before he could reach her.

'Maria,' he said, crouching down in the dirt, placing his fingers on her neck, feeling for a pulse of life. It was there. He reached towards the hair and carefully moved it back so that he could examine her face. Her eyelids were fluttering and she was trying to murmur his name. 'Hush,' he said, brushing his lips to her forehead. 'Hush now. All will be well.'

Above them, Thomas Faithly had turned on Clémence. Seeker spoke to him. 'This is your doing, Faithly. I will hunt you down, however far you run, I will hunt you.'

'Seeker, I never—'

'You brought her here!' he roared.

'No, Seeker. I didn't know. I would never have—'

'Come, Thomas, there is no time. Clémence, come!' Rupert was starting to ascend the steps to the hatch when a noise that chilled Seeker's blood came from the passageway behind him.

'What was . . .?' began Faithly, but he didn't have the chance to finish before another bestial growl filled the chamber.

Seeker turned slowly. The beast, on all fours, was emerging from the end of the passageway into the pit.

Seeker took a step backwards, trying to spread himself as much as he could, to shield Maria. An arrow of pain shot through his broken arm, again and again. The animal took a moment to raise its head and sniff the air. Seeker dived to his left and grabbed his knife from where it had fallen. The bear flicked its head to the side, roaring, and suddenly reared up on its hind legs. It must have been almost eight feet tall, and as heavy and powerful as several men. Whatever might have been the truth of the Bankside bears of days past, this one had not had its teeth drawn, nor its claws pulled out. This was no blameless cub, no dancing bear for country fairs: this bear had killed.

The men above him were shouting, but what they shouted Seeker couldn't tell. The bear paid them no heed, but roared again and then swiped a massive paw, claws fully extended, at Seeker. Seeker tried to parry with his knife, but just succeeded in angering the animal further. Another swipe, and this time the claw ripped through the leather of his doublet. There was no time to move or to think before a third swipe knocked him to the floor. Seeker rolled backwards to try to cover Maria as the huge head and gaping jaw bore down on him. And then a flash, a roar, and the beast was on him.

EPILOGUE

Monday, 19 January, 1657

Westminster

Thurloe surveyed the benches around him and stood up. The Commons were restive, had been restive too long. It was clear to anyone with an understanding of the workings of the world, what should be done, what must be done, if England were not once more to descend into bloody civil war. There were several ready to propose it – had proposed it already, in quiet corridors and secret places, but their proposals would carry no weight until they were made here. Thurloe could not do it: for all his power, for all he held the secrets of governments and nations in his hand, in his head, they looked upon him, these generals, and commons, as but the Lord Protector's shadow, and a man of no account. He would tell them what he had to tell them, and by the end of it, they would be baying for Cromwell to accept the crown.

He cleared his throat and began. 'I rise up to acquaint you with the discovery of a heinous plot, which is in part discovered, and we are in pursuit of the rest.' He told them all of it, or nearly all. He told them about the plot hatched in Flanders, at the behest of the Spanish Court, to take the life of the Protector, because the Stuarts and the Spaniards knew that while Oliver lived England would stand. He told them of Toope, who had given up his confederates, the Leveller Sindercombe and the Royalist trooper Cecil, that Toope and Cecil had confessed, whilst Sindercombe remained mute. But Sindercombe, who had gone as 'Mr Fish', would be made to speak, in time. And then he told them of Boyes. 'This Boyes is the chief agent. He is now in Flanders. It is likely that it is not his name, but he is a considerable person of the late King's party.' He told them of the intelligence received, of promised Spanish help to Charles Stuart in an invasion, if only Oliver were dead. When he had told them all he was inclined to, he regained his seat. Amongst the outrage, the clamour for justice, retribution, for a day of thanksgiving for so profound a deliverance, it was Mr Ashe, the elder, who first proposed to the Commons that day that Oliver Cromwell should take the crown.

Andrew Marvell had been charged with clearing Seeker's rooms. He felt an imposter, as if at any moment the captain might walk in, roar at him for his daring, then laugh and clap him round the shoulder and bid him sit down, all in that rolling Yorkshire voice. But Seeker would not be walking back in here again, Marvell knew that. Tomorrow another officer, Walter Strickland, he had heard, would make these rooms his, and continue Thurloe's work where Seeker had left it.

And that's all there was here, in truth, of Seeker: his work. There was nothing of the man. The man was in glimpses he had allowed a few others to see – an old lamed soldier in a coffee house on Birchin Lane, a badly injured girl in a garret in Dove Court, a widow woman who kept a tavern on Broad Street, and a young Yorkshireman come down to train for the law at Clifford's Inn. Marvell looked at the empty grate in the hearth, and bent down to sweep some wiry grey hairs onto the floor. He smiled. There was the hound too, of course, nursed back to health by the Jewess and long returned to the care of the gardener's boy at Lincoln's Inn.

The hound. Marvell had felt worst of all for the hound, when first he had heard. What does that say of a man, that on his loss it is his dog that you pity most? He picked up the last of the papers already marked by Seeker for filing by the clerks and surveyed the room one last time, before going to the door. The place was silent, and empty. 'But only human eyes can weep,' he said to himself as he turned the handle and went out.

Thomas was frozen, and exhausted. In the last eleven days, he and Rupert had eaten on perhaps one day out of two. They had been drenched more times than they'd been dry, and not slept in a proper bed once since they'd left London.

'Like old times,' Rupert had said, in an attempt to cheer him.

'Old times for old men, Highness,' Thomas had replied. 'What was nothing to me to endure as a man of twenty-five is not nothing ten years later.'

'But you will endure,' Rupert said. 'You have endured.'

The Prince's eyes were searching his, for something. Eleven days, and Rupert had not yet asked him, but as their boat at last came within sight of the Flemish coast, Thomas felt it was time. 'I betrayed the King.'

Rupert shook his head. 'I don't think so, Thomas.'

'No, you must know it. I would have you know it. I was ready to give it up – the King's cause. I traded letters in the hope that I might return home, I offered to spy on my own kind . . .'

'But you did not, did you?' Rupert said quietly. 'Those exposed in the letters you traded had done nothing but make empty promises. They were no loss to my cousin's cause. And most of all, when you saw me that night, you did not betray me.'

Thomas saw it again, so clearly that the wave of nausea he had felt then threatened to return. He was by Lady Ranelagh's terrace, sitting with Andrew Marvell, laughing and not quite whispering indiscretions about some of their august fellow guests, enjoying the best company he had found himself in since he had returned to England. Then he had seen him, an old clockmaker, at work on the clock in Lady Ranelagh's hall. Thomas would not have given the fellow a second glance, had something in the movement of the clockmaker's hands not taken his eye. That grace, that fineness of touch. How many times had Thomas seen those fingers wield a paintbrush, a tennis racquet, work on some mechanism beyond the fixing of others? And then the clockmaker had looked up, straightened himself to his full height and looked him right in the eye, and Thomas had known for certain that it was Rupert. He had never sobered up so quickly.

'I tried to find you. I spent the night looking for you. God knows what Marvell thought. And then when I went back to Sayes Court and asked Clémence, she wouldn't tell me – she denied it had been you. I don't think she quite trusted me.'

Rupert gave a soft laugh. 'No, her suspicions of you were very deep. I argued that whatever else you might do, you wouldn't betray *me*, but Clémence has never been prepared to leave my well-being to chance, when she has thought she could better protect me.'

'I wouldn't have betrayed you,' said Thomas. 'It was like a veil had lifted for me, and I saw my life, my country, for what it was. Then when I saw your handwriting on the note delivered to me at the Black Fox . . . I'd tried to persuade myself that I could make something of it, carve out a place for myself . . .'

'With the girl?' prompted Rupert.

'Yes.' Thomas's voice was all but inaudible. Even now he could not bear to think of Maria.

Rupert reached a hand across and gripped his. 'It will be well with her. Seeker's body protected her.'

Thomas nodded, and looked out towards Flanders, and his future, but his hand in Rupert's, his face, his heart, were frozen.

Lawrence folded the letter and put it away in his doublet when he heard Dorcas's step on the stairs. His little room under the eaves of the Black Fox was even smaller than his chamber at Clifford's Inn had been and would have fitted six times into the apartment he had had in Faithly Manor, but he wanted to be nowhere else. Which was just as well, for Dorcas had made plain to him that he would not be returning to Clifford's, unless he wanted her shouting his name at its gates every day. Clifford's was not safe, that was plain to see, and Lawrence was not safe to be let out on his own. He was not safe even to be let out in company. Even Seeker had not been able to . . .

And then she had stopped. Dorcas stopped, every time she tried to speak of Seeker, whereas Manon could scarcely speak at all.

He stood and went to the door when she knocked on it. The cuts and bites on his hand and arm were healing, though the stitches in his leg and on his stomach still gave him so much pain that only the apothecary Drake's preparations allowed him any sleep.

Dorcas was cold, and he ushered her to the fire that she insisted he have here as he studied at night.

'You're soaked,' he said.

'I've never known snow like it, not in London,' she shivered. 'My cloak's a puddle on the floor downstairs.'

'You shouldn't have gone tonight.'

That fire, that anger came into her eyes. She was too easy to provoke, these days, Dorcas, her anger being all that stopped her destroying herself with grief. He wished he hadn't said it.

'Damian would have done it, and he's not here to do it so I shall. How can Elias nurse the girl? He'd hardly the wit to keep her fed and warm when she was in health, and how should he do so now? Grace does what she can, but she has enough to do with the coffee house and poor Samuel near enough broken, and no one but that boy to help her. He speaks of America. America – Samuel! He and Elias, as soon as Maria is mended, they say, they'll be done with England.'

Done with England, Lawrence thought. How was England ever to be fixed if those who might do so would not stay? 'And will she be mended,' he asked quietly. 'Maria? How was she today?'

Dorcas looked into the fire. 'Her body, perhaps, I think so. I had her up today, and she managed a couple of steps. Elias wept at the triumph of it. I almost wept myself. But – I think her soul's gone.' Dorcas nodded to herself, as if it were almost a relief to say it aloud. 'Her soul is gone, Lawrence. But I told her – she has to do it for her brother, and for Grace and Samuel.' The anger was going out of her, as it always did. 'And she has to do it for Damian, for what else can we do for him?'

Lawrence watched her sink back in her seat, her eyes closed and her head raised to the heavens. No one else ever saw Dorcas like this. Least of all Manon.

He reached out a hand to pat her awkwardly on the knee, and then retracted it. 'There's Manon too, though. We can do that for him, we can look after Manon.'

She sniffed and straightened herself and smiled. 'Bless you, boy, the idea of you looking after anyone when you can't even look after yourself. But you can make the girl smile, and there's no one else in the world can do that now.'

Lawrence didn't mind that Dorcas thought him so helpless; if it made her feel stronger to have so many others to take care of, then so be it. But Lawrence wasn't helpless, and he'd have been here even if Dorcas hadn't insisted upon it. He'd have been here, looking after them in ways they wouldn't have guessed at. Because he wanted to, and because he'd been trusted to. It was all in the letter. There was money, with an agent, in Liverpool, if ever it should be needed, and there was a safe house, an address, only to be used in case of danger, which in these days, in England, might never be far off. And there was another address, in a code which John Thurloe himself had shown him, to which he might write, when the need arose.

It had been ten days ago that Thurloe had come into Seeker's chamber in Whitehall. Michal, the apothecary Drake's sister had been there, nursing Lawrence and the dog, and Thurloe had asked her to leave them alone a while. When she had left and Seeker's clerk been ordered away from the anteroom, Thurloe had shut the door, and locked it. Then he had told Lawrence, and he had explained to him the code, and given him the letter. 'Wait ten days,' the Chief Secretary had said. But as to Maria, Thurloe had been very clear: for fear of her brother's associations, she could not be told.

Ten days. Dorcas declared herself warm enough and stood up to leave.

Lawrence looked up. 'Dorcas? Can you fetch Manon? She'll not be sleeping yet, I don't think.'

'Manon? At this time of night? Whatever for?'

Ten days. More than long enough they'd suffered, and now he could tell them. He felt the edge of the letter as it pressed against his shirt beneath his doublet and smiled. 'I think there's something that you both need to know.' And after he'd told them, Lawrence would be going to Dove Court, Thurloe or no Thurloe, and he'd be showing Maria the other letter that had come to him, just today, from Bruges dated only five days ago, and written in Damian's own hand.

At Sayes Court, John Evelyn and his friends – Wenceslaus Hollar, Samuel Hartlib and Robert Boyle – were once again gathered in the elaboratory. But tonight, the furnace was cold, the stove was not lit, and alembics and funnels sat idle. Tonight, the talk was not of the new science, nor yet of philosophy, politics or religion. Tonight, all the anxious talk between these four learned gentlemen concerned what was to be done about their friend, Thomas Bushell, who appeared to have lost his wits. For, as Evelyn explained to the others, for ten days now, since Clémence Barguil had been found by Colonel Pride's soldiers, hiding in his old house on Lambeth Marsh, poor Bushell had been telling anyone who would listen that the last bear in London had been shot, dead, by Rupert of the Rhine.

AUTHOR'S NOTE

In the foregoing story, the tale of the murder of Joseph Grindle, and Seeker's subsequent investigation of it, are entirely fictional. The Bankside Bears were shot in February 1656 by a firing squad led by Colonel Pride, and the mastiffs used in the baiting shipped to Jamaica. The catalyst for this event appears to have been the death of a young child who had fallen from viewing scaffolding into the arena in September of 1655. The arena was soon demolished and the site redeveloped. Bear baiting may in fact have continued in another arena near Islington (there *was* a Bear Garden tavern at Hockley-in-the-Hole), prior to being permitted again at the Restoration.

The clandestine exchanges I have located at Tradescant's Garden in South Lambeth are also fictional, but the Gardens, and the Cabinet of Curiosities gathered by the John Tradescants were very much in existence, both as business and public attraction. The remains of the amazing collection of curiosities built up by father and son, the credit for which was appropriated by Elias Ashmole, can be viewed in Oxford's Ashmolean Museum, of which it formed the original collection. The Tradescants' tomb can still be seen at the Garden Museum in the former St Mary's church, Lambeth.

While the tale of Joseph Grindle is fictional, that of the attempts by Boyes, Fish and Cecil in the autumn and winter of 1656 to assassinate Oliver Cromwell, is not. By 1656, Cromwell's many enemies had begun to coalesce. Royalists and disgruntled Republicans alike came to believe that their only hope lay in the removal of the Lord Protector. These disaffected groups inevitably crossed each other's paths in exile in the Low Countries. The Leveller Edward Sexby, for instance, a former colonel who had once been close to Cromwell, became increasingly disaffected with the Protectorate. He began to forge links with Royalists abroad, and in 1655 met the cashiered Parliamentary soldier Miles Sindercombe (alias 'Mr Fish') in the Netherlands. Sexby commissioned Sindercombe to murder Cromwell, giving him £1500 to make the required arrangements. Sindercombe returned to England as 'Mr Fish', took up residence in King Street, Westminster, and hired former Royalist soldier John Cecil and another mysterious Royalist – 'Mr William Boyes' – to assist him. He also took John Toope, a member of the Protector's Life Guard, into his pay. Toope was able to pass on information about Cromwell's planned movements, and to pay off guards and servants at Whitehall Palace when the occasion required. One of Thurloe's intelligence sources on the continent picked up on rumours of the threat from 'Mr Fish', but Thurloe, overwhelmed with responsibilities and the endless flow of intelligence from abroad, delayed acting on the matter.

As in my story, the group made their first attempt at the State Opening of Parliament in September 1656, but were hampered by the crowd that surged around the Protector when he left Westminster Abbey. Their second attempt was from the upper room of a coaching house in Hammersmith, where they had rigged seven blunderbusses to fire simultaneously. The Protector's carriage took another route. The third attempt was on horseback, at Hyde Park. Accounts of its failure differ – either Cecil's horse took ill, or Cecil himself took fright; either way, the planned assassination did not take place. Their last was a desperate effort to murder Cromwell by blowing up Whitehall Palace with explosives set in the chapel. Toope's bribery activities allowed them to get as far as setting and lighting the fuse before being discovered, still in the chapel. In the struggle that ensued, Cecil was quickly taken, Sindercombe (Fish) overwhelmed, losing the tip of his nose in the fight, and Boyes escaped. Thurloe later confirmed to Parliament that it was Toope who had informed them of the conspirators' plan. The depiction in *The Bear Pit* of how Toope's confession came about is my invention.

Cecil and Sindercombe were interrogated by Thurloe, Cecil corroborating Toope's version of events, Sindercombe maintaining his silence. Both were tried at Westminster Hall in February of 1657 and sentenced to be hanged, drawn and quartered. On 13 February, Sindercombe committed suicide in the Tower of London, taking arsenic smuggled in by his sister. Clarendon suggests that Sindercombe's refusal to name his associates and his evasion of the Protectorate's final justice only served to increase Cromwell's paranoia. Such was Cromwell's rage on learning that Thurloe had had advance intelligence of 'Fish's' activities and not acted on it, that he almost dismissed him. Toope, astonishingly, remained on Thurloe's payroll as an agent until the end of the Protectorate.

When Thurloe stood up in Parliament on 19 January 1657, to inform the Commons of the conspiracy and its failure, he told them that interrogation of Cecil and Toope had revealed the name of the escaped plotter – 'Boyes'. 'This Boyes,' he said, 'is the chief agent. He is now in Flanders. It is likely that it is not his name, but he is a considerable person of the late King's party.'* And so, into *The Bear Pit* enters Rupert of the Rhine. The adventures of Charles I's dashing, six foot four devil-may-care nephew, son of the doomed Winter King and Queen of Bohemia, and fearless Royalist general, could fill, and has filled, many books. Those adventures are certainly too many to detail here, but a good flavour of them can be got from Charles Spencer's highly readable *Prince Rupert, the Last Cavalier* (2007).

Despite his great height, and his fame throughout Europe,

---

* *Diary of Thomas Burton Esq.*, vol.1, *July 1653–April 1657*. Monday, January 19, 1656–7. www.british-history.ac.uk

the idea that Rupert might have moved around London in disguise is perfectly feasible. The Stuarts, down to the hapless Charles Edward fleeing to Skye after the disaster of Culloden in the guise of 'Betty Burke', had a distinct flair for disguise, particularly in times of crisis. Charles II escaped England after the Battle of Worcester in a series of disguises, and rode for several days through the west of England masquerading as the servant of the courageous Jane Lane. A fourteen-year-old James, Duke of York, was sprung from Parliamentary clutches in St James's Palace, in the guise of a young woman. In 1658, the Earl of Ormonde slipped into London from Bruges, disguised as a pedlar, his fair hair dyed black, and lodged with a Catholic surgeon on Drury Lane. Unfortunately, the dye eventually turned his hair a startling orange, but due to intelligence received from spies at the King's court, Thurloe was already keeping an eye on his movements. As for Rupert, such was his reputation that he was mythologised as a master of disguise. It was said that he once dressed as an apple-seller, and went through the enemy camp, selling apples to Parliamentary soldiers. On another occasion, stopping for refreshment at an old woman's cottage, he asked her opinion of Rupert of the Rhine. I don't think it is too much to suggest that he might have moved, undetected, around London for three months or so, in 1656, by means of a series of disguises. If historical novelists are allowed to have favourites, Rupert, good Puritan though I am, is mine.

There is, of course, a vast literature around the period

of the Protectorate and the prominent figures of the Civil War era. Key general texts are Trevor Royle's *Civil War* (2004) and Antonia Fraser's *Cromwell* (2008). Regarding intelligence activity, Julian Whitehead's *Cavalier and Roundhead Spies* (2009) and Nadine Akkerman's *Invisible Agents* (2018) make for fascinating reads. Amongst other things, the latter casts light on John Evelyn's suspected clandestine correspondence with Royalists abroad in the period. References to bear-baiting and many other aspects of life under the Protectorate tend to be incidental and scattered through a wide range of books, but the shooting of the Bankside bears is specifically dealt with in *Cromwell's Buffoon*, Robert Hodkinson's 2017 biography of Colonel Pride. The Tradescants and their outstanding achievements are given worthy treatment in Jennifer Potter's *Strange Blooms* (2006). John Aubrey in his near-contemporary *Brief Lives* tells us that Thomas Bushell (alias Mr Mulberry in my book), did indeed have a very chequered career and rather sinisterly decorated home on Lambeth Marsh. The enigmatic Andrew Marvell has inspired many studies, and the *Cambridge Companion to Andrew Marvell* (2011) considers a wide range of aspects of his life and work, whilst leaving enough space for the infatuated writer to create her own version of this elusive genius. At the other end of the scale, eschewing enigma and not even attempting to elude us, is the wonderful Samuel Pepys, in whose diaries the realities of seventeenth-century life are sometimes movingly, sometimes riotously, but always colourfully laid bare. My own personal favourite rendering of them is in Kenneth Branagh's brilliant reading of *The Samuel Pepys Collection* for Hodder & Stoughton Audiobooks.

Insight into the astonishing amount of work that passed across John Thurloe's desk can be gained from the Thurloe Papers www.british-history.ac.uk/thurloe-papers

Shona MacLean, Conon Bridge, January 2019